WINGS

OF LOVE AND WAR

A NOVEL OF ADVENTURE, ROMANCE AND COURAGE

Patrick Ellsworth Taylor MD

Just as a snowflake, individually unique, melts into amorphous water, the story of an unsung life becomes as dust when those who remember are gone. Without a written account, no more than a grave marker serves for most, and for many, not even that.

ISBN: 978-0-9891571-0-0

Library of Congress Control Number: 2013906970

The Cover: "Winter, 1944-45 Over Germany" Acrylic on canvas. The author, 2012

Interior Design: Val Sherer, Personalized Publishing Services

The author is a World War II Army Air Force veteran and neurosurgeon, now semi-retired, who commutes to his office in San Francisco, across the Golden Gate Bridge. In addition to writing, painting and photography, he makes award-winning amateur wines, and with his wife, Eivor, owns and manages a commercial vineyard in the Dry Creek Valley, north of San Francisco. Next to the youngest in a family of five children, his childhood was spent under the guidance, and occasionally the brotherly oppression, of Bobby, the subject of this novel. This is his story, dedicated to his memory.

Contents

INTRODUCTION

While *Wings of Love and War* is a work of fiction, it is based on a true story. It thus is a truly a historical novel, dealing with the lives and events of a generation of another century and of a radically different era. This account touches on the heady decade of the Roaring Twenties after the First World War, the tribulations of the Great Depression of the Thirties, but mostly takes place in the Forties, culminating in World War II, ending in 1945.

Those were exciting times, and the events of the period covered in this work served to make the U.S. the dominant power on Earth. Most of those involved in that combat have since departed, only a relative few remaining to tell the story in person.

This is also a biography of a member of one of America's great generations, coming of age during that period. The story is about the author's oldest brother and of those around him, whose lives, in touching for a brief time, generated all the elements of the Classics: Ambition, Adventure, Love, Betrayal, Desperation, Courage, and Tragedy.

Some of the names have been changed for various reasons, but most of the main characters existed largely in their depicted capacity. All but a few of the events portrayed in this work actually took place. Only a handful of characters, and their connection with events, actual or fictional, are of the author's own invention.

PROLOGUE

The Awakening

December 7, 1941, soon to be plunged into death and destruction, dawned a lovely Sunday morning in Honolulu. The cumulus clouds, as usual, hung over the Pali, the steep windward bluffs of the Koolau Range, sheltering the city from the weather.

On the northwestern outskirts, Navy personnel at Pearl Harbor, and those of the Army were mostly still asleep. The blue skies were shadowed only briefly as errant clouds tore themselves away from those massed along the ridges, and rode the wind southwest. It was not yet eight, and only those pulling duty, plus a handful getting an early start for recreation or worship, were up and about.

The day starting out couldn't have been more idyllic. Half of the gray-painted battleships of the U.S. fleet were in the shallow harbor, having relocated there from previous bases on the West Coast. As usual, when not at sea, most of them were anchored or tied up in pairs along Ford Island in the middle of the anchorage. Battleship Row, they called it.

At 7:55 AM, the thunder of hundreds of aircraft engines emerged from the north, soon followed by the roar of strafing Zero fighters and the detonations of bombs and torpedoes. Heard only as dull thuds in the city, they created ear-shattering explosions in and around the harbor and other military installations. The attack was as devastating to the barracks and airfields ashore as it was to the moored ships.

It was instant carnage, unprecedented in American experience. Almost everything was enveloped in flames. Towering pillars of thick black smoke, tinted vivid crimson by the flames of burning ships and parked aircraft, soon obscured the sun. It was an unmitigated disaster, and all was confusion. Sailors, still in their skivvies, even cooks and bakers, hastily manned anti-aircraft machine guns, firing at the torpedo bombers as they bore in to launch their deadly fish at the battleships. Others aimed skyward at the dive-bombers screaming down from above.

At the military airfields, the P-40 fighter planes were lined up as if for review by the Commanding General. While at that time there had been some concern about the intent of the Japanese, the likelihood of an attack so far from Tokyo had been considered remote. In addition, the military command seriously over-estimated the risk from local Japanese saboteurs. Wrong on both counts. Wide dispersal of the planes was deemed a greater risk than air attack. Parked together, they could be closely watched.

At Wheeler Field, where the bulk of the Army Air Force fighters were, pilots frantically sprinted for their aircraft as they were being fired up by the ground crew. Many were cut down by Zero fighters before they could even reach their planes. Others, barely airborne, were shot down even as landing gear was being retracted. Less than half of the more than fifty P-40s would escape total destruction, and only a pitiful few would remain airworthy.

As if that weren't enough, more of the same resulted when the second wave of the enemy descended on the already crippled facilities. The very surface of the harbor around the ships was aflame from bunker oil released from torpedo-blasted fuel tanks. Only a handful of attackers were downed, and the toll taken of American lives in dead and mortally wounded was almost three thousand.

Because most of the fleet units caught by surprise would be out of action for many months, fear of the Japanese invading the Hawaiian Islands and even the West Coast created a near panic. The Country, although in the first stages of mobilization, had only partially emerged from its isolationist posture, and until then was still divided regarding the *Axis* powers: Germany, Italy and Japan.

The Japanese had hoped to entirely eliminate America's Pacific Fleet, thus freeing them to conquer the whole of Southeast Asia. By shifting the balance of power in the western Pacific by that accomplishment, they thought they could force the U.S. to sue for an early peace. After all, they had bested a western power in the past with their naval might. Then, it was Imperial Russia, and its key was the destruction of the Czar's fleet in the Straits of Tsushima in 1905.

In attacking the U.S., Japan made a huge miscalculation, despite initial sweeping successes. Even the Supreme Commander of the Japanese Imperial Fleet, Admiral Isoroku Yamamoto, while pursuing the war ruthlessly, feared that the surprise attack on Pearl Harbor had merely awakened a sleeping giant. And he was right.

The Pearl Harbor attack in 1941 united the disparate factions in our country as nothing else could have, galvanizing the U.S. into total mobilization. The last vestiges of isolationism were swept away that terrible day.

ONE

Los Angeles, December 7, 1941

It was a day few Americans alive then would ever forget. Most would always carry in their memories every detail of what they had been doing at the time they learned the terrible news. Bobby, a twenty-one year old college junior, was one of them.

Working out in the USC gym, at that very moment he was in mid-air, dismounting from the high bar.

Just then, his Phi Kappa Psi fraternity roommate burst onto the floor, announcing the news at the top of his lungs, the sound echoing through the nearly empty building.

In an exasperated tone, he exclaimed, "Dammit all, Dave, you could've waited another couple of seconds!" Then he added, "What was that about the Japs attacking us?"

Repeating the news, Dave, totally out of breath, puffed, "All of us at the house have been listening to the radio, and I thought it best to come and get you. Some of the guys are already talking about joining up, and I'm thinking about it too."

Stunned by what he had just heard, Bobby asked, "A fraternity meeting now? Half the brothers are away for the weekend. And why me? I'm in the midst of preparing for our next meet. You know I hate those long drawn out sessions, all that smoke inhalation, but mostly hot air the result."

Dave replied, "You know how they depend on your leadership because of your background in Law and foreign affairs, so do me a favor and come on."

Bobby couldn't help laughing at that, despite the situation. He was, after all, only in pre-law. What did he really know about that field? Most of his courses had been in Philosophy and History.

As they hurried back to Fraternity Row, on Twenty-Eighth Street, he agonized over what had happened. He'd always known war with Japan was inevitable, but much like the long-expected death of a loved one, when the end comes, it still must be faced. Shocked by the attack, he shook his head. Now, with war, his plans for Law School after graduating from USC would be out of the question.

"I'm in the middle of my junior year, Dave, and I'm going to enlist, hoping to graduate before being called up. This war is going to last a few years. That makes it important for us to have as much of college as possible. So don't get carried away by what you'll hear today, even from me. Unlike our past meetings, I'm betting today will be quite different. Even our card-carrying isolationists will have to change their minds now."

The room where the brothers had gathered was smoke-filled by the time they entered. Most of those present acknowledged him, and he was motioned to a chair near the radio, to which all ears were glued.

The man next to him said, "Hi, guy. Terrible news, huh?"

"You can say that again," Bobby replied, just as the announcer, for the fifth time, repeated the account of the destruction of the battleship *U.S.S. Arizona*.

"Damn," Bobby exclaimed, "One of my high school buddies is in her crew!"

Dave looked at him sympathetically, slowly shaking his head. "You weren't here when they gave the early casualty figures from that battlewagon. Already the estimate is almost a thousand men trapped below. Probably still in their bunks, they wouldn't have had a chance in Hell."

"Let's join up, someone shouted, seconded by several others, only to be challenged by another.

"Oh, please," he groaned, "The Yanks went last time, the Jerks go this time."

A jeering chorus resulted, and a voice called out, "We don't need another commentator, Bill. Sit down and shut the fuck up!"

Bobby stood up then, surveying the Group. He knew they were angry and not a little fearful about the morning's events, because he felt a mixture of those emotions himself.

"First, let's all calm down. We're facing a serious problem. Bill here has to be joking, but the truth is, there *are* two types of men, Let's call them Yanks and Jerks, both responding to their country's call. What he said really means that in the past, Yanks took up arms for legitimate reasons. Those were wars in which no pretext was needed. The men at Bunker Hill were the original Yanks. The troopers in blue at Gettysburg were Yanks fighting for the very survival of the United States as we know it. And only twenty-three years ago, our own fathers, in Belleau Wood and the Argonne Forest, answered the call in France. They all were Yanks, fighting and dying, hoping to preserve Democracy.

"Then there's the Jerk. By Bill's definition, he responds to the call to arms without good reason. Patriotic, sure, but enlisting whether the war is justified, or is based on a pretext, as in the sinking of the battleship *U.S.S. Maine* in Havana harbor in 1898.

"Now, I find it inconceivable, in the face of this morning's treacherous attack, that anyone can still be an isolationist. A Jerk of a different kind, misled not by a call to unjust war, but misled by himself. Whatever the reasons behind the attack on Pearl Harbor, the fact that we have to defend ourselves makes this a just war, one in which all true Yanks, and yeah, even Jerks, must fight."

For a few moments no one spoke, as those gathered there looked around expectantly at each other.

Finally, Dave broke the silence, jumping to his feet, exclaiming, "I'm with you, Bobby!"

An idea at such times can be contagious, and everyone present, even the wiseacre Bill, caught it. The attack earlier that morning, coupled with Hitler's Nazis already overrunning Europe, made it clear. Once again, America would need its people to rise in its defense.

That night, hardly anyone slept. Bobby lay awake for hours, debating the wisdom of enlisting, or in the alternative, waiting. It might be possible to graduate before the Draft caught up with him. He already had the two years of college the Army Air Force required for pilot training, but with the country now at war, Selective Service would expand, snapping up everyone. Waiting for them to draw your number could be risky, he thought. One could end up in the trenches. While it would be just as dangerous flying in combat, the thought of fighting through the mud, and then sleeping in it too, was not an attractive one.

After he and Dave decided to visit the recruiting office in the morning, he still couldn't sleep.

Soon, however, lulled by Dave's gentle snoring, his thoughts turned to his childhood, and how remote the prospect of war had seemed then.

TWO

The Early Years, 1920–1937

For a reason unknown to him, he had always been called Bobby. That name, perhaps, was more fitting when he was little than his given name, Philip, or even Phil, but as he grew into a strapping youth and then into manhood, the childhood name stuck.

Born in Los Angeles in 1920, as the first-born male of the family, Bobby was the golden boy. From the beginning he was idolized by his parents and his older sister. Named after his father, Philip Barr Taylor, and born on the Fourth of July, he was what then was regarded as the typical American boy. With his cherubic, open face, light brown wavy hair, bright blue eyes, and freckled nose, he would have been the perfect model for that painter of Americana, Norman Rockwell. And he had a personality to match. Because of his looks and charisma, movie director Hal Roach wanted to cast him in the *Our Gang Comedies,* a very popular movie series in those days. His mother scotched the opportunity for a lucrative contract then, in fear of spoiling him, but he went on to become a little spoiled anyway.

Then came the Stock Market Crash and the Great Depression. While his father struggled selling life insurance for Metropolitan, his mother and her sewing machine conserved what little income he earned. Not only would she buy cut-rate remnants to fashion window drapes and slipcovers for the furniture, she became adept at making clothes for her kids. Too adept, Bobby recalled, as she insisted on short pants until he reached the age of twelve, thereby avoiding trousers worn-out at the knees. But that forced him to learn to defend himself from the bullies who considered short pants only for sissies.

Bobby on his fourth birthday, July 4, 1924

He remembered his mother making dresses and gowns for friends and neighbors, and was not only impressed by her work, but by the extra allowance that came his way after she had been paid.

"Mom," he recalled saying, "You're too generous for your own good. Take the money and buy yourself something nice for a change. You haven't had a new hat in years."

Typical of her was the reply, "No, we need the money for the family. But that gives me an idea. I'll make one for myself."

Bobby was right. In the face of near-poverty, she was generous with her money, that is, when she had any. He never saw a hobo turned away when one came down the driveway to the back door for a handout. They were always fed in return for a some yard work, and then sent on their way with a couple of coins, however small, jingling in a pocket.

While his mother was the one to shape most of his ideas during his early years, his father too, played a role. This was both by the example of his long hours in sales, and by his oft-repeated maxim that success took hard work.

Despite being on the job more than twelve hours daily, his father always found time on Sundays to spend with his sons. One of Bobby's favorite times was playing Golf with him at Griffith Park in Los Angeles. There, he learned the game, and by example, how to behave as an adult. Unfortunately, his father wasn't good in imparting the facts of life, raised as he was by a puritanical older sister after the early deaths of their parents. He was totally incapable of frank talk about sex.

Thus, as Bobby entered adolescence, naturally looking for explanations, he soon found that his father wasn't a good source. The closest he ever came to an answer was one Sunday on the golf course, when they were a chip shot from a green, walking together.

Out of the blue, and obviously embarrassed, his father whispered, "Son, do you understand the concept of *Continence?*"

Bobby stopped, thinking for a moment. Dad wouldn't be whispering if this weren't about sex, he knew. Interested, he answered, "Sure, Dad, if you're not talking about geography, then it has to mean *Restraint,* or something like that, right?"

That was all that his father was able to say on the subject. No anatomical descriptions or other hints regarding sex, and no mention of precautions, even from disease. But heck, he decided, his mother, at least, had already explained the rudiments.

He recalled the last few holes that day being spent mostly in silence as he mused about the apparent similarity between golf and sex. In both cases, he concluded, it all came down to control.

As he reached his teen years in 1933, the nation was in the depths of the Great Depression. There was hope, as it looked like President Franklin Roosevelt's *New Deal* was going to bring about great things for the economy, but it took re-armament, beginning in 1940, to start the country back to prosperity.

* * * *

Along with the rest of his siblings, he had been baptized a Catholic, and as he grew, he continued to consider himself such, although his family, beyond a belief in God, lacked much in the way of religious conviction. His four feet eleven dynamo of a mother, raised in that religion, considered herself to have been excommunicated because of an induced abortion of an unwanted pregnancy in 1924. His father, an Episcopalian, had promised when they married that he would raise the children as Roman Catholics, and he stuck to his word. The brand of religion learned by Bobby, however, despite a couple of years attending parochial school, was nothing Rome would ever approve.

He recalled coming home one Sunday from church, excited over the news that he had been offered the position of Altar Boy, only to have his mother nix that.

Her rejoinder was, "I don't trust those priests. Just keep on the other side of the railing there in church, young man, and you'll be fine."

Puzzled, Bobby asked, "How come? They all seem nice to me. Please mom, tell me the reason."

Shaking her head, she replied, "You're too young now. I'll tell you when you're fifteen. Just do as I say."

Bobby never did become religious for obvious reasons. Part of this was because his father rarely went to church with him and his brothers and sister, and his mother never did. This left attendance at his whim as he grew older. Half the time he would end up at one of the more tempting spots along the route to church. This could be a drug store, with its soda fountain and magazine stand, or a friend's house. His father would often ask him what the sermon had been about, bringing him to answer hastily, *The Epistle to the Romans* or *The Sermon on the Mount*, or whatever at the moment came off the top of his head.

After he graduated from junior high school, his mother, never impressed with the local schools or his circle of chums, pressured him into transferring to Loyola High School in Los Angeles. This meant leaving the friends with whom he had grown up, traveling over the hills into Hollywood, and then across L.A. Her reasoning did appear sound to him since it wasn't for religious purposes, but to help him with study habits for which the Jesuits were famous. Academically, despite getting excellent grades, even he recognized that he had been coasting along. There had been little homework, and for him and his friends, the very idea of study at home had come to be regarded as an outrage.

Because he had started in the middle of the year at Loyola, having graduated from junior high in mid-year, he was exposed to the required first year Latin with the rest of the class far ahead. Try as he might, it was impossible for him, given the need to perform well in the rest of his subjects, to catch up. As a consequence, starting out in the tenth grade, Latin had to be repeated. This meant 10-D, a class made up of all those who had flunked Latin, as well as other subjects in the case of some. One might assume that the "D" stood for "Dumb," but as time would show, a better descriptive would be "Deviltry." The fact that Loyola was an all-male institution undoubtedly contributed. It seems that most of the guys were inveterate cut-ups and goof-offs.

The Geometry instructor, Mr. Daly, was a relatively young Irish "Scholastic" as those studying for the Jesuit priesthood were called. He was one of the "Black Irish," with a brogue suggesting he was just off the boat, but with an air of toughness. This was enhanced by a his piercing dark eyes set beneath beetling brows and over a bluish five o'clock shadow. The picture of authority was completed by the manner in which his black cassock hung down over his solid frame and his way of pacing about, or rather marching around. Bobby shuddered to contemplate how the class of 10-D would have behaved had they had a less imposing scholastic.

For him, Mr. Daly proved to be an excellent instructor, as were his other teachers, and as a consequence, he did well in his classes from an academic standpoint. It was also fun, due to the occasional disruptive mirth that some of his more ir-repressible classmates triggered off by their boisterous antics and joking. From the beginning he couldn't help laughing at those clowns, but as the year progressed and his academic security increased, on occasion he would join them.

One of the routines would be to make a play on the name of a fellow student named Jim House. The task was made easier by the fact that he was always screwing up in some way in his recitations, or in his answers to questions when called upon. The supposed humor was enhanced by the fact that Mr. Daly was quite straight-laced, and seemed easily shocked by anything that was, in his interpretation at least, even a little off-color. In his presence, no one dared to utter anything overtly profane or smutty, so the trick was to make a play on words.

A favorite was when a member of the class would falter, bringing someone to call out, "Help him out, House!" This was said in a way to stress those last two words. Predictably, Mr. Daly was noticeably distressed by the thought of the word, "Outhouse." This would invariably bring a high degree of juvenile mirth, as much because of the Jesuit teacher's re-action as to the silliness of it all. These were the essential fac-tors, and this particular exhortation was the one most often repeated. House didn't seem to mind, and Mr. Daly was able to quickly quiet the room, if only for the time being.

This game continued throughout the entire year, with the punishment assigned to the perpetrators either extra home-work, or cleaning the blackboards after class at the expense of their recess. It seemed that the scholastic didn't expect as much from the inveterate cut-ups as he did from the rest of the class, even though everyone had in some way come up short academically, as was Bobby's case in starting Latin six months behind.

More than halfway through the year, his behavior having earnied no black marks, a situation came up that he couldn't resist. This time House himself had failed miserably in explaining a geometry theorem. They say timing is everything.

He couldn't resist seizing that moment to call out, "You're a flop, House!"

It was the first time that combination had been used. The observation created pandemonium and raucous laughter not heard the entire year. Mr. Daly was shocked beyond belief, stunned momentarily into immobility. He soon recovered, and as the mirth continued, he was quickly able to detect the source of the disturbance. Grabbing Bobby by the ear, he led him headlong out the door to the Principal's office, or as that worthy was termed, the Prefect. It was something Mr. Daly hadn't done with anyone the entire year. Needless to say Bobby was shocked, the more when it became clear that the Irishman's definition of the term "Flophouse" was not that of his own, an extremely inexpensive place to sleep.

A stern lecture, given by Father Bellanger, the Prefect, concerned the importance of having a clean mind as well as a clean mouth, to which all Catholic young men should aspire.

What a joke, Bobby thought, as the lecture continued. Never had he heard such profanity in public school as he had encountered at Loyola High. He was threatened with expulsion should that happen again. Then he, who rarely uttered a four-letter word aside from "Hell" or "Damn" was given three hours of detention after school, which would delay his getting home until well after supper.

Mr. Sykes, the Prefect's secretary, had to assign something to do during that time, although he was seemingly more understanding of such forms of the vernacular.

"Taylor," he said, "I'm surprised at your behavior. I've noticed that you're a leader rather than a follower, yet today you acted just like the rest of those cut-ups. What were you thinking?"

Bobby thought for a moment, and then replied, "I dunno, something inside me just burst out, I guess. It was an opportunity to top the rest of the guys, after having to put up with their antics all year. At the same time, I'm really sorry for disrupting things so. But Mr. Daly's reaction! I didn't expect such outrage."

The secretary looked down over his half-glasses with the hint of a smile, saying, "Well, you asked for it. Don't you know that in some quarters a 'Flop' is a lady of easy virtue? And what would that make a flophouse? Come on Taylor. If you're to lead in the future, you have to look before you leap. Consider the consequences of your words and actions. And speaking of the consequences, you now have three hours of detention for your too quick a wit."

"Gosh sir," Bobby protested, "I don't get home until five as it is."

"Well," he replied, "You'll just have to spend the time learning a lesson."

Bobby then asked, "You mean I can do my homework, then?"

"No," Mr. Sykes answered, "My orders are for you to write this little rhyme of Ogden Nash's on the blackboard. Maybe it will cure you of your tendency to play when you should be working."

Bobby looked at the paper and the four short lines, smiling, despite himself at the humor, which dealt with the Ant's industriousness being driven by its being filled with formic acid. Relieved that the task involved writing only twenty-five words, he then asked, "And how many times in my three hours?"

Mr. Sykes replied, to Bobby's dismay, "See to it that you repeat it at least a thousand times. I'll be checking on you, and when you need more chalk, just sing out."

Needless to say, by the time he had finished that chore, it was well after six, and his right hand was practically useless, barely able to hold the chalk. He would look at ants in a different light forever afterwards.

He did continue his contrarian ways, once for drawing during Religion class, for which he was again sent to see the Prefect, and again for heading his papers "RSVP" instead of the regulation "AMDG," the abbreviation for *Ad Majorum Dei Gloriam*. He resented dedicating his work to the Greater Glory of God, the translation of the Latin, because his efforts were designed to advance his own good, and not that of God. This, of course, was asking for it, as the front office was as well versed in French as in Latin. After having used that French abbreviation all year, he ultimately got the appropriate response, again Jesuit punishment.

Despite the distractions, he was able finish the year with perfect academic grades. He actually took pride in having learned to study, and by the rather obvious method of his father's early advice, that of merely applying himself. It was something for which he somewhat grudgingly also had to credit the Jesuits.

* * * *

There in the fraternity house, the Sunday of Pearl Harbor, still unable to find sleep, he smiled inwardly, recalling starting the tenth grade at Burbank High School and another Sunday afternoon at the public course in Griffith Park.

He and his father had just finished a nine hole round, and both were pleased. It was the first time that he had matched his father's effort, a testimonial to his athletic ability and parental coaching.

"Son," his father said, putting his hand on Bobby's shoulder, for him a rare gesture of affection, "I'm proud of you. It looks like you've been practicing the game along with all your other pursuits. And now that you're sixteen, you should get your driver's license. Then, as a reward, you could drive our new DeSoto."

"Gee, Dad, thanks, that would be swell. But didn't mom tell you? I got my license last month." He didn't add that he had already driven their new blue sedan.

"I detect a certain lack of enthusiasm," his father observed, "Is there a problem, lad?"

"Well yeah, Dad. I've been hitchhiking to school ever since we moved here, and it's a pain. I need real wheels of my own."

"Okay, you have wheels. What's the matter with streetcars and that bike of yours?"

"Dad, it's three miles from our house to Burbank high, and you know there's no streetcar in that part of the Valley."

"Only three miles? When I was your age, in Minnesota, I had to walk, and it was over five miles. And much of the time it was through the snow and often below zero!"

Oh God, Bobby had thought then, how many times had he heard that, and from mom too. Still, he couldn't resist observing, "And I suppose you didn't have waterproof boots to make the trip either."

"Boots! They were unheard of in our family. I was the youngest of five. Everything I wore was a hand-me-down. I was lucky even to have *shoes*. Haven't I ever told you about the cardboard I had to insert because of the holes in the soles?"

"But Dad, this is 1937, and to be anyone at all in high school here, you have to have a car."

As they put their clubs into the trunk, his dad motioned him to the driver's side, handing him the keys. Driving back along Riverside Drive, he was surprised when his father agreed to his idea.

"I'll tell you what. If you get all A's this year, you have my permission to get a car, if it's okay with your mother."

Bobby enthused, "You've got a deal! I'll start looking around for one this summer. I want a Ford Model "A" roadster to hop up in my spare time. The work can be done out behind the garage, and it won't cost all that much."

In those days old Fords were a dime a dozen. One could get a Model "T" for almost nothing, but the standard was the 1929 Model "A," which, while not as light as the older "T," could easily be mated to the later and more powerful Ford V-8 engine and transmission. The combination, lightweight when stripped down, was a potent formula for sheer acceleration. With changing gear ratios, high top speeds could be achieved when aftermarket equipment was added to boost the 85 horsepower of the stock V-8 engine to 150 or more.

It took him a year to assemble the needed components for his hop-up in the back yard of their Burbank home. Stripping the fenders, bumpers and running boards off a slightly beat-up '29 Ford roadster, he rigged up block and tackle and hoisted out the stock four-cylinder engine. After having a pair of front engine mounts welded in, he dropped in a good 1937 Ford V-8 engine bought at a salvage yard in Glendale. His best buddy, Tommy Hunter, helped get it running. At last, he had a car of his own.

* * * *

At the Army recruiting office in downtown Los Angeles the morning after Pearl Harbor, they found that the line waiting to join up stretched halfway around the block.

As he stood there, moving at a snail's pace, he reflected on what a good buddy his roommate Dave was. He knew when to shut up, whether lost in his own thoughts, or knowing when to leave those around him to theirs. What a shame the Army would separate them, even if they both qualified for Cadet training. Alphabet soup might be common in the chow-hall, but each unit had an alphabetical roster, with "Lincoln" far from "Taylor." Their meetings would be seldom, except when the Battalion assembled for inspection, and the rare occasion when they'd be able to obtain passes together.

Bobby, then twenty-one, was physically and intellectually mature, but still looked a couple of years younger than others his age. Taller than average, he had an athletic build, his natural muscularity bred of sports and outdoor work, plus some weights. Favored with a winning smile, enhanced, somehow by two slightly crooked front teeth, he was a man's man, despite his apparent youth. This, along with his dry wit and enthusiasm, made it easy for him to befriend individuals of either sex.

Joining that line to enlist, the bright optimism that his face usually reflected was subdued, pre-occupied as he was by the enormity of the events at Pearl Harbor the previous day. Looking around him, he saw the majority were just kids, their unfinished teenage faces betraying the fact that while they were old enough to fight and die, they still were not old enough to vote. He looked at the man in front of him and regarded the one behind. Which of us, he asked himself, will be still alive at the war's end? It was a sobering thought. These others are mostly too young, he decided, to allow such ideas into their heads.

This brought to mind when he had been eighteen like them, and Europe was again moving toward war.

THREE

The Gathering Storm, 1938

As the war clouds loomed in Europe, many tried to ignore them. The First World War had ended only twenty years earlier, and until Pearl Harbor, most tended to bury their heads in the sand regarding anything international. Bobby's Burbank High School, on the other hand, immersed its students in the deteriorating world situation, leading to them becoming very conversant with the turbulent state of foreign affairs, national politics and the military.

Central to the curriculum for a time was Nazi Germany and the rise of the infamous Adolf Hitler. They studied the Nazi re-occupation of the Rhineland, and the *Anschluss*, Germany's annexation of Hitler's homeland, Austria, followed by the two-stage takeover of Czechoslovakia beginning in 1938.

His class engaged in spirited discussions of those events, but importantly, they also listened, by means of short-wave radio, to the fiery speeches of Hitler himself. What an orator! Bobby, like most of his classmates, hardly understood a word he said, but easily saw how the sheer drama of his bombast was leading the German people into another conflict.

When the speeches, translated in the newspapers, were discussed in class the following day, the message was appalling. The Nazis would never stop short of war.

* * * *

While waiting in the line, Bobby's reminiscing was inter-rupted by his stomach rumbling. The smell of the food being prepared at Clifton's Restaurant down the street started his mouth watering. It was just after noon, and they were much less than half way to the recruiting office.

Dave's enthusing about getting into the Army Air Force allayed his hunger, as he began to examine how he also had become interested in flying.

It was during the early thirties, when he read the many popular stories about the fliers of World War I, their dog-fights likened to the combat of the knights of ages past. Aces, such as Eddie Rickenbacker, Billy Bishop and Baron von Richthofen were famous. Hollywood made a number of exciting movies of the war in the air as well, such as *Dawn Patrol* and *Hell's Angels*, giving the youth of Bobby's genera-tion a taste for flying. Most of the boys, and many of the girls, considered themselves "Air-Minded," and avidly followed the adventures of contemporary aviators such as Wiley Post, Jimmy Doolittle, Amelia Earhart and Jacqueline Cochran.

Charles Lindbergh was especially admired, even regarded as a hero on the basis of his pioneer solo flight across the Atlantic in 1927. Because of that adventure, he became known as "Lucky Lindy," the idol of millions of youth.

Ten years later, Lindbergh's praise of the German air force, or *Luftwaffe,* which should have been heeded as a warn-ing to our country, led to an Iron Cross decoration by Adolf Hitler. Sadly, the medal was accepted, and worse, in person. Lindbergh was further discredited when he asserted that the Democracies, especially the U.S., were so far behind in arma-ments, especially in air power, that they would lose any war with Germany.

Through it all, despite many detractors, his reputation from his daring flight across the Atlantic never faltered in the minds of the young. This, coupled with his stand regarding the importance of airpower, provided a powerful incentive for would-be fliers to join the military. This was furthered by Britain's Royal Air Force, or RAF, which did heed the buildup of German airpower. Their timely development of the Hawker Hurricane and Supermarine Spitfire fighters, the latter matching the best German aircraft, foiled Hitler's plans to bomb England into submission after the fall of France. A cross-channel invasion by the Nazis was thereby thwarted by the heroic performance of a relatively few RAF pilots, during what became known as "The Battle of Britain," in the summer and early fall of 1940. It also helped partially reverse the isolationism that pervaded U.S. policy. Here was a Democracy that needed our support, and one that could stand up to the Nazis after all.

Like so many others, Bobby avidly read all he could about flying. Many times he would ride his bike to the local airport to watch the planes. Barely earning enough at that time with his paper route even for pocket money, taking flying lessons or even a plane ride were out of the question. But a dime could get admission to the movies, where serials about air adventure and daring, such as *Tailspin Tommy* in 1934, and later, Frank Hawks in *The Mysterious Pilot* served as further inspiration.

It was Lockheed's radical twin-engine P-38 fighter, first flown in 1939, which finally confirmed his intent to become a fighter pilot, should the U.S. once again become involved in war. Those unusual planes would often zoom effortlessly over the family home, to and from the Lockheed airport across the San Fernando Valley. The smooth whistling purr of their twin Allison engines became one of his favorite tunes.

Bobby's fellow aviation enthusiast and best buddy, was classmate Tommy Hunter. Tall, raw-boned, and open, he spoke with the soft burr of the Scottish lowlands, having emigrated with his family to the U.S. ten years before. Not yet an American citizen, Tommy vowed that he would join the Royal Canadian Air Force, the RCAF, after high school graduation, so that he could do his bit as a fighter pilot against Hitler's *Luftwaffe*. No one else in his circle of friends felt as strongly at that early date.

* * * *

As he stood there in line at the recruiting station, Bobby recalled Tommy's enthusiasm, and his pre-occupation with the war in Europe.

Tommy would say, "Don't you guys see, that if the Nazis beat the British, we'll be next?"

At the time, Bobby thought the Japanese were a greater threat, assuming that the Nazis would probably turn on the Soviet Union first, leaving a free hand for the Japanese to attack in the Pacific. They had read passages of *Mein Kampf* in class, where Hitler had written that Germany's destiny was to the East, in the great expanses of fertile land there, assuring room for the growing German population.

Another member of their little group, Warren Wheeler, known as "Wheelie," would invariably take the isolationist view, maintaining that we had no business being over there.

"We don't have to worry about the Japs either. Have you ever seen anything mechanical they make that would hold together for long? You told me yourself, Bobby, that the bicycle your little brother Terry got for Christmas, a 'Famous Flyer,' made in Japan, fell apart within a couple of months. Imagine how their battleships and planes would hold together in combat."

Sinclair Smith, or "Sinkie," the fourth member of their circle, planning on joining the Navy, chimed in.

"And what would they do for steel and oil? They get most of that from us. They're not stupid. Do you think they would try to kill their golden goose?"

Tommy and even Sinkie accepted Bobby as leader of their circle, but Wheelie did not. This inevitably led to competition between the two, usually in athletics, coming out in their workouts in the gym or on the field.

* * * *

Bobby couldn't help recalling one such occasion when he and Wheelie had just finished a hundred yard free-style race in the pool at the Hollywood "Y." He had just lost by a yard.

"Dammit," he gasped, out of breath, "I can never beat you in this pool. It must be because of your big feet," pointing to what he was certain were size thirteen. Their owner was mockingly kicking water with them, just in front of Bobby's face.

"Oh, come off it," Wheelie countered, "That just evens things up. You beat me out in the weights earlier, you know, using technique, probably, rather than muscle."

As they showered, toweled off and dressed, they were joined by the other two members of their group, who, as usual, criticized them for being so competitive.

"You guys! Always making a contest out of the slightest thing," Tommy observed.

If given the choice, Bobby wouldn't have had it that way. As with everyone else, he was convinced that basically, Wheelie felt he always had to excel. While he often did, as in swimming, he could be insufferable at times. Bobby and the other two agreed that he had to be brought down whenever possible from his smugness and his air of superiority. The problem was, the task was left to him, the only one who seemed to be equal to Wheelie's challenges. He was almost a year older than his classmates, due to earlier transfers to Catholic schools in mid-year. With this added age, Bobby's natural leadership was enhanced.

They were so alike, accustomed to getting their own way. Both learned at an early age that they were special. Wheelie as an only child from an affluent banking family and the sole recipient of parental attention, and Bobby, in his position as the oldest boy in a family of five kids, accustomed to leadership in everything.

But there were differences. Bobby worked summers as a lifeguard, at the pool at the Lakeside Country Club, where the Wheelers were charter members. In working there, he was able to save enough to start building his cut-down Ford model "A" with its V-8 engine. Wheelie, on the other hand, got his new 1939 Ford convertible as a gift from his parents for his seventeenth birthday.

* * * *

After their frequent workouts at the Hollywood "Y," They would drive, usually in Wheelie's convertible, back into the Valley, stopping first at a soda fountain for a burger and a shake, which would hold them until supper. The four would get into bull sessions, most often between mouthfuls. These were usually about girls or sports, usually girls.

When the headlines on the newspaper rack made them feel less light-hearted, they talked about the coming war in Europe, and what that might mean to their futures. The conflict in China had been going on for so long that the Japanese threat to peace at that time was given little thought, except by Bobby. His mother had frequently stressed the idea that war with Japan was inevitable, and would last four or five years, and he agreed.

When the subject was Girls, Wheelie liked to brag about a certain Denise O'Donnell. Throughout that summer he kept talking about her to the point that the guys began to tease him about it.

Bobby remembered her from junior high, when she was in some of his classes. He recalled a plump, freckle-faced girl with sandy pigtails, leaving no lasting impression otherwise. The other two boys predicted that if such were still the case, Wheelie was welcome to her.

This would bring protests from him, defending not so much the girl as his own reputation in dating her. At one point he declared, glancing in Bobby's direction, "She probably wouldn't even look at you guys anyway. Besides, she and I are already practically going steady."

It would be over Denise that Bobby's friendship with Wheelie would end.

* * * *

Appreciative whistles from the guys in line, following a woman walking by, brought him out of his reverie.

She wore a sheer, clinging green dress, jiggling a little as she walked along in a strikingly voluptuous unfettered way. 20-20 vision became 20-10 for the men in line at that moment, and remained so until she disappeared down the block. He wondered why it was that so many guys thought it important to whistle at girls. Certainly, no woman in her right mind would respond to such attention. The woman in green didn't respond either, despite passing so many appreciative men.

"Boy, that was quite a show," Dave said, giving Bobby a nudge. "One sexy dish."

"So I noticed, but the way she paraded herself down the line makes you wonder."

"I get it," Dave replied, "Not one you'd take home to meet the folks."

She was so different than Denise O'Donnell, who had become his sweetheart in their senior year in high school. Denise was sexy too, he thought, but naturally so, and in an unconscious way. But they had drifted apart when he went to Chicago for his first year of college.

The only girl he had ever loved, being reminded of her then brought that old sick feeling, turning his thoughts to when they first started going together.

FOUR

Denise, 1939

His last year in high school had just begun when he first noticed her, sitting near the front in their homeroom class with another girl. They both looked cute to him when he came into the room, the other the more glamorous, perhaps because of her make-up. At once he was attracted to Denise, who had something, at least for him, that the others didn't. She certainly had changed. Perhaps it was the way she did her blond hair, neat and wavy, framing her face so nicely. It was also her face itself, with well-scrubbed, slightly freckled cheeks, and eyes of the darkest blue. Not that she was beautiful, and her lips were, perhaps, a little too full. To him this made her all the more attractive. She was bright and seemed to have a nice personality, but there was something sad about her that he couldn't define.

That day she was wearing a light blue pullover and a mostly dark blue plaid skirt, which revealed an athletic figure. This added to her appeal, her slimness not all that common in an era of the "Stylish Stout." He had gotten there early enough to be able to sit next to her, and for him, it was love at first sight.

As he glanced her way, she gave him a smile, returning his greeting with a friendly "Hi!"

His heart was pounding a little as he offered, "You're Denise O'Donnell, aren't you? Remember me from Junior Hi? I'm Bob, er, actually Phil Taylor. They call me Bobby."

Because further talk was interrupted by the teacher's arrival, there was nothing more than occasional eye contact for the rest of the hour.

When the period was finally over, the last that day, hoping to take her for an after-school soda, he ventured, "Say, you have a ton of books there, let me help you with them. Afterwards, maybe I could treat you to a Coke."

She really looked at him then, and seeing his muscular arms, suggesting his being equal to the task, she became more interested. Besides, she could really use a Coke after the long hot day, and she thought it might be fun to renew acquaintances.

"That would be swell, there are so many of these books, and my locker is way down the hall. Thanks."

Filled with anticipation, he gathered the books up under each arm and followed her towards the door. At that point, Wheelie, who usually sat next to her in class, ever the practical joker and now a jealous one, tipped the books upward from behind. Falling forward, they crashed all over the floor.

Bobby was mortified, to say the least, while she stood there with the other girl in amusement at the mess that she thought was caused by his clumsiness. When he finally bent to pick up the books, by that time the two girls had retrieved all but one.

Taking that remaining from his hands, Denise, firmly and with a worrisome finality said, "Thanks anyway, Bob or Phil or whatever your name is."

She then strode out the door before he could say a word, becoming quickly lost in the crowd in the hallway. He knew at that point that it would be fruitless to follow, despite being worried that he might not get another chance with her.

Before he turned around, the culprit had raced out the other door, unseen by him. All that he saw were amused smirks.

Suspecting Wheelie, he muttered to no one in particular, "If I find the guy who did that, I'll kill him!"

For the next couple of weeks Wheelie would get to class early, grabbing off the only seat next to Denise's customary spot.

Bobby approached Denise again, in a manner of speaking, at football practice later that same month. She was at the edge of the playing field, trying out for a cheerleader spot. He had just caught a long pass from the quarterback, on the sidelines, but caught on a dead run requiring some great moves to avoid bowling over several of the girls going through their routines there.

At that moment, Denise was performing a little dance as part of her sequence, with her arms outstretched, spinning around. He ran into her, but was able to stop just in time to avoid a significant impact. Automatically, he steadied her with an arm around her waist.

For him, the moment was magic. All thought of the team and the practice vanished, as the one he had been dreaming about since they had first sat together in class was there in his arms. He also felt some sort of chemistry between them at that moment, which was definitely, as they term such reactions in chemistry, "Exothermic," as even through his jersey he could feel her warmth. He could have stood there forever.

Her wide-eyed look led him to wonder unrealistically, could this be like love at first sight? In the excitement of the moment, it didn't occur to him that it was merely due to shock and surprise. One look at her and he knew that he had to play football that year even though his mother had always forbidden it in fear of his being seriously injured. Hell, he thought, he'd happily break any parental rule, or for that matter any bone in his body, for a chance to be near her. His reverie was soon shattered by the laughter of those nearby, and slightly delayed squirming from her embarrassment.

He barely heard her softly but firmly say, "You again, you big oaf! Will you let me go now?"

Bobby, now contrite and ashamed of his ineptitude, couldn't say anything as he bent over to retrieve her pom-poms, only belatedly responding with a somewhat clumsily offered apology, "Gosh, I'm sorry. Are you okay?"

Shaking grass from the pom-poms, she replied, "Sure," in a gently scolding voice, "But no thanks to you. The least you could have done was to drop that darned football, avoiding all this!"

Undiplomatically, in his own defense, he blurted out, "What? Drop the ball and risk not making the team? I had to hang onto it, can't you see?"

Her features hardened a little at that, as she said accusingly, "I might have known, the response of a typical jock. And I suppose football is more important to you than human life?"

"Heck no," he replied, "The main reason I went out for football was so I could see more of you, maybe get to know you better." Then he quickly added, "I've been watching. I know you're going to make cheerleader, you've got what it takes."

He hoped this wouldn't be taken as idle flattery, because she really looked the part, and while not tall, at about five feet four, she had that willowy litheness that made her appear taller and with every movement the more graceful because of it.

At that point, he took a chance, and cautiously asked her if she would like to go for a Coke with him, half expecting the same rebuff as before. Luckily for him, she was seeing him in a new light by that time, not because of the flattery, but at second look, she thought he was kind of cute with his wavy hair and the sincere expression on his face. Despite the circumstances, he seemed more mature than the others, compatible with his eighteen years, old for early 12th grade. This made him a year older than she was, a feature that at that age she found attractive.

"That would be nice," she responded.

When he heard that, it was as if his life had just begun. She had seemed lovely to him from the beginning of the school year, with those big indigo eyes and sandy hair, but now when she smiled at him, he thought it was the sweetest thing he had ever seen.

They talked over the Cokes for more than an hour before the waitress finally shooed them out. It was past closing time at the little soda fountain across from school. They were too late for the last school bus, and he hadn't brought his still unfinished roadster that day. They walked the mile to her home, the last couple of blocks hand in hand, conversing about their ideas, plans for the future and whatever came to mind. Some of it was silly, and they laughed a lot.

When they reached her house, he couldn't linger, as it was late and he still had more than two miles to go. Next time he would have his car, but now, far more importantly, he might just possibly have a girl, and not just any girl.

* * * *

Thus the romance of Bobby and Denise began. Her mother accepted the idea that her daughter, an only child, seemed to have a steady boyfriend. Her father never did. This was partly due to his being a strict Calvinist, leading him to think a Catholic boy was not good enough for his little girl. Seeing her father's disapproval, she would often ask Bobby to attend their church on Sunday, and although definitely not a churchgoer, he went, just to be near her.

Her mother, a pretty, matronly Registered Nurse, was quick to accept the reality that Denise was falling in love. She soon accorded Bobby a degree of maternal affection, inviting him over from time to time for Sunday dinner. He, in turn, took a shine to her, because of her acceptance of him and seeing in her a pleasing image of what Denise might be like in the future.

Still, on such occasions, Mr. O'Donnell continued to regard their guest with suspicion, which made the others at the table uncomfortable until he went into the living room with his dessert to listen to the radio. This left the young couple to talk on the nearby sofa while her mother cleaned up in the kitchen.

"Gee," he said, "I wish your dad would relax about the religion thing. I'm not much of a Catholic anyway. Heck, I spent more time when I was younger at the corner soda fountain reading magazines when I was supposed to go to Sunday Mass than I ever spent actually going. The only reason I go to church with you is so we can be together all the more."

Looking at him affectionately, she replied, "My reason for our going to church together is the hope that it will help my dad accept you. I'm not trying to convert you, that's probably a lost cause." This was offered with just the slightest hint of sarcasm. She then went on, "But I definitely am trying to be seen with you. You see, I just might be showing off my future husband."

This revelation was a surprise, but with his elation came a deep warm stirring, which for the moment obscured any pangs of fear of commitment and the responsibilities that came with it. He took her in his arms then, and they kissed, oblivious of her parents in adjoining rooms, until he gently began to fondle her breasts. For a moment her hand pressed down in response on his, and then just as gently, she removed his hand, with an imploring look. She motioned in the direction of her father, but to Bobby it wasn't the emotion of fear that her eyes betrayed.

It was much too soon for Bobby when they were interrupted by her mother. Gently putting put a hand on his shoulder, she said, "You had better go now. It's a school night for both of you, and classes are early. It was nice seeing you, though, and do come again soon."

"Thanks, Mrs. O'Donnell, for the nice dinner. I enjoyed being here. Say goodbye for me to Mr. O," he said earnestly, blowing a kiss to Denise as he made a hasty exit.

As he hopped into his roadster, he felt an almost overwhelming yearning for her, filled with desire as he was. Driving home down Olive Avenue in the starlit night only intensified it, despite the cool air blowing on him in the open car. He sensed that after that night he would never be the same.

"Imagine," he said aloud, "I have the love of a real woman, me!" He still found it hard to believe.

There followed other nights when they had parked in his car on Mulholland Drive, overlooking L.A. and its carpet of light. God, he thought, it was so great, snuggled next to her with her softness in his arms. They had barely gotten beyond the necking stage by that time, but her kisses had been so delicious, that he had known that soon he would be unable to resist going further. He had hoped it would be simply a matter of time. Would completion of their love have to wait for marriage? This question remained somewhat disquieting to him, as they had never discussed that.

After that, their senior year virtually flew by, especially when she started saving the seat next to her for him in homeroom, much to Wheelie's displeasure. Bobby warned his former friend not to pull any more tricks or he would pound him into the ground. Hearing that, Denise objected, saying that if he did any such thing, she would be very unhappy with him.

He made the team, and she won the cheerleader position, which brought them together often more than once daily in school. After classes, he usually drove her home in his roadster, and they would sit on her front porch and talk until late, when one of her parents would call her in. Even then it was always too soon. Weekends they went to movies and parties together, or into L.A. for an evening of dancing, when one of their favorite swing bands, such as The Glen Miller or The Benny Goodman bands were in town.

* * * *

One Sunday morning they had driven in his newly built *Iron* to the beach. It was a warm day in the Valley, and at first they both enjoyed the breezy openness of the roadster. However, before reaching the summit over Sepulveda, they were met by a solid wall of incoming low clouds. It was a disappointment, as it meant a cold sunless beach all day, and yet it was beautiful, pouring like a gray waterfall over the divide separating the L.A. plain and the Valley. He was tempted to pull over and watch it awhile, but despite her windbreaker, he could see she was shivering in the cold wind swirling into the open car. At least he had a windshield, but there was no top.

The windiness abated some as they drove west on Wilshire Boulevard, but in the surf at Santa Monica the water was cold, and she never did warm up. Instead of sitting on their beach blanket, they wrapped it around themselves. Even that and the thermos of hot cocoa they had brought were barely enough. At least her shivering didn't recur, and the bluish cast of her lips disappeared after a while.

At that point he tried to kiss her, but she blocked him with one hand. As he looked questioningly at her, she put her other hand to his face, rubbing the stubble he had neglected to shave that morning.

"Bobby, I haven't complained about your foibles much, but the whiskers will have to go if you want to smooch. And another thing, that jalopy of yours is the worst. It's definitely out on a day like this. No top, but I could put up with that if it had a heater. And look at my hair. It's a mess now, all tangles from the wind, and maybe you wouldn't notice, but I smell like exhaust, even after being drenched in cold salt water just now. Not the answer to a girl's dreams."

"Gosh, Denise, It's all I've been able to afford. Every dime I have has either gone into this car, or for our dates together. But I promise you, the next time you ride in this roadster, there'll be at least a heater. And I'll see if I can find something to deflect the wind. I'm sorry sweetie, none of the guys have had any complaint."

She gave him a surprised look at that. "You do realize that I'm a girl, right?" It was then that she put her foot down. Dates would have to be in his family's DeSoto sedan.

They became caught up in the final festivities of their senior year, to culminate in their commencement ceremony, where Bobby was one of the Valedictorians. She would tease him about all the time he was taking to prepare his delivery, literally sweating out giving the address.

He explained to her about the rush of adrenaline he felt whenever he thought about it, just like before an athletic contest, or when he opened up his roadster on a long, straight deserted stretch of highway.

"It's a mixture of fear and excitement, a little like when I first asked you out for that Coke."

"Oh, now I understand," she responded, "I felt some of that too. But the commencement address you're giving, how does it figure in that?"

"Well, you know the class theme this year is 'He who would be great.' Of the qualities that further such an achievement, my subject is the one that allows a person to persist in his ambitions, in the face of all adversity. Despite his own fears and anxieties, *Courage* is what sees him through. To be great."

Squeezing his hand, she said, "Bobby, that's wonderful. With ideas like that, you needn't sweat out your presentation. Everyone will love it. And what is courage without fear for one's life, limb, or even reputation? Without some concern over the possible consequences, there is no bravery, only stupidity."

* * * *

In the weeks that followed their senior prom, known as the "Aloha Dance," and then graduation, Bobby and Denise were practically inseparable. They talked a lot about what the increasingly uncertain future held, with war threatening in Europe.

One balmy June evening, as they sat in his roadster, Denise asked, "How long it will it be until we'll be dragged into it, just as in 1917?"

He drew her closer then. "A couple of years, probably. Most people say we could beat the Japs within six months, and the Nazis a year after that. But I'm certain any war will last close to four years for us."

Almost in tears, she whispered, "Just as long as it doesn't take you away from me. I couldn't bear that."

Starting in June, they would drive over Sepulveda up past Santa Monica and Malibu for body surfing and tanning at Zuma Beach. They both soon sported peeling noses despite the application of gobs of zinc oxide ointment, and she freckled, a little bit more than he did. She didn't shrink from bodysurfing the huge waves there. When they would curl off their tops rather than churning down, crashing with a roar of foam and sand, she was right there with him. She was some gal, he knew, proud of her ability. You didn't often see women bodysurfing.

He imagined the wonderful life they would have as they sat together on their beach blanket one day, after a session of surfing. As he put his arm over her shoulder to draw her closer, he somehow quickly found himself in her embrace. She had turned toward him, slipping effortlessly into his arms, and, finding him clean-shaven, kissed him on the mouth. God, he thought, those soft lips.

They were totally happy together, except when Bobby discussed going for his first year of college at the University of Chicago. That threatened to separate them for months, but would make college affordable, paid for by his wealthy aunt Betty, his mother's older sister, and her husband, Joe. Conveniently, they lived only four blocks from campus.

* * * *

The street noise near the recruiting station had reached a new high, as a hopped-up roadster pulled up nearby, a few more would-be applicants piling out. As its V-8 engine idled with characteristic roughness, it caught Bobby's attention. Exuding speed, the engine had to be "Full-race."

As he stood there, the sound began to bring back the memories of his trip to the desert to put his own roadster through the speed trials at the dry lakes.

FIVE

The Roadster Crisis

He had made the decision, in the summer of 1939, to see what his own roadster was capable of. Although it didn't sport even a special cam or much in the way of other performance improvements, he really wanted to know just how fast it was. He knew it was good from the few drag races he'd had on deserted stretches of highway, but what would it do flat out? That could only mean the dry lakes.

When he had brought it up with Denise, she nixed the idea of her coming with him for the roadster meets.

"I've heard about those things. Dustily baking in the sun all day, and nothing but drunken carousing all night. No thanks."

To be eligible to participate, one had to be a member of a roadster club, leading him to join one in nearby Glendale. During the winter he had worked to soup up the engine, installing twin carburetors, or *pots,* using a *Thixtun* manifold, replacing the stock heads with high compression ones. He also changed the ring and pinion gears in the differential from the stock 4.11 to 3.78. That way he could crank out more top speed in exchange for losing the greater acceleration of lower gearing. He had calculated, that theoretically, a top speed of 110 MPH would be possible.

The meet day was July 23rd, about two weeks after his nineteenth birthday. The timing traps had been set up by the Southern California Timing Association that year at Rosamond Dry Lake, northeast of Palmdale, on the high desert. Their favorite spot, Muroc, or Rodgers Dry Lake, a much larger expanse, was out, declared off limits by the Army Air Corps when they took it over.

When Denise begged off, Bobby enlisted Tommy to drive there with him. At first his buddy was reluctant, as he had planned to take his own roadster. When Bobby pointed out that since he hadn't joined a member SCTA club, all he would be able to do would be to drag up and down off to the side, or be a mere spectator at the timing runs. Tommy readily saw the logic, and together they made plans for the drive and for overnight camping on the mud flats of the dry lake.

First, he had to see Denise, bringing her flowers to placate her for the weekend they would miss. As they sat in his roadster in front of her house, she was pouting.

"It looks like your darned love of speed in this car is more important than our being together."

He took her hand then. "A guy's gotta express himself with this sort of stuff. Would you think as much of me if I didn't have imagination and an adventurous spirit? The challenge of these time trials is part of that, a culmination of all the work I've put into this *Iron* over the last year. I promise you, sweetheart, if I'm successful, I won't leave you by yourself for even a Saturday, much less a whole weekend."

Looking at him dubiously, she asked, "Is that a promise, Bobby?"

Taking her into his arms then, he gazed sincerely into her eyes, and said, "Cross my heart."

* * * *

When he was at last packed and seated in the roadster, with goggles on because he had removed the windshield for added speed, his parents came out to see him off.

"Have fun, Bobby," his mother said in an off-handed way, leading him to reflect how permissive she could be.

"Dad and Mom, I'll be home late Sunday at some time. But don't wait up."

His father just looked at him, unable to speak, his eyes betraying the fear he felt for his eldest son. Trying to reassure him, Bobby said, "Look, Dad, I've had this roadster flat out before, you know, on that long straight on Sepulveda up near San Fernando. This time, it'll be on a smooth expanse of hard dry clay, without any traffic around, and in broad daylight. How safe can you get? And you'll note that the number they assigned me is thirteen, my lucky one."

Waving to the two of them, he backed out into the street, and drove off to pick up Tommy. It was almost a two-hour drive to Rosamond Dry Lake, and without a windshield, until they left the Valley, an occasional insect collision occurred. One such had to be a big, hard June bug, Bobby thought, as it struck his forehead, leaving a welt that lasted the rest of the day.

The dusty road off highway 14 was only three miles long, opening out onto the wide expanse of the parched flats, which in the midday sun shimmered against the distant mountains. The clay of the lakebed was baked hard with myriad cracks forming mosaics, appearing rough at first glance, but as the roadster rolled out onto it, the ride became utterly smooth, as if they had actually been launched onto still water in a boat.

Soon after they arrived, he reported to the officials at the timing stand, and was directed to take his place in the line forming at the start of the course a mile back. Entrants already there seemed to number almost a hundred, with more following.

"Look at all of them," he said to Tommy, "I just joined a member club recently, and haven't won any points. How did I get such a low number?"

With his usual deep chuckle, his buddy replied, "Thirteen? Probably because nobody else wanted it. But it's *your* lucky number. Isn't that how such things are supposed to work?"

They got out their lunches of sandwiches and Cokes as the line of waiting cars slowly shortened, and as it did, he found himself becoming more excited than ever. Tommy had gobbled up his huge sandwich, and when he offered him the unfinished half of his, he jumped at the chance.

Between mouthfuls, Tommy said, "What's the matter, butterflies in the stomach? It's really a breeze, you know. All you have to do is floor it for a mile, hope you're at maximum speed as you enter the traps, hold it for that quarter mile and then back off. But don't forget to slow down soon, because these dry lakes are kinda rough around the edges. After that, all you have to do is come back and pick up your medal."

"Medal? Come on, you know they don't give those out." As he said that, he was envisioning the little brass plate recording his speed, which they did give, for mounting on his dash.

By the time the starting flag dropped for him, Bobby had dealt with the adrenaline rush he was feeling. It really wasn't fear, but the excitement of competition, as in a track meet, or just before a big game. Certainly, he thought, it was the anticipation of a first-time adventure.

Tommy was right. It was like a drag race, he thought, as he floored it, keeping the accelerator pedal flat on the floorboard, winding out through the gears, each time on hearing the whine of the engine peaking, speed shifting. He had no speedometer, but in high, he knew he was approaching a hundred, when the usual relatively low-pitched whistle of his roadster at speed began to warble, and then, with further acceleration, became a steady high "C." He had never heard that before, even flat out on the long straight on Sepulveda. He kept it floored, as the lakebed cracks became blurs under his car. The elation he felt kept his foot on the accelerator until well after he had passed the end of the measured quarter mile. Again Tommy was right. Deceleration was too slow, and he soon found himself and his roadster bouncing over hummocks of sage and sand.

When he finally got back to the timing stand, the official took his entry ticket and marked it "106.50". Not bad, he said to himself, for just heads and twin pots. Marveling about that as he drove back to pick up Tommy, he couldn't help but fantasize about the records he'd be able to shatter with a *full-race* mill.

That night there was a celebration by his roadster club, as it seemed they had won more points on that first day than any competing group. Preparations were made for a big bonfire, Bobby being collared, along with Tommy to gather the wood from the ample dead tree branches and brush that littered the edge of the dry lake. It seems initiates were expected to do the menial work for the old-timers, most of whom were a rough lot, made to look even rougher by the grubbiness that came with all the dust and grease of the occasion.

The golden sunset couldn't have been more beautiful, and when darkness set in, the stars shone with a brightness he had never seen, even in the semi-rural San Fernando Valley. For a while the group around the fire was mellow, and when one of the club members brought out a Ukulele, most joined in singing along. As the veteran members' blood alcohol levels rose, however, they became more boisterous.

Bobby thought of Denise, especially with some of the more plaintive love songs. Saturday was always the biggest date night of the week, and he lamented that he was there without her next to him to share his minor triumph. Then he reasoned, sitting out there on that god-forsaken ancient lakebed, that he'd be seeing her Sunday night. Wasn't that soon enough?

As he gazed at the bright panoply above, thinking of her, someone threw more wood on the fire, leading to a brilliant display of sparks showering into the night sky, competing with the very firmament overhead. Becoming more sentimental, he fancied that he was just such a spark that could warm her up out there among those twinkling stars.

There was relative quiet while they downed hastily roasted hot dogs for the evening meal. Then the serious boozing began, generating at first great merriment. Later, as the burning wood began to turn to glowing coals, Bobby nudged Tommy, still sipping his Coke, pointing out the drinking of the two closest to the fire.

"Look at what they're putting down now. It looks like pure Ethanol mixed with sloe gin for flavor, and because it's pure alcohol, they're using beer to cut it."

Tommy hooted at that in disbelief, until it became evident that the clear stuff came from a five-gallon can.

"See, I told you. They inject that into their manifolds trying for the utmost in performance from their mills during the run through the traps."

They looked on in disbelief as one of them, now obviously drunk, took a swig of the unmixed liquid, leaned toward the dying flames, and sprayed the mouthful in that direction. He was like a small flamethrower, as the arc of spray caught, brightening the coals into a renewed blaze for a moment, causing sparks to again shower upward.

The gathered members, by that time unsteady with drink, cheered loudly. One of them, a mean-looking giant of a man, grabbed the can of alcohol, and staggering over to Bobby, held it out to him.

"Here, kid, drink some of this and see if you can spout fire too. It'll be your rite of initiation into our club."

Bobby was aghast. He had never touched anything stronger than beer, and then only rarely. "Sorry big fella, drinking that straight could be worse than drinking sulfuric acid. Even your buddy who started all this cuts it with plenty of Lucky Lager. And don't try it yourself. You're big, but not that big."

"Hey, Tiny!" Someone yelled from across the fire, "Leave the kid alone, for chrissakes. If ya havta pick on someone, find a guy from another club."

The hulking man became the picture of rage, screaming, "You son of a bitch, I'm coming after you!" With that, he picked up the can of alcohol and threw it at him.

All hell broke loose then, as his aim was off, and it landed in the flames.

Almost in unison came the awed communal gasp, "Oh shit!" Those around the fire then bolted in every direction. It took only a few seconds for the contents of the can to heat enough to blow off the cap. Then, as if on wheels of its own, and spewing flame from the opening, it rocketed straight for a "High Boy" '32 roadster that had been backed up and parked nearby for the celebration. It hit squarely under the somewhat elevated rear end, and became lodged there, its surge stopped by the rear axle, but still spewing flames just under the gas tank.

By that time the commotion had attracted quite a crowd. Had the roadster been built with a model "A" body, it might still have had the gas tank up front, just behind the engine compartment, and the pyrotechnics would have ended there. But beginning in 1932, Ford installed the fuel tank at the rear.

What for Bobby seemed forever, the jet of flame continued to spout, some of it licking upward against the tank. It actually took less than a second for him to realize the danger. He was the first to see it.

"Quick, Tommy, get the crowd on the other side away from there. I'll do the same over here."

The only entirely sober ones, they swung into action, shouting warnings, pushing and cajoling the crowd back. One couple, obviously spectators judging by their dress, was too close. Swaying as if to music and seemingly mesmerized by the blowtorch sound, they finally were jolted out of their dream by Bobby yanking their arms, and shouting, "Get back, this heap is going up any second now!"

The man let go of his companion and ran, as she staggered an uncertain step and fell. Everyone was running then except Bobby. Grabbing her by the arms, he dragged her away, just as the gas tank exploded, engulfing most of the vehicle in flames.

As he labored to pull the hapless woman farther away, rivulets of fire reached out for them as the burning alcohol and gasoline sped along the fissures in the baked clay. For a moment it reminded him of pictures he'd seen in *National Geographic* of molten lava flowing downslope, consuming everything in its path. But after another couple of yards, he was able to release his prostrate burden, as the last of the flaming fuel exhausted itself in the surface cracks. The hulk of the '32 smoldered on all night.

The next morning, most of those able to have slept even a little had hangovers. This included the SCTA officials who came early to investigate the incident. Only a few present could comprehensively recount what had happened. Bobby and Tommy, although nearly sleepless, filled them in on the events of the night before.

The big man known as Tiny spoke up. He was enraged because it had been his car that had been destroyed. He pointed a finger at them, saying angrily, "They started it. When I offered them a drink, those little jerks threw the can of alcohol into the fire."

Bobby jumped up in their defense, indignantly countering, "That's a bald-faced lie! Earthquake McGoon here did it all by himself. The irony is, it was his hot '32 that burned."

That got a laugh from the man that Bobby had pulled away from the explosion. "Yeah, he's right, and a hero too, saving our lives by warning us. Why, he even risked his own life, dragging my girlfriend away just in time."

The chairman of the association turned to Tiny with an accusing eye. "You know, you can be expelled for much less than this. Luckily, nobody was more than singed by the explosion, and it wasn't someone else's roadster that was destroyed. Now, do you have anything to say in your defense?"

The big man sheepishly hung his head as he replied, "I admit I threw the can of alcohol, but I didn't mean for it to land in the fire. It was heavier than I bargained for. And it was this kid," again pointing in Bobby's direction, "Who made me do it."

A chorus of jeers resulted, bringing the official's hand raised for silence. "You guys know we have to police ourselves, or the authorities won't continue to permit these meets. You're only sorry because your iron burned, but not truly contrite, falsely blaming these teenagers."

The vote took only a few minutes. The brawny Tiny was banished, meekly shuffling over to his blackened and cooling '32.

Bobby leaned over to Tommy, saying, "Let's quit while we're ahead. The rest of the meet will be going on until dark, and I have things to do at home." His buddy nodded as they headed for the roadster, and began to pack their things.

As Bobby was checking under the hood, a soft "Hi!" caused him to turn. It was the woman he had pulled away from the fire and explosion. In the daylight, despite it being her morning after, she was a knockout. Long auburn hair, and with the most striking amber eyes, almost cat-like, that held his gaze as if he were hypnotized. Obviously bra-less, she wore a man's white cotton shirt, tied by the tails with a knot under her ample breasts. Tight black bullfighter pants accentuated the curve of her hips and shapely legs. When he was finally able to control his amazement, he returned her brief greeting.

She smiled at him, and running the tip of her tongue along her teeth suggestively, she offered, "I wanted to thank you later last night, but my boyfriend was around, so here I am this morning."

"He's still around," Bobby replied, pointing, "I saw him just over there."

She then said, "We had a big fight. Someone told me he just panicked and ran, leaving me to my fate. If you hadn't been there, I would've been toast."

"Gee," he said, kicking at the dried clay, "I would have done that for anybody in danger. Last night it just happened to be you."

"But it was *me*. You saved my life. The least you could do is to let me make it up to you."

With that, she took a step forward, and putting her arms around him, kissed him passionately on the mouth, murmuring, "And I just happen to be here now."

She was still brushing her lips on his when he slipped out of her embrace, hastily closing the hood. "Tommy, Let's go!"

He was almost breathless as he turned and stammered an apology. "I promised I'd be home tonight. I just happened to be in the right place at the right time, that's all. It was nothing personal."

"Well, it's certainly personal with me. Here's my card with my number. Call me."

Since he made no effort to take it from her, she tucked the small lavender card into his shirt pocket. Smiling invitingly, and rolling her wild golden eyes, she turned, and slowly walked away, her hips swinging provocatively.

"What the heck was that?" Tommy asked, as they pulled out of the group of roadsters. "Whatta doll."

"Aw, it was nothing, just gratitude is all." The question was answered absently, as he swung the car onto highway 14, heading for home.

* * * *

Bobby learned later that when he and Denise had said goodbye, she was unhappy. Hadn't she devoted her whole senior year to him, and hadn't he just taken off for the weekend without her? For her part, she'd always been available when *he* needed *her*.

After graduation, she had secured a job at the Wheeler Bank in town, as she had during the previous summer. She needed the money but not the extra baggage of having to deal with Wheelie, the banker's son. Having dated him before Bobby, she had come to look on him as merely a friend, but his interest in her was hardly platonic.

He often drove her home after work, and on that Sunday came over, losing no time in asking her out.

Demurring, she said, "Why, Wheelie, you know full well that I'm going steady with Bobby Taylor now. Of course we can be friends, but it wouldn't be right for us to date, under the circumstances."

Narrowing his eyes slyly, he replied, "Then as your friend, I can be very handy, if only for a shoulder to cry on."

"Cry? Why would I do that?"

"Well, didn't he just take off without you?"

"Cry about such a little thing as his taking his hop-up to the dry lakes for a couple of days?" She didn't add that she did have a good cry after Bobby had gone, and that she had refused to go with him because of that car.

Wheelie didn't need her to tell him that. A couple of times, driving his new Ford convertible, he had picked up girls who had been hanging around with those roadster freaks. A shiny new car always beat out a cut-down *iron*. He even had been told by a date that many girls wouldn't be seen in a roadster, for the same reason that riding on the back of a motorcycle was then generally looked upon as a sign of their being tramps. Guilt by association.

"Denise," he said, after some thought, "I see us as more than friends. Before Bobby, we did have some fun, didn't we?"

Reminded of their previous good times together, she looked at him affectionately, playfully putting a hand on his knee. "We did, but that was then. It's different now."

With that, he put his hand over hers, and held it there. "See, not so different, is it?"

"You know what I mean," she replied, pulling away, and getting out. It was then that the idea came to her. Bobby was due back from the desert that night.

"But if you're the friend you say you are, and you behave yourself, we could go to the movies together today. I hear that big hit, *Gone with the Wind*, is playing at The Burbank."

As she entered the house, it occurred to her that she could be playing with fire, but as long as it doesn't get romantic, she mused, how could it hurt? It might be just what Bobby needed, a little competition. He's been taking me for granted, she thought, for sure. A little dose of jealousy might be good for him.

* * * *

As they drove home from the dry lake meet, there was a lot to think about. As the miles passed, the clatter of the un-muffled exhaust began to form tunes in his ears. That woman had to be ten years older than he, but he still found her exciting. As the engine noise droned on, he wondered what tune would she have sung to him? It would probably be a torch song. Inspired by that, he found he could hum along with the roar, changing the accompanying tune by thinking of lyrics of songs learned from records at home. He was reminded of one belonging to his parents, "Frankie and Johnny," about a guy betraying his girl. Why that tune, he wondered. He had been just a Saturday away from her. How is that doing her wrong, just thinking about those eyes, and well, that other stuff?

When he dropped Tommy off, his friend said, "If you're thinking of seeing Denise now, you'd better wipe off that lipstick."

He decided then that he just had to see her. So, without returning home to shower and change out of his grubby clothes, he headed over to her place. After all, she had agreed to their getting together when he got back.

There already was a car parked in front of the O'Donnell place. Dammit, That's Wheelie's convertible, he realized. What the hell is he doing here for Christ's sake?

It was still light, and he could see Wheelie and Denise sitting there talking. At least they weren't necking, he saw to his relief.

Pulling up behind them, lacking a horn, he called out, "Hey, you two, what's going on?" Then, hopping out of his roadster, he knocked on the raised window next to Denise.

"Bobby!" She exclaimed, rolling the window down, "I didn't expect you back so early."

Wheelie nervously nodded his agreement, as he pushed the starter button.

"Wait," she said, turning to him, "It was fun today. See you at work tomorrow."

Bobby then opened the door, and she got out, smiling up at him coyly. He started around the back of the car to the driver's side, causing Wheelie to hastily put it into low gear, peeling out, leaving the smell of burning rubber.

"How come after I'm gone only a single night, you're dating your old flame again? I thought we were steadies."

"It wasn't a date, and he never was a flame. There was a show in town that we both were interested in, so we went. I don't have a car, you know. Besides, you've never said anything about going steady. You just assumed that since I wasn't dating anyone else, that had to be it. You know he and I dated before you entered the picture, and now we both work at his father's bank. It's impossible to avoid him."

Bobby took both her hands then, and looking into her eyes, earnestly said, "Let's make it official. Remember, before going, I promised you I wouldn't leave again for as long as a whole week-end if I proved successful. My speed was more than I expected. That to me is success enough. From now on it's just you and me, if you want."

Denise realized then that her going out with Wheelie had served its purpose. It wasn't until she nestled into his arms that she noticed how smudged with dirt and oil his shirt was. Taking a closer look, and running a hand over his chest, she felt the card in the breast pocket. Curious, she asked, "What's this?"

He had totally forgotten its being there, pre-occupied as he was. Before he could react, she took it out, and read the print, with a voice strained with increasing exasperation.

"What's this? 'Amber Allen, Exotic Dancer and Photographer's Model.' Oh Bobby," she said plaintively, her tone betraying her pain, "How could you?"

He took the card from her and threw it to the floorboard. "It's a long story. Let me explain."

She didn't wait to hear it. "Never mind," she said hotly, wheeling toward the front door.

"But wait, I haven't told you what happened. It's not what you think."

She didn't answer as she slammed the door in his face.

* * * *

Standing there waiting his turn near the recruiting office, he was becoming frustrated. A commotion at the head of the line, still almost half a block away, had slowed his progress.

His mood returned him once more to his problems with Denise, after his return from that dry lake meet three and a half years before.

SIX

Forgiveness

They hadn't spoken for two weeks. She didn't call, and wouldn't answer the phone. He began to despair that she would ever forgive him, considering the cause of it all. He had retrieved the card, thinking of calling Amber. But after some deliberation, he had realized what he and Denise shared. He decided then that their love was worth fighting for, and tore the card into tiny bits. Real love certainly trumped gratitude. He rang Denise's bell one afternoon towards the end of that week, and her mother answered the door.

"Hello Bobby. I'm sorry, but Deenie still doesn't want to talk to you, or anyone else. You must have had a terrible fight. She cried for most of the first few days, and wouldn't even go to work. For the first time in her life, she still won't even discuss anything with me."

"I'm sorry, Mrs. O'Donnell. It was a huge mutual misunderstanding as I see it. What can I do to get the message across to her?"

"She won't talk to you, but if you bring some flowers, I'll see that she gets them. A little note to accompany them would help."

Bobby looked at her gratefully. "You're wonderful. I'll do just that, and bring them tomorrow."

"I'll see you then, but don't make it too late. Her father will be coming home from work, and he wouldn't allow her to receive anything from you."

"Thanks for the advice, I'll get on it right away." Then he headed for his car.

* * * *

That night, Denise was finally able to confide her feelings to her mother. Coming downstairs, she found her mother in the kitchen.

"Mom, I'm so sorry to have behaved so badly these last weeks. Bobby met some sort of floozy at the roadster meet, and she wants to see him again. What has upset me so much is that he kept her card, making me wonder about his plans with her. I purposely went out with Wheelie to stop Bobby from taking me for granted, but if she's still in the picture, it may mean that I've overplayed the jealousy card. Such tactics obviously cut both ways."

"I see," her mother replied, "And it seems to have cut very deeply, bringing you to constant tears, and practically driving you out of your mind."

"I'm much better now, and looking back on that night, I was so unfair, too upset even to listen to him. But I miss him too much to allow that to come between us for much longer. And he's been hurt too, I just know."

* * * *

Bobby was lucky, finding his mother's prized roses to be thriving. He cut a dozen of the purest white, and wrapped the stems in layers of moistened gift-wrap. Attaching a small card with a ribbon, he wrote:

White roses are for innocence, humility and love that's true.

All three of these, a dozen times over, I'll always have for you.

   All my Love, Bobby

That afternoon he took the flowers to Denise's mother, who, on seeing the bouquet, remarked, "How lovely. Perfect for her depression. Last night we finally were able to talk, and I think she's feeling guilty as much as betrayed. Once she starts reasoning, instead of emoting the way she's done all week, I'll bet she'll listen to you. But you'll have to go slowly and be gentle. None of your boisterous impatience, okay?"

As he started his engine, she called, "I'll have her phone you, but it may take a few days."

Three days later they did have a short telephone conversation, during which she thanked him for the roses and the little poem. There followed a more lengthy talk that evening, in front of her house, and in his family's sedan. At first she was reserved, but this changed as he explained his connection to the dancer.

"There was an explosion, and I pulled her to safety. Everyone said that I saved her from burns or worse. She was just grateful, that's all. Her entire life hangs on her looks. You have to understand that even relatively minor burns could ruin everything for someone like her."

Finally she said, "I think we should have an understanding. You're the only boy I want. If you're not going to have anything to do with that overly grateful bimbo, then we'll both know we can depend on each other. Being steadies is what we've been all along. Don't you think it's high time we made it official?"

"I thought that was us from the beginning. Didn't you once say something to the effect that you were going to marry me? I haven't been interested in anyone else since then. Isn't that exclusive enough?"

She kissed him then, saying softly, "Oh Yes," adding, "And your roadster will be fine. Just shave once in a while."

As he held her, he couldn't help comparing her kiss to that of the dancer. Denise won, hands down, but he realized by that time that their love was not written in stone. He would have to continue to work to keep the spark alive.

* * * *

As the days of summer passed, his remaining evenings with Denise were dwindling down, as he planned to leave for Chicago the First of September. She snuggled into his arms on one of those balmy Southern California evenings when late summer conditions blocked the low clouds from rolling in over the Hollywood Hills.

This time they were parked just above the reservoir, Lake Hollywood, in the hills above Cahuenga Pass, looking down on Hollywood. The moon was past full, but still bathing the hills and the lake in a magical silvery glow. The light shone on her hair, as if it were a halo, as well as outlining her form beneath the light blouse and shorts she wore. He wondered, since this would be almost their last evening together for as long as a quarter, if this could be the night.

They had progressed in their lovemaking, which was wonderful for him, and he thought, for her, as she responded warmly to his caresses. But for him their relationship still failed to bring the ecstasy that he envisioned would be the pinnacle of their love.

At that moment he whispered, "Sweetheart, why can't we go all the way tonight? I'm leaving soon, and this will be almost our last chance until maybe Christmas vacation."

Her reply was a shock despite it being so soft-spoken that he could hardly hear it, as she replied, "Because, for one thing, darling, you've never actually said you love me, and for two, we're not married yet."

"Oh, Christ, is that all? Can't you tell? Of course I love you and want to marry you."

This last came out automatically. He had never told any girl he loved her, because he really never had. But that was before Denise, and he had always associated love with marriage. At that instant he was surprised about what he had blurted out so spontaneously, and this was reinforced by a sudden awareness of his ears becoming enveloped in a burning, tingly sensation he'd never experienced before. Quite simply, it was a kind of fear, evidence that he wasn't ready, just then, for such a commitment. Oh, he thought, he did love her, and wanted to be with her forever, that was certain. He just wasn't ready for all the responsibilities that came with marriage.

He thought of the only real jobs he had ever held, all only for the summer. Work as a lifeguard or parking cars wouldn't come close to supporting a family. Even with her getting a job, it would be hard for them to live in Chicago while he studied. God, he said to himself, it would be impossible for them to get by if she became pregnant. He just couldn't see tying the knot until he graduated at least, never mind his ambition for Law School, three long years more. And with the war, who knows what all would happen?

She sensed his fears, giving a squeeze to his hand, and a brush of her lips to his neck.

"We'll get by as long as we have our love, which is more powerful than anything." Then she murmured, "Especially when we're married."

He suddenly felt sick with love for her. He pleaded, "But must we wait for a mere legal certificate before our love is complete? It's so beautiful out here tonight, why not here and now?"

"Oh, what an impatient lover you've suddenly become." Chiding him gently, "That can wait for God's blessing." After a pause, she added, "I think you better take me home now." This was voiced with a tone of firmness that was unmistakable, ending any protest.

He had nothing to say on the way down the hill and across Burbank. He drove more slowly than usual hoping somehow that the evening wasn't going to end like that. I can't see getting married for years, he thought, at least until graduation from college. I certainly can't marry now, but will she wait for me?

She broke the silence finally, putting her head on his shoulder, and tearfully said, "I want to marry you more than anything, Bobby, but will you remain true while you're away? I need the security of your love, but with your plans for college and Law School, you won't be able to support a family for years. How long will the wait really be?"

He looked down at her then, feeling her tears through his shirt. "The way things look, the wait may be years, he responded, "But what better way to unite us forever than our making love before I go? That would seal our commitment to each other. I couldn't ever look at another woman after that as long as you'll be here for me when I come home."

"I do know you love me, so what you're saying isn't just a line. But it would be unfair, somehow, to give myself to you now rather than waiting for marriage, after all my mother and I have talked about all my life."

When they pulled up to her house, he shut off the engine and turned to her. "Let's discuss this again tomorrow night. In the meantime, think about our love," adding imploringly, "And the fact that I could be back in only a few months for Christmas, if necessary. I'll write every day, and I'll be true to you. Wait for me."

She burst into tears again, her voice choking with emotion, "Of course I'll wait for you. You are the only one I'll ever love, can't you see that, my Bobby?"

He was in no condition to respond, close to tears as he was, thinking, men don't cry, do they? All he could do was walk her to the front door, where they embraced and kissed good night. When the door closed, he was left with an emptiness he had never known, and was so depressed that he considered not ever leaving Burbank for any reason, despite all the arrangements that had been made.

"Dammit all." was all he could mutter.

She, in turn, leaned with her back against the inside of the door until the latch clicked shut, then slumped to the floor in despair. It was a couple of hours before her mother found her there, still weeping quietly, and another hour before she could be persuaded to finally get into bed.

After crying most of the night, she had finally been overtaken by sleep. It wasn't until Saturday noon that she was awakened by her mother.

Denise's first words were about Bobby. "He's leaving tomorrow. Mom, what should I do? How can I let him go like this?"

Mrs. O'Donnell replied soothingly, "Didn't he say he'd write every day, think of you constantly, and not even look at another girl until the two of you were together again? You told me that last night, between your fits of sobbing and tears. Didn't you say that the two of you made a solemn pledge? Doesn't that mean anything any more?"

"Oh Mom, you can't possibly know how complex our situation is. It's practically impossible."

"Darling, I'm your mother, remember? We've always been honest with each other. Now let's get a bite to eat and talk this thing out over coffee, okay? I'll fix something while you get dressed."

Putting on jeans and a sweatshirt, she became eager to air her further concerns to the only person in the world possible aside from Bobby. As she hurried down to the kitchen, she was met by the increasing aromas of breakfast, foremost that of strong coffee.

"I'm not hungry Mom, but I really need that coffee, thanks."

After the first cup, the two just looked at each other, the older women smiling benignly and expectantly, her daughter still the picture of despair.

"Mom, I don't know what to do. If I had followed my heart, I would have given myself to him last night, but I just couldn't, when the time came, because of all the plans we've talked about my whole life. You know, the church wedding, and about saving myself for my husband, and all that."

"Dear," her mother finally offered, "As close as you and he have been, I wouldn't have been surprised to hear that you had already been intimate. I think I know how you feel, having experienced the same thing when I was your age. I saved myself for the man I married. But what did it get me? He found that I had never felt that ultimate in passion with any other man, and it seemed to have given him the idea that I had never loved or been loved. Because of that, he became convinced that I was his property, and abjectly dependent on him. With that attitude came the man you now have for a father, dictatorial, self-centered and unsympathetic. You've seen how he treats Bobby, as if he were a second-class citizen just because he's Catholic. Look how he exerts authority over you, telling you he would never allow you to marry him. You know, that could extend to any other man you might choose, unless he approves of him for some reason of his own, likely without any thought for your own feelings or what you might have to say in the matter."

"Mom, what you're telling me is that you've wasted your life. Why did you stick with him all these years, then? Why?"

"Because of you, my dearest and only daughter, because of my being your mother, and wanting you to grow up in a family with both parents. At least we didn't fight much. I gave that up early. You know how your father is. He's a good provider, keeping a roof over our heads all through the Depression. Sex, yes, there was that at first, but of a selfish kind, without much thought for me. Still, it brought you, and for that I'll forever be thankful."

"You still wasted your life for me!" Denise cried, her voice now carrying a tone of guilt.

"No dear, as I just said, I have you, but it will have been a waste if you are forever unhappy with your own life."

"But mom, the only way I can ever be happy is if I can spend my life with Bobby. He's the only one I could ever love."

Her mother looked at her with the hint of a smile. "I know that's the way you feel now. But you're only eighteen. You'll have plenty of time and other chances for happiness."

"Not the age thing, please." Denise implored, "I can't take that now. I'm a high school graduate, I have a job, and I'm old enough to make my own decisions."

Mrs. O'Donnell looked at her daughter proudly. "I know that all too well, and one of these days I'm going to lose you to some lucky, and I hope deserving, man. I think Bobby is one of those. Personally, he would be my choice among the boys you've dated. But no matter who you end up choosing, Deenie, it would still be special for you to be a virgin when you wear that white wedding dress."

Denise thought that one over for a couple of minutes as she contemplated the remaining coffee in her cup. Then, she looked up and said, "Gee, thanks, Mom, for having the patience to sit down with me like this. We haven't had such a heart to heart session since you told me about *the birds and the bees.*"

With that she bounded up the stairs, to shower and dress for her big date with Bobby. It was the last time they'd be together for some time, as his train ticket was for the following morning, and she wanted to look especially pretty.

He borrowed the family sedan, rather than driving his roadster. He knew this was a special occasion, and that she wouldn't want her hair mussed up by the wind. The outfit he had on was his best, the same one he had worn to the graduation parties and commencement. Before he left the house, his sister, Phyllis, an acquaintance of Denise's, made sure he looked his sharpest.

"Yummy," she concluded, "You'd pass inspection anywhere. Have fun."

He was taking her to the Aragon Ballroom, in Los Angeles, where their favorite, Glenn Miller and his band were playing that week. They both loved to jitterbug, but also to move to some of the slower rhythms of his ballads.

Before leaving for her place, he made a little corsage from a pink rose from the garden, a couple of leaves, and some tin foil. Not much, he thought, but she loved little surprises like that. Besides, he had just enough cash to get through the evening as it was, without plunking down more for a professional job.

Looking it over, his mother said with a benign smile, "It's lovely. Of course I would wear it, especially if given by the one I love. But I would advise you to get a big pin to hold it on. Girls don't have button holes in their lapels, or even lapels, for that matter."

While driving the two miles to her house across the Valley, he couldn't keep his thoughts from the frustrations of the night before. Although this was going to be their last time together for some months, he resolved not to push her to give in to him. He wanted tonight to end happily, whatever happened between them. Best to leave her with wonderful memories, not the agony of the previous night.

When he pulled up in front of her house, her father was out on the front lawn watering.

"Hi, Mr. O'Donnell!" Bobby called out in a friendly greeting, as he eagerly strode up the walk towards the front door. As usual, a minimal response was forthcoming, but he was used to that from him. At least he's not turning the hose on me, he thought. Still, he hurried up the steps to minimize the target his back presented.

Denise's mother came to the door, smilingly opening it for him. "My, how nice you look tonight. And a corsage! I can't remember when she last got one of those. She'll be so pleased."

Bobby felt the warmth returning, thinking, one out of two parents isn't so bad. "Evening Mrs. O'D. You're looking well, how's everything? Denise about ready?"

She replied, "Thank you, fine, almost, in that order. Do you always greet people that way?"

At that moment Denise appeared, bringing gasps in unison from the two. Her mother was the first to speak, exclaiming, "Darling, I've never seen you so beautiful."

Bobby was dumbfounded, his knees suddenly feeling a little weak, able only to blurt out, "You can say that again." God, he thought, she truly is beautiful. With a trembling hand, he pinned the flower to her dress, a low-cut strapless of white cotton, worn under a diaphanous lace jacket of dark blue, the color of her eyes. She smiled as he fumbled with the pin over her breast.

"Watch it!" She cautioned, adding, with a bit of hyperbole, "That pin looks almost as big as one of Cupid's arrows. But we all know that one of those has already done its job."

All three laughed at that, and after she grabbed her coat, she offered a cheek for her mother's kiss. Hand in hand, the couple happily went out the door. During most of the drive, he was too smitten to say much, as she contentedly snuggled next to him. Neither talked about his leaving in the morning for his school year in Chicago. To him, he was more in love than ever, and felt that he would do anything to win her, even if it meant waiting forever. Or almost forever. As they drove, he decided not to be aggressive regarding sexual intercourse, but with the lingering hope that she might still let herself go fully, regardless of her previous stance.

The first part of the evening flew, as they danced to some of the greatest swing music of the era. They did what later came to be known on the West Coast as the *New Yorker*, but without those wild gymnastic gyrations seen in exhibitions. They were able to get beers, instead of soft drinks, as they looked so mature, the waitress complimenting them, "You two make such a lovely couple."

The alcohol alleviated some of enormity of their impending separation. One of the numbers they danced to, "In the Mood," was Miller's trademark at that time. They didn't really need any tune to make them feel that way, however.

It was late, and before the last ballad was played, they left for the car. For the fun of it, they stopped in Hollywood on the way back to the Valley. As they strolled down Hollywood Boulevard, more than a few passers-by gave them admiring glances, as if they might have been movie stars, so glamorous she looked.

One young woman exclaimed as she passed, "Oh, beautiful!" Bobby's chest swelled with pride. That night, she truly was beautiful.

He asked, "Shall we go somewhere for a bite?"

"I'm not really at all hungry, are you?"

Bobby certainly was, until she continued in that special husky voice, "Let's go somewhere with a view and where we can be alone together. It's been so wonderful for me that I just want to make up for the pain I caused you last night."

Oh God, he thought. This is unreal. Is this really happening to me? He was not about to question her reversal. "But I don't have any condoms," he whispered, not intending to be heard.

"I heard that." She replied, "I thought that you were a Boy Scout, silly. Remember your motto. Just march right into that drug store over there, and get some."

As he crossed the street, Bobby thought, because they were not getting anything to eat, he luckily had enough money left, after the beers, to buy a pack of *Trojans*. But what would the protocol be, he wondered, if short of cash, in asking the girl to pay?

While she waited outside alone, enduring the soft whistles from a couple of passing men, he braved facing the clerk inside, a youngish woman who gave him the once over. It occurred to him that she might refuse his request because of his age.

Instead, she offered, "You can have them for free, if you'll take me with you." They both laughed at that, but his thoughts were only for Denise.

They drove up into the Hollywood hills along Mulholland Drive, where the lights of Los Angeles shone like a carpet of diamonds. The night was again illuminated by the still nearly full but waning moon, lending a glow to her skin and hair. As they kissed, she became more passionate, her full open lips sending a thrill through him he had never felt before.

"Wait," she whispered, as she smoothly removed her lacy blouse. Before he knew it, she had somehow opened the bodice of her strapless dress and removed her bra. Her nudity in the moon's glow then lighted the way for their increasing passion.

As they made love, despite it being the first time for either of them, it couldn't have gone more smoothly. His biggest problem was extracting the condoms from their foil. For her, the first momentary twinge of pain was extinguished quickly by their mutual passion and didn't recur.

"If only this night could last forever," she murmured after a time, encircling him once more with her arms, gently nipping him on the neck.

He agreed, with a long sigh, but added, "My Denise, as much as I love you, I don't think I would be capable of much more, at least in one night."

She giggled at that, wondering aloud, "Maybe more practice would help."

At last they came back to reality as he exclaimed, "Look, the view is gone."

She laughed, "Have you lost your mind? The windows fogged up long ago. No wonder we can't see outside."

Sheepishly, because in his ecstasy he had not realized that, he responded, "That's what you've always done to me. Make me sweat, whether in frustration, fear, or passion."

Her reply came softly, "From now on, only in passion."

Before they parted at her door, he embraced her, whispering into her ear, "Tonight was so wonderful, I'm thinking of canceling my plans to leave. To heck with them. I'll get a job here somewhere, and we can get married as soon as we have enough money saved."

Recoiling from his arms, she quickly and firmly replied, "You'll do no such thing. You have to follow your original plan, at least for the first year. Then we can talk about where we go from there. No matter what you feel now, you'd never forgive me if I stood in the way of your career, and even though I'd see more of you, I probably would never forgive myself either."

* * * *

The following day, the First of September, Hitler's armies invaded Poland, starting WWII, changing the lives of hundreds of millions of people. Britain and France declared war two days later.

The conflict was taken seriously during the *Blitzkrieg* through Poland, but most were soon lulled into complacency, despite the Nazis' easy conquest there. The hostilities on the Western Front became so tepid that it was dubbed a phony war, a *Sitzkrieg*. Life, for a time, continued the same, at least in the U.S. The war was a long way away, and many Americans became dedicated isolationists. Those who remained in favor of Britain and France still found it hard to believe that the conflict would ever affect them.

* * * *

That Monday after Pearl Harbor, waiting to enlist, filled with memories of their lovemaking, he recalled phoning Denise the morning after that last date. She had been on the way to church, and he couldn't reach her. Bobby's father had driven him to Union Station, in L.A., where he had grabbed his bags, said a final goodbye, and climbed aboard the Santa Fe "Chief."

Almost in a daze at that point, worrying about the war, and thinking back to that wondrous night almost two years before with Denise, he recalled how his destination had seemed a million miles away.

SEVEN

Chicago, 1939—1940

He'd made the trip before with his mother to visit her sister Betty in Chicago, where he would be staying for the first year at the University of Chicago. The only drawback was the fact that they were, while outwardly easy-going, quite religious, and everyone went to Mass much too frequently for him.

The forty-nine hour trip promised a degree of comfort, although sleeping in the chair car his ticket specified was not the best and most restful situation. He recalled much of the time thinking of Denise while staring at the scenery. After watching the vast expanses of the West streaming by, even on closing his eyes to rest them, the moving panorama persisted.

There was one diversion that evening. After supper, a young Army Air Corps captain, with pilot's wings on his blouse, singled Bobby out, and sat down beside him. He immediately struck up a conversation with a playful slap on the shoulder.

"I'll bet this is the first time you've been away from home, kid. You must be too lonely to be bored."

"Nah," Bobby replied, "I've been to Chicago twice before on the train." This was with the certain assurance that comes with the truth. No need with this guy to add that both times he went with his mother.

The captain, not more than five years older, looked him over, and then squarely into his eyes, observing Bobby's youthful appearance.

"You can't be more than sixteen. I'll bet you didn't travel alone before this."

In righteous indignation Bobby protested. "I'm nineteen, and anyway, it's none of your business."

A long silence ensued, leading Bobby to regret his protest. Wasn't his new seatmate the very picture of what he hoped he might become? Probably with the Air Corps, depending on which way the war in Europe went.

This brought an apology. Stammering somewhat embarrassedly, he admitted, "It's a first time all right, not the traveling, but having to leave my girlfriend."

With that the captain showed renewed interest, and genuine sympathy. That won a spontaneous outpouring on Bobby's part, thoroughly describing his position, its frustrations, and his resultant depression.

"I'm with you," the officer said, "And these things aren't easily solved in just a few days. It may take weeks or months, but there *is* something that can be done about that. Come on with me to the club car for a drink. That'll fix you up, at least for now. It's on me."

Their destination was only a few cars back in the train, but the door openings and closings at the vestibules made the trip seem longer, and definitely noisier, with the warm wind, much purer than the smoky chair car diminishing his sadness a little.

The club car was even smokier than the others, but somehow it seemed natural there, as he observed a number of passengers talking as they smoked and drank. This was what high school students would do at their parties or while driving in their cars through the hills at home. The problem was, there it was mainly soft drinks, and at the most, beer. Now he was being offered hard stuff.

They slid into chairs facing forward, and the steward, after a wink from the captain, nodded and went off to the nearby bar for the drinks. Apparently the tastes of the Air Corps were well known to him, or at least those of the captain himself.

When the drinks came, Scotch for the captain and a Manhattan for the younger man, the officer toasted to the wild blue yonder, and downed his whiskey within too short a time. Unused to such potent drinks, Bobby was definitely inclined to nurse his sweet cocktail.

"Come on, fella, down the hatch. You need more than just one to treat your present problem."

Bobby was just beginning to feel a little light-headed, with the first of the sweetness, but he also noted that much of his sadness had left him.

"Yeah, thanks, I will go for another," pouring the last of the glass's contents down his throat.

Two more, and he was definitely flying, something the steward noticed, leading him to whisper into the captain's ear. His newfound friend then suggested that they end their social hour and depart to their respective coaches.

He had hoped to dream of Denise that night in the same way his day-dreaming unfolded during the day, but somehow the train's motion and the repetitive "Clickety-clack" sound of the wheels on the rails kept coming through along with grinding sounds, transmitted from the vestibules at either end of the car, when the doors there were opened. This made for fitful sleep, devoid of any inspiration, although it came easily that night for the first time in a couple of days, if only for about four hours. On awakening, he first noted a queasiness and then with movement, a headache, his forehead throbbing away.

Great, my first hangover, he thought, and not an ice bag in sight. He craved fresh air, and headed for the front of the car, but when he opened it, the rush of air was stinking of diesel fumes, and that, combined with the accentuated motion at the end of the car nearly caused him to throw up. But as luck would have it, the train was slowing before pulling into the station at Tucumcari, New Mexico.

Saved in the nick of time, he thought, as the slowing pace reduced the car's gyrations, and with that his impending upchucking.

When the train came to a halt, he went out onto the station platform. The crisp cold mountain air was a tonic, as was the dawn sky, washed with the pink glow of the impending sunrise, promising a lovely day. Because of his headache, he still couldn't open his eyes widely, as even that soft light provoked a worsening of his pain.

As he was standing on the platform, amid milling fellow passengers, his erstwhile drinking companion approached him with a hearty greeting. This was met with a half-hearted smile and limp handshake.

He observed dubiously, "I may some day sign up for training as a pilot if we get involved in the war, but I probably never will be able to drink like one."

To that, the captain mirthfully responded, "Not spoken like a true fighter pilot, son. If you had never experienced a hangover, you'd have a tougher time with the strain and aftermath of aerobatics or combat."

"My God," Bobby murmured, considering for a moment the dubious logic. Rather than being encouraged, in his queasiness that morning, he could only reflect that maybe, even if war came, they would need lawyers too.

By the next afternoon, when the train rolled into the Dearborn Street Station in Chicago, he was well, partly because of normal recovery, but also by reason that the young captain did not again approach him with drink in mind. He hurried to the vestibule with his bags, and as soon as the doors were opened, he jumped down and was off to the station exit. How to get to his aunt's home on the South Side was a dim memory, but he still recalled the route. Take the Illinois Central to the Midway, and then across to South Woodlawn Avenue, at least a mile, no mean feat with his luggage and in the humid Midwest September afternoon. Whatta sweat, he thought.

As he emerged from the station into the bright sunlight, he heard a soft southern voice calling out his name.

"Is this the little Bobby Taylor I used to drive around years ago?"

Bobby turned toward the sound, and the beaming face of a light-skinned African-American. He instantly recognized Alfred, his aunt and uncle's chauffeur and butler. He was then in his mid-forties, tall and straight.

"Gosh Alfred," he said, "By this time I thought you would have gone on to better things, maybe with uncle Joe at the Motor Club, or playing with a big band with that sax of yours"

"Hell boy, you gotta know there's no room for us folks in the front office, and I sure am past my prime for the road. The work with your aunt and uncle suits me fine." Then, looking Bobby over, he added, "My, you're for sure not the little boy I used to call Bobboo. It does look like you've put away your share of eatments by the way you've grown! Come on," he finally said, "They're waiting for you now, and if we're late for supper, there'll be hell to pay, for a fact."

The drive took about a half hour, straight to the South Side via Lakeshore Drive, along Lake Michigan, which was an unusually smooth blue, and then onto 57th Street through the Hyde Park neighborhood.

Bobby recalled with nostalgia what he had experienced back then. There was the sensuous sultriness of the air, and the great overhanging elms shading much of the street. The memories came flooding back. He recalled the sound of the Cicadas' shrilling. He thought of the outings to the lakefront in the summer for swimming, and the Midway for ice-skating when they flooded it in winter. One summer, it was the playground for softball, with an after game ice-cream cone in that same Hyde Park neighborhood, on that very street.

Just then, the Caddy pulled into the wide driveway that described a straight line to the house before it curved to the back of the property and the two story building that proved to be the gardener's flat, below which was the four car garage. They stopped at the main entrance, along the side, with the door up several wide Indiana limestone steps, the whole area, including the car, sheltered by a large overhang, shielding everything from the notoriously fickle Chicago weather.

As soon as the car stopped, Bobby hopped out, going for his stuff, but was waved off by Alfred.

"Get on in there, boy, they're anxious to see you after all this time."

With that, Bobby, needing no further urging, bounded up the steps to the door, propelling himself inside, and fully into the waiting arms of his aunt Betty.

Things really had changed. The last time, when he was nine, he barely came up to her chin. Now, he was a head taller than she was, but still outweighed by her matriarchal figure. Beaming, she wrapped him up in a virtual bear hug.

"How good it is to finally see you, son. How long has it been? And look at you. You've become a man. Joe, come and see who's here."

Not waiting, she took Bobby by the hand, and proudly led him into the adjoining living room, over to her husband.

"Hey!" His uncle exclaimed, "I used to call you squirt, but by Christ, you're my size now. Welcome to our humble mansion, my boy, it's great to see you."

Joe habitually wore a smile, and had a sly Irish sense of humor. One wondered whether he drank too much, or was given to long hours mixing it up with Chicago politicians in smoke-filled rooms. Actually, it was both, which didn't diminish his success in business. He ran the Motor Club, including its subsidiaries, aided by his three brothers. After those four, it was anyone's guess how many cousins were included. The whole family profited. It was how they had become well off, and dwellers of their South Woodlawn Avenue mansion. It wasn't a sprawling palace, but was a great Tudor of brick and limestone block of three stories. It had numerous bedrooms and baths, as well as servants' quarters, and a spacious ballroom on the third floor, which doubled as a huge game room. The kitchen was large, and since Bobby had been there ten years before, everything had been modernized and redecorated. In the living areas, plush red carpeting harmonized with rich oak paneling everywhere. Everywhere except in the servants' quarters, and the back stairs they used, where linoleum and plaster reigned.

The value of the Motor Club connection was brought home one night to Bobby coming back from a Jazz joint on the North Side near the Evanston line, driving aunt Betty's Caddie. Due to his overly heavy foot on the accelerator pedal, combined with the wet pavement on a sharp turn on Lakeshore Drive, he spun out, ending up facing oncoming traffic. He prided himself on his driving, feeling mostly embarrassment until he found himself facing a police patrol car. Spinning a hasty U-turn, he was quickly flagged down by the red light and siren.

Christ, I can't afford a traffic ticket, was his first thought. He stopped the car at the curb, out of traffic, and was approached by two burly cops, who looked like they meant business.

After showing his driver's license to the one, he was alarmed to hear him remark to his partner, "Look, he's from out of state, maybe we'll have to take him in." The other, a big beefy man, grunted in assent, "Yeah, and since it's late, and a weekend, no telling how long it'll be until the fine can be taken care of."

At this, one of them began shuffling his feet, scuffing up some of the sand remaining on the paving, while appraising the Cadillac. It was obvious to Bobby that he was hinting at a possible solution, paying them the fine directly, to avoid jail. He was almost flat broke, and told them he had only two bucks left, opening his wallet to demonstrate. This brought the response that it looked like jail, then.

Desperate, and playing his last card, Bobby asserted, "You know, my uncle is J.J. Cavanagh, the head of the Chicago Motor Club."

Initial disbelief was written on their faces until it was pointed out that license number eleven didn't just happen by chance, and those special club medallions on the bumpers, which had been missed in the dark, meant something.

"J. J. is your uncle?" mouthed the impressed officers, almost in unison.

"Yep, and if I can have your badge numbers, I'll tell him how you've been helpful to me. Christmas is only a couple of months away."

That did the trick, and with a friendly warning that driving in Chicago was nothing like that in California, he was smilingly waved on. These guys didn't know the half of it, Bobby thought. No one could ever get away with that at home.

When he got back to the Cavanaghs', he described the incident to his uncle, still rather amazed at the circumstances. This was greeted by a broad smile.

"Sure, that's the way we expect them to treat Motor Club members. We're a strong supporter of the Police Officers Association throughout the year, and gift them generously for the holidays. Just don't expect anything from the Park Police," adding with a chuckle, "Somehow, it must be that the leafy greenery they patrol all day makes the green of the folding type less impressive."

At that point Alfred came in to announce that supper was served, reminding Bobby that he was ravenous. The dining room was set formally, a far cry from home in Burbank, with everything but place cards. The kids, Joey, and his younger sister Betty Jr., known as "Sis" were away beginning the new school year. The bedroom earmarked for his use was on the second floor, at the back, overlooking a spacious garden. He marveled at the luxury, even more than when he last was there with his mother, knowing that he would enjoy his new digs.

At his first opportunity he wrote a letter to Denise, filled with news and his longing for her, and for a time that was one of his daily activities. He also wrote home, usually to his mother, on a weekly basis, newsy letters regarding his courses and how he was progressing. Each day, he could hardly wait for the mail to be delivered, and was rewarded by Denise's answers to his own ardent writings for the first few months, to the extent that it became a point of gentle ribbing by his uncle.

On Bobby's previous visits to Chicago as a boy, he had always found his uncle to be jovial and easy-going, his humor definitely irreverent. He appeared to Bobby totally relaxed about Catholicism, and by the time the first quarter in college was finished, uncle Joe had been observed to go to mass just once.

One evening after supper, his uncle told one of those jokes about the Priest and the Rabbi. After that, the conversation developed into a discussion about religion.

Bobby had been raised to regard the Books of the Old Testament as works of ancient literature, rather than as literal accounts of history. To him, the description of Creation in *Genesis* had to be metaphorical. He had just read Darwin's *The Origin of the Species*, and enthusiastically explained his idea that each of the last three days specified for creation in the Bible in reality referred to the millions of years of each Era, the Paleozoic, Mesozoic and the Cenozoic. He enthusiastically stressed the time needed for the slow evolutionary change from the first life forming in the primordial ooze to modern man.

Frowning, his uncle retorted, "And I suppose your theory includes us as having descended from monkeys?"

Trying to reassure his uncle, he replied, "Of course not. Monkeys and the great apes may be branches of the primate family tree, as are we, but not in a direct line with us."

The resulting silence caused him to give a double take of the older man. Bobby was shocked by the change. The light heartedness and humor had vanished. His usually hooded eyes were bulging, owlish in appearance, and his somewhat pallid face had turned several shades of red, around a hostile scowl. It was plain to see that what had started as a friendly conversation had to end before either his uncle had a stroke, or he himself was thrown bodily out of the house.

Retreating up the stairs to his room, he was shocked. How can an educated man, he thought, still be rooted in the literal translation of the Bible, ignoring all the geologic and biologic evidence. He could hardly believe the change he had seen. A form of Evolution, all right, but hardly Darwinian.

* * * *

That first year in Chicago, he studied hard, not knowing his potential in college. Compared to high school, it was far more demanding. By virtue of dedicated study, his first quarter grades were all A's. After that, he was able to relax a bit, pledging a fraternity, Phi Kappa Psi, becoming an Active during the third quarter.

Because of his surroundings and his motherly aunt, homesickness was not a problem. Rather, he was lovesick, separated as he was from Denise. He was kept busy by his studies, and this helped. Still, he couldn't rid himself of the sick aching whenever he thought of her. This, instead of subsiding with time, worsened as her writing progressively became more abbreviated and sadly, cooler. He began to realize that the prospect of their having to wait years before marriage had to be telling on her. Silently, if sadly, he reconciled himself to their drifting apart.

Her letters came to a halt at the end of January, after a last forlorn paragraph-long note informing him that it would be best if they dated others, considering the circumstances. He knew his own situation, barely even looking at a girl since they had parted. What other circumstances was she referring to, aside from his being in Chicago? Wheelie?

When Bobby had first arrived there, he was given a five dollar a week allowance in exchange for doing one single chore, that of replenishing, in cold weather, the pan of humidifying water under each steam heat unit. In 1940, a fiver was enough to keep him in lunches, and on weekends to pay for beer at Jimmy's, near the campus.

Fraternity parties, with their added cost would have been too much for his budget had it not also been for his aunt, and her brand of religion. This seemed to hark back to the days of the reformation, when one of the perceived evils of the Catholic Church, the only Christian church in Western Europe until then, consisted of paying cash for what was known as an Indulgence. After death, one's years of punishment in Purgatory could be reduced, and if a person came across with enough, he or she might be allowed to go straight to Heaven. Purgatory was supposed to be a Hell-like way station, where the equivalent of civil punishment associated with the commission of sin was meted out, even after the sin itself had been forgiven by confession and holy communion.

Dear aunt Betty, it seems, had been afflicted for years with a severe intermittent facial pain, taking her to most of the famed medical centers of the day, where a large number of tests had been carried out, and multiple medications tried, without relief. Somehow she escaped surgery, more a testimonial to her luck than anything else. When her pain continued, she finally went to the shrine at Lourdes, and there made a promise to the Virgin Mary, that if her pain were relieved, she would attend communion daily for the rest of her life, and bring everyone she could to the good offices of the Church. As a testimonial to her faith, it was not long before the pains ceased, further reinforcing her beliefs.

True to her promise, she, who had been a bit of a hellraiser in her younger days, and prior to the trials of facial pain was relaxed to some degree about religion, became a devout churchgoer early every day, attending confession as necessary in order to take communion each morning. To her credit, but also to Bobby's good luck while he was in Chicago, she remained faithful to her promise throughout the years.

It was as if she saw that her pledge could be further realized by the recruiting of further souls to the benefits of the sacraments. Like an indulgence, she decided that cash was important, and using what was for Bobby a scarce resource, a willing participant was found. He considered it somewhat hypocritical, but being a pragmatist, very happily partook of her gift, or bribe, as it really was, on every occasion possible. Expediency thus won out over ethics. The added ten bucks went much farther than his usual fiver.

In this religious environment Bobby became more and more confused. Where was the simple religion he had learned—or thought he had learned—at home? Was he really a Catholic after all? His education had indicated that no truly thinking person felt anymore that the Bible was to be interpreted literally. And, he wondered, what spiritual good ever came from paying for a plenary indulgence, or, for that matter, bribery of the type he was accepting?

He was shaken in this way, and he began to challenge even his previously held beliefs, however relaxed they were. He had never believed in dogma such as Original Sin, the Immaculate Conception, Christ's ascension into heaven, or the concept of Limbo and Purgatory. Hell, and the various mortal sins one could commit to get there, such as merely having "Carnal thoughts" about girls, also tested his credulity. Heck, he thought, a normal guy might spend half of his free time thinking about girls and sex.

Early in March, as he arrived home from study on a Saturday evening, just before dinnertime, he was surprised to see, coming down the stairs from one of the guest bedrooms, a pretty, willowy blonde of about eighteen. Her bearing was particularly winning and—as he gasped at the unreality of it all—it was almost as if he were seeing his lost Denise right there in Chicago.

Looking raptly at this vision in a powder-blue suit, he was further enthralled as she spotted him for the first time. At that moment, her face lit up with wide-eyed pleasure. He knew it couldn't be Denise, and as she smilingly approached he could see there were no freckles, her eyes were sky-blue, and although her hair was in the same style, it seemed too evenly colored to be naturally blonde. But, he thought, who would care about such details at a time like this?

She had an Irish name, Fiona Harrigan, another thing she shared with his lost love. Needless to say, the meal was a great success, and they hit it off beautifully. If their ignoring the other diners were taken as bad manners, they would hardly have noticed.

He learned that she had been tutoring the Cavanagh children. She was a sophomore at River Forest, one of the Catholic women's colleges in the northwestern suburbs, and was an occasional houseguest even with the kids away at school.

After dinner, everyone went to the Ballroom on the third floor for music. When the older adults retired, the two young people danced to popular records of the big bands. Soon, they were moving to some of the slower ballads.

Gathering her in more closely, he whispered, "What's that perfume you're wearing? It really does things to me."

"It's called Temptation. Do you like it?"

It was during the playing on the phonograph of a sentimental ballad that Bobby decided to kiss her. To his delight, his lips were eagerly met by hers, finishing the actual dancing for the evening, substituting instead that other step, sometimes called the "Why dance," a sort of swaying, arms around each other, to the rhythm of the music. Then, giving up the dance floor altogether, they moved to the nearby sofa for substantial necking.

This went on for almost an hour, until she decided it was time to part, this decision spurred by his hands gently beginning to roam. Her instincts appeared to kick in at that point. Bobby knew it was usually the way with women. Taking things more slowly was important to most of them.

The following morning he arose, eager to continue their new relationship, and after breakfast together, again oblivious of the rest of the family, she announced that the two of them should go to Mass. For the first time in months he actually wanted to go, and was able to arrange his driving one of the family Caddies.

The church they attended was not too far, on South Clark Street, which even then was beginning to change, as many of the more affluent, virtually all white, were leaving, mostly for

the North Side and the suburbs such as Evanston just across
the line. As a consequence, the people moving in were of a
much lower economic status, but what they lacked materially,
they seemed to make up spiritually.

This was the case with their Parish at that time, where
most of the faithful were black. The Low Mass, not elsewhere
marked by singing, was in this church accompanied by a chorus of a size that neither Bobby nor Fiona had ever heard in
church. The symphony of voices, much of it sung in the style
of upbeat negro spirituals, lent a joy to the occasion, making
the ceremony a real celebration, far beyond the usual meaning of that term in referring to the Mass. This served to bring
the young couple closer, as they held hands and exchanged
amazed glances. He was swayed mostly by the music and her
nearness to him, and that perfume again. So sexy, he thought,
She's definitely my type. Still, he was thinking of Denise.

* * * *

Raised in the usually balmy climate of Southern
California, he was accustomed to immediately donning light
summer attire with any warm weather. He looked forward
to the very pleasing reciprocal wearing of colorful summer
dresses on the part of the co-eds, but was amused to see that
most of the students, male and female, merely peeled off a
few layers of the clothes they had been wearing all winter. In
some cases, it was evident, if one didn't stay upwind of them,
that neither the clothes nor their wearers had been washed
much during that time, either.

That spring in Chicago promised a wonderful season,
starting slowly in April, suddenly bursting on the scene in
early May. Emerging everywhere, from the ground and in the
trees, were fresh covers of green, and above, flights of birds
and honeybees. Puffy clouds, floating in the blossom-fragrant
air, lent another dimension to the yearly renewal of life. This

is not to say that all this was uniform on a daily basis, and in the case of Chicago, the saying, "If you don't like the weather, wait ten minutes," couldn't have been more appropriate.

This was brought home to Bobby one school morning on the First of May of that year. He noted the beginning of a balmy day when he arose, and missing the weather report in the Chicago *Tribune* and on the radio, brought out his California casual summer outfit of light cotton slacks, a colorful rayon short-sleeved Hawaiian shirt, and the favorite in such weather, woven Mexican leather sandals, or Huaraches, worn without sox. A perfect outfit for the day, and one he was certain would evoke envy and admiration. Nobody ever got a chance as it turned out.

The weather continued balmy for only a quarter of his usually leisurely four-block walk to school, when he detected a chill on his lightly clad back. Looking over his shoulder, he saw dark clouds coming in from the north, soon covering the sky above like a shadow. As he began to walk faster, the temperature dropped at least twenty degrees, and by the half-way mark the wind picked up, and with it, in addition to the fall of some newly-formed leaves, drops of cold rain began to splatter around him, along with a further chilling drop of the thermometer. In no time the rain was replaced by snow flurries, which in the last block were succeeded by big cold relentless flakes. The last hundred yards were covered in an all-out sprint in an inch of snow to his locker, which luckily contained a thick woolen sweater his aunt had insisted he wear a month before, thus saving that day for him, and possibly averting a case of pneumonia.

As he left his locker, some guys were cynically singing about one of the rites of spring, "Hey, hey, hey hey! It's the first of May. Outdoor fucking starts today!"

He couldn't help but envision the outrageous predicament in which amorous couples would have found themselves under such circumstances, given his experience that day on his way to class.

* * * *

Bobby and Fiona had been writing each other regularly since that first weekend. Her letters were perfumed, which made things all the more interesting. One contained an invitation to visit her at home in downstate Illinois. Although he had planned to head west as soon as the school year ended, she pleaded with him to delay his trip until their reunion there, for a week or so.

The chance of seeing her again appealed to him, as the promise of the love expressed in her perfumed letters had grown during their three months apart. This clouded his judgment, and he failed to grasp the significance of the invitation, which mentioned meeting her parents and the rest of the family. The enticements overcame any misgivings he might have had, and he proceeded with the arrangements for the trip.

It seems that the only passenger service there was the Gulf, Mobile and Ohio Railroad, which connected Chicago with New Orleans. He was undeterred that her town, about thirty miles from Springfield, the State Capital, was little more than a whistle-stop. Worse, they stopped there only briefly at two AM. The train, either the *Abraham Lincoln* or the *Ann Rutledge,* named for that great president's first love, left Chicago at eleven PM, alternating nights, passing each other on the return trip. Bobby mused that this seemed romantic enough, but what of the lady that Lincoln married, Mary Todd?

Alfred drove Bobby to the station, and despite the late hour, was very solicitous regarding the impending trip.

"Now don't let the train get you down, as it will be a rough ride. At least that'll keep you awake for your arrival there when you'll need all your marbles. Can't you see boy, this gal's after you? I saw it in her eyes when you first met. You know you're too young to settle down, dontcha?"

Full of that bachelor's advice, but unconvinced, thinking only of Fiona's charms, and flattered by her attention, he was armed with the young man's certainty that he held all the cards in avoiding being trapped by feminine wiles. He remained convinced of that, although his mother had always told him otherwise.

At the conductor's "All aboard!" He bounded up the steps into the train, the *Abraham Lincoln,* in a state of great excitement, anticipating only the pleasure of another adventure.

Never was a stretch of track so uneven, as it soon became evident after Chicago was left behind. At times it was like a rollercoaster, and, he thought, threatening to put him and the other passengers in the aisle. It seemed to him it was either that or derailment. With sleep impossible despite the initial period of adjustment, it seemed an eternity before the stop at her town came.

When he queried the conductor about the condition of the tracks, and how anybody could stand such a rough ride all the way to New Orleans, the reply was that after the train crossed the Ohio River, they would no longer be on these neglected Illinois Central tracks, and the trip would thereafter be of normal smoothness. This was scant consolation for him, getting off the train well before that, still facing the return trip. Perhaps it would be on the *Ann Rutledge.* Somehow that seemed more comforting.

He was met by Fiona and her mother at the station. They then drove through the still sultry darkness to their home, in a quiet section of town. There, instructions were given regarding Bobby's quarters, leaving the two of them on the living room sofa.

They were both happy to be together once again, but too sleepy and tired to carry on much of a conversation. This left them with the only alternative to retiring, that of the renewal of their previous smooching. She was enthusiastic, and as they became more involved, she the more passionate. Noting the smoky look veiling the blue of her eyes, and the invitation of her seductively reclining, he hesitated. He just didn't feel comfortable in that open living room, and with that, the lack of sleep caught up with him.

God, he thought, I need sleep more than sex, yet another demonstration of the primacy of the first law of nature. Tired as he was, sleep nevertheless came slowly, in a strange bed in a room down the hall from her. Too soon, the darkness changed through shades of grey to a beginning pink heralding the dawn of another summer's day.

The week started out well enough after Fiona was able to induce him to get up with the promise of breakfast, aromas of which were invitingly wafted into his room by her cheery entry. She was wearing a light blue cotton dress, which he found attractive, as it accentuated her slim but sexy curves. After hastily putting on Levi's and a short-sleeved shirt, and slipping into his huaraches, he joined her in the breakfast room. There, he was met with friendly interest on the part of her mother, with a hint of affection. Her father was cordial, although a little stiff in his manner. Bobby ascribed the coolness to a father's natural attitude when first meeting his daughter's boyfriends. Besides, he reminded himself, Mr. Harrigan, was, after all, a mortician.

Things went well, the bacon and eggs in sufficient quantities to satisfy even Bobby's outsize appetite. The conversation, despite his residual sleepiness, soon picked up. The usual topics were discussed, and with more coffee, a strong brew, explored in a more animated fashion.

When breakfast was finished, Fiona was given the loan of one of the family's Buick sedans. Black, of course, but thankfully, it wasn't the longer model that carried the bereaved behind the hearse. Bobby was invited to drive when the two of them toured the town. That morning, they drove over to Springfield, where the highlight was Lincoln's Tomb. Set in a lovely green park on a slight hill, it was impressive in its white marble classical style, but surprisingly small, considering the stature of its occupant.

The county fair was just starting, and after a lunch of hamburgers and sodas, they took in the sulky races, having fun betting between themselves on the horses. The stakes were not high, but could get heavy, as they agreed that the currency was to be in kisses. Because of the crowds, most of them had to be reserved for later. She was obviously uncomfortable with such a show in public.

As she explained it, "These are, after all, mostly small town people."

Needless to say the debt would be settled later, as he kept score very carefully. Later, while they were holding hands, he offered his fraternity pin, which she took eagerly, saying, "I was hoping you'd do that."

After their return, she gave him a tour of the funeral home. This was in the house just next door, with the two buildings connected through their basements. First she took him upstairs to the ground floor, where a number of coffins and caskets of varying weight and cost were displayed in the showroom. Bobby, who had never been to a funeral, was impressed by the ones cast in bronze, polished to a mirror finish, and padded luxuriously in satin inside.

When he remarked how comfortable that looked, she replied laughingly, "Would you like to try it?"

"Thanks, but not for about sixty years."

She proudly showed the little chapel, with a dozen seats and an altar at one end, over which a stained glass window allowed colored light to shine down on the altar cloth. He thought it odd that she crossed herself and genuflected as she entered, but was relieved that she failed to notice that he did not. Next she showed him the big black hearse in the adjoining garage, and the long, black limousine that would follow it. Her father obviously favored Buicks.

Before returning to the residence, she opened a door in the basement passage, which led to the embalming room. They were conducting no funerals that week, and the room was empty of occupants. Off to one side was an open closet, holding shelves lined with the jugs and carboys containing various chemical solutions used in the embalming process. These she pointed out to him.

Nodding, and then pointing to rows of bottles of red liquid, he asked, "What are those?"

"Oh those," she replied, "They're *Ruby Fluid*. Corpses, you know, are really pale. That solution is injected to pink them up to augment the makeup."

That evening there was a special dinner at home, even though it was a workday, to introduce Bobby to the rest of the family. She wore his pin proudly, showing it to each of those present, basking in their approval. The company seemed easy-going, consisting only of brother John, his wife

Grace, and their infant son, John Jr., who livened things up by crawling all over, drooling on the rugs, and making joyous gurgling noises. Everyone, particularly the grandparents, doted on him, and gave him most of their attention, while the parents and Fiona looked on in satisfied pride. Bobby gave what he thought were the proper compliments to the family, and played with the infant a little, but raised in a family with three younger siblings, all boys, his level of enthusiasm failed to match that of the others.

After dinner, while it was still light, Fiona's brother suggested that he and Bobby go for a walk, ostensibly to burn off the excess calories put away at the table. Bobby caught her eye, and receiving a nod in the affirmative, off they went. The walk took them under those typical elms that seemed to line the streets throughout the Midwest, and which gave a decidedly park-like ambience especially to the residential neighborhoods.

It soon became evident that the purpose of the walk was not just for exercise. After the obligatory small talk, regarding the baseball season and the county fair, John spoke of his years at his *Alma Mater*, Notre Dame.

"You know," he began, "I was quite an athlete, running track and consistently doing the hundred in ten flat." Bobby supposed that this came out in connection with his own interest in athletics at the U. of C.

Then John came to the point. "As you've seen, we're a tight-knit little family here and Fiona is my only sib. I hope you have nothing but the best in mind for her. I heard that you were thinking of going home soon. Are you continuing on at Chicago? You know, if you break her heart there'll be more than one Harrigan after you."

This last was added half-jokingly, but the message was clear. Bobby couldn't help but wonder if her brother had a shotgun in mind.

It was then, despite his chronic naïveté that he finally realized he was being seriously courted with the invitation downstate. Alfred was right when he had warned him at the train station. Oh jeez, he thought, giving her his fraternity pin, which he regarded only as a token of their going steady, was to her a symbol of a greater commitment. An engagement? He almost said it aloud. I'm still too young for that. Then he wryly considered John's ten flat hundred. It would be hard to outrun her irate brother, even with his added age.

That evening, after the walk and the talk, a much less enthusiastic but wiser nearly twenty-year old sat with Fiona on the front porch, facing the canopy of trees lining the avenue across the lawn. The green grew greener in the dusk as the shrilling of the *Cicadas* gave way to the flickering of the fireflies, milling about in delicate profusion. The sensuously sultry air, deprived of the last rays of the sun, was stirred only by a languid breeze, which felt velvety on the skin.

"God, how romantic," he whispered. Wary from the earlier encounter with her brother, he was still unable to hold back his affection and yearning. Maybe it was that perfume she was wearing then, which in the past had done things to him. Part of it was his age and the beginning of summer.

She leaned closer to him as they sat together on the porch swing, and gave him a soft kiss in the ear, which sent a shiver through him. "That's a partial payment for now, but I want to talk about *us*. We certainly are compatible emotionally, and wearing your pin, I feel secure in your love. But we haven't ever discussed anything really important, like the plans we have to make for our future together."

Bobby had a sudden Déjà vu feeling, and much of his frustrations with Denise came over him then.

Fiona sensed his reaction, but continued. "We haven't even discussed religion in all our time together. You call yourself a Catholic, but I don't think that your heart and your soul are really in it."

A little defensively, he replied, "My God, how so?"

"Because among other things, you use the name of God in vain. A good Catholic is supposed to avoid that."

Where has she been all her life, he thought, recalling his year and a half at Loyola High, and the most profane language he had ever heard.

"Oh, is that it? I am a Catholic, but the way we were brought up, we're not fanatics the way my aunt and uncle in Chicago are, for instance. We go to Mass sometimes on Sundays and to confession and communion as necessary, but we don't expect any boy in the family to study for the priesthood or a sister to become a nun. We just take it more casually than that spelled out by Rome."

"And that's what I worry about," she retorted, holding his arm, drawing him closer. "I've been raised a strict Catholic, and have been schooled by the nuns all my life. To me there are no exceptions to canon law, and what the Pope decrees is the law of the church."

Bobby asked, "So you believe the Pope is infallible?"

She responded with conviction. "In matters of faith and morals he most certainly is." Adding, "Now I see what we have to do. Before going to the lake to swim tomorrow as we planned, you're going to have to sit down and have a look at my books on religion if we're going to get along." Then she added somewhat ominously, "That's the way it has to be from here on out."

Hmmm, he thought, what is that supposed to mean? He was certainly disappointed, in contemplation that religion was threatening to come between him and what could become something serious. Still he was not deterred in his ardor, as her tone softened to end the evening on a positive note. He collected completely, and more, on his day's sulky race winnings.

The next morning, after breakfast, he was herded out to the back yard where she deposited him, along with three sizable books on Catholic dogma, philosophy and history. Their apparent weight discouraged him even to look at them, but to please her he began to go through the first in earnest, getting through a chapter which dealt with Augustine and the concept of original sin.

There's no zealot like a convert, he thought, recalling his history studies at the U. of C. about the dissolute ways of that Saint in his earlier years.

He dutifully read, but found he still couldn't believe any of it. The sun was hot when he first chose to sit there, but he rationalized that at least it would help with his summer tan. When he was forced by the heat to move into the shade of the nearby arbor, he continued to sweat uncomfortably in the increasing humidity. He was reminded of the concept of Purgatory by the combination of his reading and the heat. Mercifully, as from that Catholic way station to Heaven, and just as he was about to say to hell with it, he was rescued from his torture.

Fiona's attitude had softened, and she suggested going to the beach at the lake as previously planned. By that time, nothing would have suited him better except quantities of cold drink.

He got both, as they stopped on the way for malted milks, and then a swim out to the buoy that marked the limits of permitted swimming. On the way out there, the combination of the rich drink and his showing off his speed made him a little sick, putting a damper on his conversation. In the process, it did evoke an outpouring of sympathy from her.

After they had slowly swum back to the beach, he had to lie down for a time on the sand, with her kneeling behind him, softly stroking his head and shoulders. As she removed her bathing cap he felt her long thick hair falling over the back of his neck, tickling slightly. Then there was the brush of her breasts on his back as she leaned over, kissing him on the side of the neck. Needless to say, he quickly forgot his minor nausea, and turning over to face her, he pulled her quickly but gently down on top of him. They kissed passionately for a moment.

"Let's continue this in private tonight after dinner," she murmured, "I've the promise of the Buick again, and we can go dancing, have a beer, and then drive out into the country and park somewhere with a nice view. The moon will be full and I'm feeling very romantic just now."

He was struck by her breathless tone as she uttered those last few words, and that evening he could hardly down his dinner in contemplation of what the night might bring. She was extra attentive and affectionate, enough to cause her mother to exchange questioning looks with her, and her father to remark about Bobby's not asking for the usual second helpings. There was extra warmth at the table besides the lingering heat of the day. She told them she was looking forward to their dancing at the country club that evening to explain her mood and the neckline of the light silk dress she chose for the occasion. Bobby saw all this as well as the cleavage that the dress revealed, and more than ever was torn by his desire on one hand and the warning signs on the other.

They did indeed dance later, not at the club, but to juke box music at a roadhouse just outside town, drinking the promised brew and talking about his plans. He told her that he had to finish college, and then Law School, but was undecided about whether to remain in Chicago or to return to Southern California. She squeezed his hand tightly as he mentioned leaving Illinois, indicating her desire that he stay.

Pulling out a rare cigarette, she asked, "Do you have a match?"

While lighting it, he said, despite his previous concerns, "I do have a match. My heart and yours."

As she exhaled the first puff, he could see a change in her face, all soft and with those smoky blue eyes again. As if by a signal they wordlessly got up for that drive into the country. He paid for the beers and joined her outside. The moon was just rising, and seemed much bigger than ordinarily as it hugged the horizon briefly. He took her hand as she kissed him, and for the first time he felt the tip of her tongue brushing his.

On the drive out into the countryside the sky was suffused with a veil of silver, which seemed to light her face in the most angelic yet sexy way. The glow reflected in her eyes almost like stars when she looked at him. They found a roadside park and selected a spot facing east so that the pale light would bathe them both as they basked in it together.

The air had become cooler, but not enough to lose that sensual heaviness that can be so wonderful about a summer night in the Midwest. He supposed that any night under similar circumstances would give the same feeling, with the air fragrant with the aroma of clover, and the occasional stirring of a gentle breeze bringing with it a delicate sweetness from somewhere, reminiscent of night-blooming jasmine.

It was almost too much. It brought back memories of his evenings with Denise, and their night of passion. It also stirred his pent-up frustrations, for before him was a scene promising the fulfillment that he had experienced with his first love, but posing the same problem of possibly ending up married much too soon.

The attractions of his companion would have proved too much for his inhibitions in the end, but any wavering was cut short by her gently pulling him over to her. Wordlessly he gathered her in his arms and kissed her, lightly at first, but with her response, their kisses swelled into passionate soft-lipped open mouth caresses. Still holding his lips to hers, he put his hand on the inside of her thigh just above the knee, where somehow her skirt had been displaced upward. As he gently stroked the warm, incredible smoothness, she went limp in his arms.

Oh God, he thought, this has to be it, as he gently caressed her. As he moved his hand a little further upward, she moaned softly into his ear, and then, abruptly, spread her legs. Sudden as it was, completely out of the rhythm of the lazy tempo of his advances, it shocked him to involuntarily falter momentarily. He withdrew his hand and straightened up in surprise.

Reading his hesitation as rejection, she mumbled, "You're right Bobby, I got carried away." Stammering, "Maybe it was the moonlight. I don't know what came over me. It was like I was dreaming. Now I'm awake, thanks to you."

This last she added somewhat ruefully, he thought. He didn't know what to say, but recognized his mixed feelings, not only of frustration from the interruption of their mutual seduction, but also just a trace of relief.

He knew then that their moment was lost beyond repair. He kicked the starter, putting the car in reverse, and with wheels spinning in the gravel, turned onto the highway for town. He didn't want to talk, but listened as she explained her behavior. Once more he heard the refrain about how unfair, somehow, their consummating their love before marriage would have been to her mother.

Why did women think that way? He wondered. He had never made any such promises to *his* mother.

The following morning she was quiet during breakfast, and afterwards when he sought an answer, she handed him his pin. Hurt, more in his pride than in the apparent loss of her commitment, he asked why.

"Don't you know? Last night was just another clue that your heart wasn't ready for me. And there's more. I was awake most of the night and was able to put it all together."

A little indignant, he asked, "Well, what else was wrong with us before last night?"

"Oh, poor Bobby, it may be unfair from your perspective, but don't you see, even though you regard yourself as Catholic, we're not compatible religiously, and judging by your lukewarm interaction with my baby nephew, you're also suspect as a prospective father."

"That's it? We're both Catholics, yet our religion can come between us? And look, all my life I've had little kids, my younger brothers and cousins, underfoot. It's no wonder that I didn't give your baby nephew more adulation. Well, okay, if that's how you feel. It has been fun, but you know, it really hurts."

Still, he thought, He wasn't ready for a commitment of that type, and sure as hell he couldn't take her brand of religion. With that he went upstairs to pack his stuff, calling back over his shoulder.

"Do you think I can get a lift to the station tonight? I'll catch the train back to Chicago when it comes through."

She drove him there, softly singing the Gershwin song, "Just Plain Bill," over and over, making it clear that another guy still had a place in her life somehow. Bobby marveled about this, and the implication that all the apparent passion she had invested in their affair of sorts must have been based in large part on rebound. He had to chuckle out loud at the irony. It had been the same for him.

The hour was late, and she didn't want to wait for the train, its plaintive whistle just beginning to be heard in the distance. As he got out of the car, smiling at her, she reached for his hand.

"I'm truly sorry Bobby, but look at you. It seems you're not too unhappy, are you?"

Gazing at her a moment, still a little sick at heart, he considered that question, but rather than answering he wheeled to leave, saying, "Thanks, and good luck with Bill."

And then he walked slowly and deliberately to the platform without looking back.

* * * *

By late in the afternoon, those ahead of them in the line to the recruiting office still numbered over a hundred. A burly sergeant came by, handing out numbered cards, so that they could keep their places in line the next day.

"You men won't get through the door by five, so you can leave now without losing your place."

That night, back at the Phi Psi house, supper was eaten with more than the usual din of voices. Most of those who had been waiting to enlist that day seemed compelled to voice their concerns about where they'd be going for training, once called up. Bobby, hashing at mealtimes to save money towards his tuition, was too busy serving and too pre-occupied with his own thoughts to participate much in the conversation then. He did hear talk of the oft-repeated Army habit of sending men seemingly as far away from their homes for training as the confines of the Continental U.S. would permit.

He had to laugh to himself at the thought. They'll send us halfway across the country, for sure. Join the Navy and see the Great Lakes, join the Army Air Force, and see Texas.

After finishing his kitchen duties and studies, dog-tired, and returning to his room, he found Dave already asleep and snoring.

Despite his fatigue, he found sleep elusive, and began to reflect on his last journey across more than half the Country, driving home after his freshman year at the University of Chicago.

EIGHT

Driving Home

His task was to drive the newly purchased family sedan, a brand-new 1940 Oldsmobile, which the folks had arranged to be picked up in Chicago. The savings in price would more than make up for the cost of gasoline, food and lodging, and provided an extra hundred bucks, really big money in those days, to pay for his further education.

Readying the car after it was shipped to Chicago took a couple of days, as Bobby caught up on his sleep and said his goodbyes. After thanking his aunt and uncle for all they had done for him, he tried to give Alfred and the cook tips, but they wouldn't take the proffered bills. Saying goodbye to his uncle was easier than with the rest. It had seemed that he would be just as happy with him gone, ever since their differences surfaced with the discussion of evolution.

With his aunt it was tough. She had been his mother for a year, and a source of both affection and generosity. He hoped he would see her again, but he knew somehow it wouldn't be soon, if ever. He did promise to write to keep her up to date.

He picked up the car early in the morning at the Motor Club, where he was furnished with maps and advice about the best routes to take to the West Coast during the summer heat. He could hardly wait, and showed it, but was given careful instructions regarding driving slowly during the break-in period of the first 500 miles. The shiny blue car had the all-steel top, a new development, which impressed him, but much less than did the powerful engine, with the speedometer indicating up to 110 miles per hour. He wondered how he could keep it below forty-five after he reached the highway.

He hit the road as soon as the lecture ended and was given the keys. Consulting his map, he headed west for Rockford and the Iowa border, planning on taking the northern route, at least to Salt Lake City. Concentrating on the directions, breathing the wonderful aroma of the new car, and distracted by the thrill of his first driving it, he missed most of the passing scenes of the great city, which, counting his earlier visits had been his home for more than two years.

He was so eager that he drove for twelve hours, stopping only for gas and lunch outside Des Moines. The Olds drove like a dream, a little Cadillac, he reflected. It was in western Iowa that he finally began to bring the revs up to highway speed. Amazed, he thought, how this baby can roll. He was anticipating driving next in Nebraska, where there was no speed limit at all.

Almost through that state, twenty miles from the Wyoming border, at a traffic light at one of those small town crossroads, a State Police cruiser pulled up next to him. My God, he thought, as the trooper called over to him, saying that he was wanted in that little town thirty miles back. He wouldn't, or couldn't, say why, and seemed to be so disinterested in the situation that Bobby was tempted to keep on going, with the state line so close.

Some time was spent pondering whether he would be arrested in Wyoming for evading the law, and still be forced to return. And why in the world they were interested in him anyway was a mystery. The problem was all the more puzzling, because of the lack of a speed limit. Sure, he had opened it up over the last couple hundred miles, but he'd been careful never to cross the double line initiating passing, and in slowing down for the towns along the way, warned about those notorious speed traps. It wasn't long before his conscience and fear of arrest got the best of him, and he turned the car around and headed the other way.

"Damn," he exclaimed aloud, "Just when it looked like I could get well into Wyoming tonight."

Driving back was depressing, and even more so when he reached the city hall, where he was told that he would have to wait for the Sheriff himself, who handled all highway infractions. What infraction? No one could give him any information as he sat twiddling his thumbs for over an hour, with nothing to read, looking at the green institutional paint on the walls, decorated only by a portrait of their Governor.

Finally he could see shadows behind the frosted glass door of the magistrate's office, marking the return of the Sheriff. The door soon swung open, its frame filled by a large man, in a khaki uniform, with a sizeable pot, necessitating the use of wide suspenders to hold up not only his pants, but also his gun-belt.

"Come in," was the command. "Sit here," he said brusquely, indicating an uncomfortable looking cane-backed chair in front of the desk.

"So what's this? Unsafe passing? You know what the double line means don't you?"

Bobby replied, "Yes sir, I always observe them. Honestly, that's the one thing that's most important to me, since at highway speeds safety depends on that."

"So you maintain that all the way across Nebraska you never passed over the double line?"

He stammered as he answered, "No sir, I mean yes sir. I would never do that. Please believe me."

"Well, you know son," came his reply, "You may not have passed over the double line, but it must have been that you didn't get back in time after passing when the double line resumed."

Bobby was dumbfounded. "You mean it's illegal not to get back before the double line starts again, even though you can't see that point when you begin to pass?" Recalling a pre-law course he took, he then asked, "Isn't that something that cannot be anticipated, and is thus not enforceable? And another thing, who was it that observed all this? I have a right to know my accuser."

"Now you leave that to law enforcement, young fella," the Sheriff replied rather pointedly, "We here in this part of the state go strictly by the law, and no upstart from out of state is going to tell us how our laws are to be interpreted. By the book, your fine is twenty dollars."

"My God, that's half my budget to get home," Bobby exclaimed, "Can't you just let this stand as a warning? After all, I came back all this way to answer your charges, doesn't that count for something? This car is my parents' and all they gave me to make the trip to L.A. was forty bucks"

"Sorry," came the reply, "The law is the law, and there's nothing I can do to change that. Just give the money to the clerk." At that, he pointed his arm in that general direction.

Just then, Bobby noticed the ring on the Sheriff's finger, with the shield, in black and gold, with the omniscient eye and the lamp of learning of Phi Kappa Psi. Good Christ, he suddenly realized, a Brother!

"The clerk will take the twenty now, and you can be on your way," the authoritative voice continued. "He'll give you a receipt for your dad, to keep this all legal and above board, regarding the letter of the law."

In desperation, Bobby played his last card. "Would you still fine me, a brother Phi Psi for such an infraction?"

"A Phi Psi? You?"

"Sure," Bobby replied, "I couldn't afford a ring, and my pin is in my bag." Offering his hand for what passed as the fraternity handshake, he followed up by pulling out his wallet, showing his membership card.

"Well, in that case," the Sheriff replied, looking warily around him, apparently worrying about the open wallet, "I guess we *can* let you off with a warning, sort of probation, you know."

Bobby was told he was free to go. After some further talk of their respective chapters, he again hit the road heading west, trying to make up for lost time, of course watching that double line more than ever, but chuckling to himself about justice under that rigid letter of the law.

* * * *

Things went well all across Wyoming, where, too sleepy to continue, he slept in a motel for almost twelve hours. Even more behind schedule because of that, he didn't stop again until he reached Salt Lake City. Problem was, according to the gas station attendant there, the Nevada State Police were extracting a twenty dollar transit fee for new cars being ferried on the main routes passing through that state, again something he definitely couldn't afford. His doubts about whether his driving role would be considered ferrying the Olds forced a revision of his plans. No big deal, he reflected, as he selected a much less-used highway across Utah to Fallon, and then into California, where he would come out on U.S. 395, along the east side of the Sierras. There, it would be unlikely to have anything besides a California agricultural inspection station. That way he could reach home in Burbank via the high desert from the North.

Progress was smooth as he crossed Utah and the semi-desert that made up that segment of Nevada geography. During the whole day, driving that road, he saw only a rare jackrabbit in the endless sage, or a wheeling buzzard, high in the sky. There was little other sign of life, except for an occasional crossroads huddle of weathered buildings.

It was at one such place that he stopped for gas and lunch. The single pump gave only one choice, *Blue Green Gas*, which was shown to be actually that by its display in the calibrated ten-gallon glass cylinder that topped the pump. The thing was gravity-fed, and because the Olds took more than ten gallons, Bobby refilled the cylinder by using the pump lever attached, under the watchful eye of the aged attendant, who seemed almost too feeble to do the job himself. After checking the oil and paying, he asked about something to eat.

"Across the road," was the laconic reply, accompanied by a nod in the same direction. It was the usual weathered gray wooden building, displaying a sign on which a single word was printed: "Eats."

These people aren't given to wasting words, and probably that also holds for this café, Bobby thought, as he swung a "U" and brought the car to a standstill beneath the sign.

The afternoon was hot, suggesting it would be the same inside, but as he entered, he was welcomed by a cool draft.

The light was subdued, even when his vision, accustomed to the glare of the summer sun, accommodated, lending a further atmosphere of coolness. He could see a long polished bar counter, complete with brass railing, at the end of which was the expected spittoon of the same metal, and on the other side of the room, a couple of checkered oilcloth-covered tables, each with those same Spartan cane-backed chairs. The creaking planked floor was well worn, this accentuated in places by the nails, each polished by many feet and protruding on the little plateaus of wood their heads protected. Between many of the planks, apparently of shrunken century-old pine, were spaces, and it was from these openings that cool air was issuing. It smelled nearly fresh, but with a hint of mustiness he couldn't quite place, but which whetted his appetite somehow.

There were no other customers present at the time, lunch hour being long past, but it did take the waitress, an attractive thirtyish brunette, a couple of minutes to come to the table he had selected, one he thought closest to the source of cool air from below.

Obviously she was a native of the area, as there was no greeting, although she had a friendly smile.

"What'll it be?" She opened with, slapping down a frayed typed-up menu. He was thirsty, and asked for a Coke.

"We only carry R.C. Cola. Why not a beer?"

"Well," he replied, "Firstly, I'm driving and have to stay awake, and secondly, I'm not twenty-one yet." This last was added reluctantly.

"Shoot" she replied, "That don't mean nothin' in these parts."

"I'll take an R.C. anyway, and a hamburger with the works," he responded firmly.

"Okay," she replied, "But today's special is fried rabbit, and it's tops."

Bobby laughed, "Nah, I'll bet it's not anything but Jackrabbit. From what I've seen, that's the only living thing on the ground around here for two hundred miles. I'll still have the burger," he replied, wondering whether the meat would, after all, turn out to be rabbit anyway.

When the plate came with the burger and the R.C., she sat down in a chair opposite, looking at Bobby expectantly. He wasn't sure what that was all about, but when he bit into the burger he was surprised it was so good.

"You like it? The seasonin' is sage," she chuckled, "Almost the only thing that grows in these parts. The mushrooms are a specialty of the house, or maybe the tunnel? The catsup and relish are from California."

While he ate, he wondered about the tunnel she mentioned. As he washed a second burger down with the last of the cola, she told the story of their settlement.

"There was a minin' center a half mile up that dirt road outside, a ghost town now since the silver ran out. This place is over an old tunnel, the openin' directly under the floor. Gives the buildin' its air conditionin', and serves as our mushroom cellar."

Of course! He thought of that musty quality, but where does the breeziness come from?

As if reading his mind, she offered, "The air comes from the tunnel, built for drainin' water from the mine, just like the one that engineer fella, Sutro, dug in Virginia City. Here they hit an underground stream, and decided the extra pumpin' would be a waste of money. They thought they could supply water 'round here, but they had no takers. After that, grandma and grandpa homesteaded the land. They built this place over the tunnel openin' for its coolin' and water."

Bobby was fascinated, and seeing that, she invited him to take a tour of the shaft and the mushroom caves, seductively looking into his eyes while bending over the table invitingly, her loose blouse showing almost everything she had. He was naturally attracted, but a little embarrassed, averting his eyes to look at his watch. Concerned with the late hour, he begged off.

"Gotta get going, maybe next time."

"Next time? Are you kiddin'? The war's gonna come before you get the chance. You ain't comin' back." Seeing his dismay, she added hastily, "At least along this way, anyhow."

When he paid the bill, including a tip, she shoved some of the coins back across the table to him, smiling, "You're not supposed to tip the owner, kid."

As he opened the door to leave, complementing her on the burgers, she called after him, "Yeah, you guessed right. The meat *was* Jackrabbit."

She knew what I was thinking, he reflected. And what did she really mean about my not coming back?

As he headed for California, it was soon evident that aside from the soaring buzzards, nothing moved, except for the illusion of the panorama of distant sagebrush moving with his progress, and shimmering in the summer heat waves. It did occur to him that where there were buzzards, there must be carrion. Little did he know just how much there was, and what its source would be.

The heat of the day was followed by a balmy night as the moon rose behind him. The highway continued straight west for miles, surrounded on either side by the nearly flat sage-dotted land. So monotonous, bringing the conviction that he'd have to work to stay awake for the rest of the trip across Nevada.

That might have been a problem but for the appearance just then of spots before his eyes. His first thought was *flock dots*. But the splatter of insects on the windshield didn't quite fit. Suddenly it became clear that these were objects on the road, masses of small animals milling about, as he braked to a crawl. Amazed, he saw Jackrabbits, hordes of them, frolicking in the moonlight. Forced to proceed slowly, he honked the horn as he went. This succeeded in getting only a few off the paving ahead of the car. For the rest, it was as if they were hypnotized not only by the full moon, but also by the headlights, with some of them falling under the wheels after being nudged there by the front bumper.

He thought they would soon move on, possibly following the moon across the sky. Problem was, the lunar path was also due west, directly ahead. He decided it would be best to wait them out, and pulled over onto the shoulder, turning off the engine and lights. Still they gathered all around, although for a reason that was not entirely clear to him. Was it a mating ritual or perhaps a lemming-like gathering in submission to the dangers of the highway? Sometimes over-population would do that to rodents as their numbers out-stripped the forage. With those thoughts, he dozed off for an hour, expecting the orgy to move on.

When he awakened, the moon was approaching the zenith, but the rabbits were just as numerous, gamboling in swarms of brownish-gray fur in the silvery light, seeming to prefer the warm asphalt pavement for some reason. There he was, frustrated by a swarming blockade of bunnies. He worried about his shortage of cash, as there was barely enough to buy the gas needed to make it home. Time was becoming critical because of his need for prodigious plates of food at mealtimes.

After waiting impatiently for another hour, he finally decided. Enough! Pulling back onto the road, and honking the horn, this time driving without lights, he was able to pick up some speed, with only an occasional "Thunk!" that came with impact of the bumper on a fleeing jack. They would still run ahead of the car instead of veering off the road, even at forty miles an hour. Hoping that speed would scatter the rabbits, Bobby turned on the headlights, accelerating to sixty. This brought out the futility of the rabbits trying to match speed with the car. While not increasing the number of impacts, they did become more forceful. He shuddered at the mayhem brought down on the rabbitry as well as the potential of damaging the new car, if not the bumper or grille, then the hydraulic brake lines. He thought of the reaction that his father might have, both elements concerning his own personal safety.

After about an hour, the gathering thinned out, with more of the rabbits giving up the contest in front of the car and escaping into the roadside sage. Whew, whatta relief, he said to himself. But now, without them, how to keep awake?

The experience was exhausting, and he was punchy. This made him think of it all having been a form of Darwinian natural selection. He was convinced that the car had killed close to fifty of those less intelligent. Maybe, he thought, the survivors would impart their genes, as rabbits are known to do in quantity, to brighter bunnies. In any event, he was then certain of the reason for the gathering of buzzards. Despite the unsettling carnage, he had to laugh about jackrabbit being the special for the day.

As he neared home, his anticipation grew. It was a beautiful day, and, tired as he was, his mood matched it. The typical low clouds had been chased by the summer sun hours before, bringing an afternoon pleasantly warm. He needed his leather jacket only to cover his dirty tee shirt as he drove down the block to the white stucco house that was home. It looked much as when he had left, separated from the concrete-paved street and the sidewalk by the front lawn, with the tall poplars on the grassy parking strip, their leaves shimmering glints of gold and green in the gentle breeze.

He parked in front, hoping everyone would be there to greet him, as he had called ahead with his last nickel when he got to Studio City, a couple of miles away. His expectations appeared fulfilled, as he caught the movement of the drapes in the big front window as he pulled up, showing that his arrival had been noticed.

Before he could get out, the front door of the house burst open, and the family excitedly emerged, led by the two youngest, Patrick, or Paddy, who was fourteen, and twelve year old Terry, he sometimes called Ted. That Saturday, his parents were home, and joined the clamor to hug their welcomes. The younger boys, after their brief greetings, had eyes only for the new car, fondling the sweep of the full fenders and hood.

"Look at you, Bobby, how you've grown," his mother murmured with a tearfulness that conveyed the thought that she had lost one of her little boys.

"Heck, Mom," Bobby replied, "I'm still your boy. I've only grown an inch and gained only ten pounds in all the months of my stay in Chicago."

Stroking Bobby's chin, his father observed, "Just look at that stubble. I never saw that much before. You're certainly not the boy you were when you left."

Joey, the next oldest, just graduated from high school a month before, wasn't home to greet the new arrival at that time, because of a summer job. Phyllis, the eldest, who among all the kids idolized Bobby the most, spotted him, and running up, flung all five feet and ninety pounds at him, sobbing happily. He fielded her deftly, kissing her on the forehead to avoid the tears streaming down her freckled cheeks.

"Why cry Sis?" he asked softly, "This homecoming is supposed to be happy."

Everyone was beaming except for his poor sister.

"You've been gone so long you must have forgotten how sentimental she can be," Paddy called out. "She cries over everything, even sad clowns."

Joey came home from his summer job at about five-thirty, but ever the technician, didn't come in until after he had given the new car a thorough going over. He and Bobby then spent an hour comparing notes about Chicago where each had spent a couple of years on multiple visits.

His mother prepared a meal of Bobby's favorites, including a lettuce, cottage cheese and pineapple salad, and fried chicken with mashed potatoes and gravy. For the vegetable, it was string beans, always a challenge for her for some reason. She also served him the cream from the top of the bottle of milk, another of his preferences.

As all gathered around the table, everything looked and smelled great, except for the beans. They were a little burned, and virtually inedible as was often the case with her vegetables. But that night she made up for it with a dessert of her special apple dumplings topped with raw sugar syrup and cinnamon.

The conversation naturally focused on Bobby, who gave a vivid account of his adventures on the trip west. Intending to spare those at the table, he mentioned only that swarms of Jackrabbits had been encountered crossing Nevada.

Hearing that, Joey remarked, "Yeah, and you must have hit a few, judging by the fur you missed on the inside of the front bumper and the A-frames when you cleaned up the mess. Did you bring any rabbit home?" Winking slyly, he added, "You know how Sis loves fried rabbit."

At that, Phyllis dropped her fork. "Mom! You didn't foist rabbit off on us again, calling it chicken, did you?"

"Of course not dear," her mother replied, "Can't you see those wings? I wouldn't do that again, knowing now that you can't stand even the thought of eating a bunny."

The rest of the meal went well until his father sneezed, leading Phyllis to offer the routine "God bless you."

Evidently upset by the possibility of rabbit damage to his new Olds, he retorted angrily, "I don't need God to bless me."

Jumping from her chair, she cried out with emotion, "Well then, God damn you!" Fleeing to her little back room, again in tears, she was followed by a chorus of young voices claiming dibs on her dessert.

Unfazed by the commotion, Bobby continued eating, happy to have avoided more tears for the hapless rabbits, saying, "Chicago was never like this, but it is sure good to be home."

* * * *

One of his first moves was to drive into Los Angeles to register at USC for the fall semester. He was able to get his old summer job back as a lifeguard at the Lakeside Country Club, only a few blocks from home.

Using his savings, much of which was from the sale of his roadster before leaving for Chicago, a 1933 Ford V-8 three-window coupe was purchased for transportation, since a car to get around Southern California was more essential than ever, especially in the case of the Valley. He was still hooked on hot rods, but he remembered well that the open ones were disliked by most girls, not only because of their hair being blown every which way, but also in the process leaving them smelling like exhaust fumes.

The family was back at full strength, all seven crowded into the seven room, one bath home. Phyllis, for privacy, slept in the little converted sewing room in the rear of the house. How everyone was able to co-ordinate their use of the facilities, especially with the presence of the younger boys, stands as a tribute to American ingenuity, and most certainly, firm parental rules. Oftentimes, especially on a school morning, the bathroom was like Grand Central Station, requiring co-operation otherwise impossible in the case of siblings. For Bobby, this was a radical change from the privacy he had enjoyed in Chicago, but as he was expected to be the role model for the other boys, for a time he dutifully faced up to the responsibility, and in so doing came to realize a certain satisfaction over his new-found status. He was a leader of sorts once again.

* * * *

Bobby was jarred out of his daydream by what would become a frequent occurrence over Los Angeles just after Pearl Harbor, when fear of an impending Japanese invasion gripped the West Coast. A flight of P-38 fighter planes, flying low, suddenly appeared over downtown. Most of those in the line at the recruiting office, admiring that advanced fighter plane, began talking about combat, and how in their planes they would make short work of the Japs and Nazis. Bobby felt some of that also, but was more realistic.

Turning to Dave, he exclaimed, "Listen to those kids. You'd think by their talk they were already aces. The younger one is, the more belief he has in his own invincibility. Death in war is inevitable, but always for someone else. Risks are dwarfed by dreams of glory and the spoils of war. Fame, fortune, and women."

"You forgot patriotism," Dave replied. "But all that makes them more aggressive warriors than older guys. But it also helps make aces of veteran pilots among the enemy. In a way, it's like sports. Those more experienced usually have the edge over the freshman, and those more physically gifted an even greater advantage. A pilot already an ace, especially one with the natural ability of a top athlete, would feast on these kids.

All that reminded Bobby of his buddy, Tommy Hunter, who had been the first of their little group to go to war, and the first to die.

NINE

Tommy and the Blitz, 1940

He and Tommy had hung around in the driveway of his home together a lot the summer of his return from Chicago in 1940, working on their cars. Mostly, aside from roadsters, they would discuss the war, or brag about their love lives. As with most males of that age, they were not entirely truthful with each other regarding their experiences. Tommy knew that Bobby had been close to Denise before he left for college, but he had never spoken of that last night to him. He would never kiss and tell when it came to Denise, and he had never stopped loving her. Not wanting to appear backwards, Tommy bragged that he could make out with his girl, Billie Jean, anytime he wanted, but for the fact that they had vowed to save themselves for marriage.

One morning, after the overcast had cleared, they had again parked in the driveway. There was little talk for a time, the silence punctuated only by the clanking of wrenches tightening the new chromed acorn stud nuts that would further dress up the flat heads on their V-8s. After they were satisfied with their work, the talk finally came around to girls.

Bobby asked, "Isn't your girlfriend only fourteen? She's in my brother Paddy's class in junior high, I think, and he's six years younger than I am."

"Yeah," Tommy said, ruefully, "She's way too young to get married. Her parents don't approve of me anyway because of our age difference. Her father says I'm robbing the cradle."

Bobby let the subject drop, and then, for the first time, Tommy came out with his decision. In a low voice, he said, "I'm joining up! The RAF is accepting high school graduates from the U.K. and the Dominion countries for flight training with the RCAF in Canada. Pilots are really needed now, with the German Blitz making London and other British cities hell on earth. You've been reading the newspapers. You've seen the photos and the newsreels. I can't stand by any longer. I have family over there, you know," he added, "But not in Scotland. An aunt and three cousins, in Coventry."

Everyone knew what that meant. The *Luftwaffe* had bombed that city into virtual oblivion.

It wasn't long before Tommy was called up. The farewells were congratulatory and optimistic among the guys, in anticipation that they might soon be brothers in arms. Not so with the women, and least of all in the case of Tommy's girlfriend, her face stained with tears. Despite her attempts to put on a brave front, it was evident to all that she regarded his enlisting as a disaster.

Bobby and Tommy occasionally wrote each other, about how the training in Canada and then in Britain was going, and how Billie Jean was holding up in Tommy's absence. He was apparently thriving on the routine of pilot training, as expressed in his enthusiastic letters, both to her and to his buddy. But she was not doing well at all, a fact she and Bobby glossed over in their letters to Tommy. He phoned her each time he heard from him in fulfilling his promise to look after her.

It was barely a month after Tommy had entered combat that his mother called tearfully to announce his being killed in action in his Hurricane fighter over London. Her words hit Bobby as if cold steel were being thrust through him.

Billie Jean, along with the Hunter family, was devastated. Hoping to console her, he went over to her home off Magnolia the first chance he got. Her pretty face was stained with tears, as she kept harping on a single theme.

"It's your fault, all you guys. Sure, Tommy was one of you, but all you ever thought about was speed and more speed. It wasn't enough to tear up the roads or the dry lakes. You had to take it into the air. He just beat you to it. Now you're next up, and if you die too, you'll prove my point. Tommy admired you too much, getting his pilot's ambition from you. I just know he'd still be here with me without your influence."

Bobby tried to explain that Tommy's motivation to help defend the country of his birth was the deciding factor, and that his choice of military services, as with Bobby, was always because of a desire to fly. At that, she began to weep uncontrollably, showing him further words would be useless.

As he realized that and stood up to leave, she blubbered, her voice choking, "Get out! I never want to see any of you engine nuts and speed crazies ever again."

Tommy's parents more graciously received Bobby's condolences. In their grief, they blamed themselves for permitting him to enlist in the first place.

Bobby observed, "Billie Jean is beside herself, blaming me for his joining the RCAF."

Mr. Hunter, putting a comforting hand on his shoulder, replied. "Nothing could be farther from the truth, lad. He always wanted to fly for the RAF, even before we came to the States. It was all he ever talked about, even after we settled here."

"I know that all too well, but try to convince his girl of that." Bobby replied.

"Why bother?" Tommy's mother said, "Remember, she's only a child, and will get over it quickly. She's hardly old enough to understand these things, the reason we never approved of her anyway. Very bright, yes, but so young! Much too young for our poor Tommy."

It took Bobby weeks before he could free himself from the constant ache. Thoughts of Tommy's death lingered even longer, recurring whenever his mind came back to recollections of their experiences together. A lot like his losing Denise. It was that same sick feeling of depression, that huge emptiness. But the finality of death was far worse than a mere lost love. Tommy is dead, he lamented. It seemed so unbelievable. And hadn't he been convinced of his own immortality? He would say repeatedly, "There's no way a bullet could have my name on it." A lot of guys thought that way, but as a believer in free will, Bobby knew that one's choices were almost everything. The rest was blind luck, as he had tried to convince Tommy.

"Every bullet has your name on it only if you get in the way. Just keep your head down, and an eye out behind you."

His death sobered the guys who had known him, diminishing to some degree their young man's belief in indestructibility. The loss of his closest buddy led to Bobby's deciding that continued education would be best. At the time, the Army Air Corps, as it was called then, required two years of college training for prospective pilots anyway.

* * * *

Tuesday, December ninth dawned clear and cool, promising a pleasant day, their second in the line to the recruiting office.

Accommodating to the expected long wait, Bobby soon was lost in reminiscing about his earlier experiences at USC, when things were more carefree.

TEN

Living In, 1941-43

His stay at home lasted over a year, but took its toll scholastically after the semester began. Renewed friendship with old high school buddies, not so academically inclined, was a mixed blessing. More often than not they ended up enticing him out for the evening, at the expense of his studies.

Finally, that and the crowding at home became too much. Sharing the bedroom with his three brothers brought some difficulties. Bobby was dissatisfied by his lack of privacy, after all he had enjoyed in Chicago. One afternoon, a letter from a friend there was opened and read before he had even seen it. In it was reference to some affair he was reputed to have had. His mother, while passing the thing off as the idle boasting of a young male, sternly lectured him that to kiss and tell was betrayal of an important trust. He had to agree with her, but he was rightly outraged that his mail had been opened. He was sure his sister was the guilty one.

When his mother then unfairly said, "It was one of the young males," he stormed out of the house, shouting, "Those little twerps again. Mom, with them around, this may be a house, but it's not a home!"

All this led Bobby to move to the Phi Kappa Psi fraternity house on Twenty-Eighth Street, adjoining the USC campus in Los Angeles. The added expense, a concern of his parents, mostly would be defrayed by his "Hashing" at the house, serving at mealtimes, in return for which he received his meals and half the cost of his room. This enabled them to come up with the balance, calculated to be not much different than the cost of having his ravenous appetite at home, coupled with the expense of the daily commute.

With the start of his junior year, things really picked up. Living at the frat house, almost two hours a day of driving time was saved, and life on campus, geared to class schedules, made study easy, whether in his room or at one of the school libraries. This efficiency allowed him time for writing and reporting for *The Daily Trojan,* the school paper, where he later became an editor, occasionally also contributing to the *Vulture,* billed as the "Alleged humor magazine." There was also ample opportunity to socialize, with the house next door to two sororities, and across the street from two more.

As usual, almost everyone was excited about the football season, which was always a big deal at USC. In 1941, despite the increasing ferocity of the war in Europe and the worsening relations with Japan, the football spirit still affected the students. Every year, in playing either Cal or Stanford, much of the student body would trek north, many by train, to take in the game and to party in San Francisco.

Bobby at first thought he would be too busy, thinking he'd stay home, listening to the game on the radio. But at the last minute, he hopped on the Southern Pacific "Trojan Football Special," heading for San Francisco.

It seemed like half the student body was aboard, as almost the entire train was reserved for SC rooters, with more than half the cars just for students. He hardly knew a soul, but he felt somewhat at home as he cruised the aisles of the several student cars, casting friendly looks at groups of coeds, who, mostly engrossed in their own thoughts of the coming weekend, gave him little attention. Returning to his seat in the regular part of the train, he decided that the best way to get started was to have something to drink, and to be able to offer one to a girl who attracted him.

His opportunity came when the train stopped at a small town a couple hundred miles north of L.A. Getting off his coach, he approached a conveniently located grocery store just across the street, and entered. Spying the liquor shelf, he said to the man behind the counter, "Gimme a pint of that Old Crow, will ya please?"

The proprietor's answer was quick and decisive. "Not on your life, young fella. I doubt that you're of drinking age, and even if you are, no way will I sell you any alcohol to take to those kids on that train."

Bobby indignantly replied, "I'm twenty-one, and I'm sure not going to share a measly pint with anybody."

"You bet you're not, because you're not getting any from my place," he tartly replied, and then pointing, "Look, your train is pulling out. G'bye!"

Bobby's frustration was exceeded only by his effort in sprinting after the train, jumping aboard just before the steps were pulled up. Christ, he thought, I've gotta be at least a couple of years older than most of the gals on this train, and I can't even get a drink.

The bartender in the club car was very hard-nosed too, and didn't believe him either. In a funk, he sullenly retraced his steps forward to the student section, which by that time was swinging, everyone drinking and singing college songs, including that derogatory one about the University of California's dirty golden bear losing all his hair. People were passing around bottles, and filling paper cups with the same stuff that he had tried to buy. He certainly didn't appreciate the irony.

Standing by the door, he was noticed by one girl, who had just accepted a cup of whiskey from another coed. Catching his eye, she called out, "Care to share this with me?" Still feeling uncomfortable, he sat down next to her, managing a smile.

"Thanks, a friend indeed."

"Is a friend in need," She answered, "Did I get that right?"

Bobby thought of the mixed up cliché, but smilingly nodded. Whether she would have been as friendly were it not for the booze, he didn't know, but her interest in him was the antidote to his frustration.

She offered, "I'm just a freshman and a KKG pledge, and I see by your pin that you're a Phi Psi. But I don't recall seeing you, even at the pledge presentations."

"That's odd," he replied, "We're just next door to each other. But I just started living in last month, after almost a year at home and my freshman year at Chicago."

"What a coincidence," she exclaimed, "I'm from the Midwest too!"

He looked at her, amused at her lack of guile, replying, "Well, I'm not *from* there, actually, I'm from just over the hill in Burbank. But I've got tons of family in the Midwest. My dad is from Minnesota, and my mom was born in South Dakota."

Her gray eyes lit up with enthusiasm then. "I'm from North Dakota. Fargo, you know, the Pony Express, the Wells Fargo stage, and all that?"

Tongue in cheek, Bobby ventured, "Small world, isn't it?"
He regretted his sarcasm, but she appeared not to mind. She
seemed really sweet, in a simple disarming way.

"Say," she said, "After the game we Kappas are having a
party, at the Drake Hotel in San Francisco. Why don't you
come? I'm just a pledge, but I'm sure you'll be welcome."

He knew about those hell-raising fraternity affairs, where
drinking, dancing to records, and water bombing people on
the sidewalks below were the usual aftermath of the game.
Would it be different at a sorority party? The thought about
Kappa Kappa Gamma calling itself a fraternity led to a
chuckle.

"Hey, great," he exclaimed enthusiastically, "But what
room number? And I don't even know your name. Mine's
Phil Taylor, but everyone calls me Bobby."

"That's cute. Mine's Rhoda, a good old-fashioned name.
Rhoda Thomas. We're farmers, but don't hold that against
me."

He surprised himself, responding to her candor, confiding, "I'm no city slicker either. I grew up in the San Fernando
Valley, where every other person is either a horse or a cow."

She laughed at that, took his hand and held it, enthusing,
"We'll be two farmers in the big city." Then, writing the room
number of the party on a napkin with her other hand, she put
it neatly into his shirt pocket, patted it down, smiling sweetly.
"Now, this may seem stupid, with all these distractions, but
I've got homework to do." With that, she reached down to the
floor, pulled a large book out of her bag there, and quickly
became lost in it.

Bobby was amazed, and at the same time intrigued. She was seemingly so simple, warm one moment, and all business the next. He decided he had to get to know her better.

In San Francisco, he was able to share a room with some brothers, also at the Drake. On arrival at the hotel, he thought, God, even checking in is an experience not to be forgotten. Standouts were the Bellboys in their red uniforms and the people at the front desk in impeccable black. And the lobby was decorated as if for a holiday.

"Wow," he said half aloud, "This is swell, just like the Palmer House in Chicago."

The women especially caught his eye, with those white gloves and fashionable dresses. No bobby sox among them. He thought about the crowd on the train, and the clothes he had on. How could any of us fit in here?

Their room was not high enough to see the Golden Gate Bridge, and on the west side of the building, away from a view of the Bay Bridge too. Oh, well, he mused, it wouldn't be bad, sharing it with a couple of other fraternity brothers, who had driven up together. Heck, hardly any time would be spent in there anyway.

In the morning, after breakfast, they all went over in the car to Berkeley, first to see the campus and visit the chapter there. The fall colors were just turning the leaves to lovely shades of red and orange, and there was a clean, crisp something in the air not evident much in L.A. There was also much more green than ever there was around campus at SC.

The fraternity house was decked out in the school colors, the blue and gold of the University of California. After brunch, thanking their hosts and inviting them to visit the house at SC next time, the guys all headed for Strawberry Canyon and the football stadium. As usual, it looked like it would be full by game time, because this was always a huge contest between perennial contenders, often deciding which team would go to the Rose Bowl. This year it was different, with the Trojans under their new interim coach, Sam Barry, but still the rivalry was evident everywhere. It was fortunate that the rooting sections were on opposite sides of the stadium, as encounters with fans, who made it known they didn't like the visiting team's colors, would sometimes lead to blows.

Across from the Trojan side, the Cal rooting section was especially rowdy, and while the card section was much more disciplined, rows of mostly blue-dressed men above it were not. This became especially evident at half time, when after the hard-fought first half, the score was seven to seven. Those guys would hoist huge cardboard phallic symbols in the form of purple shafts, or others more explicit. As usual there were insulting signs with the usual play on words regarding the Trojan brand of condom. Bobby was in the card section, and attention to that busy routine, invented at USC, kept him from taking in all of that, but everyone, at least the young men of either school, thought it was hilarious.

The second half was equally contested, but was scoreless, ending in a frustrating tie. It was not the kind of game that gave the SC teams of the great Howard Jones, who had retired that year, the name, "The Thundering Herd." Still, that was thought an appropriate term, especially by Cal supporters, prone to look down on Southern Cal's academic ranking in comparison to their own. Naturally, this didn't bother Bobby one bit, and it hardly dampened the spirits of any Trojan fan contemplating the promised night's revelry in San Francisco.

Back at the hotel, after showering, he put on slacks and a white shirt under a burgundy sweater. He preferred blue, but among SC fans after a game, that would not go over well. As he left the room, the thought crossed his mind that there would be plenty of Cal students around, some of them sore-heads. Well, he thought, we'll just have to outwit them. We sure as hell can't outnumber them.

A smiling coed opened the door where the KKG party was, saying, "Hi, come on in. I see you're wearing the right colors, but do I know you?"

Bobby thought she had to be the holder of the room key. "Hi. I'm Phil Taylor, and my invitation came from Rhoda. Is she here yet?"

Looking him over with new interest, the hostess said, "Oh, you're the cute boy she met on the train. Come on in, she'll be here soon enough. Want something to drink?"

Bobby answered, "Sure, I'm parched, if you don't mind."

"We've got beer or whiskey, and if you'd prefer, both."

"Nah," Bobby answered, as she led him across the room to the makeshift bar, "I'll just have the beer, thanks."

Enjoying their view, he half emptied the bottle of Lucky Lager. Just then, he noticed Rhoda entering the room. Could he be mistaken? There was the same long, wavy dark brown hair, and the striking gray eyes. No, he'd not likely forget that. But, in heels, with a fluffy blouse that accentuated her ample bosom, and in a red jacket and skirt, she was a knock-out. Excusing himself, he rushed over to her just as two other guys cornered her.

Quickly coming across the room, thrusting his beer be-tween the two men, Bobby said, "I've been expecting you. Here's your beer," steering her away from the two dumb-founded guys.

He asked, "Who are they, friends of yours?" Then, releasing her slim waist, he handed her a fresh cold one. The other bottle had served its purpose and was getting warm.

Ignoring his question, she answered only, "Thanks."

Like the beer, he was getting warm also, but it was more of a reaction to her nearness, where he could smell her perfume and look into her smiling face. Until then, she hadn't said more than that one word, just smiling sweetly at him.

Then she said simply, "I was hoping you'd be here."

They danced a bit to the record playing, rather sedately, as the room was too crowded for jitterbugging. During a break, they were admiring the view and a smoke at the open window, until the same two guys pushed in and started dropping water-filled balloons aimed at the people below.

"Jeez, guys," he said, "If one of those hits, it could cause a real injury."

One of them, glowering at him, retorted, "Who asked you, anyway?" Then he turned back to the window, with a full balloon in his hand. Seeing his opportunity, Bobby touched the end of his cigarette to the distended latex, causing it to burst, the water spilling all over the guy's front.

"Shit, man, look what you've done," he exclaimed.

The hostess, observing the scene, interjected, "Only saved somebody's life maybe, or at the very least kept us from being kicked out of our room."

"Aw, we were just trying to have a little fun," he complained. Then to his crony, "There has to be some real partying somewhere in this hotel. Let's go, Don."

As the glowering two left, Bobby said, "Don't hurry back."

The gathering became normal once more, and he became the center of attraction, surrounded by a couple of interested sorority sisters. Giving them scant time, seeing him basking in their praise, Rhoda took his hand, telling them, "Sorry girls, he's my date." And then she led him out into the hall.

Once outside the room, she looked admiringly at him with that winsome smile. Bobby was happy to have won points with the girls, but his stomach told him it was suppertime.

"Say, let's go get a bite, and then hit some of the clubs in North Beach. I've heard there are some really good ones."

They settled on Bernstein's Fish Grotto, off Union Square. Its white ship's prow façade attracted them, and the food was good. As they sat at the table across from each other, the candle in the table's center lighted her face in a most sexy way. Bobby wondered if she realized that. They talked of the game, enthusing about the hard-fought contest, and the fact that, despite the score, the Bears had been out-played.

The day had been exhilarating for her and her sorority sisters, but more in anticipation of the weekend away than for the football itself. For Bobby it was both, with, as things went at the parties, a chance to raise a little hell as well.

"Let's go somewhere and dance," Bobby suggested, after the dessert of pineapple sherbet.

"I've a better idea," Rhoda answered, "I arranged for us to double with my girlfriend Betty and her boyfriend Ron. She's from Fargo also, and we grew up together, although she's a little older. I haven't seen her for almost a year. She's a nurse at the University Hospital. You'll like her. Anyway, I called her when we got here, and they'll pick us up outside." Disappointed, Bobby paid the bill. So far, he thought, it had been great. But doubling with a couple of total strangers?

He needn't have worried. Betty turned out to be a perky little blond, who kept things going, and Ron was a tough-looking first class Navy gunner's mate. He obviously took pride in what he called a great ship, the battleship *U.S.S. California*.

Betty remarked, "You would think he was married to that ship, he talks about her so much."

At that point, Rhoda decided that some sightseeing was in order, and the place to go on a clear night was Twin Peaks, where a view of the entire city could be spectacular. They drove up Market Street, and then after turning a few corners, there they were, looking out over the panorama of San Francisco and the Bay Area. The City was blanketed in the glow of myriad lights, as well as their reflection from the fog that hovered just off the Golden Gate. Everything was lit up, both bridges outlined by the lights of the traffic, which formed a kaleidoscopic display of moving white specks and red, from the vehicles crossing.

Bobby would have enjoyed it more if he hadn't felt a little queasy. He never became carsick when he drove, but the back seat was his nemesis. The couple in front immediately start-ed necking, leading Bobby to put his arm around his date. The radio was playing his old favorite, Glen Miller's "In the Mood," but she opened the door and got out.

"Come on, the view is better out here," she said light-heartedly.

He followed, to the log that marked the end of the park-ing area, onto which she stepped.

"Yep, you're right about the view," he whispered, as he took her hand, finding it a nice fit, but cold.

When he remarked about that, thinking of offering her his sweater, she said, "Cold hands, warm heart. You've heard that I'm sure."

"Repeatedly," he replied, thinking of his family, where clichés were a second language. "I've heard a million of them."

Facing her, he put his other arm around her waist, and there they stood for a few minutes enjoying it all.

Just then they were interrupted by Betty calling out, "Come on, you two, Ron and I are starving, Let's go to my place. I know you guys just ate, but there's beer there if you want it."

A disappointed Bobby lifted Rhoda down from the log, taking in the fragrance of her hair. "That would be great," he said, thinking mostly of her body momentarily pressed against his.

They took the winding way down, continuing over to the upper Haight to the little place on Belvedere where Betty rented. On the way, she pointed out Moffat Hospital where she worked as an RN, but by that time he was beginning not to care. The ride, in the back seat, with the stop and go jerkiness was proving too much. He was getting carsick. First, there was the sweating, and then the nausea. Whatta way to end what could have been a perfect date, he lamented to himself. When they finally arrived, he couldn't wait to get out into the fresh air again. Forget the beer, all he wanted was to lie down. Rhoda led him into the living room to the couch there, arranged a pillow, and taking off his shoes, lifted his feet onto the cushion.

Betty and Ron were chattering in the kitchen when she went in and got herself a beer, and it was then that they quieted down, much to Bobby's relief. God, but he felt awful. When she came back with the now half empty beer, she curled up on the floor beside the couch, looking at him in the most concerned way.

"Aw, don't worry," he said, "I'll be okay in a while. I'm sorry to put such a damper on the fun."

She smiled at that, and finishing the rest of her beer, gently whispered, "Why don't you move over." As he began to sit up, sliding to one end of the couch, she said, putting a restraining hand on his shoulder, "No, stay down. Just move back." Then she lay down beside him.

There he was, so close and facing her, with her blouse unbuttoned just enough to reveal her inviting cleavage. Her lips were next to his, as if asking for a kiss, but he felt so sick that his desire had temporarily left him.

"Rhoda," he whispered, worried about his nausea blowing his chances with her, "I'm so sorry. Sorry for ruining your weekend."

Snuggling even closer, she said softly, "We'll have other weekends."

He finally began to feel halfway human by midnight, but by then she was sleeping, her face angelic, still next to his. He kissed her on the lips, and in her sleep, she stirred, returning the kiss a little. He got up carefully, so as not to awaken her, and stood fondly looking down at her. Just then Ron came in and offered a ride downtown, on his return to his ship.

"Okay," Bobby said, "But I get to sit in the front seat."

* * * *

He had meant to continue where he left off in his romance with Rhoda, but their promising beginning didn't lead anywhere. They dated a few times, and after the first snow fell in the mountains, they skied together, getting along beautifully.

During the next week, he missed seeing her on the way to classes, and that evening enquired after her at the Kappa house. Her roommate, answering the door, looked at him quizzically.

"Oh, didn't she tell you? Her father pulled her out of school. She left in a hurry yesterday, and in tears. Seems he doesn't approve of anyone dating his daughter, especially a Catholic boy."

Bobby had been through that before, but to lose her was almost too much. Any religion, Catholic, Protestant, or any other, coming between two people in that way was definitely not for him.

* * * *

One Saturday at home, who should come over, but Sinkie, in his uniform of a naval gunner's mate. In their conversation, Bobby recounted to him how in 1935, when the fleet was in Long Beach, the family had spent a Sunday there, visiting aboard the *U.S.S. Arizona.* Sinkie's face lit up at that.

"Yeah, that's how I became interested in the Navy as a career. And that's my ship. Isn't she a beauty? With more modernization since then, she's a match for anything."

Bobby, having read *Jane's Fighting Ships,* the international authority on the world's navies, when he was younger, was dubious. He was thinking of the many arguments he had engaged in with his Nisei classmate, Hideki Fujikawa, who had guaranteed that Japan's Imperial Fleet would make short work of ours.

"But she's only fitted with fourteen inch guns, and displaces a mere 33,000 tons, and what about the Japs building 73,000 ton battleships, while we stuck to the terms of the Washington Naval Treaty that limits capital ships to 40,000 tons, and heavy cruisers to 10,000. How would our battlewagons match those Japanese monsters with their eighteen inch guns, and almost twice the tonnage?"

"It's all just crap," Sinkie protested, "You've seen the workmanship of the Japanese goods they sell us. Do you think they make their own things any better?"

Bobby had to agree that most of the goods from Japan had turned out to be junk in his own experience, and that was well known, to the point that "Made in Japan" had become synonymous with shoddiness. Their marketing suffered, to the extent that they even tried the subterfuge of renaming one of their islands Usa, stamping everything "Made in USA."

He did tell him again about his little brother's old bicycle. "It was made in Japan. It literally fell apart within a few months."

"That's what I'm saying." Sinkie went on, "Besides, look at the trouble they've had subduing the Chinese, who have only antiquated equipment. The word in the Navy is that if they attack us, they won't last six months. Everyone knows they depend on us for their oil, and on our scrap for their steel."

Bobby had heard all that before. It seemed a national delusion then. No one dreamed at the time that our recycled metal would be coming back to us in the form of artillery shells and bombs, and that the Japanese would quickly sweep through mineral and oil-rich Malaysia and the East Indies to secure those riches there for themselves.

He asked, "But what about the battleship's vulnerability, demonstrated by General Billy Mitchell back in the Twenties with the German battleship *Ostfriesland?*"

Sinkie hotly answered that. "I've heard that story. Do you really think they recreated actual combat conditions? An obsolete World War ship, anchored and motionless, without adequate deck armor, built before aerial bombing was even thought of? Come on. I probably shouldn't be telling you this, but the reason we're in port in San Pedro is for a refitting with more anti-aircraft guns than you can shake a stick at. Let the bombers try. We'll show 'em. And our deck armor is plenty thick enough."

Bobby could see then that there was no point to further discussion, and the conversation ended on that note.

It was less than two months later that the uneasy peace was shattered on December 7th by the Japanese surprise attack on Pearl Harbor. The *U.S.S. Arizona* was a total loss, a bomb having somehow pierced the armored deck, setting off the ship's magazines deep below. Like the *Ostfriesland*, along with most of our battleships, it was tied up and motionless, and there was little time, because of the total surprise, for anyone to fire in defense before the damage was done. 1,177 men aboard the *Arizona* died, close to half the toll of American lives for the entire day, as much of our Pacific Fleet was put out of commission. Sinkie, listed as missing, is probably still in the sunken hulk of the ship he loved so.

* * * *

A newsboy interrupted Bobby's reminiscing, waving the Los Angeles Times and shouting, "Japs attack the Philippines!"

Grabbing a copy for the price of a nickel, Dave shouted, "Another disaster. They've destroyed most of the planes at Clark Field and bombed the Naval facilities at Cavite and elsewhere on Manila Bay, inflicting heavy damage. Can you believe it? Another Pearl Harbor."

Bobby questioned, "Weren't they in radio contact with the Military in Hawaii and Washington? How could we have been so badly surprised twice?"

Reading on, Dave replied, "According to this, there is no good answer. But between you and me, our commander there, General Douglas MacArthur, will have a lot of explaining to do."

It was more terrible news, but it confirmed the mindset of everyone present. They would be needed more than ever. Numbered cards in hand, and after a couple more hours in line, they finally were able to complete the sign up process for the Army Air Force.

* * * *

A week later, they reported for the general physical and other tests. The routine was rigorous, designed to select only the best men for any combat training, and the very best, physically and mentally, for Aviation Cadet.

Bobby's teeth passed as the soundest the doctor had ever seen, as he ran a wooden tongue blade noisily across them. He stumbled only on his introduction to the *Short Arm* exam designed to detect gonorrhea.

"Okay men, skin it back and milk it down," was the barked order from the sergeant at the head of the line.

Skin it back? What's with that? Despite his momentary difficulty in grasping the concept, the mental exam was a breeze for him. He received the highest score of the two hundred taking it that day, 314 out of a possible 320.

ELEVEN

Cadet Training

He was finally called up in the spring of 1943, midway through his senior year. Orders were to report to Santa Ana Army Air Base, just sixty miles from home. There wasn't enough time to sell his car and his record collection, much to the glee of his two youngest brothers, who got the rare chance to drive his 1939 Ford Convertible, bought the year before, and to play his many platters of swing and jazz.

The Army routine was well organized and things went smoothly, considering the numbers, from assignment to their respective barracks to being issued G.I. uniforms. Amazingly, most of the clothes fit despite the seemingly arbitrary way the uniform sizes were determined by the supply personnel. Instructions were given about arranging their footlockers and making their beds, so that the blankets were taut as bowstrings. Dog tags for identification were issued and they were subjected to the first of innumerable orientations, the Army's term for practically everything.

After learning about Army Regulations, and the penalties should they stray, another treat was in store, their first G.I. chow. So much food, great ingredients treated very badly. There were great quantities of lumpy mashed potatoes, greasy gravy, tough meatloaf and overcooked peas and carrots. The milk had been powdered and then reconstituted, as were the scrambled eggs at breakfast the next day, a little like foam rubber, garnished with chunks of Spam. And the cornflakes did poorly with the powdered milk. He couldn't tell what the juice was, and neither could anyone else.

The first days were occupied with more testing, this time with the *Army General Classification Test,* or *GCT,* and the *Mechanical Aptitude Test.* Others were tests of co-ordination, to separate out potential pilots from those less physically gifted.

They were told not to look at their test scores, but naturally everyone did, as each cadet carried his folder between the different stations. Bobby's aptitude for flying was graded 9-10-9-8, best for bomber pilot, and while still acceptable, least suited for navigator. Needless to say, he was disappointed that fighter pilot came in second.

After that, they were assigned to companies according to their classifications. Somehow, his was company A, although their names were all R to Z. It was then that he became close friends with a fellow cadet, Danny Thunder. During pilot training they would be together, placed in the alphabetical order typical of the USAAF. They studied together, marched alongside each other, and when the chance came for Bobby to get home for a weekend, he took Danny along.

Danny was an American Indian, a *Sioux*, from the Black Hills of South Dakota. He was one of the lucky ones who were able to escape the poverty there. Very bright, he was recognized by the tribal Elders as the most likely among them to represent the Sioux Nation in the white world. Small wonder. One would never in a million years have thought he was anything other than a typical Caucasian. Not tall, around five nine, he was built like a truck. This belied his cat-like quickness, which accounted for his having excelled athletically. His mind was cat-quick too.

It had been easy to believe his story of having been a curiosity. A red-haired, green-eyed Indian? His father, with the same coloring, had also been a genetic anomaly in the tribal gene pool. Somewhere, in the distant past, the blood, perhaps of a French trapper, had become mixed with that of The People, as they called themselves. Or maybe he was a descendant of the union of a captive immigrant Scandinavian female and a brave.

Born on the Pine Ridge Reservation, Danny had been both shunned and idolized. He thus grew up in the tribe somewhat of a misfit. Perhaps it was that factor that molded him early into an achiever, in a society of so much indolence and despair. After finishing high school, he obtained a scholarship from South Dakota State University at Brookings. He excelled there scholastically as well as athletically, and the combination soon labeled him as an academic Jim Thorpe, that greatest of Native American athletes.

At the end of his second year, the war in Europe changed him. In 1939, when Hitler's troops invaded Poland, he decided that it was time. Somehow, his being a racial misfit at home goaded him to fight. He had become fed up with the Nazi theory of racial superiority.

That year, he answered the warrior's call. At the time it was illegal for an American citizen to join another country's military, a fact that kept many a young man in white America at home. It was different with Danny. As an Indian, he felt bound only by the law of the *Sioux* Nation. So in 1939, he made the journey into Canada, enlisting in the Royal Canadian Air Force. He would fly for the cause of Democracy, never mind the inequities his people suffered at the hands of the one at home.

Training didn't take long. Twelve weeks in Canada, where he learned to fly, and another three months in Britain, polishing his technique in bombers. His arrival was too late for the Battle of Britain, that epic defeat of Hitler's bid to conquer Great Britain, but it was perfectly timed for the retaliation the British planned. How it happened that Danny ended up in flight training again in the Army Air Force, rather than being placed immediately into an American heavy bomber unit was a story that came out only later.

Within six months he had completed a hundred sorties over occupied Europe in twin engine Wellingtons. He would never forget that raid on Hamburg in 1942, when the firestorm created by incendiaries combined with high explosives killed tens of thousands, and left nearly a million homeless.

As with most British bombing missions against the *Reich*, the attacks were carried out under cover of darkness. That gave a certain protection against the defenders, with their fighters and anti-aircraft guns. It was still not easy, as navigation at night was iffy, the target seen only when burning, or when the moon reflected identifying rivers or canals. That light worked both ways, also illuminating the raiding RAF bombers.

* * * *

Only once did Bobby ever get close to aircraft at Santa Ana, but they did a lot of close order drill. While he was leading his squad one day as assistant drill instructor in the direction of the airfield, an awesome display for those would-be pilots took place. Just then, a flight of rakish, hot little low wing monoplanes, painted an unusual red, peeled off and landed, coming in right over them. To a man, all wanted to fly that particular ship until the instructor informed them that the red color meant that they were used for towing targets.

The academic training was intensive, emphasizing math and basic science, along with all the elements of flying, including navigation. Aerodynamics and the characteristics of the aircraft they would be learning to fly were stressed, particularly the concepts of fuel consumption, power, and speed. Many were disappointed when they learned they would have to cruise most of the time to extend range and engine life, rather than to fly at full throttle. For the *Hot rocks* among them, meaning just about Bobby's whole company, that took some getting used to. The concept of lift versus gravity requiring planning ahead for pulling out of dives was drummed into them. Compensation for torque in single-engine flight, with control adjustment, especially at full power, as in taking off, or in sharp banking close to the ground was not to be forgotten. All this was new, and sorely needed, in preparation for actual flight. Those who forgot their lessons wouldn't last long.

After ten weeks, he finished Preflight, and was sent to Primary Flight Training up in Visalia, in the San Joaquin Valley, two hundred miles to the north. Again there was the usual orientation, still very much needed to control the impulsive men. Like Bobby, they were all itching to fly, and damn the formalities. In Preflight they had anticipated training in the sleek all metal Ryan PT-19, a monoplane that had been represented in a training film shown them as the plane they would use. Their expectations, however, were soon disappointed.

The Stearman PT-17, a fabric-covered, stodgy-looking biplane would be their primary trainer. Reminding him of a First World War S.P.A.D. pursuit plane, it did handle beautifully. Despite that, it had caused much distress in earlier cadets, leading to the nickname, *The Washing Machine.* Not just because it sounded that way, but because it led to so many washing out, and for some, far worse than that.

Bobby did especially well in primary, soloing in just under four hours, but did find that he had a tendency to airsickness. This came out while his flight instructor was demonstrating spins and recovery. This had him worried, something temporarily put to rest when he was able to weather his solo spins without difficulty. By the time primary had run its ten weeks, and he graduated, things were going well for him.

Sadly, one of his buddies was killed when his plane stalled out while practicing takeoffs and landings. This letter was written that night.

December 1, 1943

Dear Paddy:

There's almost no time to write, with our constant study and flying around here, but I just had to pen this to get a huge weight off my chest—actually, off my heart. One of my closest buddies, Bill Talley, was killed in a crash today. Jus' stalled out turning into his short final.

Remember when you were a little kid, you told us you saw that happen at the Glendale Airport? We lived on Alameda then. I didn't believe you at the time, but the awful truth of that was brought home to me today.

After the crash we had to help clean up the mess, and some of it was poor Billy. I packed up his clothes to send to his wife. My hands were still warm and moist from rinsing off the blood that stained them after I wiped off the ship in which he died. He was convinced that God would be there to protect him. Didn't he pray when he saw he was going to crash, and didn't his wife pray every nite for his safety?

It's to be hoped that you'll learn from this as I have, and never let a turn of the wheel of fortune get you down if such is ever the case. One thing is clear to me now, and I hope, little brother, that it will be clear to you. The only one you can trust at a time like that is yourself. Just keep your head out, and your nose down, and, unlike poor Billy, you'll never stall out.

Rite now I feel like getting a bit smashed, guess we all do after today, but tomorrow means more flying. And so to sleep, perchance to dream—but to be hoped, not a nightmare like today.

Keep in touch, kid, and you'll have my love,

Bobby.

* * * *

After successfully completing Primary, Basic, the next step, was only a few miles away, north of Fresno, California. He looked forward to continuing his flight training there. Often, while in Primary, simulating combat, the faster low wing Vultee BT-13s from that school had "Bounced" them in their slow biplanes, much to their envy and chagrin. The planes were hot looking, but they did have some bad features, the least being the reason they were called "Vultee Vibrators."

He got along well for the first month, checking out in the new plane in a shorter than average time, when one night he awakened with a pain in the abdomen. He'd had something similar three years before, for which his mother had given him copious amounts of olive oil to drink, which seemed to do the trick. But this time he had a fever, causing him to report on sick call in the morning.

He was given *APC*, the standard G.I. remedy for pain and fever, by the enlisted man on duty there. That didn't help, and the pain worsened as it shifted down and to the right, over the appendix. When he returned to the dispensary, he was accused of goldbricking by the same enlisted medic. Bobby objected that as a cadet he certainly wouldn't be feigning illness, and demanded to see the doctor. In that way he got the attention he needed, and an ambulance to the local hospital for an emergency appendectomy.

The surgery went well, and for recuperation, he was transferred back to the Base hospital at Santa Ana, for a few weeks. It was during this time that he wrote again.

January 12, 1944

Dear Paddy:

I hope you will forgive the pencil because I ain't got no pen. Is a bit of a scribble. Don't, however, feel obliged to scribble rite back because I'm so prompt. I know you're busy with high school and I have nothing to do.

They brought in three more lads yesterday with hernias. One of them is about 18 years old and cries at night. He's hardly old enough to be out of the cradle, emotionally, anyway. He hadn't been operated on when Mom and Dad came down to see me the other day and he noticed them. The first thing he said when he woke up from surgery was in a tear-strained voice.

"Were those your folks that visited you Sunday?"

"Yeah, that was my Mom and Pop," I rejoined briefly. "You come from Louisiana, don't you?"

"No," I corrected him, "From Los Angeles."

"Gee," he began, with tears on his adolescent eyelashes, "All the way from Louisiana. I wish my Momma and my Papa would come from Connecticut." I couldn't convince him that he was off the beam. He just kept crying to himself and repeating the last statement over and over again.

I hope he snaps out of it soon. You'd think he had been shot full of holes taking Berlin single-handed instead of having a mere hernia repair, the way he looks and moans.

Guess I'm getting a little coarse for my own age but I'll tell you something. Even the little I've seen of this war and of this Army has acted as quite a conditioning agent for things to come. When I was up at Visalia in primary training, and they were getting killed like flies, the Captain would have the ship hauled in for us to take a look at it and hear a lecture on same. The sight and smell of the blood on the ship and his telling how it was the kid's fault, while the boy was dead or dying teaches you that sympathy in the Army is outmoded—it just ain't. You feel as tho it would never happen to you, that's your egotism, but if and when it does, you'll know from past experience what others will be thinking—it's just T.S.

So you learn to shut up and not cry when things go wrong. I tell you man, it's funny how your philosophy changes. You come to feel that things that happen just happen. They don't necessarily happen for the good or the bad, they're just true. You may or may not be the cause, but it doesn't matter. There's still the effect, which can seldom be altered. So when you get a tough break, T.S. But everything goes on just as it ever did, and the things that happen don't really count, they're settings on a stage that are changed only by fate. God is in heaven and for all your prayers, if a thing is going to happen, God will still be in heaven when the payoff comes. He may be with you for your own mental or religious stability, but you still have to convince yourself he's there. There'll be no outward sign. The wheel still turns on its destined way and all things will still be run by a law that is governed by no one, I wonder if even by God. This kid next to me doesn't know this, and after you read this you won't either.

I guess I kinda got off my stick, but this is just what I'd like to tell that kid if he were my brother but it's not any of my business.

Well, so long pal, take care of yourself,

Love, Bobby

* * * *

Recovering from the appendectomy, he returned to flight training, a couple of weeks behind his class. The first day back, his flight instructor took him up for aerobatics. As before, when he took the controls, he would do fine, but having to endure the instructor's loops and rolls, he soon became airsick. Because he wanted his student to catch up with the rest of the class, the instructor, Lt. Sheridan, kept the controls too long for Bobby. When the plane was finally turned over to him, he was able to do the same maneuvers, but not with the smoothness he had learned in primary.

"Taylor, you might as well pack your bags, because I'm giving you thumbs down. You just can't cut it"

Then, as the shocked Bobby pulled off his helmet and goggles, the lieutenant saw the pallid skin and the beads of sweat.

At that, he observed, "Airsickness, is it? That accounts for a quarter of our washouts."

"Wait until tomorrow, Sir, then let me fly the Vultee myself. You'll see. I never get sick when I do the flying. I did all this stuff in primary, with the PT-17, and did well. Look at my record from Visalia. I was near the top in everything."

"Sorry, Taylor," was the crisp reply. "In a dogfight the maneuvers are far more likely to create airsickness than a few planned aerobatic figures. If you get sick in combat, you'll be dead meat in an enemy gun sight, considering your very shaky routine just now. And what would happen if you upchucked into your oxygen mask at thirty thousand? That stuff would freeze, and you'd have to tear the mask off. Do you know how long you could remain conscious then?"

"You know the story of Bob Hoover," Bobby responded defensively, "He learned to fly before enlisting in the Army and had a problem with airsickness too. He practiced aerobatics until he cured himself of the problem, like a sailor getting his sea legs. Now he's regarded as the greatest stick and rudder man who ever lived. And that comes from no other than General Jimmy Doolittle himself."

"Taylor," he replied, "I've heard that story a few times. Just like what Eddie Rickenbacker, our highest-scoring ace in the First World War went through. But getting over it takes time, and that's something you don't have. My judgment stands, and no more argument. The Captain will review my report, of course, but he's never, to my knowledge, reversed an instructor's decision. I'm sorry. I wish I could still rate you for flying bombers, but at this stage that's impossible. However,

with your vision and co-ordination, you'd make a great bombardier too. Why don't you go for it?"

And so Bobby's ambition to be a fighter pilot, along with
that of so many others, was left in the cockpit of the Vultee
Vibrator.

* * * *

Bitter at the time, his instructor's words stayed with him.
He had scored well for bombardier in the initial classification tests. After pilot, that was his second choice anyway, because he had become thoroughly impressed with the Army
Air Force dogma of high altitude precision bombing. At that
time it was coming into its own as a potent weapon in the war
against the Nazis. His role of pinpointing industrial targets
with the super-secret Norden bombsight, surgically destroying German targets without killing civilians living nearby,
immensely appealed to him.

He was appalled by the loss of life among non-combatants in Europe as seen in the newsreels and in the papers.
Photographs of the destruction of Coventry and Rotterdam
both galled and saddened him. He couldn't believe that the
wanton destruction of those cities by the Nazis could ever be
justified. He was repelled equally by the methodical British
firebombing of Hamburg and other German cities. Too many
lives of innocent women and children were taken there. Of
course, all that was done at night, making precise targeting
impossible, and vengeance was an element in those raids.
Still, envisioning the accuracy that could be achieved in daylight, it was a relief for Bobby to receive his orders to report to
the Army Flying School in Victorville, California, for bombardier training, in the high desert a hundred miles east of
home.

Before they parted, Bobby had a farewell beer, along with burgers, with his buddy Danny, at the local bar and grill.

"Of all our class," Danny observed, "You were the last I ever expected to be washed out. I had you pegged as a natural. Hell, even with never having flown before, you soloed in Primary almost as soon as I did with all my previous experience."

By that time, the post-washout depression had softened, with the help of a bottle of *Lucky Lager*. Bobby smiled appreciatively, "Thanks pal, coming from one helluva pilot, that's quite the compliment. But I should have taken precautions with *Dramamine*. I always had a tendency to motion sickness, but thought I was outgrowing it until we went through that series of slow rolls my instructor was demonstrating. Ugh."

Danny regarded Bobby with a reassuring smile, saying, "You'll do well in the nose of a bomber. It's certain that I'll finish up in multi-engine, and if you handle that bombsight the way you fly a plane, you'd be the choice for my crew."

* * * *

At The Army Flying School in Victorville, they flew twin engine Beechcraft AT-11s, dropping practice bombs, but in a far different environment than he would ever encounter overseas. Above the Mojave Desert, their bombs were filled with sand, but also carried a charge that would explode on contact with the ground, showing where it hit. Their plane, piloted by a bored veteran, was equipped to allow one student to sight and drop a single bomb while the other would photograph the results. Then they'd switch roles.

His instructor was amazed at Bobby's accuracy, and put him in for a commendation. He consistently came close to that impossible feat of dropping his bomb into the proverbial barrel from ten thousand feet. But that was with perfect visibility and under non-combat conditions. Almost three months were devoted to bombardier training, much of it learning the intricacies of the super-secret Norden bombsight. He carried it in a satchel to and from his plane, and practically had to sign his life away each time he checked it out.

Receiving the commission of Second Lieutenant was for him a great occasion, his chest swelling with pride. Anticipating at last a contribution to the war effort, he thought, precision bombing, here I come. After celebrating winning his bombardier's wings with his fellow graduates over a couple of drinks, he picked up his bags and bummed a ride into town. There he hopped on a Greyhound bus, excited over completion of that phase of training, and the prospect of seeing his family and old friends.

His bus ride from Victorville, spent mostly napping, ended at the depot in Hollywood. He was jarred out of his reverie by the hiss of the airbrakes and the clatter of the bus's doors opening. As he hitched a ride over the hill into the Valley, his elation gave way to a lingering thought. Tommy and Sinkie both gone. There wasn't much remaining of their old high school gang. He and Wheelie were the only ones left.

Bobby, just after receiving his commission as a Bombardier,
May 20, 1944

TWELVE

Reunion

With two weeks to enjoy before reporting for further training, he was able to borrow his brother Paddy's 1936 Ford convertible. Gas rationing limited his range, so his old digs around USC, past downtown L.A., were out of the question. Everyone there probably had been gobbled up by the services anyway, he figured. Even Hollywood, just over the hill from the family home in Burbank, was a stretch if one made a habit of it. An "A" gas rationing card, the only one Paddy, a senior in high school, could qualify for, allowed just four gallons of gas a week, providing only eighty miles of driving.

So he drove across the Valley to downtown Burbank. He was still thinking of Denise, and it occurred to him that he might run into her. It had been more than four years since he'd heard anything about her. That was when the news of her marriage to Wheelie had saddened him so when he was at the University of Chicago that first year.

I've always loved her, he thought, although even after promising to love only me, she married another guy. But asking her to wait seven years was a tall order. I thought that love would find a way, no matter what. Why couldn't I have seen that the only way to keep her was with a ring?

Just then, he passed the bank where she had worked. He wondered, could she still be there? Many women had taken work in the defense industries to help the war effort, and even his mother worked at Vega, the new plant where Lockheed was turning out B-17s, the bomber in which he thought he probably would fight.

On the chance that she might still be at the bank, he parked the car. Hopping out, he impulsively rushed in, squarely into a woman who was just leaving. He was half-blinded on his entry into the subdued light of the interior, and he nearly bowled her over.

Talk about Déjà vu. There he was again, looking into the startled deep blue eyes that he had nearly given up ever seeing again. She saw him too, and her lips parted in surprise.

Giggling a little, she breathed, "We've got to stop meeting like this."

Her elation was only momentary, and as he stood there, wanting to kiss her, she hastily extricated herself, bolting through the door out onto the sidewalk.

"Wait!" He cried, "Please don't run off like that. We at least have to talk."

She was hurriedly distancing herself from the bank, but finally, down the block, she slowed so he could gently catch her arm.

"Please, Denise, don't avoid me like this."

Turning to face him, with tears in her eyes, she sobbed, "Oh Bobby, I'm not running from you, I'm worried, and running from the people at the bank." Looking nervously over her shoulder, she continued, "I'm married to the boss's son, you know, and people talk. If we were wise, we wouldn't speak to each other at all." With that, she pulled her arm away, looking imploringly at him.

"Please," he said, "Can't we have a bite together, for old times' sake? You've been on my mind and in my dreams all these years. I've been busy, but I've missed you so. Please don't go." Exaggerating a little, he continued, "I've only got two weeks before I go overseas. Let me back into your life just for a little while."

She turned to face him then, tears still in her eyes, but with a smile on her face. "Okay, I would like to hear about what you've been doing, and where you go from here. A girl has to be nice to our boys in uniform these days."

They drove to Mel's Drive-in farther down San Fernando Road, where they sometimes would have a soda or a malted milk after school. Their conversation was at first tentative, as if each were afraid of real communication. By stages they exchanged details of their lives apart, until they were confiding in each other about their hopes and fears concerning what the future held. The war was certainly affecting them both. Bobby was poised to go into action, excited about the coming adventure, with little thought of the physical dangers.

"You know, don't you," she said, "That Wheelie was finally drafted, and he has been in Italy for a year with the Army. I worry so much about him, even though he's only in a supply unit. And you're going back to duty in two weeks. You'll probably see action soon, and who knows what then? I know they'll be shooting at you. That would make two men I care for in danger. I'm not strong, and I know I couldn't bear it if anything happened to either of you."

God, Bobby thought, maybe she really does love me still. Turning from his tray and the half-eaten hamburger, he took her hand.

"Say, let's go over to the Fern Dell in Griffith Park, and talk some more. The brook will be running in that shady glen there, and everything will be in leaf by now. How wonderful it was there after our graduation. Remember?"

That thought seemed to hit a chord with her, and on an impulse, she leaned over and kissed him on the cheek.

"You're so impractical. Don't you know that I have a job, and the time we've spent already was supposed to be my lunch hour?"

With that, he kissed her back, but on the mouth.

"Okay," she said, slightly more huskily, "Give me a nickel to call from the pay-phone here to let them know I won't be in the rest of the day. Banker's hours, you know."

They drove to the park, and to the little bridge that crossed the stream, where he parked the car. Up the canyon was a profusion of ferns and water-loving trees, including his favorite, the fragrant California White Alder. They made their way along the well-beaten trail that wound slowly upstream among the boulders and ferns that lined the brook, which tumbled over the rocks in a steady murmur. Even in his lightweight khakis, in the warmth of the early afternoon, the shade was welcome, and it was there that they rested, on a flat rock by the clear, cold water.

At first they just sat facing each other, with smiling mutual acknowledgement. The slight breeze brought with it the distinct aroma of the trees, dominated by the sweet nut-like vanilla essence given off by the alders, usually in the cool of the evening, but also when the shade of nearby trees cloaked them.

Feeling a pleasant nostalgia, born of their last visit there, he whispered, "Remember that scent? Does it have the same effect on you as it's having on me?"

A pause, while she considered the question, occupied them both. Then she cautiously ventured, "Yes, I do remember, Bobby, very well. We were just kids then when you carved that heart on one of these trees. Do you think we can find it? It's only been five years."

He tried to take her hand during their hunt, but she avoided contact, until they found the tree. And there it was, on the trunk, still standing out among lesser carvings, a large heart enclosing their initials. As he stood, lost in thought, she softly murmured the initials, as if anything louder would break the spell.

Bobby whispered, "Don't you think it's beautiful?"

With that she straightened up, her puzzled frown giving way to a warm smile. "Yes, it is lovely. It shows what we meant to each other then."

"But what about now? Don't you feel that love still?"

A frown came over her face. "Of course I feel it, just as the scent of the trees brings back all those wonderful days in my memory. But I still can't forget that I'm married to another man, who is away serving his country in the war."

He could think of no rejoinder, except that he soon would be in the fighting himself, but elected to avoid the comparison with his one-time friend, ambivalent as his relationship with Wheelie had been. He couldn't help but recall that it was their very rivalry that had brought him Denise in the first place.

They walked up the Fern Dell a little ways more, and sat down on a park bench under another fragrant tree. Reaching up, she took a sprig of leaves from it, rolling them between her fingers, sniffing them in appreciation. She then placed them under his nose.

"You have to smell this, Bobby."

He took her hand in his, kissing the tips of her fingers, and said, "Umm, and they taste even better."

He then took her other hand and held both to his lips, looking into her eyes. Again there was silence, until she turned fully to him and began to talk. At first it was a little disjointed, with a confused account of her feelings starting when he had left for Chicago. She spoke of her initial reluctance with Wheelie's courting her, his overcoming those barriers, finally leading to their wedding. In Bobby's absence at the time, she explained, marriage made sense to her. Her father was for it, and her mother didn't object. When he had taken the train to Chicago, the morning after that last date, she had been depressed, left with a huge feeling of emptiness. With time, the only solution seemed to be Wheelie, working with him every day.

"Can't you see? When I recited those marriage vows, it was to heal the hole you left in my heart. That didn't mean that I ever stopped loving you. Now Wheelie's away, and probably will be for the duration, and sadly, I'm alone again. You probably don't want to know this, but until he was called up, we tried desperately to have a baby, but nothing worked. The doctors couldn't find anything wrong with me, but decided anyway that it was a deficiency on my part. Well, look at how athletic and virile-looking Wheelie is." She went on, "So I'm destined never to have a child, a totally important part of being married for me."

With that she began to cry, accepting his handkerchief, and the arm that brought her gently over to him. Bobby was again at a loss for words. How could he reassure her? He too, was close to tears, empathizing with her.

Finally, he offered, "This is now, and you've got me for the next two weeks if you want. And remember, we were married in our hearts before you ever had any real feelings for him."

She nodded in agreement. "I'm terribly lonely, since my husband had been gone for so long, and you're right. I realize now that I still feel the same way about you. The only thing that has changed is that the men in my life have traded positions. Before, when you were in Chicago, Wheelie was there when I needed someone, and now it's you. It seems so simple."

They walked arm in arm to the car, and as she cuddled up to him there, he put his right arm around her. He wanted to make their time together something extra special. But he realized that all the swing bands were touring the war zones, entertaining the troops, and even without gas rationing, the big ballrooms in L.A. were out.

He asked, "Isn't that restaurant still open up in Big Tujunga Canyon? Lets go there for dinner and dancing."

"The Wildwood Lodge? I think it is. That would be fun, but I'll have to change and get ready. Give me an hour or so."

With her reply, she gave him a warm kiss and they parted. All the way home, savoring that kiss, her lipstick still on his lips, he found himself whistling that popular tune, "Besame Mucho."

At home, after showering, and putting on his new forest-green jacket, or blouse, as the Army called it, and "Pinks," those mauve-gray trousers, he gave his mother a peck on the cheek, and the advice not to wait up for him. On the way back to Denise's, he stopped at a florist's shop for some red roses and then at a drugstore, where he purchased a pack of cigarettes with a couple of books of matches, as well as some condoms. He was still concerned that he might be rushing things, but after all, hadn't she once brought up that Boy Scout thing herself?

When he got to her place, she came to the door absolutely radiant, in a dress that did little to conceal her lovely figure.

"Oh, flowers, aren't they beautiful," she exclaimed, and then, admiringly looking him up and down in his new uniform, she added, "And they're not the only thing beautiful here." With that she kissed him, and took the flowers into the kitchen. As he stood in the living room of the small studio apartment she had shared with Wheelie, she called out, "I'm so looking forward to tonight. Except for a show occasionally with my mom, I haven't been out in more than a year. We can dance the way we used to. Tonight, don't you think we can pick up where we left off?"

"Sure we can," he replied hopefully. "I'll have no trouble, I'm sure of that."

When she emerged from the kitchen, she had a confidence he hadn't seen before. Taking his hand with a particularly inviting smile, she pulled him to the door. The twilight was cool, as it often is in the Valley, despite the heat of the day. She snuggled close to him in the open convertible as the road wound up the canyon. He felt the old passion overcoming him, and wondered why he had ever left her.

Looking down at her, he said simply, "I love you, Denise."

There was a pause, and he began to worry that he had gone too far, and too fast. Then she stirred from her position against him, and looking up at him, responded, "And I love you too, Bobby. I always have. I did marry Wheelie, but I see now that hasn't changed my feelings for you. He's away, and may never return. You're here for only a short time, and how do I know you'll ever come back either? That will have to be faced some day, but for now we should make the most of the present, don't you think?"

Just then they arrived at the restaurant, a rustic timbered lodge-type building, perched on the edge of the canyon, high over the Valley. He pulled into the parking area, while reflecting on what she had just said. She loves me, he thought, and how wonderful that felt. But he recalled her previous reluctance regarding sex before marriage. He began to worry about how she would react to the idea outside of it.

He brought the Ford to a stop in front and shut off the engine. She sat upright, apparently inhaling the aroma of cooking in the cool hillside air.

He asked, "Hungry?"

Her reply was a smile and a nod. He got out, and came around to open the door, but not before she was half way out.

"Here," he said, "You have to let me be the gentleman tonight, Okay?" She laughed, admitting that she had forgotten such niceties because of the war and the resulting shortage of men of any persuasion, gentlemen or otherwise.

As they entered the crowded restaurant, all eyes seemed to turn to them, as in a small town when strangers enter. It was more than mere curiosity, however, and Bobby noticed approving looks coming their way from both the men and the women. Very few were their age, as in the song of the wartime absence of eligible men, "They're Either Too Young or Too Old."

A waitress showed them to the best table, next to a picture window overlooking the nearly dark Valley, which with the wartime brownout furnished only the fading afterglow behind the distant Hollywood Hills. It was away from the small dance floor, and would be private and quiet enough to talk. After they had been seated, Denise leaned towards Bobby.

"I'm going to enjoy our being together here, but look at the menu. It's 'Meatless Tuesday,' and I left hamburger in the refrigerator. How are you with spaghetti or vegetarian food?

I seem to recall the big appetite you used to have, and mostly for red meat."

He replied with a laugh, "You saw what was left of that appetite at lunch today. When I'm with you, it seems, I'm not very hungry."

They each had a beer, and while waiting for the food to arrive, he offered her a cigarette. She declined graciously, saying it would be fun to take a turn or two on the dance floor first, since someone was feeding nickels into the Wurlitzer for the music. They had always been great together jitterbugging, and the pieces were fast enough, rhythmic, and designed just for that type of dancing. They especially enjoyed "Take the 'A' Train," along with the other popular swing rhythms.

It was as if they had been the entertainment of the evening, as when their food was being served, they left the floor to an appreciative applause. Denise was visibly affected, shyly putting a hand to her face, but Bobby, after looking down at her reassuringly, thanked the crowd with a salute.

"I can see we won't have any privacy here tonight," he whispered as he pushed her chair in.

She replied softly, "There'll be plenty of time for that later."

There went what was left of his appetite. He toyed with his food, as they made small talk, skipping the dessert to go back to the dance floor, now to some of the slower ballads, much to their enjoyment. He closed his eyes, taking in the wonderful feeling of her nearness, and breathing in the fragrance of her hair. It seemed only a short period of time that they danced, but it turned out to be over an hour. The jukebox player had only then run out of coins to feed the machine.

"I think I'll have that smoke now, Bobby," she said, as they returned to their table.

He pulled his chair closer to hers and produced a pack of *Lucky Strikes,* opening it. He tapped the cigarettes out a little and offered them. As she drew one out, and put it to her lips, her eyes on his, it struck him as being so sexy. In his distraction, he forgot which pocket held the matches, and pulled out the small packet of condoms instead. Dropping his cigarette in embarrassment, he hastily hid the condoms in his fist.

"Well?" She enquired, leaning over to receive the expected flame. "Isn't that a book of matches? What does a girl have to do to get a light, anyway?"

Not quickly enough, he switched hands, producing the expected matches, and, hiding the condoms in his other hand, he struck a match and lit her cigarette. As her *Lucky* flared with her first pull, he could see her eyebrows arching with curiosity, her mouth in a faint smile. He realized then that she knew. Resigned, he showed her the packet of *Trojans.*

"So?" She said, passing it off as a joke, "I know you went to USC."

The humor surprised him, as it had when they first ran into each other earlier at the bank. But he detected a slight catch in her voice, and, looking into her eyes, saw tears forming.

"I hope it wasn't premature of me to buy these for tonight, but you see, all during the day, as we became closer, I couldn't get the memories out of my mind of the glimpses of paradise you showed me just before I left for Chicago in 1939. Denise, can you forgive me?"

"Forgive you for what?" She finally asked, tears still welling up. "Blame you for wanting me? No. I can't help crying because of the irony of the useless condoms. I'll never be able to bear a child anyway, whether Wheelie's or anyone else's for that matter, remember?" At that point, she whispered, "Let's go to my place. Maybe we can talk more about this on the way."

After he paid the bill, they went out into the cool night. On the drive down the canyon, she clung to him wordlessly. He wondered how much of that was affection for him, and how much was due to the cold. Either way, his gentle squeezing of her shoulder from time to time would bring an answering kiss to the side of his neck.

When they arrived at her place, he parked the convertible down the street. When they reached her front porch, she unlocked the door, and taking his hand, led him inside. Rather than turning on more lights, she gave him a hug, suggesting he get them beers from the kitchen, while she visited the bathroom.

He had just finished half a bottle of *Golden Glow,* when he got a scent of her perfume.

"Hi," she whispered just behind him, as he put the bottle down on the counter top. She was so close, that when he turned, it was right into her arms, his lips easily finding her upturned mouth. It was then that he noticed that she was wearing only the sheerest silk robe, which did little to conceal anything. She then led him to the studio couch, now converted into a double bed, and sat down on it invitingly.

"Well, don't just stand there," she admonished, "An Officer and a Gentleman doesn't keep his lady waiting, you know."

Bobby needed little further encouragement to get out of his uniform, and to join her in bed. In his enthusiasm he smothered her in kisses, caressing her with hands that had held the beer bottle, the cold totally ignored by her, her arms and legs around him in passion.

She huskily said, "And remember what the doctor told me. You don't have to bother with the *Trojans*."

They stayed in bed together all night, and like a honeymooning couple, most of the next day. She called in sick, and naked together, for food they fried eggs and bacon as well as that hamburger, while drinking beer. They cautiously avoided the hot splattering grease, reluctant to put their clothes back on.

She finally persuaded him to call home, to allay parental worry, and did call her mother, but otherwise monopolized his attention completely, and repeatedly. She, in turn, found such pleasure that she regretted ever marrying anyone else. They spent much time looking into each other's eyes, and talking about the future. All of this at the expense of adequate periods of sleep, leading to some of their talk being silly, as it often had been in high school. As the beer ran out, she agreed with him that they probably didn't need more anyway.

And so it went for the next couple of days, until they had to go out for groceries, and sheer fatigue took over, extracting from them longer periods of sleep. They were settling down as if they were newlyweds, but she had to get back to work, in order to pay the rent, and he knew he owed his parents and the extended family time over that first weekend.

After that, they went out to dinner a few times, and to a show once, a love story about the war, during which she cried, contemplating Bobby's all-to-soon departure. Every night they danced at her place to her records, and made love in bed, on the carpeted floor, and once even in the bathtub. They couldn't get enough of each other, after those years apart, and the knowledge that it would soon end spurred on their passion. When the time finally came, they embraced one last time, each promising to write faithfully and often.

"I'll always love you, Denise," he said softly, "To my dying day."

In response, she put a finger to his lips to hush him. Eyes glistening with tears, she tried to respond bravely, stammering, "You have my love forever, my wonderful Bobby." All the while she was squeezing his hands with hers until their fingers were white and almost bloodless.

THIRTEEN

Flying Fortresses

Returning to Victorville, he was able to get a flight on a C-47 transport plane, flying personnel to several of the northern bases, including his destination. At his window seat, he gazed downward as the dry sage-dotted terrain of Nevada passed beneath, bringing back memories of his trip west after his year in Chicago. Then, thinking of Denise, and the wonderful furlough he had just spent with her, he drifted off to sleep, aided by the drone of the plane's twin engines.

His dream, not of her, but of endless driving across limitless plains below, was suddenly shattered by the rumble of the plane's flaps and landing gear, signaling their approach to their first stop, an air base in Idaho.

Awake, he was left with the thought of the jackrabbits and what the waitress had said after lunch that day in the little café. "You won't be coming back." That had worried him at first, and he had wondered what she had meant. Hell, he said to himself, as the plane touched down, she was already wrong. We just flew over the same part of Nevada I drove back in 1940.

* * * *

His transfer to the AAF Base in Lincoln, Nebraska was for transition into crewing Boeing B-17 heavy bombers. He was particularly happy about that, knowing them to be the most rugged bomber in the Army Air Force. When he arrived there, he eagerly absorbed the Tech Manual's data about the plane.

It wasn't a new design, coming off the drawing boards in 1934, but as with many classics of aircraft design, such as the Messerschmitt BF-109, and the Supermarine Spitfire, it carried with it the potential for almost unlimited development, and it shared durability honors with that all-time great, the Douglas DC-3, the same plane, in Army olive drab, which just had flown him there.

The later models of the B-17 were ideally suited for the role they would play when it came time to expand the air war over Europe. Its four Wright R-1820 engines could propel its fully loaded thirty-two tons to a maximum of around 300 miles per hour. Its bomb bay could hold three tons of bombs, and its tanks enough fuel for a flight of 2,000 miles. It had early been dubbed the "Flying Fortress," bristling as it did with twelve or thirteen Fifty Caliber Browning machine guns for its defense. But unlike a true fortress, its walls were mostly of thin aluminum, and as with any aircraft, as well as fortifications on the ground, it would prove vulnerable to cannon fire.

Still, Bobby was impressed, as were all the new arrivals there. Most of the bombers available for training were older "F" models, which actually had a top speed slightly greater than the craft he would fly into battle. This was because of the added weight and wind resistance of the new chin turret and other improvements. Hell, he thought, no one flies at top speed anyway, and the added forward protection the turret gave was well worth it. Still, he was disappointed that cruising speed was not much over a hundred and eighty.

It was there that Bobby and his close buddy, Danny Thunder, were reunited. They had started together in preflight, separated when Bobby washed out in Basic. Danny had gone on to win his pilot's wings at about the same time Bobby graduated from Bombardier School. When combat crews were being formed, it was simple for Danny to select his crew from the roster available. Almost all were unknown to him, but when he saw his old buddy listed, he grabbed him.

After formation of their crew, they all came to agree that Danny was a great pilot. This was because of flying skill due to his athletic ability as well as his extensive experience over Nazi-occupied Europe. They took pride in that, as well as in their name, "The Thunder Crew."

He was affectionately referred to as the "Old Man," not only in his role of plane commander, but also because of his age of twenty-eight. Bobby was no kid either, at the time nearly twenty-four, otherwise qualifying him for elderly status, except that he didn't look any older than the gunners, who were all nineteen.

The two would occasionally get into town, usually just to sit in a bar over a beer, while Danny, at first reluctantly, told war stories at his buddy's request. This was an education for Bobby, who could never understand the Army's reasons for forcing Danny to train all over again.

"Corkscrewing. That was the key to survival in those days." It was Danny's answer to one of Bobby's questions. "You couldn't do that safely in formation, nobody could, especially at night. Being close at night is suicide. So our bombers flew individually, dodging the flak and night fighters by evasive maneuvers."

"How could you accurately hit your primary target?" Bobby asked, thinking of the need for a stable platform for precision.

"Not a problem," came the reply. "We did what we called 'Carpet-bombing.' So your drop is a mile off? It still hits the built up areas of the city. If not factories, then you hit the homes of the people who work in them."

Bobby asked, "But what about the women and children?"

Danny nodded as he continued, "This is war. Total war, not like in romantic stories. And in failing to rebel against the Nazis, in the estimation of men in the RAF, every German deserved what he or she got. I went along with that, even though I'm not British. Revenge for London, Coventry and their other cities? No, that wasn't for me. For my part it was war against the racist Nazis. Aryans, Hitler calls them.

"Maybe it was my warrior blood that saw me through, but more likely it was just luck. By the time I finished, I had flown a hundred sorties. I'd had it with the night. Had it with the searchlights and the night fighters. They would sneak up on you from below without warning and kill. That was not the way of the warrior. And our aircraft were almost blind in that direction, making it easier for them.

"I wanted out of the night war. Well, I had finished more than two tours, but the job was far from over. Applying for a transfer, I was told for some reason that fighters were out, and the only daytime work available was antisubmarine patrol, which I knew I would hate. So, after Pearl Harbor, I made the decision to transfer to the USAAF."

"So here you are," Bobby commented, "But I still can't figure out why you had to retrain."

"My RCAF commandant, Major Drummond, met with me about that. He told me that Bomber command was expanding, and there would be room for leaders in the increased intensity of the air war against the Germans. He told me that they would need every man like me they could get. The Avro

Lancaster four-engine bombers were then being produced in quantity, with twice the range and three times the carrying capacity of the Wellingtons or other types. They'd be consistently taking the war all the way to Berlin, and with significant bomb loads. He told me there was a place for me in command if I wanted."

Bobby exclaimed, "Hey, after a hundred missions I'd sure go for that!"

Danny ignored that, and continued, "Everyone there was evidently convinced that if we'd had more of my kind in the Revolutionary War, the whole of English-speaking North America would still be part of the Commonwealth." Then he laughed, observing, "They had plenty of red men then. They just didn't use them properly. I told him that they weren't using me properly either.

"I was informed that I could have my discharge from the RCAF, but the way things were, I'd have to start from scratch in the USAAF. I was shocked, needless to say. I pointed out that *Eagle Squadron* fighter pilots had been transferred to the U.S. Eighth Air Force directly, joining the Fourth Fighter Group. Why, I asked, wouldn't the same be accorded my transfer? The response was that because I was a lone individual, not an entire squadron, no arrangements had been made for that sort of thing. I still remember Major Drummond's observation, 'It is odd that a nation of individualists would work it that way.' But there it is."

Taking a gulp of beer, Danny continued his story. "Well, I hitched a ride on a returning tanker, can you imagine, zigzagging across the whole damned Atlantic in a convoy. The only saving feature was my hope of seeing my wife, and kids. They were toddlers when I last saw them. When we got to New

York, I immediately hit the closest Army recruiting station. They really wanted pilots and my credentials were good."

"Yeah, I would think so," Bobby offered, "How often would they ever get a chance at someone with your experience?"

Danny shrugged his broad shoulders, and went on.

"No, they liked that I had some College. But they were suspicious of the training and combat I'd been through. Not enough of the former, and too much of the wrong type of flying in the latter."

Bobby looked up from his beer in surprise. "I'll bet they didn't believe you were an Indian for starters, and they went on from there."

"Wrong," Danny replied, "They didn't give a damn about that. It really was my RCAF experience. Can you believe it? When I gave my papers to the sergeant at the front desk, I was ushered into the office of the lieutenant who was in charge. I was wearing my slightly worn uniform, looking every bit the seasoned veteran, with all my campaign ribbons. It was a joke. Sitting at the desk was this jerk, wearing his hat well back his head, like 'Hot Shot Charlie.' Remember the fighter pilot character in *Terry and the Pirates* comics? And get this, he had removed the stiffening grommet from inside the rim, affecting a 'Thirty-mission crush,' despite probably never having worn earphones, or even been up in a plane. It was all I could do to keep a straight face. He didn't have wings of any kind, and must have been just out of Officers' Candidate School, a Ninety Day Wonder for sure. Oh, he did wear his ribbons. I should say ribbon. It was the Good Conduct Medal.

"You know," Danny said, continuing his story, "I remember that recruiting officer looking down his nose at me, telling me that I'd have to learn to do everything the Army way. Right out of the manual, he gave me the theory of precision bombing of industrial and military targets, and in broad daylight. He seemed to think I had been sneaky to operate at night. He also said that because I had no experience in flying the tight formations that daylight bombing demanded, I would have to train all over again. But not just the nine weeks of Advanced Flying School, where real formation flying is learned, but also the whole damned thing, even Preflight, in addition. Can you imagine? But I wanted so badly to continue flying, and in daylight, and since the RCAF didn't want me as a fighter pilot, here I am."

As Danny finished his beer in disgust, Bobby replied sympathetically, slowly shaking his head, "That's the Army for you."

"I'm happy despite still being in bombers. In my opinion, the B-17, about the same size and power as the Lancasters we flew, is a little more rugged, and it sports the ball turret in the belly, with those twin fifties, covering us from below. Also, it's easier to fly. Not just because you have a co-pilot and dual controls, but because of its responses in flight. It practically flies itself, trimmed properly. Of course the Avro carries twice the bomb load, but pays for that by its service ceiling being restricted to a good ten thousand feet lower than our Forts. Even at night, you know, the higher you fly the safer you are."

"How about another beer?" His buddy asked, "This story is getting good. I'd like to hear some more, especially about your experiences in London. I had my hands too full in training to get the whole story out of you then."

Danny stared at him balefully. "You know my limit is only a couple. You do recall that bar fight in Visalia during Primary?"

The Thunder Crew, Army Air Force Base,
Alexandria, Louisiana. Summer, 1944.

Back Row, from left, Gunners: Zito, Cardone, Kelly,
Pearson, Firof, Demers

Front row, Officers: Danny, McCauley, Lynch, Bobby.

Demers transferred out when B-17 crews were reduced to
one waist gunner. Zito also served as engineer.

Bobby remembered only too well. Danny had one too many that night, as they both celebrated soloing. For Danny it had been a breeze, after those years in the RCAF. They still made him go through the Army Air Force routine, although he was a better flier than any of the instructors.

He recalled his own joy and relief that day. They both were in a partying mood. He remembered Danny taking one too many toasts to the Lady of the Wild Blue Yonder, forgetting his sensitivity to alcohol. As with everyone else, he found it hard to believe that Danny was really a *Sioux*. He should have known better. If not a pure blooded Indian, he must have had some Viking in him. They didn't call those adventurers *Berserkers* for nothing after they'd had their fill of mead. Either way, he recalled, the near-riot that had ensued was his fault. What were buddies for but to keep each other out of trouble?

There had been a woman who had sat down next to Bobby at the bar, beginning to flirt with him. Her date, a burly Navy gunner from the Air Station at Lemoore, not far north of there, became very upset. The guy was about to slug him, when Danny grabbed his arm. That could have stopped things then and there, but the plains warrior or the Viking, or both, decided otherwise. Danny lifted the two hundred pound gunner over his head, and threw him onto a nearby table, causing it to collapse to the floor, taking its Navy occupants and their drinks down with it. When Danny had been attacked by that knot of men, a bunch of Air Force guys jumped in, and a classic bar battle ensued.

It had been all he could do to protect his friend's back, and then, before the MP's arrived, to drag him, much against his will and still swinging, out the back way and down the alley. Nothing ever came of that, but if they'd been caught it could have meant being washed out then and there, certainly in Bobby's case.

* * * *

He continued to hone his skills with the supposedly super-secret Norden bombsight, while studying navigation, as a possible backup in an emergency. Danny ridiculed the security measures the bombardiers had to take with the bombsight while in training, carrying it in a locked case from the safe at headquarters to the plane.

When he was questioned about his skepticism, as usual loosened up over beer at the Officers' Club, the older man looked at him with an amused curl of his lip.

"Come on, you think the Jerries don't know about it? By now they've gotten quite a number of them from our downed bombers, not that they need them. They've had the secret for years. Their spies have been in our factories since the Thirties. Even before the war they were smuggling the plans of our secrets out of the country on that liner, the *Bremen,* which was used by their diplomats. And can you believe that our government won't let the British have the sight?"

Bobby looked at him in disbelief. "You mean that? What about Lend-Lease?"

"When I was over there, I got the dope from an operative of MI6, you know, British Intelligence, that the Germans were able to build a replica that worked, from the stolen plans, plus some improvements of their own. They had high expectations for it, judging by the name they gave it, translating as *Eagle Apparatus.*

"Luckily, It never really helped them, in part because so much of their bomber fleet had been destroyed by the RAF during the Blitz. Anyway, after that they were forced to concentrate on fighter production for defense against RAF night bombing, and now, the Eighth Air Force daylight heavy bomber raids as well."

* * * *

B-17 transition continued, despite the weather, which was rough at times. Their Fortress was so stable that at his station in the nose he had no problems with airsickness. Their flights took them over the Great Plains, as well as the Rockies to the west. Always, at high altitude, the cold was intense, giving some hint of what could be in store for them. They were organized into squadrons, and practiced the tight formation flying that was necessary to provide the maximum protection of their defensive guns.

During that period of training, while most of the recently minted pilots of the squadron were still unfamiliar with handling the big four engine bombers, it was Danny's skill and experience that averted disaster for them.

Their element had been a tight flight of three planes, when they entered a particularly rough stretch of air over Denver. In the turbulence, the other planes lost their positions in the formation, and the two Forts collided in front and slightly below, in Danny's blind spot.

Seeing it from his vantage point in the Plexiglas nose, Bobby shouted over the intercom, "Danny, left, go left!"

One of the stricken bombers was veering towards them in a climbing turn. As Bobby and Lynch, the navigator, hung on helplessly in sheer terror, Danny, with his quick reflexes and not a little intuition, whipped the big ship into a vertical bank away from their wounded mate. Somehow this maneuver saved them, but it was only by inches.

Gene Pierson, the ball turret gunner in the belly, and who was the closest to the oncoming B-17, exclaimed, "Holy shit! They're so close, I can count the individual rivets in their wing!"

The waist gunners couldn't hang on in the unexpected and violent maneuvering, and were thrown into a heap on the deck, as Danny calmly righted the diving Fort. Along with the groans of the crew, one could hear a chorus of similar sounds from the unusual stresses on the airframe of their weary old F-model Fortress as it was pulled out of the dive. It was their first taste of disaster, but it wouldn't be their last.

Both planes that collided crashed, but not before the lucky crew of one ship were able to bail out. Bobby had become close to both bombardiers, as they had studied and bunked together for almost a month by that time. It was a lesson, learned early. Sad as it may seem, it was evident that aside from one's own crew, friendships were to be avoided. The loss of even one buddy was just too hard to take.

After Lincoln, they flew to Alexandria, Louisiana for further training. They were assigned a newer Fortress, a B-17G, flying out over the Gulf of Mexico, as Bobby wrote, "Looking for clouds." No problem with that. They were everywhere. Along with their main pre-occupation, that of simulated missions with tight formation flying, there was also training for the bombardiers in the operation of the new remote control chin turret. These had been fitted under the nose of the B-17G because of new tactics, which had become popular with the enemy, attacking head on.

Before enlisting, Bobby had never fired anything bigger than a .22, but he became quite adept at operating the new turret with its twin Browning fifties, as well as the single cheek gun on each side, one of which was manned by the Navigator. Proficiency was developed mostly with targets on the ground, but he did as well as any of the gunners on the few aerial targets offered them.

They had only one pass into town, aiming for a taste of Cajun cooking. Bobby and Danny both loved the stuff, popularized in that song about Jambalaya and Crawfish Pie. They had hopes of hitting New Orleans after that, but time ran out. It was just as well, as that night in town they almost came to blows with a couple of southern crackers over the use of a water fountain reserved for colored people.

The bus that came from the base dropped them off at the station. The heat of the day was lingering, giving the air of the evening more than the usual heat and humidity. Throats parched, they both spied the nearest water fountain simultaneously, and raced each other to get to it. Danny had a step on Bobby, and, eager for a drink, he bent over happily, noisily slurping.

Just then a loud guffaw was heard, coming from a group of the locals who had been drinking whiskey in a brown bag on the steps just outside. One florid-faced redneck pointed at Bobby, and in a loud southern drawl, unleashed a torrent of ridicule.

"Hey, fellas, look at that! Goddam flyboy nigra lovers, I swear. Whaddya say we teach 'em a lesson about the South?"

Danny, finished, yielded the fountain to Bobby, and turned, still in a crouch, facing them with fists clenched, the picture of rage.

Bobby restrained his buddy, saying, "Come on, we can't let them ruin our night on the town. Drunk as they are, we could easily handle them, but that booze will have them choking on their magnolias any time now."

Danny, undeterred, his warrior face darkened at least three shades of red by that time, glared at them. He seemed about to launch himself at his nearest tormentor, when a paddy wagon, driven by the local police, teamed with an MP, pulled up, intent on the drunken rednecks and them. It was close.

"Run!" Bobby yelled, as the police collared the southerners. The two then out-ran the MP, and soon lost him by ducking up an alley.

After their overnight pass, they returned to base, visiting the Officers' Club for a beer. At a table, they found the co-pilot and navigator of their crew, and began to recount the incident at the bus station. All were from states that had fought the Confederacy in the Civil War, and they still couldn't get over the rigid segregation they had found there.

Their conversation was overheard by a Mississippian, Quigley, a gunnery instructor, sitting at the next table. As with many of those from south of the Mason-Dixon Line, he was a crack shot, and thus in gunnery instruction he was a natural. The problem was, he was also known for shooting off his mouth, and that day was no exception. As he followed the tale about the rednecks in town, he seemed increasingly irritated by what he heard.

Danny, still incensed, was especially outspoken, as "Colored" also meant him, or at least his fellow tribes-people.

"Dammit," he exclaimed, "If I didn't pass for white, I'd be relegated to the back of the bus, too. What would I be fighting for, anyway?"

At that point, Quigley came over uninvited and sat down, bringing his thick Mississippi drawl to the table, along with his corpulence. "Y'all are in a southern state, now, ya hear? Accordingly, y'all should respect southern traditions in these parts. We keep the nigras in their place for a reason."

Bobby quickly responded, "Remember, this is the U.S.A., not the Confederacy. You'd think you guys won the Civil War, the way you carry on."

Quigley sneeringly replied, "Well, you muthas wouldn't have won except that you outnumbered us two to one. And look, you can't possibly think the colored are your equals can you? Shuckin' and jivin' all the time, why, they're barely human."

Bobby, who had never gone to school with non-whites aside from a few children of local truck farmers, Mexican and Nisei, hotly objected. "They're humans like the rest of us. Even a redneck bigot like you should be able to see that. Your laws put them under your thumb, keeping most of them in ignorance and poverty. You may be an officer, but you're no gentleman, that's for sure. Poor white trash is more like it."

Danny then added, "Speaking of being out-numbered, it's now *four* to one here. So take your confederate flag and get the hell out of here before I flatten you."

As he got up, the sullen Mississippian growled, "Goddam Nigra lovers, ya'all are welcome to them. Marry 'em, for all I care."

With that, Danny leaped to his feet, bringing their adversary's hasty retreat.

"One more word from that jerk," he grumbled, "And I would have throttled him, the fat bastard."

* * * *

As the completion of their training drew near, there was no end to the speculation of where they might be sent. Most thought the Pacific theatre was likely, considering the latest experience over the Gulf. But everyone knew how contrary the Army Air Force could be, and rumors were rife. No one was forgetting the extreme cold over the Rockies, either. So, after ten weeks of the balminess of Alexandria, in true Army fashion, as many of them had guessed, they were ordered to England, ultimately to serve as replacements in the Eighth Air Force, and as it turned out, for the 390th Heavy Bombardment Group.

They were ordered to fly a new B-17G to Britain by way of Bangor, Maine, and Gander, Newfoundland. The entire crew was understandably excited, even Danny, since it would also be his first flight over the Atlantic. And they loved their new plane, its shiny aluminum skin bright against the mid-continent fields and forests of green.

Ferrying bombers across the Atlantic during the war was almost always at night, allowing celestial navigation, plotting the course with fixes on the stars. And the weather was perfect, although the full moon dimmed all but the brightest stars. Lynch, the navigator, specially briefed on the route, had told them he expected their first sight of land would be Greenland, and was able to plot a perfect course.

In the nose of the Fortress, Bobby was the first to see what appeared to be a long white cloud in the northeastern gloom, causing him to give Lynch, the navigator, a congratulatory cork on the shoulder, shouting gleefully over the intercom.

"There it is. Land Ho!"

Even the sleeping gunners in the rear were jolted from their slumber at the shouting coming through their earphones. As they flew on, they were all treated to a breathtaking view of the vast icy expanse of southern Greenland in the silvery moonlight. Later, they would agree that the sight was the frosting on the cake of the whole flight.

After refueling at Prestwick, Scotland, instead of flying to a replacement depot, they were ordered to proceed directly to their new base, Station 153, near Framlingham, in East Anglia. Because of the weather, their landmarks grew progressively uncertain, with their destination becoming partially obscured by a ground-hugging mist as they approached.

Like most of the Eighth Air Force fields, it was laid out in a standard pattern that led to the bases appearing almost identical from the air. It was the sighting of the prominent ruins of Framlingham Castle, on its low hill, rising above the fog, which confirmed to the newcomers the location of their new station at the nearby little village of Parham.

FOURTEEN

Depression

When Bobby had driven away at the end of his furlough, Denise, after their torrid interlude, was relieved that they hadn't been discovered. They had ignored the doorbell ringing on two occasions during that time, and the phone more than that. She was left with mixed feelings. Their being together, while more wonderful than anything she had ever known, had been all too brief. Now there were guilt feelings, submerged before, of having betrayed her husband. She had anticipated a let down when Bobby left, but the real world was beginning to close in on her.

She walked over to her parents' home, up the hill across San Fernando Road. Her mother was on the front porch when she got there.

"Mom!" She cried, bursting into tears as they embraced.

"We've been wondering about you," her mother said, "And we missed you at church on Sunday. What's been going on?"

Afraid to look her mother in the eye, she responded, "You remember Bobby. Well, he was home on furlough before finishing his training, prior to going overseas. Although we met by accident, we ended up sleeping together."

There was a long pause as Mrs. O'Donnell considered that. "Bobby Taylor?"

"Yes, mom, but now he's gone, and God knows if he'll ever come back. You have to understand, he's never stopped loving me, and after we literally stumbled into each other, I found it was the same for me.

"Poor dear little Deenie," her mother said, using the childhood name Denise had answered to. "You led with your heart again. I saw that during your rebound romance with Wheelie after Bobby left for Chicago. But your happiness is what is most important to me, dear, and if Bobby is your true love, then I'm for it. Remember, he was my favorite anyway. But how do you expect to face it when they both return from the war? You'll have to make a choice sooner or later."

"Oh, mom," she plaintively replied, "I can't send Wheelie a 'Dear John' letter now. It wouldn't be right, with him so far from home and depending on my support."

"I know dear, it's a hard choice, and it's best to wait. We can figure something out when the time comes."

* * * *

All through those first weeks of their separation, Denise was on the job, her life otherwise devoted to communication with Bobby and her mother. She had only one real girlfriend, but the only one she could discuss her romance with was her mother.

She paid little notice at first to missing her period, as that had happened before, particularly early in her marriage, when they were trying to conceive. It was usually in conjunction with the emotional roller coaster she had been put through, and was always attributed to that by her doctor. Here again, she thought, was another emotional crisis. What could one expect?

When she missed her next period, however, she became alarmed. Rather than going first to her mother, in whom she had always confided, she decided to find out on her own, with the help of their family physician.

An appointment was obtained over the telephone, but it couldn't be for almost a week. With the wait, and further worry, she became certain that she was pregnant. Lying awake at night, she contemplated her long-sought motherhood on one hand, while torn on the other how this would play out with her family.

She knew that adultery, and worse, bearing another man's child, was regarded by most as too shameful even to discuss. People at that time were especially strict on the subject, especially when the adulterous affair ended in pregnancy. Shotgun weddings were for single couples, but the penalty for one already married could be far worse.

Denise worried that a mistake like that was ample reason for exclusion from society as she knew it. She would certainly lose her job, well before advanced gestation forced her to take maternity leave. Her father would come down especially hard on her, at a time when not only would a physical haven be necessary, but when she would be more in need of the emotional support from her family. My God, she thought, almost everyone will desert me!

The Doctor's examination was an anticlimax after all that mental turmoil. When her lifelong family doctor, a fatherly man who, in fact, had delivered her, finished his examination and turned with a concerned look on his face, she knew.

"Deenie," he started tentatively, "Because you couldn't conceive, I became convinced that you were infertile, but I have to admit that my diagnosis was dead wrong. I can't explain it. Has Wheelie been home recently? Something certainly has changed, and it looks like for the better."

She reflected for a moment on the "Better" part, trying to decide whether to confide in the doctor. Hadn't he taken care of her minor ills all her life? Won't a doctor keep any confidences to himself? Finally, she gave the expectant G.P. the missing puzzle piece.

"Dr. Baker," she said, "Wheelie is still in Italy, and the baby isn't his. It's a long story, but this has changed everything, and I just don't know what to do."

The doctor's frown covered his surprise. "Deenie, you're almost family to me, and what I have to tell you comes from the heart. You have a choice. Keep the baby, or put it up for adoption. Or—I shouldn't be telling you this, because it's illegal—get an abortion. I even know someone good at that, if you want."

"Doctor, I can never give up this baby." She responded tearfully. "Never!"

"Then think of the wonderful future the three of you could have," he replied. "All you would have to do is ask your husband for a divorce and marry the baby's father."

"Thanks, Dr. Baker, I'll talk this over with my mom."

"Great," he said, "Mothers are always good for that."

Despite the doctor's ideas, which were initially comforting, Denise couldn't help but obsess over her predicament, and the anxiety and depression returned. She wondered how long it would take her to show, and what would happen when the truth became known. It had been easy to conceal her affair with Bobby, but pregnancy could not go undetectable long. At that point, she invited her mother over for a talk.

It wasn't long after her arrival that Mrs. O'Donnell said, "I can tell that something is wrong. Come on, you can confide in me, you've always known that."

With that, Denise broke down, giving only a partially coherent account of what had happened. Getting control of herself, she exclaimed, "I'm almost three months pregnant now. Bobby's the father, after all these years trying to have a baby and failing with my husband. In my marriage, I wasn't the deficient one after all. But because I'd been led to believe that I couldn't conceive, I talked him out of using protection."

* * * *

Denise continued on the job for a month more, but as her midriff began to bulge, she gave notice. The reasons given were perfectly valid for that era. As she explained, with her husband and so many of our boys in the service, she felt it necessary to support him and the war effort by finding work in one of the nearby war plants. She knew of openings in the smaller companies that sub-contracted for the big corporations, as some of them did their banking downtown. Many were located well away from there, even in other towns in the Valley, where the likelihood of her being recognized would be almost nil.

It was during this period of emotional strain that Denise awakened one night from a fitful sleep. This was not unusual given her depression, but that night it was different. The moon was new, and it should have been dark, but instead, the room was bathed in a soft eerie light. There, at the foot of her bed was Bobby, sitting in a chair, smiling at her. She was jolted fully awake by the sight, and sat up in bed. The light showed that there were tears in his eyes despite his smile. There he was, although she knew by then that he was in England. She even pinched herself to make sure it was not a dream.

She called out softly, "Bobby, How did you get back so soon?" He seemed about to answer, when his image just slowly faded, along with the ghostly light. Now in the blackness there was no sound. She switched on the bedside lamp, revealing the room as it had been. Of course, not even the chair was there.

She couldn't sleep the rest of the night, trying to make some sense out of her experience. What did it mean? Could it have been a dream? It seemed so real, she was certain it was not. She worried that she was going crazy, and through it all a great sadness began to come over her. Was he dead?

"Oh God, please let him be alive," she repeatedly prayed aloud.

At daylight, after dressing, Denise walked hastily over to see her mother, mulling over what she finally decided must have been a hallucination. Good lord, she thought, maybe I *am* insane. It's becoming too much for me. This depressed her further, compounding her upset, already stoked by guilt, fear of discovery, Bobby's possible death, and the uncertainty of it all. Her mother tried to reassure her, but the effect was only temporary.

As her mood deteriorated over the following weeks, she began to lose interest in almost everything. She couldn't sleep enough without a sedative to function, and her appetite left her. Her depression continued worsening, and was compounded by the minor problems of pregnancy, which otherwise would have been taken in stride. For the first time she began to feel absolutely empty, except on those days when Bobby's letters arrived from England. One such arrived close to her birthday.

October 9 1944

Darling Denise:

Happy birthday, my love. I hope this finds you in keeping with the occasion, and that you're warm and content, altho missing me, as much as I miss you.

Jeez it is cold! Damn, sweetheart, I'm freezing to death. We're all huddled down in one end of our hut with a stove and blankets plus some G.I. flying clothes trying to keep warm. Our efforts are not too availing. I'd love to be snuggling here with you, as that would help in more ways than one, but I wouldn't wish these conditions even on my worst enemy.

Our Quonset, or Nissen, whatever these huts are called, are of corrugated iron, and directly in line with the prevailing winds and in not too sheltered a spot. The wind howls thru the place with the screech of a fast express, thru the chinks and open spaces and under the door at one end and out the other the same way. The stove has a rather fancy base, but is a mere extension of the stovepipe, and we find that all the heat goes whipping right up same. And so? So we shiver in the cold. I am just learning the value of John L's or long handles and the blessing of G.I. wool socks.

Outside the snow's beginning to fall and 'tis a lovely sight. A rather unusual phenomenon for this time of year, the old hands tell us. Everyone is singing "White Christmas," but to hell with that. I want some of that California sun, ya lucky gal.

How I wish we could be together now. All the cold would be gone in a second. When I can't sleep some nights because of it and the noise on the flight line, I think of you and of all the wonderful times we've had together. Not just last April, but before, in those months after our graduation. I hoped then the summer would never end. Next time, when we're together again, we'll have to see to it that while the seasons will come and go forever, we'll be there for each other, through them all, no matter what.

Now I will bid you adieu, sweet love, and toddle off to bed. I miss you so. They say we'll be in action soon. Give my best to your mom, and jus' keep those letters coming. Be good, my darling, and I'll sign with love and kisses,

Your ever-loving Bobby

* * * *

The next night, her mom called, announcing her intention to visit over the weekend.

Her opener was, "Hi, honey, how are you doing?"

Denise replied, "Physically, barely acceptable, but emotionally, I'm a disaster. By now Bobby is due for his first mission, I think, judging by the letter he wrote that I got yesterday, but dated three weeks ago. That means he is in more danger. I just can't shake the thought that, heaven forbid, he's not going to make it."

Her mother, trying to cheer her, offered, "From what I hear, the Nazis are on their last legs, with our boys advancing through France, and the Russians closing in from the East. They're not going to be able to put up of a fight much longer. Some are saying it's going to be over by Christmas."

Denise sighed, "Oh, wouldn't that be wonderful. But how does that protect him, when every bullet sent his way would be just as deadly, even if it's the last one of the war? Think of all the men who will die on that final day."

* * * *

Her health held up from a physical standpoint, as she neared the middle of the second trimester, by which time it was impossible to conceal the inevitable changes. Her mother came over each Sunday, when the family car wasn't being used for her father's work. She looked forward to the visits, as it seemed that with her depression, her mother's support, plus Bobby's letters were all that were keeping her going. Of course, Wheelie would frequently write, but in her guilt, his letters were all the more depressing.

One Sunday, while she was busy tidying up in her small studio apartment, she noticed the family sedan pulling up. The anticipation of seeing her mother again gave her a warm feeling, but that quickly turned to ice, when it became apparent that her father had accompanied her.

Good God, what can I do? She thought. He doesn't know I'm pregnant. A near panic overtook her. Her first thought was to flee, but the apartment had no back door. She resigned herself to facing her father's outrage, but she knew the scene wouldn't be pretty.

Her mother was the first through the door, and hurried to hug her daughter, apologetically whispering, "He insisted on coming for some reason, don't ask me why."

Mr. O'Donnell wore a smile as he entered, but this changed immediately to a shocked scowl as he laid eyes on her.

"What the hell? What's happened with my slim little girl? You've gained weight." Then, "Oh my God, are you pregnant?"

He just stood there, beginning to shake. As the realization sank in, he clenched his fists. Turning to his wife, he angrily shouted, "How long have you known? Why wasn't I let in on this abomination? I'm her father, you know!"

Softly, his wife answered, "Because I knew you'd react this way, and instead of being understanding, something your daughter needs now more than anything, there would be recrimination."

"Recrimination?" He shouted, "How can a man act otherwise when his daughter turns out to be a goddam whore? And with her husband fighting overseas. What did he do to deserve this? Who was it, Bobby Taylor, that damn mackerel snapper again?"

"Again?" Mrs. O'Donnell answered, in Denise's defense, "It has always been Bobby. If you were half a father, you would have known that."

Never tolerant of her parents' fighting, her depression enhanced by her father's terrible reaction, Denise burst into tears, throwing herself onto the studio bed, burying her face in a pillow.

"Yes, it was Bobby," her mother continued. "She loves him more than anything, and if you have any feelings for her at all, despite your foolish pride, you'll support her now, when she is so in need of your understanding."

He was livid, invoking in both women the fear that he was about to have a stroke.

Denise tried to calm him, crying out, "Daddy, I love you, but I knew this would upset you so much that I wanted to have the baby without your knowing."

That didn't calm him in the least. Grabbing his wife's arm, he headed for the door. She pulled away, exclaiming, "I'm not going. Our daughter needs me now more than ever because of your attitude."

With that, he shouted, "Suit yourself. But your staying here tells me whose side you're on. And I won't tolerate it. From now on, she's no daughter of mine, and if you support this awful sin of hers, you're not my wife either!"

FIFTEEN

Combat

During his first weeks with the 390th, Bobby had to concentrate on his bombardier's duties and brush up on his gunnery, at the expense of his thoughts about Denise and his letter writing. He slept soundly at night, but despite his last thoughts before sleep being of her, his dreams were of frustration and lack of fulfillment, as well as excitement and not a little anxiety about impending combat.

All was not work during that period, because of the poor weather. They were allowed to go into town, where some time was spent at the local pubs, getting used to English beer. Not warm as reputed, but at English room temperature, in other words, cool. Usually they didn't even remove their overcoats, it was so cold inside.

It took some practice to learn the British monetary system, but their hosts were patient and honest in cash transactions. Bobby also learned the slang of the friendly locals, who were touchingly thankful to him and the other "Yanks" for coming from so far to help out. The young women among them were especially friendly, and he had to constantly remind himself that he was already spoken for.

The local socializing was interrupted by their completion of training in October. There was also a change in the weather, which, while clearing only a little, became much more frigid. This brought out not only the terrible cold of high altitude flying, but also more flaws in the construction of their quarters and the ill-planned orientation to the wind of their corrugated metal Nissen huts.

At that point, the timing of his baptism of fighting was fitting. He and the rest of the crew were actually itching to get into action, despite the realization that with their designation as crew number one, they were there in the 390th as replacements. The question was, had the previous crew assigned that number finished their tour of duty, or had they been shot down?

Before he and his crew entered combat, the 390th Bomb Group celebrated its 200th mission. As with the earlier festive observation of their 100th, preparations had been made well in advance, and with great anticipation. Unlike combat crews, who remained there a few months at most, the supply, maintenance, security and command personnel had been there since the establishment of the 390th two years before. They would not see home for another year at the earliest. For them, especially, the opportunity to party was a real morale builder.

Women from surrounding towns and neighboring British auxiliary units were invited, many lodged in Parham Hall, the stately manor house that existed on the Base. It was run like a hotel, with cots borrowed from the Base quarters, and supplied with surplus bedding. Because the previous celebration had been so wild, MPs were assigned as a precautionary measure to keep order, but outnumbered as they were by about a hundred to one, they were largely ineffective.

A big band from London supplied the music. Individual supplies of whiskey and gin were supplemented by copious amounts of beer supplied by the Quartermaster. Needless to say it was a gala affair, spurred on by drink, music, and the mix of Air Force men and British women. The revelry went on far into the wee hours, and while the MPs were able to empty Parham Hall of amorous airmen overnight, it took more time to clear some individual Nissen huts of friendly females.

Danny, who was married, and Bobby, committed to Denise, were not followed to their beds, but such was not the case with some officers and men around the Base, and several more days would elapse before the MPs could discover and oust the last tenacious lady.

By the time of the celebration, with the crew's training completed, they were deemed ready for combat. They had practiced the intricate assembly process after takeoff until they knew it by heart, starting with the uniform climb rate through the obscuring clouds and mist, always with their eyes straining through the murk for some other plane that might be too close. The Group had been involved in a couple of collisions previously, and that was an ever-present danger.

At last, the day arrived for their first mission. Bobby's excitement was at a high level, as was that of the rest of the crew. Most of the men were young, and still imbued to some degree with the young man's sense of indestructibility. Paradoxically, that didn't seem to help when a mission loomed, carrying fear of the unknown and the realization that combat could kill.

Very few slept much that night, at least in Bobby's officers' quarters, concerned as they were with what the day would bring. Their reveille, if having a flashlight in the face shocking one awake could be called that, came at four AM, after only a couple hours of fitful sleep. Slipping his clothes on over his "Long handles," the term for long woolen underwear, doubling as extra-warm pajamas, he visited the freezing ablutions hut, or latrine and washroom, taking care to shave so that his oxygen mask would fit properly. They all then hopped the waiting truck that served as their shuttle to officers' mess.

Fliers on a mission almost always were given the treat of fresh eggs to go with their bacon and oatmeal, but Bobby was able to down only one, which he put on the cereal. Thirsty as he was, he had been warned against drinking too much liquid, in case the route took too long. No bomber was known for its toilet facilities, and using the "can" back towards the tail was too dangerous because of frostbite at high altitude, the origin of a number of jokes about freezing one's ass off. To compound the problem, the same sub-zero temperature made using the relief tubes a virtual impossibility as well, at least the second time, as they froze solid in seconds and stayed that way.

After their meal, it was on to briefing. The map of Europe, which occupied the entire wall behind the Briefing Officer, was always covered with a curtain at the beginning of the session. Only the Command Officers knew their destination beforehand. It was with the greatest anticipation that the audience awaited the dramatic unveiling of the map with the attached ribbon stretching from Framlingham to the target and back. The longer the route, the bigger the sweat, and when distance was combined with a notoriously well-defended objective, the revelation would always bring a chorus of groans.

That day, the first mission for Bobby and his fellows, was revealed to be Cologne, Germany. They were filled in on the details of the city, known for its medieval Gothic cathedral with its twin spires, to be avoided if possible. Somehow, in the midst of all the destruction, that grand structure still stood, giving rise to the joke that it had been spared due to it being the aiming point for the bombardiers!

It was the fourth largest city in Germany, and before the war boasted a population of over 750,000 people. Situated on the Rhine River, not fifty miles from the border with Belgium and the Netherlands, it was one of the targets closest to England. That was a plus for the anxious fliers, especially for those on their first mission.

Their momentary elation was quickly dashed by the information that the area was one of the most heavily defended by anti-aircraft artillery, or "Flak" guns. They would learn that the defense put up by the Jerries over their cities was often, although not invariably, proportionate to the importance of the industries there.

The Group Intelligence Officer filled them in on the importance of their destination, which had just been revealed. They learned that the city was a transportation network, with connections to and from the enemy's great industrial Ruhr Valley and elsewhere. This was coupled with the importance of interrupting the *Wermacht's* supply lines as they faced the Allied armies in the Low Countries. Thus their primary and secondary targets would be rail marshaling yards, as well as bridges.

When the Weather Officer told them there would be heavy cloud cover all the way, but with some breaks in it expected over the city itself, he and Danny looked at each other as if to say, "What's new about that?" They had been flying in and through that stuff in training for so long, they had almost forgotten what the ground looked like, at least from high altitude.

Details of their bomb load, along with certification of their defensive guns, were covered by the Group Ordinance Officer. Engineering pronounced the planes to be airworthy and described their fuel load, around 2200 gallons of Hundred

Octane. What to expect by way of weather conditions, fighter and flak resistance, as well as the time of rendezvous with the expected Mustang escort were also important items. There was no way they could remember all the briefing officers' names, but they knew they had better get the figures right.

During the customary question period that followed, because they were so occupied by anxiety and excitement over their first mission, they could think of nothing to ask. But they knew that they had to learn, and despite their apprehension, listened intently to the answers given to the questions of the more seasoned crews.

A shorter session was then conducted for the bombardiers and navigators in separate rooms, while the pilots stayed for their specialized instructions. The co-pilots left early to check out the enlisted crews. Bobby's task then was to pore over reconnaissance photos, maps and reports on Cologne to familiarize himself with the layout of the city, its bridges, and the marshaling yards of the vast rail network.

After briefing, they grabbed their bags of equipment, and were taken by truck back to their quarters in the 568th Squadron area, where they got into their flight clothes. They had been told that they'd be at twenty-five thousand feet, and that the temperature would be around fifty below. They all piled on the cold weather gear, being very careful, despite their excitement, to connect all the heating element circuits together carefully. They were then dropped off at their plane, situated on its concrete apron, or hardstand.

In the cold faint glow of the pre-dawn, they hoped that the B-17 G they were to fly would be the one they had flown during combat readiness training. Every Fortress had a slightly different personality, and just once, they all agreed, they would be content if only they could crew a plane long enough to feel at home in it. But no, this one, as seen on her nose, was an older craft, dubbed *Powerful Katrinka,* a comic strip strong woman.

Unlike practice flights, the ponderous process of start-up, taxiing into position for the timed and orderly takeoff took all the concentration Danny and the co-pilot possessed to carry it out smoothly and safely. Unlike a solo takeoff, it had to be done with all the precision of an orchestral performance. The problem was, there was no score, only their hastily scribbled notes and their constant practice, and for most of the squadron, no baton, and often, no view of the leader.

They were "Tail-end Charlie," the last plane of the twelve B-17s of their Squadron, which was also the low Squadron of the three put up by the 390th. It was just follow the leader, hoping that the pilot of the next plane had it right from the guy ahead of him. While their position in the bomber stream would be one of the most vulnerable to fighter attack and flak, at least they had the consolation of not having to worry about one of their numbers chewing off their tail during the vital climb through the clouds.

While Danny filled out the pre-flight checklist form with the Crew Chief, Bobby inspected the bomb-bay doors, and then, after heaving his equipment bag through the front entry hatch, swung himself up, always an effort despite his gymnastic abilities, over-stuffed as he was with bulky flight clothes.

He checked out his station, with its Norden bombsight, and various connections. Inspecting the control yoke operating the chin turret and the twin fifties he would be firing should enemy fighters appear, revealed everything was in order. This extended to his oxygen connections and those to the intercom. He emptied his equipment bag, hanging his parachute nearby, ready if needed to attach to the harness he wore. Then he placed his flak vest and steel helmet on the deck, where they could be reached easily. Some officers, who spent most of the mission seated, wore their parachutes, but Bobby found it put him too high on his bombardier's stool for easy viewing through the bombsight, and was an encumbrance moving around the craft. This was necessary when he had to get past the navigator's station and up onto the flight deck and beyond to check out the bomb load and the safeties on the bomb fuses before take off. Later, they would be armed, and verifying that was a duty he didn't want to delegate, either.

After each was satisfied with his respective checklist, they all left the plane for a few minutes before engine start. Those who had the need relieved themselves on the ever-present Brussels sprouts that lined the outside edge of the concrete hardstand. Raised by the local farmers, the crop occupied every square foot of tillable soil available.

Most of the crew, talking nervously among themselves, joked to relieve their own tension. That day the play was on the name of the target city, and the stink they hoped they would create there. One young gunner was over by himself, nervously coughing himself to the point of gagging.

Bobby went over to calm him. "Come on chum, we're all scared, something the old boys say is 'First mission jitters.' They didn't say anything about the fright that comes with each added combat, but remember, you're not alone, and as long as we work as a team, we'll make it out okay."

The engines, previously warmed up and checked out, were restarted, as the aircraft of the entire Group came to life almost in unison with the roar of over 181,000 horses. The lead planes first, each squadron then formed its line of twelve planes, proceeding down their perimeter taxiways. There they joined with the others at the downwind end of the runway, each ship waiting for the signal for takeoff.

In the nose, Bobby could see the control tower, and the green light given every thirty seconds to each Fortress as its turn came. He could feel his pulse race with added adrenaline, when at last the green light flashed for them, and Danny pushed the throttles forward. The surge of power was reassuring. Well before the end of the runway, despite the B-17 being fully loaded, they were airborne. As the wheels and flaps came up, and they began to climb steadily, a collective sigh of relief clearly could be heard over the intercom.

He never got over the excitement of taking off and landing, partially because those times were so critical, but also because of his seat, foremost in the plane. There he was, hanging out over the bombsight, and with nothing else between him and the outside elements ahead but the fragile Plexiglas nose. This perspective magnified the perception of speed, especially when they were near the ground.

In practice, in groups of only a few planes, he hadn't appreciated how lengthy the process of assembly could be, but now, at the tail end of thirty-six big birds, the slow climbing turns east of the base seemed to take forever. Actually it took only thirty minutes by his watch to reach Rally Point altitude, where the group, fully assembled, headed out over the North Sea.

The co-pilot, Lloyd McCauley, using the intercom, gave the gun check order, followed by the noise and vibration of the other ten guns each firing a few rounds. After getting off a short burst with the cheek gun on his left, Bobby pulled down the remote control yoke for the chin turret, and tested those guns too. He then polled the gunners over the intercom, learning that all guns checked out.

At ten thousand feet, oxygen masks were donned and connected, and after about twenty more minutes, the word came from Danny that they were entering enemy airspace. It was time to keep their eyes peeled for bandits, he said, and cut any extraneous talk. They had been told to expect the Mustangs of the fighter escort to join them about that time. Danny cautioned everyone not to fire on our "Little Friends," who appeared from a distance similar to the Nazi Messerschmitt BF-109.

They attained their planned twenty-five thousand foot altitude by the time they reached eastern Belgium, but the clouds below them at around six thousand feet still blanketed everything. Of course, Bobby, with his map out for reference, had it practically memorized by that time, in case of a break in the cloud cover. He waved to Lynch, the navigator behind him, who was using his sextant through the astrodome above. They both knew that the lead navigator ahead would be responsible for plotting the course to Cologne, but it wouldn't hurt to verify that the big boys up front were on course. It wouldn't be the first time they were off in their calculations.

They all felt a keen disappointment when no breaks in the layer of white appeared below as they neared the Initial Point, or IP, where they turned toward the objective. There the bomb run began, the plane's controls taken over by the bombsight in conjunction with the automatic pilot. Bobby, especially, felt frustrated, as he would have to depend entirely on the Group's lead plane, with its radar, when to drop their bombs.

Switching on the Norden, he said to Danny over the intercom, "Now you can have a short rest."

"Ha, very funny," his pilot buddy replied, "Have you seen all the instruments and controls we have to mind up here?"

Bobby then opened the bomb-bay doors, having already armed the fuses. He continued to scan the skies for Jerry fighters.

At that point the tail gunner, Dale Firof, reported contrails from single-engine planes at six o'clock high, reassuring them all when he quickly added, his relief evident, "They're ours!"

At that point black irregular patches of flak bursts began to appear up ahead, much too low to be effective. Apparently the German radar, aiming the deadly 88s far below, was being misled by the reflective aluminum "Chaff" released by the planes up front.

Bobby said aloud, to no one in particular, "Let us hope the flak stays low." Over the intercom came the word, "Amen."

Seeing the signal from the lead plane, he flipped the bomb release switch then, calling through the intercom, "Bombs away!"

Someone observed, "As if we couldn't tell, with the plane suddenly making like an elevator."

Danny commanded, "Quiet down, back there. Can the idle talk. We're not out of this yet!"

They made a slow banking ninety Degree turn, away from the greasy-looking bursts, then another turn, to pass well north of the city, calculated to take them out of the flak belt. Before the second turn, the barrage again commenced. This time the aim was accurate, severely damaging a Fortress ahead, which started down in a steep dive, trailing smoke from two engines.

"Come on, guys." Bobby urged, "Hit the silk!"

They did see four parachutes open before the clouds swallowed the wounded plane. Did any more make it out? That was the question of everyone witnessing the chilling event.

As soon as they were over friendly territory, their descent began and they were thankfully able to shed their heavy flak vests and helmets. Upon reaching ten thousand feet once again, restrictive oxygen masks were pulled off. Bobby came on the intercom to call for a final check on the crew as he periodically did. When all responded as before, Danny commented that they could now chatter all they wanted until the final approach.

The landing itself was a dream, as was usually the case with Danny in the left seat, and as the ground came up, Bobby leaned on the comforting support of the gun control yoke, and was further reassured by the sharp bark of the wheels touching down soon after the runway was seen to be speeding beneath them.

After deplaning at their hardstand, and congratulating their ground crew for the plane's flawless performance, the relief was palpable. Kelly, the waist gunner, even kissed the concrete. They were then taken with their gear by truck to debriefing. In exchange for the routine shot of Scotch whiskey, they reported the apparent effectiveness of the "Chaff " dropped during the bomb run, along with seeing at least four men escaping from the stricken Fort. No enemy fighters were seen. The Squadron's lead bombardier reported unknown bombing results, due to the clouds.

As it turned out, later reconnaissance flights showed only limited damage inflicted on the railroads, although severe destruction was seen in the previously bombed nearby factories and surrounding built-up areas. Better news was that the damaged Fortress had crash-landed in Belgium, mostly liberated by that time, all but one man surviving.

That night, after supper, tired but elated by the completion of his first combat, Bobby wrote another letter.

October 15, 1944

Dearest Denise:

We just finished our first flight over Germany, and while I'm so tired I can hardly stand it, I just had to write you, to tell you that I'm alive and well, and love you more every day. Your last letter was waiting when we got back, and I spent most of the time at mess reading it over and over. The scent of your perfume is still with me, filling me with an indescribable longing. I think I'll curl up with it in bed tonight. My dreams are sure to be pleasant.

You'd be amazed at the preparations we have to go through to survive these flights, which are so cold. And whenever I speak of the cold temperature, think of the lovely clime somewhere near the stratosphere, let us say, 30,000 feet, shall we?

So you're gonna fly a mission? First let me lead you thru the routine that you have to go thru to stay healthy and what has been done for you in that line. First of all, after you are awakened at four in the morning, fed in a manner of speaking and transported to the briefing room, briefed and turned loose, you find yourself confronted with your day's work. We have just learned all the particulars of what we are to do and what we will expect en route and home. Also they told us that the temp would be 65 below zero today and we think that is cold. Now, in the miserable light of the cold, drizzly, half-hearted dawn, we shiver for a moment while the facts seep into chill-benumbed brains. 65 below, gad that's really cold! Well, gotta get dressed.

And so our hero goes thru his attire and puts on more layers than worn even by the many petty-coated belles of the 1800s. He doesn't have a thing to wear? He better have plenty, believe me.

Next to the skin, come the ever-loving long handles. Of pure wool, they are pulled on and secured, giving the wearer the nightmarish appearance of a misshaped ballet dancer. Next comes the nylon electric suit. This is a very practical piece of clothing looking like the Hollywood conception of a farmer's pair of overalls. Of a pretty shade of green and with the overall-like straps, the ensemble has a jacket to match. Complete with zoot legs and stuff cuffs! The suit has a maze of tiny wires sewn into the cloth. The jacket looks for all the world like the conventional dinner jacket, which plugs into the pants to complete the circuit. Now comes the winter flying suit, a heavy cloth jacket with Malacca lining and pants of the same order. For the feet are the ole heavy wool socks, then slip on a pair of electric booties that look like house slippers, connect them to the trousers and put the feet into very heavy winter fleece-lined rubber boots. Finally, pull on the electric gloves with rayon lining and snap them into the connections on the sleeves. There! You're all dressed for thirty thousand feet. Stylish, no?

I have so much more to describe, but I just can't stay awake any longer. I'll write soon with more details. In the meantime, just know that I love you, and think of you constantly. I'm living for the day we can be together again.

That new defense job of yours sounds like it's speeding that day, so keep it up, sweetheart. And just keep those letters coming.

Be good, and you have all my love forever,

Your Bobby

* * * *

After a day's well-earned rest, his crew was again selected for their second trip to the *Reich,* mission number 205. They now had been under fire, and while not blooded personally, with their plane suffering no damage, they felt a new confidence for at least a whole day. Bobby spent the 16th in the sack, sleeping, and then writing letters, including another to Denise, filling him with longing.

He could use a beer, he thought, as he mailed the letters at the PX, but drinking was forbidden for those flying the next day. He went to the Officers' Club in the cold drizzle, and sat by the fire, gazing at the mural of the comely mermaid above the fireplace, seeing in that fanciful picture a reflection of his love at home. He had a couple of cups of hot tea before hitting the officers' mess, where his feelings kept him from eating much. Tomorrow was too close for comfort.

The shocking wake-up flashlight and terse personal address came again at four AM, and the preliminaries were a repeat of the first mission. Briefing revealed the target, again Cologne, a repeat because of the failure to significantly damage the rail network, which was of primary importance. They flew the same plane, which was encouraging, as they had done well in their first mission in her, and without any malfunctions. Instead of a route aimed almost directly at the city as had been carried out before, they were to head to the north, coming in on their target flying a southerly leg. The routine preparation for takeoff was identical, as was their position in the twelve craft from the 568th, except that their Squadron would be the high, or "B" element of the Group.

As would prove to be almost invariable that autumn, the cloud cover over the city was complete, and again the bombing was by pathfinder radar, with results unobserved. The flak was intense, but no losses were incurred and no enemy fighters were seen, probably kept away by their "Little friends," the Mustangs from the 567th Fighter Group.

At the debriefing interrogation, they had nothing to report in exchange for the shot of Scotch each was given. They were told that a key bridge across the Rhine had been dropped into the water by a near miss. Only later was it shown to be due to German demolition charges, triggered by the concussion of their bombs.

It was plain to them that they were on a roll, when another mission was scheduled for them the very next day. Bobby felt particularly beat, and learning of their selection, he retired to his cot just after supper. The mission, leading all to be awakened again in the wee hours, was to Kassel, at briefing said by the Intelligence Officer to be a manufacturing center for battle tanks, aircraft engines and airframes at the Henschel and Feiseler plants, as well as a communication and transportation hub. Its pre-war population had been around 250,000, although what the number was at that time, with refugees and slave laborers, was anybody's guess.

On their flight there, the city proved to be covered by clouds, as usual, and the Group's bombs were dropped as before, on signal from the Pathfinder ahead. Bobby was shocked by the density of the "Box" of flak they flew into over the city, and not a little bit frightened, although that quickly passed for him and the rest of the crew, as there were no serious hits.

They had been escorted by the checker-nose Mustangs once again, a factor in keeping *Luftwaffe* fighters scarce. Some of the escort tucked in close to the B-17s on the way home, allaying some of the anxiety aboard the bombers regarding being attacked by German intruders after leaving hostile skies, while availing themselves of the skills of the bombers' navigators.

Things continued busy for Bobby and the Thunder crew, with more missions under their belts. He, like all of his buddies, could never really get over their fears on combat missions, but oddly, for him at least, one of the worst parts of a mission was being awakened from a fitful sleep in the wee hours, hastily dressing, and having breakfast on top of a resisting stomach. It reminded him so much of when, as a kid, he had to get up early to deliver the *Burbank Shopping News* and later the *L.A. Times*. Then, the only danger was the unlikely jumping of the curb by a passing car at the corner where he was folding his papers. Hardly the risk of flak and fighters, but still, he hated the feeling.

Missions over Germany continued, despite the bad weather. On October 19, their fourth was to Mannheim, which, they were told, was the enemy's second largest river port, at the confluence of the Rhine and Neckar Rivers. Their job was to destroy chemical plants there, part of the huge I.G. Farben complex, repeatedly hit previously, but still an important producer of explosives and chemicals used for synthetic rubber and oil production.

After assembly, tense as ever during the climb through the clouds, they found the same layer obscuring the target, and went on to bomb nearby Darmstadt, with the help of the lead bomber and its radar, again with unknown immediate results. The decision was made to unload over a relatively undamaged area of the city, rather than re-bomb old ruins from previous raids. The lack of landmarks, even with the aid of the "Mickey," or radar unit, was a continued problem.

Bobby wrote Denise again at his next opportunity.

October 21, 1944

Darling Denise:

Here's hoping, Sweetheart, that this finds you in good health and in good spirits, of course, thinking of me. My thoughts keep going back to when we discovered that the love we had was still alive. I only wish my dreams were as filled with that as my memories are during the day. Been very busy lately, getting little sleep, and such thoughts are all that are keeping me awake.

I'm reminded that you mite like to hear the final account of the fly-boy's preparations for zooming into the frigid blue yonder, started in that previous letter.

I gave ya the dope on the clothing we wear to ward off the cold, and now comes the heavy stuff. You aren't really dressed just yet. You still need some very important accoutrements. But first, climb into your parachute harness and buckle all the fastenings. Now, if you can, climb into the plane and worm your way into the nose—this is a job. You know how cramped you are. But the payoff comes when you take your station at the bombardier's devices. Getting into that seat is a feat of strength and I need every ounce of heave-ho I have to move my feet around and get them in place.

You're sitting down now, and get comfortable 'cuz you won't be able to move much for about six hours. Pull on the winter helmet with the heated goggles and heated oxygen mask and earphones. Buckle them on and plug in all the connections, have your armor suit and steel helmet ready, along with your life jacket and parachute, plug in the connections, turn on the rheostat for warmth and les' go. By this time you look like a football practice dummy and feel like you're inside a mattress. All the connections, hoses and wires make you think of the back of a telephone switchboard. But wait, you gotta put on the armor. Nuts. How can you swing all that steel around when you can't even move? Well, you put that on, and quickly when the shooting starts and tho it bends your already broken back you really like the feel.

Well, that's the stuff, the true info. When it's all over and you're down, a beaten fatigue steals over you and you're ready for the sack. Eight hours of fifty pounds of clothes sitting in one position with the oxygen mask clamped tite, the pressure of the helmet plus the strain of the constant vigilance—damn, Denise, I'm bushed.

Your comments remind me of a joke I heard recently. Seems as tho the war was going to be over by Xmas. Ha! That's a good one. It would be nice to return to you soon, but I'm afraid, sweet, it's no dice. You only have to look around over here to see that Jerry is still very potent. It'll be a much briter sunny morning in another year and another season before we can shout, "huzza we won!" I don't want to hang too much crepe, just want to set things rite.

I can't stay awake any longer, Denise darling. But not to end on a negative note. We'll be together again, and then we can make up for all these months apart. Until then sweetheart, just continue loving me as I do you, and keep those letters coming.

All my love, always,

Bobby

* * * *

Reveille on October 25 as usual was at four AM, and after breakfast in the officers' mess, briefing. The primary target was the *Rhenania* oil refinery, which supplied fuel to the aircraft and defense installations of northern Germany, and thus was marked by the Eighth Air Force for obliteration, in the new campaign to drain the *Reich* of its life-blood fuel and oil. It would be heavily defended by batteries of 88s and swarms of fighters, attesting to the importance of the facility.

Hamburg was the secondary objective, and they were filled in on its importance, the second largest port in Europe after Rotterdam. It was astride the Elbe River, unmistakable with its networks of canals, and over two thousand bridges, making it a bridge buster's paradise. Also, it was noted to be Germany's third most extensive railroad and highway center. Bombed mercilessly by the RAF in night raids since early 1942, it had suffered devastating damage to its built-up sections, with great loss of life, yet it still functioned as a German transportation and manufacturing center.

As before, the impenetrable cloud cover necessitated dependence on the pathfinder, or PFF plane, for the signal to drop. For some reason, maybe Gremlins, as one skeptic suggested, the radar unit didn't function. Rather than dump the deadly load in the general neighborhood of the small primary, they went on to bomb the sprawling secondary, Hamburg itself. That they were on to something worth defending was attested to by the accurate anti-aircraft fire, which while knocking down only a solitary Fortress from the Wing's 95th Bomb Group, damaged over ninety, half the entire bomber effort, several being from Framlingham. The escort from the 357th lost a single Mustang, as they kept the Jerry fighters so far away they were not even seen by Bobby or his crew.

The very next day, on the 26th, the primary target for their sixth mission, the oil refinery in Misberg proved too small for the Mickey radar unit in the lead plane to outline, so they bombed over the city of Hannover through the clouds, again with unknown results. At briefing, they had been told that the city, the secondary target, was known to have a number of military vehicle factories, and thus was an important objective in its own right. It was apparently important to the Nazis also, as the flak was as thick as it had been over Hamburg. While no B-17s were lost, sixteen were badly damaged, two from the 390th, and several crewmen were killed, one from the 568th.

All the way back from Germany, sitting in the nose of the aircraft, Bobby's mood matched the nearly impenetrable gloom below. Well, at least he had survived, he mused. Those dense clouds worked both ways, didn't they?

After a day's rest, they had a mission to Hamm, an important communications center, and positioned to be a key transportation link to the Western Front. It had been attacked previously a couple of times with minimal damage inflicted on the all-important railroad marshaling yards there. As had become invariable, visibility was almost nil because of the multi-layered clouds, forcing the Group to bomb on instruments once again at the lead plane's signal. While the heavy haze permitted photos of the flashes of explosions on the ground, landmarks were so unclear that bombing accuracy could not be assessed.

A plus was that of the one hundred and eighty-four planes sent up by their Air Division, the Third, not one fell to the enemy defenses. The Thunder crew had a rough time passing south of Münster on their return, when flak damaged their plane and four others. They were all thankful for their armored vests and helmets, as the aluminum skin of their ship rattled with the impact of a number of fragments, and one gunner came away with a souvenir, a razor-sharp shard of steel that bounced off his helmet.

It was around this time that Bobby sent another letter.

November 1, 1944

Dear Darling Denise:

I do hereby dash off a response to your letters written a month ago that just came in. Yes, I do miss you, and pray daily for our victory so that we can be together again, just as you do. It will be a glorious day, let me tell you.

I received a letter from my aunt Betty in Chicago, and got a big bang where she said that she was glad that I was over here on the tail-end of the fighting. Ha!

I can't write about the missions we go on, except in an offhand sense. Too much of that stuff, when you recall a certain incident, brings to mind events that might best be forgotten. I recognize your anxiety and I know of the human element, but I guess you'll have to sweat it out. I can't give you any details, even tho I'm my own censor.

This patter brings to mind the treatment the movies give combat. I just wish they'd film more real footage. They'd give the public an idea of the complex mental situation that this presents. But enuff of that, my love. Tell me how you're doing. Do you think of me all the time? Thinking of you is what I do, and I don't mean just in my spare time.

The weather over here is not exactly the stuff you could ask for as far as flying is concerned—clouds, fog and haze galore. Indeed, the works. Monday we really had an early preview of a white Christmas. During the nite it turned exceptionally cold and come morn we were greeted by a wonderful sight. The entire countryside was mantled by a beautiful covering blanket of frost. It gave the barren terrain a lovely, virgin appearance. How I wish we could have been together here to enjoy the scene.

I miss you so, and look forward to when we can be together again. I know that'll come in time. Just pray for me, sweet love, and it will happen that way.

I think I'll close this as of now and I wish you my best. If you have the time, I'll take you up on your offer to send some goodies. Ritz crackers will do, along with stuff like peanut butter, honey, sandwich spread, or cheese. A good book and some tobacco wouldn't hurt either. Well, here's the list and you can enclose items that you deem best. Just use your own judgment, but don't spend too much. Save some for yourself for a movie or a hair-do. Too bad you can't send some of that Lucky Lager or Golden Glow. I could really use some American brew.

Well, I'm turning in now, hoping to dream of you, and that you will dream of me. Keep all my love, my wonderful Denise.

Your Bobby

* * * *

After his first seven missions, the targets almost totally obscured by cloud cover, he was becoming extremely frustrated. The concept of precision daylight bombing again became foremost in his mind after becoming more accustomed to the excitement and fear attached to the forays over hostile territory. While he had been at the top of his class in training, Northern Europe was not the cloudless Mojave Desert. It was then that the lack of palpable results got to him.

On all their missions they had triggered their bomb drops on the lead ship carrying the radar unit, seeing nothing of the results. Their primary target on one mission, Mannheim, an important industrial center, was so obscured by clouds, that they again couldn't see a thing. With the radar unit in the lead plane not functioning, they went on to dump their deadly cargo on Darmstadt, the city itself, since their secondary target, railroad marshaling yards there, could not be seen.

That night, although especially fatigued after four missions in five days, instead of falling into the sack after debriefing and chow, he decided he had to talk to someone about his doubts. It is one thing to risk one's life when the results were certain, but thus far, his experience, and that of everyone he talked to, suggested that their recent efforts had been useless from a military standpoint. Equally likely, as in the case of Darmstadt, he feared their efforts were probably a cause of slaughter of many innocent women and children.

He headed for the Officers' Club when he saw that the flag color indicated that there would be no mission the next day. A couple of beers certainly would help, he thought, and being able to sleep in was a plus. He knew there would be willing ears to listen to him there.

That day's mission had been particularly rough for the whole squadron, as the flak had damaged almost all the planes, and, although there had been no serious casualties, many of the crews had been particularly shaken, flying through the deadly curtain of steel.

On entering the club, he saw a buddy, with whom he had trained at Victorville, Monty Tishera, who seemed particularly upset, talking to the Catholic Chaplain, Captain Lenahan. Bobby sat down with them unannounced, although receiving a brief acknowledgement from the priest.

Monty was saying, "What's the point of being shot at, and maybe dying, when we can't even see what we're doing? For all we know those bombs are going into the woods and swamps."

"Son," the Chaplain said, "There are many risks one takes in war, and I know how it is when your plane is hit. I've been on such a mission, with the metal skin sounding like a can of rocks being shaken, along with the plane. The fear that the next one will be a direct hit or will bring a deadly fragment through your flak vest or helmet is pervasive. You just have to say your prayers and put your faith in God. The odds now are in your favor, not like it was when I first got here in 1942, when the weather was almost as bad, and radar units to help put our bombs on the targets were still experimental. Then, the enemy radar for their anti-aircraft 88s was just as effective as now. Your efforts, as uncertain as they seem to you, have had a telling effect, you can be sure. And have you stopped to consider the many thousands of aircraft, troops and artillery pieces the Air Force is tying down in Germany, weakening their defenses against our armies?"

Monty finished the last of his beer, nodding to Bobby, and on leaving the table, said, "Thanks, Father, you've put things into proper perspective for me. At least I'll be able to sleep better now. Goodnight."

When he had gone, Bobby leaned forward, saying, "Father, I'll bet this seems just like the confessional."

This was met by a wink of the Chaplain's eye. "All in a day's work, son. Now, what's bothering you? It seems there's something else, or do I have it wrong? Did your plane get flak too?"

Bobby knew the Chaplain had done his homework since their arrival at Framlingham, and that he had been to the Colonel's office at Group to learn the biographies of the replacements for each squadron. It was well-known that he had been interned in a Japanese prison camp in the Far East before Pearl Harbor, and while with the 390th occasionally went on combat missions, a factor that lent confidence to the men, not only those on whose ship he flew, but also for the rest of that squadron. He was a man's man, making him the Group's foremost Chaplain, even for many of the non-Catholics.

His thoughts were interrupted by Father Lenahan's question, "Hello, lieutenant, are you still there?"

Embarrassed, he replied, "Sorry Father, I guess I got lost in thought. Flak? Yes, a little."

The Chaplain then asked, "Well, then tell me, what else is troubling you?"

"I was listening to your reassurances to Monty, and your advice regarding bombing blindly with radar was comforting, but my problem gets more complex. It's about bombing populated, built up areas. When we can't spot a small precision target, we usually then go on to dump our high explosives on a nearby large town, most often totally blindly, like the proverbial broadside of the barn we can't miss. This happened again today, dropping on Hamm, after failing to locate our actual railroad targets. Father, that's what hurts. How many innocent people, women, children and old folks, did my bombs kill?"

A thoughtful pause followed, as the Chaplain put his prayerful hands to his lips. Finally, he nodded his reply, "That *is* a tough one. You were trained in precision bombing, which has always been the pride of the Army Air Force as the best way for strategic bombing to win the war, without purposely killing civilians. That has always looked good on paper, and has been a contentious issue in our dealings with the RAF. Some others have even accused them of war crimes for their so-called carpet bombing of big cities, killing hundreds of thousands. The priest in me decries that. Didn't God decree *Thou shalt not kill?*"

"But Father," Bobby interjected, "What about during wartime?"

Slowly shaking his head, with his hand elevated for silence, Captain Lenahan continued, "Nowhere on those stone tablets was there anything banning war, and from the wings of war comes death. Kill or be killed. It's true that the concept has changed, back to the way it was in ancient and even medieval times, when entire cities were torched and destroyed, all the males killed, and the females and children enslaved. Look how the histories describe Rome's treatment of the defeated Carthage. They even tried to ruin the soil with salt to kill future crops. So now Hitler has brought total war back. There is no way that we can respond except in kind."

"Father," Bobby protested, "If we reply with total war, aren't we bringing back that concept from the Old Testament, an eye for an eye, a tooth for a tooth? Are we Americans out for retribution for what the *Luftwaffe* did to Coventry and

Rotterdam, not to mention London? I know through my RAF contacts that such a factor is part of their motivation. But Nazi Germany is a totalitarian nation. The people have no voice in the government. Any protest by them concerning the continued waging of even a losing war can mean death. Are we out for vengeance, punishing the German city-dwellers for the crimes of the Nazis over whom they have no control?"

The Chaplain's reply to that semi-rhetorical question came quickly. "Certainly not. But remember, the way things have gone, however appalling it seems, in the long run fewer people will die, and that applies to German children, certainly innocents, and to our fighting men, possibly even sparing you, as the war will end all the sooner."

Watching Bobby sip his beer, he continued, "And when it comes to innocents, are the people that work in the factories that produce the armaments for Hitler's legions really not culpable somehow? Doesn't the housewife in the city do piece work on small parts that feed the factories, and don't they prepare the meals for those who work in them?"

He paused, as if gauging the depth of Bobby's concerns. "No, Taylor, I know you're at best a lukewarm Catholic, but you still have a duty to do what is right. Intent is all-important, and in your work even more so, in bringing down those ruthless Nazis. You must use the tools you've trained with, dropping bombs that damage their war effort. Your duty, if our radar malfunctions is to drop your bombs on the secondary target.

"The sum of these missions, however uncertain or brutal each one seems to you, has brought us to the point now where the enemy is running out of fuel and lubricating oil. Soon they won't even be able to supply what little they have left of those essentials to airfields where they're needed because your bombs have destroyed almost everything."

Bobby took this all in, just as in the Confessional. Smiling inwardly, while swirling his beer, he then said, "Father, most of what you say is more military than spiritual, and it's good logic. But contrary to Catholic teaching, in this war, what you're telling me is that the ends do justify the means, however reprehensible the latter are. Still, what you say helps. Thanks, Father, for your time. I know I've taken too much of it, as there are plenty of others needing your counsel."

The Chaplain smiled at Bobby as he got up and headed out the door, towards the "Rocker Club," reserved for enlisted men above the rank of buck sergeant. He would be welcomed there, especially by the young gunners, mostly staff sergeants.

"Get some sleep now, Taylor," he called back, "And come to confession, it's been a while."

Replying, Bobby asked reluctantly, "Is that a Direct Order, sir?" Then he got himself another beer.

He continued to brood when the second brew did little to soothe his concerns. He began to feel even more pangs of conscience about the deaths of women and children that their bombs must be killing. The news photos he had seen in the past came back, and gory thoughts of shattered bodies of children began to plague him. I can't give up, he thought. The war must be won, and what we've been doing has to be getting us there. He realized that the main problem was visibility. The weather in Northern Europe in the fall of 1944 was the worst in more than fifty years.

We've gotta improve our accuracy, he thought. For some time he had been thinking about the role the lead crews were playing, and he wasn't impressed. It occurred to him that maybe if he were the Squadron's lead bombardier, things might be different. The idea grew on him, and before he slept that night, he vowed to talk to the Colonel.

The next morning, after chow, and donning his best uniform, he visited the Squadron Commander's office at headquarters. Lt. Colonel Armstrong was out at the time, so he waited an hour, while the orderly room corporal eyed him curiously over his noisy typewriter. When the Colonel arrived, another hour passed before Bobby was ushered into his office.

As he stood at attention in front of the desk, he could see his superior was perusing his service record. After a minute, the Colonel looked up, and then, giving the order, "At ease, Taylor," he asked crisply, "What do you have in mind lieutenant? Make it brief, please."

Bobby had harbored hopes of broaching his concerns in detail, but on hearing that, he blurted out, "Sir, I want to apply for lead bombardier."

The Colonel looked at him with some surprise and replied, "Well, you were brief as ordered, Taylor, but crew don't volunteer, they are chosen. Most don't want to be in the lead position anyway, as that often is the first plane attacked in combat. But I am curious. Let's hear your reasons."

Bobby explained his belief in the doctrine of precision bombing, and the problems he was having with justifying dropping bombs blindly through the clouds into built-up areas.

The Colonel asked gravely, "But you're not telling me you want out?"

"No sir, I'm asking for a chance to help improve the Group's bombing accuracy, with the aim of better target saturation, minimizing civilian casualties. I think that I can do a better job than we're doing now if given half a chance. If that can't be arranged, I'd like to apply for duty in the Pacific, where the visibility might allow greater accuracy."

Colonel Armstrong held his eyes on Bobby for a minute, and then asked, "Don't you know that the ultimate goal there is Japan, and that with their dense population, we'll hardly be able to drop a single bomb without killing a thousand civilians? How would you feel then?"

"Yes sir, I understand that. But this is here and now. All I'm asking is to be given the opportunity to prove myself."

"And if you can't, what then, lieutenant?"

"Sir, I have no doubts about improving things."

The Commander stood, indicating the interview was at an end. As Bobby came to attention, he saw a smile on the Colonel's face. "We'll see," was all he said.

The next morning was November 2nd. It was all too early as usual, despite being alerted that there would be a mission that day, their eighth. He was rudely awakened from a sound sleep at three AM, and climbed into his clothes, shivering constantly. After paying a visit to the latrine, and shaving in the ablutions hut, he hopped the truck to officers' mess.

The briefing gave them the details of a potentially rough mission, to Mersberg, just about as far as Berlin, but ninety miles southwest, in the eastern part of the country. It would be quite a trip, their deepest penetration yet. To everyone's consternation, besides the distance, it was well known that the target there, the *Leuna* synthetic oil complex, was the most heavily defended one on the Continent, ranking with Berlin itself. Some consolation was gained from the knowledge that there would be an escort all the way by Mustangs from the 567th and other fighter squadrons from the Eighth.

Due to the southerly location of the target, his old favorite, twin engine P-38 Lightnings from the Ninth Air Force, based in Italy, were to meet them there as added protection.

As their turn came to take off, it was encouraging to feel the power of the four Wright R-1820s accelerating the heavily loaded plane into the air well short of the end of the runway and the menacing woods beyond. Assembly was achieved without mishap, although the climb blindly through the dense clouds was always a sweat.

The steady drone of the engines would have lulled anybody to sleep, but for the impending combat. For Bobby, had it not been for the shivering with which he started the day, and couldn't quite shake, along with the need for vigilance, he might have been drowsy as well. He was again reminded that the P-51 Mustang could be easily mistaken for a Messerschmitt Bf-109, with their clipped wing tips and inline engines. The other German single engine fighter, the FW-190, also could also be taken for one of ours, the Republic P-47 Thunderbolt, the blunt noses of their radial engines giving them a similarity from a distance. So, despite the comforting presence of their little friends going in the same direction, their vapor trails describing wide arcs overhead, he had to keep on his toes.

When they were within fifty miles of Mersberg, they were diverted from the *Leuna* complex because of clouds and coalescing contrails from the aircraft that had already bombed. That, in addition to a highly effective smokescreen, had totally obscured the target area to later flights. When Bobby heard over the intercom from Danny that they were being diverted, it sounded all too familiar. Their secondary target was Halle, on the Saale River, another transportation hub and the largest city in the province. Despite his misgivings, he toggled *Little Butch III's* bombs over the mostly obscured city on signal from the lead. It was the same old story, no visibility, no immediately confirmed results, but no losses.

That they had avoided possible disaster didn't occur to them until after debriefing. They learned that those reaching the *Leuna* works encountered withering flak and fighter resistance, and while the Fortresses and their fighter escorts bagged a large number of their attackers and scored well on the oil production facilities, they lost over ten percent of the bomber force.

Bobby was able to sleep in the next morning, a rare luxury. After a late breakfast, they all went over to the Officers Club to relax, and to get away from their freezing Nissen hut. They had access to the news there, in the form of civilian newspapers, as well as the Army's *Stars and Stripes*. There was also BBC on the radio. They never really knew just how they themselves were doing, however, since what was fed them, as with the civilians at home, were just generalities. They knew the experience of their Group, the 390th, but what was their Wing accomplishing over all, and how did that fit in with the bombing results of the entire Third Bomb Division or of the entire Eighth Air Force, for that matter? Ruminating about their last mission, and contemplating the daunting possibility of twenty-seven more to go dominated the conversation. After a couple of beers, the talk came around to the question of what was really going on, and what was in store for them.

Plunking down his half-empty mug, Danny said, "They're going to train us for lead crew, you know."

"No, I haven't heard," Bobby smilingly replied, wondering about his role in the selection.

Navigator Lynch and McCauley, the co-pilot, asked in unison, "Why us?"

Gulping down the rest of his beer in an effortless chug, Danny's answer was the flattering reason given to him by the Squadron Commander.

"Because we're the best. We've been selected for training after only eight missions, yet. After this week, over the six weeks following, the rest of November and most of December, no combat! We'll learn the functions of the position, and fly practice runs over the Wash and the North Sea, to learn the niceties of the new combination of radar and bombsight technologies. Here's hoping the new guy, our Mickey operator, knows his stuff. As you know, the radar dome replaces the ball turret in the lead planes, making us more vulnerable from below, but I understand that the Mickey man will also handle one of the waist guns too, if necessary.

"The other guys we share our quarters with don't think much of the honor of leading, as our plane may be the first the Jerries will go after. As compensation for the added responsibility and danger, we'll have our own quarters, separate from the other crews, definitely a step up. At least we'll be awakened only when we're actually flying that day, and maybe in a more civilized manner. Oh yeah, during the training period, there'll also be more time for London."

Bobby reflected on their selection, staring into his beer, knowing that two or three other crews in the Group would also be singled out for such training. These were the crews thought to be best suited by the way they had performed in training, coupled with how they carried out their first combats. He had heard that every new crew was considered for this position after up to ten missions, but of those finally chosen, roughly half were rejected and returned to the ranks, as it were, even after the six or seven weeks training period. He wondered whether his request was part of it, but he decided not to bring that up.

Somewhat belatedly, he said, "Well, they know you're the best pilot in the Group. No one can lead a tight formation the way you do, but what about me, your bombardier? We haven't even been able to see any of our targets with that damn cloud cover. All that work with the Norden in training has been useless, so what happens, we bomb the crap out of a bigger target nearby, like a city, full of non-combatants. Precision bombing, hell, that's something we only did on the California desert. With these clouds we might as well be bombing at night, like the RAF, and it might be a bit safer for our planes in the dark."

Danny, in the firm tone of the plane commander, responded, "Whether we like it or not, with the poor visibility over the *Reich,* each lead plane will be equipped with a factory-installed radar, and there'll be one for each squadron, ours included. No more loaned radar-equipped planes from the pathfinder people at Alconbury or Snetterton Heath." Turning to Bobby, he continued, "While this will include me and our co-pilot, plus Lynch, our navigator, you, my friend, will be the key. The bombardier working with the radar operator is the most critical link."

Bobby mulled that one over, sipping his warming brew slowly. He'd had no experience with the unit officially known as *H2X,* which had originally been called "Mickey Mouse," due to its somewhat ridiculous appearance when first experimentally installed in the B-17s nose, just behind the chin turret. Somehow, the name, "Mickey" stuck.

He returned to the concern that the radar antenna had been relocated, replacing the ball turret with its twin 50s. That's where the covering fire of the other craft in the squadron came in. All were aware that tight formation flying was of the utmost importance to form that protective umbrella. If the other planes were still there.

To Bobby, the idea of using the radar appealed to him. "Danny," he said, "I've told no one except the Chaplain and Colonel Armstrong about this, but dropping bombs blindly because of the conditions on all our missions so far has for me been a source of pain. Recall, that when we couldn't find our primary target yesterday because of nil visibility, we dropped our bombs on the nearby city of Halle. How many innocent people did we kill? That kept me from sleeping well last night."

Ordering a second beer, Danny replied, "I don't worry about women and children, and not just because my wife and our two little kids were evacuated to Canada during the London Blitz."

Bobby nodded, recalling Danny's waggling their plane's wings over that Canadian border town when they were still training out of Nebraska.

"The Germans are getting back what they started when this war began. And by now they've gotta know that they're defeated, but where is their will to bring down that madman Hitler? They need more of an incentive."

"But I still hate the idea of blind bombing," Bobby replied. "We have to do something about that."

"Yeah, I agree, it's better to wipe out their factories, rail yards and oil facilities, but if those can't be found because of the damned cloud cover, what are we supposed to do with our bombs? Drop them in the drink? Bring them back here? To hell with the people that stand behind those Nazi bastards."

* * * *

The dangerous pattern of forays over Hitler's *Reich* continued for the Group, bringing to mind the oft-repeated description of missions in combat being hours of boredom punctuated by moments of sheer terror.

At times the flak was intense, making their uncomfortable armor welcome, in the face of fear that the next one might have one's name on it. Despite the added frustration on the part of the gunners, the virtual absence of fighter resistance that had so bedeviled the formations earlier in the war was welcome. They had heard reports about the new German twin-engine jet, the Me-262, but had seen only a few single engine fighters, effectively kept away from them by their escort.

It was rough enough with just the flak. Bobby couldn't help but be reminded of what the Chaplain had said about the effectiveness of their efforts. Their bombing, however uncertain the immediate results, was surely taking its toll on the enemy. That the cloud cover they so decried had protected them almost as much as it obscured their German targets, again crossed his mind.

Their last assignment for November, before they were to begin training, was on the sixth. While the distance was not anything like Halle, it was much farther north, in the more cloudy northern part of the country. At briefing, they were introduced to an added factor. Their primary was the large airfield array at Neumünster, north of Hamburg. They were warned of the complex's ring of flak batteries and their potentially deadly accuracy. As for the threat of interception by fighters, that was left to their imagination. It was, after all, a military air base.

When they hopped out of their truck just at sunrise, they were again greeted by their beloved but well-worn *Little Butch III,* now for the sixth time. They had been given her since their fourth mission, to Hamburg, and the big bird seemed almost like home, so familiar by that time. At first they had been assigned a different aircraft almost each time, without any apparent pattern, getting whatever happened to be available. They never even got close to the beautiful new Fortress they had flown over the Atlantic.

Regarded with affection by all, *Little Butch III* didn't *appear* lovable. Look at her, he thought, all beat up, with her aluminum skin trailing the engines deeply oil-stained, and flak holes patched with what looked like tin can tops. But her moves just seemed right. He knew it was weird to invest any plane with human qualities, but still, as he performed his inspection before hoisting himself up through the front hatch, he would barely whisper as he stroked the Plexiglas nose. "Hi, gal, I'm back."

Sadly, his romance was not to last, as after that sixth mission in her, the brass decreed a change, making him feel a little wistful in the parting. Oh, well, he thought, there'll be others, as he took in a flight of new unpainted silver B-17Gs that had just arrived. But, he thought, how can they measure up to *Little Butch III?* Yeah, they're pretty, but do they have any personality?

Bobby could have saved himself the concern. He wouldn't fly those new beauties soon, having to settle again for some war-weary reject too beat-up for the crews with seniority. His optimism came through then, as he mused, if they give us the lead position, it'll be like dating the prom queen again.

The puddles of water from the night's rain around the plane reflected the pink of the eastern clouds on the cold November morning. There was no trouble starting the engines, taxiing into position and becoming airborne. The weight of their B-17 was extremely important, especially on takeoff, but actually varied little for each mission, as what was needed for fuel determined the bomb load. He checked the maximum of twelve five hundred pound high explosive bombs, which he would arm on the narrow catwalk in the bomb bay, after they had left the coast behind.

They passed over Denmark, which lay beneath the ubiquitous clouds, coming down on the target from the north. The flak was surprisingly light and inaccurate, and the Jerry fighters were nowhere to be seen, likely saving their precious fuel for another day. Bobby dropped the bombs again on the signal from the lead bombardier, having no certain idea himself as to where the target was aside from that signal and the presence of anti-aircraft fire. But it was a *Luftwaffe* airbase, at least, and not a city.

On landing back at Framlingham, it was learned that the results of the mission were largely uncertain, and later, when the news filtered down that reconnaissance photos showed only minor damage, Bobby felt a renewal of his previous frustrations.

On the way to debriefing, he said to the co-pilot, sitting next to him in the truck, "Wait until we get to lead our Squadron, there will be improvement, I kid you not. That was our last mission before we go into training for lead crew."

McCauley looked at him in silence for a moment, and then replied, "As lead bombardier, you could be in for a promotion, but as co-pilot, they could put a command pilot in my seat, and if I fly at all, it'll be in the tail as an observer-gunner. I'll never get my own plane and crew that way, no matter how many missions I fly. So count me out. I'm applying for transfer to another crew."

SIXTEEN

Despondency

Denise's mother stayed with her for several days, trying to help with her problems. It was evident that the previous few months had been a battleground for her daughter, pulled emotionally in every direction.

Bobby's letters were a boon to her flagging morale, but the letters from Wheelie, while expressing his love, continued as a source of despair. That day, Denise had received one from each, and in her mother's presence, she began to open one.

Mrs. O'Donnell, seeing the two, offered, "I'll bet the first one you're going to read is Bobby's, am I right?"

"Oh, mom, of course you are. His letters always cheer me up. Even though he's in the thick of the fighting, he gives an optimistic, even poetic outlook, while my husband, well, not only does he groan and moan about the miserable weather and the muddy footing, the very fact that he writes becomes an accusation. Sure, that's me, and my paranoia, but the fact that I love another and am carrying his child makes me so guilty and depressed that not only do I want to cry, all sorts of other horrible thoughts occur."

Concerned, her mother put her arms around her, saying, "Don't think of those things, Deenie, just be like Bobby and accentuate the positive. Look, you're having the baby that Wheelie could never give a start to, and its father loves you, his letters making your heart soar. Go with that. He'll come back to you, and your having his baby will make him love you all the more."

"Mom, I agree that would be best, but all of this is sapping my energy. My boring job, living here away from you, carrying a baby whose father may never come back, and depression about a husband who will never forgive me are all too much. I don't know if I can take it much longer."

Holding Denise even more closely, Mrs. O'Donnell said, "Dear heart, I can even feel your gloom. My advice is to see Dr. Baker. Maybe he'll have something that will help, or even a referral to a psychiatrist for some counseling."

"Mom, I asked you this before, you don't think I'm crazy now, do you?"

"No, dear, certainly not," she replied, "But things are piling up emotionally that only a professional can help unravel." Looking into Denise's sad face, she then entreated, "Come on, let's see a smile. Things will work out, I just know."

"Okay mom," she said resignedly. "Don't worry. I'll call the doctor in the morning. Along with my constipation and poor appetite, I haven't been sleeping well. That prescription he gave me a couple of months ago did help. I'll get a refill of that too."

When the feelings of optimism her mother had implanted proved temporary, Denise's depression soon made its appearance again. It was a horrible feeling, like being damned to hell, and not just until her mother visited again, but for all eternity. Consciously she told herself that nothing of the sort could take place, but emotionally, she felt it, and to her very bones. It was a free-floating thing, much of it derived from the Bible, something her father had drummed into her since she was a little girl.

She began to think that she was worthless, and that soon expanded into the thought that life was not worth living. Never mind about the new life she carried, or that her loving Bobby was out there, his hopes anchored to their future together.

While feeling nothing but love for him, a distressing factor was that almost all of her problems were because of him. Were it not for their affair, in which they had been so happy, she might at least be content, with a husband, a life, and a future. But that was before she read Wheelie's letter.

She finally got around to reading it that night. She was already bored with it before she began reading, but it was in a woman's handwriting. If that weren't enough, the first words jolted her to attention. He was coming home.

Her first response, out loud was, "Oh God, no!"

Reading on, the reason became clear. He had been badly injured in a jeep accident. His legs were completely paralyzed, and his hands partially so, due to a spinal cord injury from a fracture of his neck. He would soon be transferred to the nearest V.A. hospital, which was over the hill in West Los Angeles, off Wilshire Boulevard. It finished with a note that a Red Cross worker had written it for him.

She certainly wasn't expecting to face such a crisis until after the war's end. But now she saw that she was trapped. How can I desert Wheelie now, she agonized, as more guilt overtook her. He would need her now more than ever, just at the time when everything in her own life was already unraveling.

Sitting there, on the edge of her bed, alone in her small apartment, her world, already crumbling, was falling out from under her. The letter dropped from her hand as she fell back onto the bed in tears. Curling up on her side, she wept almost the entire night.

She hardly was out of bed for the next two days, almost unable to think. Then the dilemma that had blocked her reason gave way to clarity. The motto, *Duty, God and Country,* as if it were a voice from within, became a recurrent thought. She pondered the significance of each element, although not quite able to place its origin.

Her first thought, after she had reread the letter, was to *Duty.* Wheelie, after all, was her husband still. Praying to *God* for both of them was something she was doing more than ever. But, she reflected sadly, it seemed her prayers were worthless. Bobby was risking his life even then for *Country,* while Wheelie had been badly injured serving it.

Rationalizing, she decided *Duty* was most important, duty to her husband and to her family. He was here again, and needed her. It tore her heart as she wondered why *Love,* essential in any such equation, was not included in the sequence. Wrestling with the decision was exhausting physically and emotionally draining, but after another couple of days, she decided what she had to do.

She took out pen and paper, and wrote a tear-stained letter to Bobby, explaining her need to be there for Wheelie. In closing, she wrote that while she realized it would be as painful for him as it was for her, it would be best that they end their relationship.

That message somehow relieved, at least temporarily, the guilt she felt about betraying her husband, but was all the more depressing because she knew she was again betraying Bobby.

The next day she went to the drug store and refilled her prescription, thirty more Phenobarbital capsules. The directions read, "One nightly as needed for sleep." One certainly promoted an uninterrupted slumber, she thought. What would thirty do? God, she thought, she couldn't kill herself, even as depressed as she felt. But oh, to get some real sleep. She took one that night, and a good night's slumber, even if it had been slightly drugged, did help. As hoped, she awakened rested, but the depression was still there.

Wheelie's arrival came only a few days after that last letter. He was on the Neurosurgical floor, D-1 West, at the Veteran's Administration's Wadsworth General Hospital, in West L.A.

She made plans with her mother, despite misgivings about how her still early pregnancy would be received, to visit him that weekend. Driving over Sepulveda Boulevard, the way she and Bobby had always gone to the beach in the past, she brought along some flowers, and dressed colorfully to welcome him back.

On the way over, the conversation at first was casual, but as they neared the top of the winding grade over the Santa Monica Mountains, leading into West L.A., she started to weep.

Her mother, who was becoming increasingly distressed at Denise's deterioration, laid a comforting hand on her daughter's. "I know what you're going through, dear. Just know that I understand and am here for you, whatever happens."

"Thanks, mom," she sobbed, "But I don't think you or anyone else can come close to imagine the way I feel."

Those words brought to mind the elements that had reduced her to the present state. Guilt in the betrayal of her husband, shame because of her adultery and becoming pregnant, deceit in hiding her condition from her father. At that moment she realized the enormity of her predicament, and that her mother's attempts at comforting her were almost useless.

In a quavering voice, she said, "What'll I do when he sees that I'm pregnant? What'll *he* do?"

Her mother looked at her, "Why, of course that won't make him happy, but he's not in a position to choose any more. I'm fond of Wheelie, and his injury appalls me as much as it does you. As a nurse, I've dealt with quadriplegics, men who are unable to move their arms and legs. Self-pity is a huge factor. He won't even notice your pregnancy until he comes to grips with that."

Gasping audibly, Denise sobbed, "Mom, I don't think I can stand much more of this."

As they turned into the entrance to the parking lot, becoming more tense than ever, pale and almost physically sick, she cried, "I haven't seen my husband in a year. How he must have changed, not only physically, but emotionally too. I'm frightened about the way he'll feel towards me after all that has happened. Unless he's blind, he'll soon notice my condition. How will he take it, with rage, like Dad? Will there be any understanding? After all, he always knew I was Bobby's before he and I married."

Getting out of the car, they walked to the front entrance of the brick and concrete building, built in the institutional design of the WPA projects of the Great Depression of the Thirties.

Her mother took her hand, and holding it firmly, led her up the steps. At the reception desk, they were directed to the "D" wing on the first floor of the far side of the hospital. The dark brown polished floors smelled of antiseptic, which served to partially disguise the other less pleasing odors of the wings they passed. At the end of the corridor was an office, where they checked in.

Holding the flowers, Denise nervously asked, "Where can we find Corporal Wheeler? I was told he's on this wing. I'm his wife, Denise, and this is my mother, Mrs. O'Donnell. She's an RN."

The secretary smiled and nodded, calling to the head nurse, across the shared office, seemingly more as a warning than merely announcing their presence.

"Mrs. Gorman, the Wheeler family is here to see bed four. Can they visit now?"

The trim, gray-haired nurse said grudgingly, "Visiting hours aren't until six." But, then reflected, "Maybe your seeing the patient will help calm him, and allow the other three in that room to rest. He's been moaning and groaning all day, despite sedation. Actually, he's not in much pain. It's because of his quadriplegia, and the need to keep him strapped to that Foster Frame, the type of bed we use for turning these patients."

Looking them over, she added, "If he's happy to see you, maybe everyone will be able to get some rest." But she raised her eyebrows a little on recognizing Denise's pregnancy. "Wait," she said, "I think he's face down now. I'll have the orderlies turn him up, so that you can see each other."

Ten minutes later, they were ushered into the four-bed room, well-lighted by windows along the wall, but smelling of urine. Denise was shocked at the sight. Two of the beds were identical, and at first she had difficulty telling which one held her husband. One man was short, and as she turned, she saw that the other's feet touched the end of the frame. There was Wheelie strapped into the narrow cot-like affair that passed for a bed, with the top of his head clamped in traction tongs. The end of a catheter emerged from under the blankets and connected to a half-filled urine bag hanging down from the frame.

Seeing them, and not immediately recognizing them through the prism glasses furnished him, he petulantly said, "Well, God dammit, don't just stand there and stare. What are you bringing me? Oh, flowers. How nice," he added sarcastically. "Are you Red Cross, or maybe church people? Either way, take your stuff and get the hell out of here!"

With that, her mother stepped back, but Denise hesitated. She was shocked. This wasn't the man she'd married. He had been kind and not profane then. She found it almost unbelievable how he had changed.

She stepped over to him, and looked down into his thin, depressed face. Those strange prism glasses that allowed him to see his surroundings, instead of staring at the ceiling all day, interfered. She still saw some of Wheelie there, but he had lost fifty pounds and it was as if he had aged twenty years.

Breaking into tears, and removing the prisms, she cried, "It's me, Denise, don't you recognize me?"

He was then able to focus. After gazing up at her for a few moments, he turned his head away as much as the restrictive traction device allowed, averting his eyes. With a grimace, he began grinding his teeth the way he did when he was angry.

Trying to be light-hearted despite her tears, she said, "Is this any way to greet your wife after all these months? Your letters never gave a hint of anything like this."

His reply was quick, and in a steely tone he retorted deliberately, "What a stupid thing to say. That was before this God damned thing happened to me. Are you blind? What the

Christ is wrong with you? Can't you see, I'm not a man any more! Talk about a helluva way to be injured."

Wilting before the tirade, she felt her knees weakening, but was kept from collapsing by her mother quickly reaching her side. Recovering, she stepped back to the bed, leaned over, and kissed him on the cheek, saying, "I understand." Putting the flowers on his little bedside table, she added, "We've brought you flowers to help cheer you up. They're the same kind you often brought me, remember?"

He ignored her after that, and the two women sat down, in an uncomfortable silence. After a while, a younger nurse came into the room telling them it was time to again turn him face down. Taking the flowers, she indicated she would find a vase.

Denise, who had taken a chair next to Wheelie's bed, got up, saying, "It's time to go now anyway." Giving him another kiss on the cheek, she added, "I'll come again next Sunday. My job is six days a week now, and that's my only day off. See you then."

A doctor, wearing whites, met them in the hall. Introducing himself as Dr. Jordan, the Neurosurgical Resident, he asked if they had any questions.

She already knew, but for Denise's information, her mother asked, "Doctor, what is my son-in-law's outlook? What are the chances of recovery?" Leading the young resident aside, after glancing at her trembling daughter, she added, "Please give it to me straight. I'm an RN, and have some experience in caring for this kind of problem."

Looking at her gravely, he replied, "We can never be absolutely certain in this type of case, but seldom is there return of voluntary motion or sensation below the level of the injury when the paralysis is complete in the beginning, as it seems to have been here. The exception is in the upper extremities, and that's not due to recovery in the spinal cord, but in the nerve roots at the injury level. Even with some return of motion in the arm, sensation may not follow, making motor improvement almost useless. There is often some return of sphincter function, not on a voluntary basis, but by an automatic mechanism, so that the urinary catheter may be dispensed with later. Decubiti, bedsores that is, and nutrition are a great problem, as are kidney infections, although we're hopeful that the new Penicillin and the Sulfa drugs will control that part of the problem."

At that point, Denise, overhearing, in a voice choked with emotion, said, "I'm sorry, but I can't take this!" Then she started down the hall.

"Forgive me, Mrs. Wheeler," the resident called after her, "I was just giving your mother the statistics. Each case has to judged on its individual merits, and there's always hope. You and he both have to remember that."

Mrs. O'Donnell then asked, "How long will he be here, doctor? Is there a chance that he'll be coming home at some point?"

Still following Denise's retreat, he replied, "After the V.A. has done what it can, it might be possible. I hate to say this, but unless you're very wealthy, and can afford around the clock care, home management will be a nightmare. He'll have to be attended to like an infant, night and day.

"He'll be stable as far as the fractured neck is concerned in another eight weeks. Let's hope acceptance will be possible at the special unit at the Long Beach V.A., where they're big on bladder and bowel training, as well as in controlling urinary tract infection and bedsores."

Thanking the doctor, Mrs. O'Donnell caught up with her tearful daughter, and they returned to the car, retracing their route back to her North Hollywood apartment. At first there was no talk, as both were depressed by the prospects, and Denise was sickened by the added guilt, anxiety over the depressing visit, and even angry at the cold clinical approach of the nurses and the doctor.

After a time, she asked her mother plaintively, "How is Wheelie going to act when he recognizes that I'm pregnant? Sooner or later, he'll be able to turn his head fully, when the healing of his broken neck progresses. That'll allow him to get a good look at me, and by then there'll be no confusing my condition with mere weight gain. Even if he does improve emotionally, it'll still be a terrible blow for him to recognize that I've been unfaithful. How can I put him through all that?"

After a pause, her mother answered, "Only you can be the judge of that, Deenie dear. Which would be more distressful for you, his reaction to your pregnancy, or your guilt from neglecting him?"

Denise had to think that one over. She was already so depressed, that she could hardly deal with that question then.

It was only three weeks later that Wheelie recognized that she was pregnant, and became enraged. He called her every name in the book, including the term used by her father, leading her to retreat in tears. That was when she first seriously considered a way out. How could she even visit him, much less care for his every need at home? She thought of divorce, but couldn't bring herself to solve her problem that way, with the war still on, deserting her injured husband at such a time. She already could hardly face the reality of having been unfaithful while he was overseas. She could never rid herself of that shame, even if Bobby did come home to her. And the idea of having to nurse a man who hated her, every day of his life, was so repellant that she became violently sick.

Driving home, overwhelmed with guilt and shame, and the hopelessness of her depression, she nearly drove off the highway and down a precipitous slope. As it was, she was barely able to find her way to the family home to return the borrowed car, half-blinded by persistent tears.

Her mother was alarmed at her mood, but when Denise insisted that she had to get home, she drove her there across the Valley. On the way, Mrs. O'Donnell suggested that she talk to their minister about her problem. That brought a torrent of new tears. Her mother no longer could do anything to cheer her up, even after staying a couple of hours with her, cuddling her in her arms as she did when Denise was a little girl.

That night, as she turned down the covers, she thought of Bobby, while becoming more depressed and irrational than ever. The names Wheelie had called her when he noticed her condition kept coming back. Taking not one, but two of the red capsules with a swallow of water, she lay back on the pillow. She was savoring the certainty of sleep, and the hope that the relief would not be merely transient. How could she face the morning if the awful reality of her situation were still there?

After a couple of hours, despite the double dose, or perhaps because of it, her depression awakened her. It was deep, and she was defenseless. As she lay there in bed, the darkness surrounding her, she tried to make some sense of the way she felt.

Now, reflecting on her childhood nightmares, long suppressed as mere unpleasant memories, it all came back to her.

When she was young, she had nothing on her conscience but the teachings spoon-fed at Sunday school and by her puritanical father. Humankind was by nature evil, and for all but the most righteous, eternity would be suffered in Hell. She never could understand how innocent children could be born with sin, but somehow the constant repetition of the idea led to its being firmly ingrained anyway. And there it was again. But now it was different—far different.

She vividly recalled when she was little, and in the midst of a bad dream. Then, it was horrible too, as if the world, with her loved ones, had collapsed around her. Some awful, unnamed evil, like a sinister giant octopus, was dragging her into the depths, where she couldn't breathe, and where some unspeakable end awaited her. The message then permeating her forlorn thoughts was the overwhelming fear that she would be eternally damned to that fate. She would awaken screaming, requiring her mother's soothing embrace for the rest of the night before she could come to grips with reality.

Now she began to pray, sobbing, "O My God, please forgive my sins. My deadly sins—she couldn't find words to say them aloud. But there they were—Lust, Betrayal, Adultery, Deceit. And now—she could barely think by then—Suicide. But, she shuddered, at another awful thought, the murder of her unborn baby.

She recalled the warmth and comfort from her mother that had set everything right after her nightmares. Mom, she said to herself, you're still there, but you're no help now. Then she groaned aloud, "It's not just a bad dream anymore." That realization grew horribly then, and in her irrational despondency, her already failing stability left her entirely. She found herself tingling all over, and she broke out in a cold sweat.

Good God, she thought, it's already hell on earth, how could it be worse? As if on cue, all the reasons for her depression and anxiety, her guilt and shame, were laid out in front of her, no longer mere thoughts, but as in a ghastly abstract painting, overwhelming her. She realized then what she had to do.

She struggled to scribble a last letter to Bobby, expressing her love for him, and the revelation that she was pregnant with his child. She apologized for her earlier decision to go back to Wheelie because of his extensive injuries, but without explanation added that she now knew she couldn't continue. She begged his forgiveness for what she was about to do.

Even if she had cared, there was no need even to put on her robe, as the mailbox was just outside the door. After depositing the letter and putting up the flag, she went to the kitchen, filled her glass, and washed down the remaining capsules. Returning to bed, she was soon pleasantly sedated, and at one point even found herself smiling, feeling the warmth returning that had been absent since Bobby left. It was a form of twilight sleep, as her life slowly and dreamily slipped away. Her last impression, as oblivion overcame her, was one of Bobby leaning over her, enfolding her in soft angel-like wings. Wings of Love.

Denise's mother had been awake all that night, sleepless because of her own increasing anxiety over fears for her daughter. She became alarmed because she had not called as promised. Finally, well before dawn, she dressed and drove the few miles to her apartment. Sick with dread when she couldn't get an answer at the door, she aroused the landlady, who, all the while grumbling because of the early hour, opened the door for her.

Her heart in her throat, she rushed in. Switching on the lights, her worst fears were realized. There was Denise, in bed, cold and lifeless. Kneeling at the bedside, she looked down at her daughter's face, so peaceful in repose. Burying her face in the covers, she sobbed out her anguish, for her daughter, and for the only grandchild she would ever have.

* * * *

Bobby's sister, Phyllis, serving as a WAVE in the Navy, was home on leave at the time of Denise's suicide. She had heard the news from an old chum from Burbank High. The first thing she did after the funeral was to sit down and write Bobby.

At Denise's wake she had been given a packet of Bobby's letters by Mrs. O'Donnell, and naturally curious, couldn't resist reading them.

She had always idolized him, and ever emotional, she was quickly brought to tears. It was in that frame of mind that she was driven to put into words the way she felt. She had always liked Denise, but she adored Bobby, and knew the news would affect him as it did her.

She wanted badly to express her support for him, but then, after only a line or two, she dropped the pen in despair. How could she be the one to break the news? Tears staining her writing, she seized the sheet of paper and crumpled it up.

"Mom," she cried, "I just can't be the one to tell him."

Mrs. Taylor, who was in the next room, hurried to Phyllis's side to comfort her. Putting her arm around her, she said, "More bad news from the home front? He has enough to contend with in the fighting without another blow about her. It was bad enough when she went back to Wheelie. Don't you think that's enough to last him?"

"But mom, it isn't right that he learn of this reading the obituaries. Shouldn't it come from his family? He knows we love him, and want the best for him."

"Ordinarily, that would be ideal, but he doesn't need more distractions now. My advice to you and to your other brothers is not to mention it at all. If you love him, spare him more heartache."

And so, Phyllis wrote all her brothers that day. A benign newsy one to Bobby, and to the others, all away in the Service, letters pleading not to pass the word about Denise along.

SEVENTEEN

London

The late autumn flying conditions over Europe, while extremely cold, allowed Bobby and his crew to fly their ninth mission before the weather deteriorated in mid-November. The first and foremost factor remained the frigid conditions at the high altitudes where they flew, training for lead crew. From mid-November until late in December, they were checked out in the new Mickey-equipped planes. These were mostly brand new, unpainted craft that had only enough hours on them to have been ferried from the West Coast aircraft plants to Britain. After they were delivered to the base near Framlingham, they had been tuned to perfection, and functioned flawlessly. Bobby became conversant with the radar equipment, which was linked to the bombsight, and got to know the Mickey operator assigned to their crew. A second lieutenant, he had been specially trained in radar maintenance and use, and took the place of one of the waist gunners when they were not on the bomb run.

Daily practice flights were flown against mock targets. They sought out cloudy regions, impossible to avoid along the shores of the North Sea, practicing their radar bombing techniques. The training was intensive, involving the entire complement of each plane in the special process of being shaped for the lead.

As Bobby perfected his use of the Mickey on these flights, he derived a special pleasure in taking part in the sessions they all attended, held after each of the missions flown by lead crews in combat. He found that most of his frustrations about bombing blindly had also been experienced by those veterans. By the time they had become lead crews, their frustrations had been largely put to rest, if only by gaining confidence in learning the technique.

It was during that period that he received Denise's letter informing him of her going back to Wheelie. For weeks it was all he could do to concentrate on his work, sick at heart as he was over her decision. He had practically memorized her words about going back to him, but although its message was abundantly clear, he still couldn't believe the reality of it. After all they had meant to each other, hadn't her solemn and heart-felt promises meant anything?

He tried to put the heartache away while studying or on training flights, but his concentration was repeatedly broken by the thought of her name. There it was again, *Denise,* and the sick aching would hit him anew. His sleep, which had always been fitful during his previous period of combat, became even more so, punctuated by dreams, invariably of frustration and loss. He thought of taking his woes to the Chaplain, but discarded that idea at the thought of a priest giving advice to the lovelorn.

He did confide in Danny about his feelings, receiving sympathy, and the suggestion, "What you need, pal, is some social life. And I don't mean anything local. London has everything you could want."

At the end of November, just after Thanksgiving dinner at the Base, and upon completion of two weeks of training, they were given a three-day pass. Down in the dumps as he was, it was just the diversion that Bobby needed to help cheer him up. London was a great city, and despite the destruction by the *Luftwaffe* during the Blitz, it remained *the* destination.

They'd been there overnight only once on first arriving in England. Now the two had some time to enjoy it. They took the rickety little train, cynically referred to as the "Framlingham Flyer," which stopped at the little nearby village of Wickham Market on most days. They knew of the famous Red Cross canteens in London that offered all the amenities of home, but hell, they concurred, they hadn't been away long enough by that time to be really homesick. For them, the sights of the city were more important, as was a sampling of the nightlife.

London had been relieved of the scourge of the V-1 flying bombs, Allied forces having overrun their launching sites on the Continent. Nazi V-2 ballistic missiles were still creating destruction, however, bringing home to them scenes such as they had been creating in German cities. As the train rattled through the suburbs, he observed the signs of increasing devastation as they approached the city center.

Turning to Danny, he said, "This is what our bombs are doing when they stray from our intended industrial targets."

His companion, an old hand at dropping bombs, merely shook his head. Long before that he had become inured to such concerns.

While much of the debris had been cleared, with neat stacks of bricks attesting to the buildings that once stood there, in other districts the rubble was overgrown with weeds, obviously from the Blitz of 1940 and 1941. This brought back thoughts of his high school buddy, Tommy Hunter, who had died in Britain's defense during that time.

As the train pulled into Liverpool Station, they discussed their plans anew. They decided on seeing Buckingham

Palace, as well as visiting Hampton Court, Saint Paul's, and Parliament the next day. Each had his camera supplied with film for the touring. Danny favored staying at the Strand Palace, where they had spent their previous night in the city. That hotel, along with the Regent Palace in Piccadilly catered to American fliers.

"Come on, Danny," Bobby urged, "We've got cash saved up, let's splurge and stay at a really nice place, with a private bath, and still enjoy everything, the sights and the fun."

Taking only a little time to check his wallet, his buddy agreed.

After registering at the first rate Grosvenor, on Buckingham Palace Road, they visited a nearby pub where they had a meal of steak and kidney pie, washed down with some English stout, which by that time they had begun to appreciate.

Night was just falling when they entered the establishment, but on their exit, the blackness was shocking. This was often the case around the airfield, but here it was unexpected. After a little time needed for their eyes to accommodate, shadowy shapes could be defined, occasionally signaled by a glowing cigarette or tiny flashlight. Then too, there were the occasional taxicabs, with slit headlamps marking their presence, but only feebly lighting their way.

They had studied the neighborhood map thoroughly with the hotel concierge, and decided to check out Piccadilly. They hadn't gone a block in the near blackness, when Bobby became aware of the clicking of high heels and the scent of perfume, quickly followed by a cockney-accented woman's voice.

"I say, Yank, where ya headed?" Before he could answer, he felt her hand on his thigh. He had heard of the methods

London prostitutes employed to tell the type of serviceman they had latched onto in the dark. To them, looks meant little, and any officer, particularly a well-paid American one, was especially prized, as her price was set by ability to pay.

As soon as the texture of his dress *pinks* was sampled, she softly murmured in his ear, "Cor, Yank, come with me and we can do a little flying together, whatcha say?"

Bobby hadn't come to London for the streetwalkers. He was reminded of that anti-V.D. poster that the Army Air Force tacked up everywhere, with the message, *"She may look clean, but…"* The woman shown in that picture was a smashing brunette, and would have been tempting enough to lead almost any man astray regardless of the risk. But, he thought, not this or any other whore.

Danny, having received the same treatment, grabbed Bobby's arm, and pulled him off in the direction of the nearby Red Cross Canteen, the *Rainbow Corner,* muttering, "There'll be women there, and we'll be able to see them, besides."

As he said that, jeers came from the two disappointed prostitutes, who could only prepare for the next prospective customer.

On entering the busy canteen, a couple of hostesses came over to greet them, but Bobby was immediately distracted by a scene that was unfolding at a corner table nearby. As Danny obligingly took a woman on either arm, Bobby stood there looking, almost as if he had seen an apparition. There, a blond young woman was being rudely treated by a couple of drunken Eighth Air Force gunners.

Going up to the two airmen, glaring at them briefly, he faced the lady, and hearing the band just starting a ballad, enquired politely, "May I have this dance?"

Only too eager to be rescued from those two, she smiled, and was happily led out onto the dance floor. The two sergeants started to get up in pursuit, only to be blocked by Danny. Temporarily releasing the two hostesses, he stationed himself in the men's way, gravely shaking his head slowly at them, leaving them no recourse but to sit sullenly back down to their beers.

Once on the dance floor, Bobby's partner smilingly offered him her outstretched arms, and then looking up into his face, said, "Thanks for saving me from those two thugs. I didn't want to blow the whistle and disturb the entire club."

He looked at her apologetically, "Oh, they can't be that bad, just a couple of homesick nineteen year old kids. If you could see them sober, you'd probably mistake them for your younger brothers."

Glancing at the pair, she asked, "Nineteen, you say?" Then, looking him over, she added, "You're not much older, are you?"

Bobby chuckled, "You're wrong, but first, let's get to know each other better."

Her reply came softly as she nestled her face against his shoulder, "I'd like that."

The rest of the evening was spent doing just that, over a beer or two, with some more dancing. He learned that her name was Diana Howard. He had seen that she was educated and a cut above the few English girls with whom he had become acquainted, as her accent was at least that of the professional class, possibly even more refined.

She explained that she worked for the Air Ministry, and usually wore the uniform of the Royal Engineers, except on certain occasions. On their short acquaintance, she wouldn't divulge to him just what she did, or her rank. She told him that her father was involved in the war effort, but for the same reason, his work was not further discussed. She shared a flat near Hyde Park with a girlfriend, commuting to work from there via the Underground.

He asked how she happened to be at *Rainbow Corner*. "This is a haven for homesick Americans," he went on, "I would think you'd have better things to do than entertaining kids such as those two, in any event."

She smiled as she replied, "I've never been here before tonight. My duties keep me too busy to volunteer as a hostess anywhere, even in the canteens for our own boys. My father had just returned to London today, and I joined him for a late luncheon. Afterwards, I was on my way to the Underground for the return home, and was passing in this direction. Those two boys seemed lost when they very courteously asked for directions here. My mistake was to join them for a drink when we arrived. Perhaps I felt sorry for them, as they seemed so lonely. But evidently they were already well on their way. I thought they would behave in here, but I was wrong indeed." Then she gazed up at him with her dark green eyes, adding, "On the bright side, if I hadn't come in with them, we probably never would have met."

All this information was naturally interesting to him, but through it all, he still couldn't help marveling at how closely she resembled Denise, and did call her by that name once, as he offered her a cigarette.

She smiled a little at that. "You'll just have to get used to me, I'm Diana, you know."

"Sorry, my mistake," he replied apologetically, trying to cover his embarrassment with a laugh. "You remind me so much of someone I know. I'm sorry."

Feeling an understanding with her he had seldom experienced, he filled her in about Denise, and how, despite her marriage, they had still loved each other, and until recently had planned to marry after the war, once her divorce became final. He went on to explain that her last letter, received a couple of weeks before, however, had revealed her decision to return to her injured husband as a matter of duty to look after him.

"Certainly a different twist to the usual 'Dear John' letter," she commented.

Rainbow Corner was open around the clock, but when the band folded, and he asked to escort her home, she graciously demurred. Finally, after exchanging numbers, they agreed on a date for touring the highlights of the city the next day. She did accept his accompanying her to the steps of the Underground.

In the dim light of the entry, he attempted to kiss her, but his advance was deftly avoided, as she smilingly told him, "You must remember, Leftenant, that a worthwhile relationship is like a sound dwelling. It should be built slowly and solidly, brick by brick."

Where had he heard that defense, or something like it before, he wondered. But she laughed when he countered, "I don't think there's anything against demanding immediate surrender of a besieged castle." Then he added, "Sorry, but this war tends to speed up the process, however one looks at it. How much time do we have?"

Momentarily frowning, she reflected on the truth of what he had just said. The situation in wartime London had indeed relaxed most of the rules.

She replied, "I get your meaning. But we'll see each other tomorrow, isn't that soon enough?" Then, turning, she stepped briskly down the stairs, her long blond hair bouncing slightly.

Watching her go, he couldn't help calling out after her, "Not nearly."

Danny was already asleep, but for Bobby, that came with difficulty, his thoughts awhirl with a mixture of thoughts of Denise, and of the warm feelings he was developing for Diana. He recognized this as a rebound romance in the making, the result of his separation from Denise, and the desire he was now feeling with this new female. When sleep finally came, the two had, in his mind, merged into one lovely and desirable woman.

The two days that were left of the three-day pass turned out to be idyllic, but woefully short. They hit it off so well on that second day while on their tour of London, that she consented to go to dinner with him and dancing later.

As she showed him the highlights of London, she told him more about herself. Her mother was American, he learned, giving her an interest in the people from the "Colonies," as she dryly put it. It was her natural affection for Americans that had led her to direct those two lost gunners to *Rainbow Corner*, and to join them for a drink.

She explained that she had been married, but her husband, a bomber pilot in the RAF, had been missing in action since a night raid over Hamburg two years before. Nothing had been heard about his being a captive, and the RAF had officially declared him killed in action.

From her work, she knew the odds of a pilot escaping from a burning four engine Lancaster bomber was much less than even, and her intuition told her he had been killed. She explained that her job with the Air Ministry, as an officer in the Royal Engineers, entailed inspection and maintenance at airbases in East Anglia, including Framlingham, the home of the 390th.

That evening, they had supper at the hotel restaurant. As the music began, they were lured onto the dance-floor. The band was Australian, marooned for a time in London, and their leader played the sweetest alto sax that Bobby had ever heard. The pieces they played in that set, sentimental as they were, encouraged slow cheek-to-cheek dancing, much to his enjoyment. He felt as if he were in a dream, holding Denise at last in his arms. Even Diana's perfume reminded him of her. While attracting him even more, the scent made him a little jealous. He wondered how an English girl was able to obtain French perfume in a time of the greatest shortages.

Drawing her closer, he whispered, "I like your perfume."

As she looked up at him in that sexy way of hers, she said, "I figured that, but do I detect some concern as well?"

"Correct. Like chocolates and nylons, it must have been a gift from some appreciative guy."

"You're right about that, Leftenant, it was a gift from my father. But would it help you to hear that I've had it for some time, and have been saving it for a special occasion?"

During the break, they drank their Scotch, giving a warm comforting feeling as it went down, contrasting to the some-what cool temperature of the place. The candle in the center of the table lent a nice warm feeling also, he thought, as it illuminated her face exquisitely, leading him to recall how restaurants and bars worldwide sought that effect.

"God, I'm a lucky guy," he murmured. He hoped she was feeling the same way. At that, she looked at him with the most radiant smile he had seen in months.

The band's next set was made up of fast Swing. He led her onto the floor, and picking up the beat, they began to jitterbug, just like with Denise when he was last at home. Diana had learned the steps quickly, and they worked their way through the routines with a smoothness that made him all the more proud of her. He felt all eyes of the crowd on them, but although he was a bit of a show-off with his dancing, as with other things he did well, he began to think only about the two of them being alone.

After another drink, equally warming, and well before midnight, by a form of wordless acknowledgement, they headed back, hand in hand, to the lobby. At the desk, the clerk handed him a note from Danny, telling him he was visiting his wife's parents, and wouldn't be back that night.

"Let me call a taxi for you," he said, hoping she would reject that. He was still uncertain, despite the developing warmth between them, that it might yet be too soon. At that, she looked at him with a hint of amusement.

"Taxi? No," she answered with a sly smile, "but you can get me a lift." This was confusing to him, until she added, "I believe you Yanks call them elevators."

Happily, he encircled her waist with an arm, and guided her to the somewhat antiquated, ornate piece of equipment behind them.

After he closed the room's door, she turned to him with an inviting smile, kissed him passionately on the mouth, and then began to unbutton first his forest green blouse and then his shirt, pushing against him gently at the same time. He could hardly contain himself.

She whispered, "Excuse me a moment, I'll be right back."

Taking his blouse with her, she stepped into the bathroom, closing the door behind her. Anticipating what would come next, he sat down on his bed, beginning by taking off his shoes and tee shirt.

When she again opened the door, he felt almost faint at the sight. There she stood, wearing only the blouse, unbuttoned to the waist. He was entranced. With her flawless skin, she looked more beautiful than an angel to him. He couldn't help thinking of the white wings expected of an angel being replaced by wearing the silver ones of a bombardier. Wings of love and war. The picture was completed by the color of his blouse seeming to match that of her eyes, green and sparkling even in the subdued light.

Smilingly, she softly asked, "Well, what are you waiting for, Yank? Lend-Lease, or some other Anglo-American pact?" This jarred Bobby into motion, standing up and gathering her into his arms.

"Wait a moment." he whispered, "Those darn brass buttons."

She knew it was a pretext for opening the blouse fully, but said, "Right you are, they are indeed truly cold on the bare skin."

They didn't sleep until the wee hours of the morning, and when they did, it was not soundly because of their sharing the relatively narrow bed. He earlier had offered to get into the one on the other side of the room, but she would have none of it.

"Lord knows when we will be able to see each other again after tomorrow," she commented, adding, "I want us to be as close as possible." So they slept off and on, in each other's arms, between sessions of lovemaking, until well after noon.

* * * *

In the hotel restaurant, after a late English breakfast, they sat holding hands, lingering over tea.

"I love England," he said, and then added impetuously, "And I love you."

She looked at him warmly, responding, "That makes two of us, I'd say." Then adding with amusement, "But it's plain to see that you don't like everything about England. You didn't even touch your kippers."

Laughing, he replied, "That's probably the reason my branch of the Taylor family left here in 1636. But think of it, if they hadn't emigrated to Georgia, we probably would never have been thrown together here in London."

She found his logic obscure, and asked, "How does that hold? Seems to me there would have been, in fact, more chances to meet had your forbears remained here."

"Not likely," he replied, "You see, they were probably debtors or indentured servants, and with the class system here, we could, of course have met, but not socially, as we have now."

"In that you're correct in principle, but a bit off on the facts. My father is in an influential position now, yes. He was well on his way academically as a mathematician when he joined up at the beginning of the Great War in 1914. He was one of the rare rank and file that received a commission. And then it was for his work, in helping to break the enemy's naval code. That breakthrough aided in our Grand Fleet's victory over the Germans in the Battle of Jutland in 1916. Due to his brilliance, he rose rapidly, and we escaped the lower rungs of the class system, but only then.

"So you see, the Howard family was indeed a humble one the last few hundred years. And isn't it wonderful what a good education will do, bringing us together? When I first saw you, I thought we would be a good fit. My only reservation about us is that although you are obviously educated, you still appear too young for me."

He thought about the "Fit" part, but decided to discuss age instead. "Well, that runs in my whole family. We all seem years younger than we are. I may look nineteen like those gunners, but I'm twenty-four, certainly your senior by a couple."

"No," she replied, "We're the same age. The anniversary of my birth is the same as that of the King, George the Sixth. December 14. But then that's so late in the year, I suppose you'll be able to top that. You know the old saying, 'The first liar hasn't got a chance.'"

He saw a certain irony there, and chuckling, he told her, "Mine's July fourth. In the U.S. we call it Independence Day, celebrating when we colonists broke with another King George of yours, the Third."

"Odd how the Americans and English have come together after all that," she observed.

Bobby replied, "It's probably in part due to our common language, the fact that we both speak English. It does seem to bring people together, as in our case, don't you think?"

Looking at him with a twinkle in her eye, she couldn't help herself, responding, "It was Oscar Wilde who said we English have everything in common with America but our language. And from my own experience, I sometimes wonder whether, in fact, you Americans do indeed speak English!" Seeing his look of surprise, she quickly took his hand and added, "Present company excluded, of course."

It was with such small talk that they spent the afternoon until it was train time. He picked up his bag, and they walked to the station together. The day was gray and cold, but despite that and the ache he felt in their parting, he was warmed by her presence, and her promise that they would get together again at the earliest opportunity. As they kissed good-bye, he slipped her a package.

"Oh Bobby," she cried, "Nylons! How did you manage to get these? They are like gold these days."

"Well," he replied importantly, "It did take some doing, you know, pulling strings with the Quartermaster, an effort just short of bribery, using my influence."

"I'm even more impressed than ever, if that's possible. Many thanks. They will be put to good use, let me tell you." She beamed at him, kissing him again, "But I'll save them until we're together again."

They could hardly take their eyes off each other, until he had to board. He waved as the wheezing locomotive began to move the train, and she waved in return for some time, until the last car disappeared down the tracks.

* * * *

December found him once again busily training, thoughts of Diana occupying most of his spare time. He had neglected writing home, so a few days later, he wrote his mother.

Dec. 3, 1944

Dear Mamacita,

Have little time to write, hence these scrawls. Hope all is as well with you. I note today is Ted's birthday, and I hope you're celebrating it, altho not so much in his honor, but in your own, and for all the love and effort you've put into our family all these years.

Many thanks for all that, and also for the goodies you sent. About those nylons. The only thing that bothered me was when I first asked for them, just whom did I have in mind at the time—the scene so changes y'know. Along with the nylons, I now have a little girl who fawns on me, revering me as a source of the gems of Solomon. Of course, cad that I am, I gave her some long line about how I got them and didna tell her me wee mother was the one.

I'm still sick about Denise going back to Wheelie, and I don't think I'll ever get over that. It's so depressing. We had even made plans to marry when I get back, after she received a divorce from him. But she just didn't have the heart to send him a 'Dear John' letter, tho, especially while he was overseas. Maybe if she had, her coming out with the truth, good for the soul as confession is reputed to be, might have helped her free herself from him, before his injury trapped her.

The destruction from the Blitz is still in evidence, along with more recent damage from the Nazi 'Vengeance' weapons, buzz bombs and rockets. The former have now mostly been eliminated. Despite the bombed-out buildings, and all the casualties, the morale of the plucky British is higher than ever, and I like to think that our own efforts have played a role in that.

I'm enclosing a money order for you, to bank for me or to spend on yourself. It's much less than the usual remittance, but you have to understand, London is an expensive place.

Now, I must straggle off to mess, ere I go hungry tonight. Oh, would that I could have a nice home-cooked meal by you know whom. In the meantime, keep those cookies coming. I love those date-coconut jobs. But even without the goodies, Lotsa Love,

Bobby

EIGHTEEN

Daughter Christmas

Almost four weeks of December were spent in intensive training, with practice flights becoming more stressful, under the critical eye of the Squadron Commander accompanying them. As he occasionally did on combat missions as a command pilot, he would fly in the co-pilot's seat.

They sweated it out, but he particularly approved of Danny's flying skills, and he was complimentary of Bobby's work and that of Harold Lynch, the navigator.

They were told that their next mission would be as the Squadron lead, promising the same new Fort in which they were training. Members of the crew began to suggest possible names to christen their plane as was the custom. As it turned out, these new bright metal ships they would fly would remain identified only by their official serial numbers, because they had a different one on each of their missions in 1945.

He wrote this letter one night.

December 20, 1944

Dear Paddy:

Got your letter, little bro, and believe you me it was welcome. My mail call has been sadly deficient of late, what with Denise rejoining poor Wheelie. I know you're also away from home, and not in on the latest dope from

Burbank, but I'd give anything to know all the reasons behind that.

God, Paddy, I still miss her. I guess I'd be totally depressed, except for London. What a City. On a recent three-day pass I met a wonderful gal who really was attracted to me. We hit it off immediately, again that love at first sight thing, where you just know, with a look from her that mite be called amazement, and the indescribable warmth that follows.

I don't know if you've ever been in such a situation, given your tender age, but I did feel it first at eighteen, just the age you are now. Then it was with Denise. Now it's gotta be a rebound romance, but who cares? This is the here and the now, and we have a war on.

Regardless, it seems to have blossomed into something straight out of that quatrain from Khayyam about paradise, complete with everything but the wilderness. Needless to say we spent every precious minute we could together, however woefully short the time. Unlike my first six weeks of combat, after some ruff missions, I'm not now so eager to get back into action except that we have to pound those Jerries until they cry 'Kamerad!'

I guess I've gotten a bit off the track, with my own problems. Here's hoping you understand. How's it going there? The plan is Infantry Basic and then 'On-the-line-training,' waiting for pre-flight? Never heard of it. I can't imagine a shortage of facilities to start potential pilots off. Maybe they envision a diminished need for us flyboys this next year, unlike earlier in the war. Let us hope.

You asked about my having seen any of the Nazi jets or rocket planes. Not yet, and I hope I never do. There's enough to worry about with the flak and the 109s and 190s around. I'm reminded of that song the guys sing around here, that goes: "I wanted wings until I got those goddam things."

I know you're in the preliminaries of pilot training now, and can't wait to get on with it. But take it from an ol' hand. Jus' don't rush it, okay? To be hoped is that you'll heed the voice, or in this case, the pen, of an older brother's wisdom.

Thanks for writing. Good luck, and merry Christmas. And if you behave yourself, you have my love,

Bobby

* * * *

There was another three-day pass on Christmas Eve, and despite the lingering sick feeling over Denise returning to Wheelie, or more likely because of it, he headed immediately back to London, anticipating the wonderful way Diana enabled him to forget his cares. At the reception desk at the *Grosvenor*, the clerk handed him an envelope that held a message from her, awaiting his arrival.

Eagerly tearing it open, oblivious of the clerk's smirk, he quickly read it. It was an invitation to her flat for a holiday party that evening, beginning rather early, he thought, probably timed to afford some daylight remaining for finding the place, which was out past Hyde Park, to the west.

Checking in for that one night, showering and shaving, and then putting on his forest green tunic and pinks, he could hardly wait to see her again. The weather was cold, and he knew she would wear her new nylons. But he thought, would her skirt, in this wintry weather, be short enough to show off those great legs? He'd just have to wait, and resolved to act as expected of him. At least until they were alone.

He took the underground to the next station, Kensington, after picking up a scarce Bordeaux at a nearby bottle shop. Carrying it as a beribboned present, he then headed back a block to the address given him.

It was only four PM, but it was already twilight. He could see how one's mood could be affected by the short daylight in that part of the world in late December, even without his sadness about Denise.

As he rounded the corner, a cheery scene dispelled such thoughts. Her flat was decorated, instead of with colored lights, forbidden because of the continued blackout, with shiny red and green ribbons, still colorful, especially the green, enhanced in the increasing twilight. There were mistletoe strands and holly branches around the door, and from within, came the sound of music. He heard the lovely refrain of "Ave Maria," causing him to softly join in.

It was in this mood that he happily knocked on the door, which was soon opened by Diana, smiling radiantly, and surprisingly, wearing a long green robe and a matching conical cap. Bobby was thrilled by the combination of her beauty and the robe matching her green eyes. The garment itself, trimmed in white fur, was reminiscent of a Santa Claus coat, except for its color and length.

Handing her the bottle, he drew her to him, and tenderly planted a lingering kiss on her lips. His face turned red, as he suddenly realized the possibility of an audience. Hurriedly looking around the room, he saw the only other festive thing, the lighted Christmas tree, almost like home. And there was a delicious aroma of something wonderful cooking in the kitchen.

She smiled at his reaction, and putting her hand on the back of his neck, whispered into his ear, "Don't worry, we're alone. I asked you over early so that we would have some time to get to know each other even better before the other guests arrive. How do you like me as Father Christmas?"

He had to admit, "You do look great, but I'd much prefer to think of you as *Daughter* Christmas, if you don't mind. You must be wearing high heels, but do you have the nylons on under all that?"

Holding the Bordeaux protectively, and answering with a dazzling smile, she replied in a husky voice, "Shall we discuss that over a glass of this?"

He followed her into the little kitchen, where she handed him a corkscrew and brought over two glasses from a group of a dozen on the counter. After pouring the claret, they raised their glasses, toasting, "Cheers!" in unison. The wine went down smoothly.

Nodding appreciatively, she whispered, "Now what was that about the nylons?"

Sipping from the glass, unable to take his eyes off her, he softly replied, "Do you have them on? You know, I got them especially for you, to keep those legs warm this winter."

"Is that all? Nothing more?"

"Well, yeah," Bobby replied, "Your legs are so sexy, they do things to me that make me forget this war."

Setting down her glass, and leading him back into the living room by the fire, she said, "That's what I thought, so I did put them on for the first time tonight, and just for you." With that, she took off her cap, allowing her long hair to cascade over her shoulders, and opened the robe a little.

She did have the nylons on, fastened at the upper thighs with a filmy garter belt and panties. My God, he thought, could anything be more beautiful? His gaze traveled up past her revealing sheer vest-like blouse to her slim neck, and just above, to where her lips were curled in an inviting smile.

"Here? Now?" He stammered, smitten by the sight, but still concerned with their being alone.

"Don't worry Bobby, the Christmas party won't start for another two hours. Remember why I wanted to be alone with you before hand? Come on," she murmured, leading him into the bedroom. "You must by now think I'm a terrible exhibitionist."

Over the next hour, she made him forget his fears and worries. He hoped the guests would never arrive, and said so.

"Silly," she said, "Of course, the best things can't last, but this is only the beginning of our Holiday celebration. Now come on, we had best wash up, dress and put out the food and drink. My housemate is visiting her family in Surrey, and won't be back for a couple of days. We'll have the place to ourselves until after Boxing Day, if you like."

The evening's celebration was fun, and the people who came were extremely friendly, all appreciative of his coming so far to help defeat the Nazis. The loving glances the two gave each other were not missed by her guests, and the warmth was palpable, especially after drinks and generous portions of cheeses and brandy-laced pastries. Bobby could see their love for Diana. Taken with the scene, he mused, if this is what an English Christmas is like, why did the Taylors ever leave?

The supper's main course was roast goose, fat enough as it was, made fatter yet, covered with bacon. The goose was served with the usual Brussels sprouts and new potatoes. Bobby had never liked the sprouts the way his mother cooked them, merely boiled, but these, sliced and grilled, were exceptional. All this was served with more red wine. Dessert was a Christmas "pudding" reminiscent of American fruit cake, liberally soaked with brandy, and topped with something like that sweet white confection, known at home as *hard sauce*. The fare was hearty and very tasty, a far cry from the usual military cooking, and was much enhanced by the wine. Had he not been paying so much attention to Diana, he would have been concerned about the congealing fat around the goose on the platter, with its promise of indigestion. Definitely not his mother's cooking.

The talk was lively, at first avoiding reference to the war, partly perhaps, because of Bobby's presence. But it finally came out that there was a great deal of concern over the surprising German counter-offensive in the Ardennes Forest in Belgium, which had been launched just two days before.

Diana offered, "We depend so much on airpower to defeat the Nazis, it's no wonder they've found success this time of year, with the weather so inclement." All eyes then turned expectantly to the airman among them.

Wary of saying too much, Bobby observed, "Diana's right, I'm afraid we'll have to wait for clear skies. Even with radar, it's impossible to distinguish between a Tiger tank and a farm tractor. But they'll get their come-uppance very soon, for sure. This fog can't last forever."

One of the men, a cousin who worked with Diana in the Air Ministry, nodded in agreement. "I hear," he said, "That they can't get far because of shortage of fuel. You Yank bomber boys have seen to that with your daylight attacks, knocking out their synthetic fuel facilities."

Not wanting to expand on the topic, Bobby merely nodded his agreement, changing the subject to the fighting in the Low Countries.

"It's great that your troops have overrun the launching sites for the V-I and some V-2 weapons. For you Londoners, the relative peace and quiet must be deafening."

He got a laugh from that, both for the humor, and his reference to the British contribution, which, since D-Day in June of that year, had been partially pushed out of the headlines. The press had been playing up the American effort, particularly by the Third Army, under the fiery General Patton, leading the breakthrough across France.

Diana looked at him proudly, and squeezed his hand. Toasts were made to victory, and then, at Diana's insistence, to Father Christmas.

As all raised their glasses, Bobby said, looking at Diana in the green robe, "I still prefer *Daughter* Christmas."

The celebration went on until midnight, when the wine and the brandy-laced pudding had been almost exhausted. After the farewells, Bobby helped Diana with the dishes, learning the niceties of the on-demand hot water heater, which required the deposit of a coin to turn on the gas, just enough to heat a couple of gallons.

"What does one do if there are no more coins to put in the slot?" Bobby enquired.

Diana answered, "Oh, we just knock up the landlady upstairs, who gives us more change quite happily. You see, the gas costs her only half what we put in."

"What happens if she's away when hot water is needed?"

"Why," she replied, "heat isn't essential, it's a luxury these days. You just run it cold, or if you've a fire on, a pot of water is put on. You've heard of cold-water flats, haven't you? Most London dwellings are like that, you know. This one is relatively luxurious, but not only because of the kitchen water heater. There's one in the bathroom also."

"So I noticed," he said, "But I can think of better ways to get warm on a wintry night than that."

Going to bed, theoretically an avenue for further love making, was at that point merely an opportunity to sleepily snuggle together, deriving not only warmth, but also contented feelings, soon leading to their being overcome by sleep.

Christmas Day dawned gray and cold, quite usual for that time of year, but it seemed a balmy and bright morning to him, awakening with her in his arms. They made love then, afterwards lingering in bed enjoying their closeness. She was beautiful, with that flawless English complexion. And her face seemed to light the room, as he gazed at her smile.

"Your skin is so lovely," he said, "I've never seen anything like it."

She turned to him then, smiling. "You must not have seen very many English girls, then. That's the first thing one notices. It's because of the climate, which except for our summer, is mostly cool and cloudy."

"I'm not just talking about faces here," he replied, drawing the bedclothes down, exposing her shoulders and breasts, kissing her there. "I mean all over. Mostly, regardless of the weather, aside from your face, you're almost never exposed to the elements. Your skin everywhere is flawless, and I love it."

Reflexively, while responding to his kiss, feigning modesty, she covered herself with the sheet, and pulled up the quilt.

"Stop that!" She exclaimed laughingly, "I'll freeze if you keep that up. All this cold, and then the thrill your kisses create. I have an idea. I'll get the fireplace going and you draw hot water for a bath. And together, we can discuss skin all you want."

It took ten minutes to fill that big British tub, with all the coin he had to feed the hot water heater. By that time the flat at least wasn't cold, and the tub, easily holding the two of them, almost full of hot water, more than made up for the air temperature. The water was only part of the warmth as they embraced each other. They lazed in the hot water for an hour, occasionally inserting a coin from those she had lined up on the rim of the tub, to maintain the temperature. There were caresses, and more kisses punctuating their discussion about the rest of his three-day pass.

"After breakfast," she said, "We just have to go to church, of course, and then to luncheon. There are some good restaurants within walking distance. After that, we can come back here and enjoy a nice bottle of Port in front of the fire. And there will be leftovers again from last night for supper if we get hungry."

Bobby looked at her, her skin glistening in the water. Taking her face in his hands, he kissed her tenderly. Then he whispered, "The way you make me feel, food is the last thing I think about."

They rinsed each other, and dried off quickly, seeking refuge once again in bed, but not to rest. As they lay in bed together afterwards, she heard his stomach rumbling.

"You say food is unimportant, but your stomach tells me otherwise," she said, and with that, she threw off the covers, turning onto her side, exposing her slim waist and curvaceous hips, rolling away from him, out of bed in a most fluid and poetic motion.

"God," he exclaimed, "If I could capture that picture on film or canvas. It would rival all the nudes ever painted. A more beautiful *'Naked Maja,'* than Goya's, but seen from the other side of the model's couch, and with all the smoothness of a dance."

"Thank you, kind sir," she smiled back over her shoulder, "I did learn some Ballet in school, but always to music, and never while horizontal."

After a filling breakfast of warmed up goose and potatoes, followed by hot tea, they sat smilingly looking at each other. All he wanted was to spend the day with her in the flat, but she had other ideas.

"It's Christmas," she finally said, just before the clock struck eleven. "And we must go to church to observe the occasion."

He recalled attending midnight Mass at home, early on Christmas Day, which finally was abandoned, in his Parish, at least, because there were so many drunken worshippers.

When he mentioned that to her, she replied, "Indeed, it's the same here, except that rather than being inebriated, almost everyone will be hung over. Most churches here don't, in fact, hold midnight services, thereby giving everyone more time to drink on Christmas Eve."

After dressing, and putting on his camel's hair overcoat, he helped her with her knee-length greatcoat, of thick gray woolen fabric, trimmed in soft black mouton on collar and cuffs. Bundling up like that disguised her slimness to a degree. A regal element was added by the matching hat, eminently practical, but giving her the appearance of a Czarist princess. He had watched as she put on her precious nylons, and marveled at how much feminine beauty could be concealed by even the most becoming clothing. Except for her face, the only other exposure was of her knees, emerging from her coat just above the tops of her boots as she walked.

It was good they had dressed so warmly, as the north wind was penetrating. The gray overcast was breaking, but with it the mercury was dropping. He couldn't help but think that clear weather returning would mean an early return to action. He thought of the GIs on the ground, fighting the *Wermacht* in the Ardennes, where they had barely contained the German offensive. Now, with the approach of flying weather again, air support would soon spell the difference.

Diana looked at him quizzically, correctly interpreting his silence. "I'll wager that your thoughts are about finishing your training as lead crew and getting back into action."

He had always been amazed at how women could almost read his mind, saying, "What is it about me? Is it my face you can read, or is it my very thoughts? Whatever it is, it's a gift, for sure. Maybe you inherited that from your dad, with his talent for code-breaking in 1916."

"No, love," she replied, squeezing his hand. "I got that from my American mother. I think I learned from her how to read open Yank faces. And you know, Bobby, yours is one of those, and to me, a most lovable one, as well."

He wanted to take her in his arms then, but their arrival at the church squelched that. Entering, they found the interior much warmer, but not nearly enough to remove their coats. They could still see the condensation of their breaths, but at the same time, the bright lights of the many candles coupled with the singing and the incense made it seem much warmer.

Still holding his hand, she led him to a nearby pew. Picking up a pair of hymnals there, she handed one to him, having quickly found the place. They were in the midst of "Amazing Grace," which he thought unusual, as he had never heard it sung during a Catholic Mass. And while it was an old English hymn, he had expected something more from the Church of England.

But then, he thought, enchanted as he had been earlier, they do have an angel here, as he listened to her lovely soprano voice rising flawlessly in the cool air.

After the service, and her obligatory acknowledgement to the Vicar, they braved the cold once more. Deciding against the more distant restaurants, they found refuge in a nearby pub. There was a roaring blaze in the fireplace, fed by logs, which, as it turned out, were from a dead tree that the wind had downed just the previous night.

"Otherwise," the serving woman remarked, "We'd have to do with just our meager ration of coal, and a pitiable fire that would be."

They decided on that staple of pub fare, fish and chips, accompanied by a pint of stout for each. As they awaited the food, they toasted each other with their beer, finding the room temperature of the brew quite pleasing.

"Icy drinks would not do, now would they?" She offered, to Bobby's agreement.

Three young British enlisted men and a woman, all four in RAF uniforms, were drinking beer in one corner of the room, and singing that ribald song, "Roll Me Over in the Clover," through multiple verses.

Bobby leaned over to Diana, and remarked, "I only know the words to twelve of the verses, but they must have gone well beyond that number, although for the life of me, with their accents, I can't make out much of the words from here."

Diana replied, "Oh, there are many more verses than twelve. Someone once told me there are almost a hundred."

"My God," he said, "That must be where the term 'Sexual Athlete' comes from."

"More like sexual imagination, if you ask me," she laughed.

Their hearty fare came then, and both found their appetites. Somehow there was nothing that could rival that kind of pub meal on such an afternoon. He'd had fish and chips before, too often in batter that when fried became almost impenetrable, in combination with the fish, otherwise a great Icelandic cod, cooked to shrunken dryness. The offering there was done perfectly, and was enjoyed by both, as they capped the meal with a shared third beer.

As they sat enjoying each other's company, the tipsy female of the quartet of singers stopped by the table. Eying Bobby with interest, she observed, "We're all grateful to you Yanks coming here to help fight the Nazis, but it is sad, that unlike the rest of us, your fancy lady here chooses to avoid government service." Then, looking at Diana, she added pointedly, "Universal service is now the rule for patriotic women of our age, you know."

Before Bobby could react, Diana replied firmly, "Corporal, it's Christmas, and in the spirit of the season, as the holiday carol goes, one should wish not only for peace on Earth, but good will to men. And that includes women, you understand. If I choose not to wear my uniform when off duty, it is my business alone, and fully permitted for commissioned female officers. Now, you'd best rejoin your friends and be a good girl. And let me give you a bit of advice, corporal. You've already had too much to drink. Keep it up and all three of them will be rolling you over in the clover, and that type of ground cover is freezing right now."

Diana was upset, despite her objective manner and restrained humor in dealing with the drunken woman. She leaned closer to Bobby, and in a confidential tone, said, "I run into that a lot. If a woman of my age is in civilian clothes, the assumption is that she is someone who has avoided the military, and is out for what she can get from men on leave. My God, do I look like a good-time girl?"

He quickly and earnestly reassured her on that score, replying, "Hardly. You look so elegant, that the only woman you would likely be confused with might be one of the Royal Princesses. And let me add, you're a hell of a lot lovelier than any of them."

They lingered by the fire a little longer after he paid the tab, taking in more heat to armor them against the wintry afternoon. When they finally emerged, she cried, "This cold is just too much," barely heard over the sound of the wind. "It's back to the flat, right? I know you didn't want to leave there in the first place."

"It really has been a wonderful afternoon," he replied, "But I'm all for that too."

As they walked along, each with a gloved hand in the other's coat pocket for added warmth, they sang Christmas Carols and other songs. Somehow it seemed to help with the chill. When they got to "Ave Maria," he could only marvel again at her beautiful voice, which caused passers-by to stop and listen, and then, for those going in their direction, to follow. Because of that, a moderate-sized troop of carolers soon formed. The men couldn't take their eyes off Diana, except to glance at Bobby in apparent envy. He wondered how he came to be so lucky. His winning such a woman was a continuing source of joy.

When they reached her flat, they serenaded her landlady upstairs, who finally came to the bay window in front to listen appreciatively. But it wasn't long before the cold became too much to stand outside, causing the crowd to dwindle. Finally, after leading the singing of "God Rest You Merry Gentlemen," they waved to those remaining, and entered the front door, followed by a chorus of good wishes.

The flames over the coals in the fireplace had died down, but the residual warmth was comforting when they removed their overcoats. She quickly re-established the fire from the glowing embers, using bellows and a couple more lumps of coal.

"Remember the Port? Whilst you open it, I'll freshen up. The glasses are in the pantry with the bottle. The last time I had some of the same vintage, it was mellow, and had a lovely warmth as it went down."

Opening the bottle, coincidently a *Taylor* twenty-year-old Tawny, he carefully poured some of the golden brown liquid into the glasses, avoiding the sediment. Along with the bottle, he then placed everything on the hearth, away from the heat, along with a large *Hershey* bar that he had recently received from home. The semi-sweet chocolate, something she hadn't tasted for a long while, he thought, would go well with the sweet wine.

When Diana returned, she had her hair down, and her face was more than a little flushed.

"Are you okay?" He asked. "Your cheeks are so pink."

Going back to the mirror, she called back, "Oh, that's just the glow one gets with the rapid change in temperature.

I'll wager that being from California, you never experienced that. Here in Britain, the apple cheeks of the lasses, as with the roses of our English summer, are mainly due to the climate. Maybe you haven't noticed, but a lady's legs are often mottled red on the outside of one thigh and on the inside of the opposite calf. That's due to sitting with one's legs crossed, with that side toward the fire too long. We come in from the cold, but forget to turn the other way. We call it 'Half Warm.' Rare is the apartment or office that has central heat, where you're warmed on both sides at once. Cheery as they are, the English fireplace is to blame, with most of the heat going up the chimney, and what gets into the room due mostly to direct radiation."

Bobby drew her down onto the rug in front of the hearth, playfully requesting seeing her legs, lying a little with, "The only legs I've found really worth noticing are yours. Let's have a look, maybe they're pink like your cheeks are now." She sat up on the rug, beside him, stretching out her legs together in front of her.

"Well, take a look. You seem to have become quite the leg man," she said, drawing up her skirt. Encouraged, he reached down to unfasten the hose from her garter belt.

"Hey, Yank, not so fast," she exclaimed, parrying his hands expertly. "I'm counting on that Port and some conversation first."

Sheepishly, he smiled up at her, apologetically replying, "Just trying to check out your theory of half warm legs. Can't do that with those nylons on, you know."

"Oh, I see," she responded, as she leaned forward to kiss him, "All scientific and clinical now are we?"

They toasted each other with the usual "Cheers," and then began to sip the wine. "Mmm," she murmured, "Jolly good." He had to agree, and the welcome warmth it traced as it went down lived up to expectations.

"Have I got a surprise for you." Bobby then said, as he reached for the chocolate bar, passing it under her nose invitingly. "I'll bet you haven't had any of this lately. My mom sent it, but I've saved it for us. Don't you think it will go well with the Port?"

She snatched it from his hand, laughingly saying, "You really do know the way to a girl's heart. Wasn't it an American who wrote, in the same context, that candy is dandy?"

"Yeah," he replied, as he held his glass to hers, "But as with so many other sayings, that's not all. The rest of it refers to liquor being quicker."

Diana laughed at that, and then said in that husky voice, "Well, now we've got both."

After savoring the nice combination of the chocolate and the wine, they happily lay back on the rug together. He drew her close, and started unbuttoning her blouse.

"Wait." She whispered, kissing him again. "Remember that conversation of which I spoke? What better time than now, all warmed inside and out."

He hid his disappointment, deciding he could wait. She must have something important to talk about, he thought. Sitting up, and looking at her earnestly, he said, "Okay, shoot."

"I know we've known each other for only a month, but in that short time we have become very close." Smiling warmly at him, she continued, "We get along marvelously in every way, wouldn't you agree?" Not waiting for his reply, she mentioned the war, and the uncertainties awaiting them. "For me, it was love at first sight, as perhaps it was with you as well. This means to me that we must be together, now and later, whatever happens."

He thought that over carefully, pouring more wine for each of them, and taking a swallow. She watched him expectantly as he replied. "I see. Since we first met, God knows I've done all I can to see you here in London. For me, being with you has become the most important thing in my life, although at first I thought it was just a rebound thing. Are you thinking of an engagement? My answer would be an unqualified 'yes,' but I think marriage should wait until I complete my thirtieth, or if they up the magic number again, my thirty-fifth mission."

With that he took her into his arms, and held her, his lips brushing her forehead, saying softly, "I'm not the love 'em and leave 'em type. Until now, it's been quite the opposite. I love 'em and they leave me. After this war, I hope we can be together always."

They lingered in that embrace for a time, and then she said, "I'm thrilled to hear you say that, and the 'always' part of it sounds fabulous to me. This does call for one more step before the ring, however. You must first meet my parents. It's the proper thing to do, don't you agree? It just wouldn't do to exclude them."

He thought for several moments. "No," he said, concerned about how he would be received by her upper-crust family. "But I'm worried about our religious differences. You know I'm not really a Catholic, but how will they take it? I've been through that too much already. And I'm not about to join another church."

"Well, you did meet two of my cousins just last night, and they seemed to approve totally of you. That wasn't so hard was it?"

He had to admit to her, recalling all the merriment, "Yeah, that was easy, but I would expect your dad to be wary of any guy seeking the hand of his daughter. Fathers are that way. Beyond that, I don't know if I could stand disapproval on the basis of religion, either."

"It won't be all that bad," she replied, "Father, in fact, is indeed a regular chap. He came up through the ranks, you recall, and mother, well, she will love you, I just know. Neither of them is very religious in any event. You'll see. I'm usually right about this sort of thing."

"Then it's a deal," he said, thinking that if he could survive those missions over Germany, he could survive anything, even the scrutiny of a parental introduction. Raising his glass to hers, he whispered, "To us."

Boxing day, the 26th, was new to Bobby, something that wasn't carried over from pre-revolutionary war times, at least in the U.S., anyway. Diana explained the tradition to him.

"It started with giving gifts to the poor, later becoming an occasion to unload un-needed things, and then it evolved as a time for tipping the various menials who collected the trash, or ashes, or delivered the coal. More recently, it has become a day to pay visits to friends and family elsewhere."

As it happened, while in the process of helping clean up the flat, Bobby was accosted by a pair of scruffy-looking men as he emptied things into the trash barrel outside, under the front stairs. One thrust out his hand, obviously for a handout, but asking for it in what was, for him, an unintelligible tongue. It was a guttural speech he had never heard. His best guess was that it was Welsh. He knew it wasn't Gaelic, at least from the little he had learned from his mother, mostly swear words she had learned from hers. As he had no coin on him, he finally was able to direct them, mostly by sign language, up the steps to the Landlady. Let her take care of it, he thought.

On re-entering the flat, he recounted the experience to Diana, who laughed. "Now you know why people use Boxing Day to get away. Problem is, we didn't leave soon enough. Those were just the first, the dustmen, I believe, from your description. We still have several delivery people, and some of those actually expect to be entertained."

"Well, that does it. What are we waiting for?" Bobby asked, and then in feigned alarm urged, "Get your things quickly!"

The noontime temperature had risen to above freezing by that time, and with their winter clothing, the walk to the Underground was actually warming. The smooth transport took little time for the train to emerge into the daylight, and travel the few miles to the station that she indicated.

"It's only a short distance to the house, just across the park, there" she said, as he helped her down from their coach.

As they walked along, his mood seemed to match their surroundings. The park was barren, the many trees twisted, leafless grotesques, clawing at the gray skies, as if to match his anxiety about the meeting.

"Come on now," Diana chided, "Stiff upper lip! This is not a dangerous mission. You've overcome the most frightening part already."

"What's that? He asked.

"Why, your proposal, of course," she replied.

"My proposal?" He asked quizzically, "but you—."

She interjected quickly, "It's the gentleman who always proposes, don't you know? I thought Yanks in your position were not only officers, but gentlemen as well."

"Mea culpa," he replied, giving her hand a gentle squeeze, "How could I have forgotten?"

"There it is." Diana observed, smiling at his amazement. He was looking at the imposing Georgian mansion, presiding over a grove of evergreens. It was surrounded by a tall, ornate wrought iron fence enclosing the wide lawn, just across from the broad avenue at the edge of the park. It was far larger, and more stately by far than the mansion where he had lived in Chicago. He couldn't help being impressed, but would have been almost cowed by this emblem of wealth and power were it not for that year with his wealthy relatives.

As Diana looked for Bobby's reaction, she understood his thoughts, which were written in the play of emotion on his face. In reassurance, she squeezed his hand, and said, "Come along, you'll love them."

It took a while for the massive door to open after she rang the bell. It was the butler, a tall but frail looking man in his late fifties.

"Good day, Hughes," Diana said warmly as the man smilingly bowed. "I believe my parents are expecting us, am I right?"

"Indeed you are, Miss Diana. You will find your father in the library. May I take your coat and hat?"

Nodding affirmatively as he helped her out of her coat, she said, "This is my fiancé, Leftenant Taylor, who pronounces it 'Lieutenant.'"

The butler nodded. "How do you do, sir?" Then, smiling, he added, "Lieutenant, you must forgive us. We English make a game of butchering foreign names, and if we don't change the spelling, we pronounce them so that even the natives don't know what we're talking about."

Bobby took an immediate liking to Hughes, and by association, knew he would feel the same about Diana's father. He wasn't worried about Mrs. Howard. He had always gotten along well with the mothers. For the first time, he was actually looking forward to meeting them both. His only concern was that he had come empty-handed, confiding that to Diana.

"Don't worry, love," she replied, nudging him gently, "They'll be so busy being nice to you, they won't even notice. Besides, speaking of presents, you're bringing me."

Just then, the butler, opening the door to the library, announced, "Your daughter has arrived, Sir Robert."

They were escorted into the spacious room, which had a huge fireplace, large enough for more than one to actually sit in it. Opposite, across the lofty arched ceiling, the high wall was solid with books. A ladder on a trolley furnished access to the topmost shelves, where a middle-aged man, with a shock of white hair, appeared to be just replacing a volume.

Peering down over half-glasses, he smiled broadly, and in that polished accent of Mayfair, called down, "I say, Diana, there you are! Your mother and I didn't expect you so soon. Do make yourself and your Leftenant comfortable, while I finish up here. Have Hughes bring in the Sherry, and then call your mother. We shall sit in front of the fire, of course."

They remained standing until Sir Robert clambered down, with another book in hand. Putting it down on an end table, he embraced his daughter warmly, kissing her on both cheeks, and then expectantly turned to Bobby.

Extending his hand, he said, "It's indeed a great pleasure to finally have a chance to meet you, my boy. Diana has spoken so much about you at our weekly luncheons, that in fact I feel as if we already were old friends."

Bobby returned his firm handshake, and replied, "The pleasure is mine, sir. I'm afraid, however, that your daughter would not be a great publicist. She told me only that you had been honored for your work in the Great War, omitting that you had been knighted."

"Well," came the reply, "That was a long time ago, and the Empire stumbles along, in the process bestowing honors often due to the halo effect."

"Father!" Diana exclaimed, "We all know that with you such has certainly not been the case. No false modesty now, do you hear?"

Just then Lady Howard made her appearance, and to Bobby's surprise, she seemed almost identical to her daughter at first glance. They had the same beaming smile and graceful bearing. As he approached her for the introduction, he saw the expected thinner woman, still lovely, but with certain facial lines appropriate to her middle years, and the mandatory much shorter silvery hair. She kissed Diana, and, without waiting for the formal introduction, she turned to Bobby, stretching up on tiptoes, giving him an affectionate hug and a kiss on the cheek.

"So this is your dashing young flyer," she said, turning to Diana. "I like him already. He reminds me of when I was your age, before I left America as a volunteer in the last war." She turned to her husband and exclaimed, "Don't you think they look wonderful together, dear?"

Bobby silently exhaled in relief, as Diana took him by the arm, escorting him to one of the great chairs that had been arranged in a semi-circle in front of the fire. He was a little embarrassed when she ignored the one next to his, and squeezed in beside him. A sidelong glance at her parents told him he needn't have worried. They seemed to be enjoying it all.

The conversation over the Sherry was animated, covering the war, Bobby's plans for peacetime, and his British heritage. The topic of Religion didn't come up. The older pair exchanged loving glances from time to time, reflecting their obvious approval of the match with their daughter. Lady Howard apologized for the substitution of Sherry for the traditional tea. Both men obviously approved of the idea, and Bobby assented to a refill at Diana's father's suggestion.

Sir Robert observed, looking into the amber liquid, "You saw me exchanging books when you came in. It might interest you to know that I've become a great Winston Churchill fan, and have contrived to amass quite a collection of his works. I plan to read The *Island Race* next. The man is indeed a prolific writer and orator. And did you know that his mother was American, and a Catholic?"

Bobby and Diana exchanged smiling glances then.

Her mother added, "That is just what I've been trying to tell your father, Diana. Behind great British men you will often find a great American woman."

Her father seemed a little uncomfortable with that, and said, "Ignore the first 'Great' in that statement, you two. You know Diana, hyperbole is your mother's middle name, and here you have an example of it."

"Hyperbole is it?" His wife retorted, acknowledging the young couple with a smile. "Why do you think you were knighted and later elevated to such a high position? I'm saying it was because of your brilliance in mathematics and ciphers, just as Winnie's political acumen, imagination and gifts in the use of the English language got him where he is today. And remember, I was behind you all the way," adding slyly, "All the way to Bletchley Park."

Diana and her father exchanged distressed glances at that name which temporarily killed the conversation. Bobby was puzzled, and sitting close to him, Diana sensed his concern, giving him a reassuring squeeze of the hand. What was Bletchley Park? It must be classified, he decided, but was afraid to ask. It had to be, with the sudden freeze at the mention of the name. He knew that Diana's father had earned his commission with code breaking during the First World War. Could he still be at it?

Whispering to Diana, he asked, "Is it about code breaking?" Diana was surprised at his question, but nodded.

"Father," she said, Bobby here thinks your work now is the same as it was in the Great War. Won't you fill him in a little on some of the details so we can get on with our visit?"

Sir Robert turned to Bobby, fixing him with his cool blue eyes. "You understand, Leftenant, that what I tell you cannot leave this room. As you now have deduced, Bletchley Park is in fact the center of British code-breaking efforts, producing most of the breakthroughs in deciphering German messages. I shan't tell you how we do it, but in the Mediterranean Theatre, it was so successful, that oftentimes, British commanders there could not act on the intelligence, lest the Nazis' suspicions be aroused. I believe my American counterparts have achieved something comparable in the Pacific, with the Japanese *Purple Code*. Mind you, this is all top secret. I know I can trust you to keep it under your hat."

"Yes, sir." Bobby replied, "I know all about security in these matters. But I'm surprised the enemy hasn't stumbled onto the truth, as they seem to know so much about what's going on in the Eighth Air Force, anyway, especially at our airbases in East Anglia. We hear the most surprising insights from that propagandist, Lord Haw-Haw, over Radio Berlin. I'll bet by now they even know my shoe size."

He got a smile out of Sir Robert then, with the observation, "Quite so. They do excel at details, but their fatal flaw is arrogance. They think their codes are too superior to be broken. So they continue to communicate, without the precaution of changing their ciphers frequently enough. They should know that there has never been, and never will be, an unbreakable code."

Changing the subject, Diana turned to her parents. "Listen you two, I've the most marvelous news. The Leftenant and I have become engaged. We've known each other for over a month now, and haven't the slightest reservation. He still has a number of missions left to fly, so we'll probably delay marriage until those are finished." Snuggling up to him, she asked, "Do I have that right, darling?"

Bobby looked into her eyes, and through a broad smile said simply, "Amen."

Lady Howard got up and put her arms around them, saying, "You certainly have our blessings." She smiled warmly at Bobby, adding, "Anyone who can make our Diana happy must be an exceptional person."

Sir Robert arose from his chair to join them. Obviously approving, he quipped, "Of course this will upset the current British-American ratio in the family, forcing the vote into a tiebreaker. We'll need Hughes more than ever." With that, overcoming any remaining English reserve, they all joined in a group hug of celebration.

The impromptu rejoicing was interrupted by the butler's announcement that dinner was served. Diana's mother took Bobby's arm, escorting him into the spacious dining room, indicating that he was to sit next to her,

As he pushed in her chair, she looked up at him, remarking, "You will be the perfect son-in-law. That's something one rarely gets from one's husband," indicating across to where Sir Robert was doing the same for Diana.

"I learned this sort of thing at finishing school," Bobby said playfully, "While at the University of Chicago."

"Chicago!" Lady Howard exclaimed, "The heart of America. You must know that I'm from Milwaukee. Went to Northwestern before the Great War. When the call from Canada for volunteers went out, I left immediately for Toronto. All my male friends were joining up, and I couldn't see myself just rolling bandages at home for the duration. So I joined an ambulance company, which shipped over here. We never got to France, missing the great battles there, but that led to meeting Diana's father."

Sir Robert smiled across the table at his wife then. "We hit it off immediately, partially due to my wounds not being critical. I was young then, about the age of the two of you, and, well, it was spring, with all those things that take a young man's fancy. I was wary of foreigners for some reason then, but she seemed suitably English to me."

Pausing to take a sip of wine, he continued, "I was let down in stages, first when I learned that the volunteers were a Canadian unit. Still not so alien, you see, and while not U.K., from one of our most loyal Dominions. By the time I learned she was really a Yank, my initial bias was no more."

Winking at Bobby, he said, "But my parents had to be convinced, despite my pointing out that Randolph Churchill,

Winnie's father, had married an American woman. At the time, you see, the Churchill name was not as popular as it is now. Still, for my parents, when they met her, it was love at first sight. There seems to be something about you Americans for us Britons, more than just gratitude for people like Sylvia here and you, Leftenant, who came over to help in wars when we sorely needed you."

As Bobby nodded acknowledgement of Sir Robert's gesture, Diana commented, "That brings out an amazing parallel here, don't you think? History almost repeating itself."

Lady Howard, basking in the story of their courtship, observed, "Even in the absence of such heroics, this Anglo-American affinity happens under other circumstances, most famously in the case of Edward the Eighth, now the Duke of Windsor, who gave up the Crown for his American divorcée, Wallis Simpson."

Diana exclaimed, "And thank God he abdicated! Just think what could have happened had he remained King, with all his Nazi sympathies. And imagine giving up the Crown of the U.K. for a woman. It is indeed a testimonial as to how politics and love can addle one's brain."

Bobby, gazing fondly at her, observed earnestly, "I may be addle-brained myself, but I do know one woman who would be more than worth it."

Sir Robert nodded approvingly, and then reflected, "Despite the Duke of Windsor's shortcomings, I've always admired his style in attire. He makes an ordinary necktie look almost like a true cravat with that knot he uses. It may be the only good thing for which he will be remembered, but ironically, it isn't even his doing. You see, he borrowed that from his grandfather, Edward the Seventh."

Still reliving the tale of their transatlantic romance, Lady Howard noted Bobby's last observation, and said, "I'll wager that tens of thousands of other British girls will follow you Yanks back home."

Not totally secure about Bobby's flying, and uncomfortable with that line of talk, Diana cautioned her mother. "Let's not talk about that. This war is far from won. We can contemplate such things when the time comes." Looking across the table at him, she asked, "Do you think it will be soon, darling?"

He glanced at her mother, and then responded, "For Germany, it will be by the summer of next year, I think. They're running out of fuel for their engines and oil for their bearings, and the Soviets are overwhelming them in the east. But we'll still have Japan to deal with, and no telling how long the conquest of their home islands will take. Before that happens, there'll be a need for more bomber crews for sure. Even my finishing thirty or thirty-five missions out of Framlingham will be no guarantee I'll see no more combat. It'll take time to defeat the Japs on their home ground."

The meal was finished on that note, but it seemed not to daunt his hosts, who so stoically had endured five and a half years of war by that time. But it was depressing to Bobby as he found it hard even to look past the next mission, much less contemplate years more of war.

NINETEEN

Clouds, Radar, and Diana

After the Christmas holiday, Bobby's return to Base was occupied with more classes, some given by guest lecturers. Occasionally, a fighter ace from a nearby base would give information on German tactics and equipment, and then the entire crew would sit in.

One such presentation was by the Commander of the 357th Fighter Group. After his introduction by the Colonel, he leaned for a time on the podium surveying his audience.

"I know most of you haven't ever faced fighter resistance, because for some months the massive numbers put up in bombers have diluted the German defenses. And now we have enough long-range escorts to prevent most of them from closing on you.

"I've chosen this topic because as we advance toward the heart of the enemy, and their remaining forces become more concentrated, the likelihood of their eluding our fighters will be greater.

"My focus is the Berlin Defense Force, based within a fifty-mile radius of the Capital city. It includes two Fighter Groups, JG 300 and 301, which we've encountered increasingly as our missions penetrate ever more deeply.

"Originally organized as a night fighter force to counter the massive RAF raids on their cities, since early 1944 they're being deployed increasingly for defense against the daylight bombing of the Eighth Air Force.

"Initially they used the nimble BF-109s as night fighters, which easily carried sufficient armor to counter the British rifle caliber defensive machine guns. It soon became apparent, however, that the thickness of armor needed to stop a fifty Caliber slug from a Fort or a Liberator, plus the extra wing-mounted cannons needed to be effective added too much weight to the little Messerschmitt for it to remain competitive in dogfights.

"They turned to the newer and more powerful Focke-Wulf 190, mounting a more potent combination of twin 13 mm machine guns firing through the propeller and a 20 mm and even a 30 mm cannon in each wing. This combination was a sure bomber-killer, if they could get close enough, but the lack of side and belly armor still left the pilots vulnerable to defensive fire as they flew through our formations.

"They added more cockpit armor, and later, when they began to deploy the FW-190 A-8s, they used plates almost an inch thick to shield the pilot from the sides and below. They even added bulletproof glass to the canopy sides. All that weight added up, and fully loaded for combat it weighed over five tons. The pilot was protected as never before, but despite the 1,700 horses delivered by its BMW engine, the performance of the planes, *Sturmbocken,* as they call them, suffered. This was especially evident when, early this year, our Mustangs in quantity began to arrive, now escorting you all the way to the target and back.

"It was then that the tide of the war in the air began to turn more rapidly. The Germans losses became more telling. This was not so much because of the loss of planes, but despite the armor, they were losing veteran pilots, many of them aces, in their attempts to reach the bombers. And with the accelerated rate of attrition they're now having problems training replacements, due to destruction of their fuel production facilities.

"They do have better protection in their cockpits, and their cannon array can down a four-engine bomber with a single burst, if only they can get close enough. But first they have to get through the escort. None but the very best pilot in an FW-190 A-8 can out-fly a Mustang, weighted down as his *Sturmbock* is by armor and armament. And while heavily armed, their cannon, particularly the 30 mm ones, have such a slow rate of fire that they're less effective against a fast-moving fighter.

"The remedy the *Luftwaffe* command now employs is to escort the heavy 190s with a top cover of Messerschmitt 109s. In theory, that could work. If the 109s can fully occupy the escort, the *Sturmbock* pilot is free to work on our bombers without the distraction of having to keep one eye out behind him. Defensive gunfire still is downing some of the incoming 190s, but because of their armor, half the pilots are surviving to fight again.

"At present, while usually repelled by our fighter defenses, they still break through occasionally to score heavily. Just over two months ago, on October 6, a *Sturmbock* force was able to down eleven B-17s of the 385th over Rathenow, and the very next day scoring as heavily on other elements in the Third Air Division."

Danny raised his hand then. "Sir, I have questions about the disaster that happened to the 385th and the others. Is there a common denominator, or is it mere chance? Somewhere there must be an explanation."

"Good question, lieutenant. Usually there's a failure in coordinating with our fighters, or the victims somehow leave the protection of the rest of the bomber stream. You pilots, keep it closed up, and as for you gunners, aim for their engines or fuel tanks."

Hell, Bobby thought, from what he had heard, those Jerries came in so fast, in line abreast from the front or abeam, it was all anyone using a machine gun could do to hit anything at all.

That night, Bobby and Danny discussed the problem as they sat on their cots.

Bobby said, "Why didn't we hear about German fighter tactics when we first arrived as replacements? After nine missions, never even seeing an enemy fighter, some of the gunners couldn't even stay awake during the lecture. I think the Jerries are just saving themselves and their fuel for more important installations in their heartland, like the Leuna synthetic oil complex or Berlin. We haven't been to either of those targets yet."

Danny nodded his agreement. "I'm just waiting for it to hit the fan. You're right, I'm afraid. We missed Leuna because the landmarks were so obscured by smoke, and haven't yet drawn the short straw regarding Berlin. I just can't believe they haven't got something up their sleeve. So far we've lucked out, but it can't last. You heard what he said about their fighters breaking through to shoot down Forts in wholesale numbers here and there along the bomber stream."

"Yeah," Bobby agreed, "Even if it is composed of a thousand bombers, the fifty or hundred mile long stream might only be as wide as a Group—thirty-six measly planes at some points. How thinly would a similar number of fighter escorts be spread out over those miles? And what if they're away chasing the Messerschmitt top cover?"

"That reminds me of Murphy's Law, or at least one of them," Danny observed. "Lessons like today should help us stay alert to the possibility that something that can go wrong will go wrong."

"Let's hope we get some more input from our fighter pilots to drive the lesson home," Bobby added, "To keep our young gunners awake. Something exciting, like the record toll taken by the 390th on the Münster mission last year."

Danny grunted at that, as he fluffed up his pillow, mumbling something about another lecture after their flight the next day. Then he was almost immediately asleep. Bobby could only envy that, something always impossible for him.

* * * *

As the P-47 Thunderbolt, its nose bearing the name *Lucky,* lifted off the runway at Halesworth, and the landing gear came up, its pilot ruminated about the session he would put on for the bomber boys at Framlingham that day. Colonel Armstrong, the 568th's commander, had asked him, as a leading ace, to give a lecture on advanced fighter tactics to the three crews that were just completing their lead training.

As he headed northeast toward Station 153, he decided to wing it in his lecture. How much better would it be, if instead of a didactic talk, he could give them a real demonstration. Well, he thought, the logistics of getting them into the air so that he could give them a good lesson by surprising them today would be just too much. There was nothing he liked better than "Bouncing" an unsuspecting pilot.

Why hadn't they officially adopted that technique anyway? They had tried other imaginative ideas, even to gunners practicing by firing ceramic bullets at specially armored

P-63s. He had pushed the idea of dummy firing passes by fighters with his boss, the colonel commanding the 56th Fighter Group, although mainly to help in the orientation of their replacements, soon to be in the role of protecting those same "Big Friends."

He recalled bouncing B-17s from a nearby base while he was in advanced training. Stateside, you could safely do that because they'd not fire at you. Here, in Britain where Nazi intruders were not uncommon, a hail of fifty caliber slugs would be their answer. Not healthy.

It was a rare clear day, with only a layer of ground fog mantling the low-lying fields. Soon, the ruins of Framlingham Castle, rising out of the fog, could be seen, just to the west of his destination. He had plenty of time, so he decided to fly around a while.

Radioing the tower of his intention, he eased the stick back for more altitude. This allowed him a view of the coast, and in the distance, he could just make out the Continent. Always the fighter pilot, with the swivel-neck and the 20-10 vision of a surviving one at that, he continually scanned the blue in all directions.

To the north there was a brief flash of light, then two more, a sure sign of the sun reflecting off the bare aluminum skin of friendlies, or—possibly—from the flat panels of Jerry fighter canopies. He relished the idea of an unscheduled combat, and pushed the throttle forward to full power.

Soon, the silver glints assumed the form of a flight of three B-17s. At first a little disappointed, he turned his transmitter to the appropriate frequency, identifying himself. Seeing the radar antennas of the planes, he wondered, could these guys be those I'm supposed to lecture? That would be some coincidence. Then he had an idea. On the radio again, he made an unusual proposition.

In the lead plane, Danny's voice was heard over the intercom. "Boys, this Jug driver wants to play. Put your guns on safety. This is a great chance to practice your gunnery tracking. He'll come through our formation, acting the part of an attacking *Sturmbock*. I don't know what direction he'll come from, although I expect it'll be from the front. Heads up, now! See how well you can follow his path with your fifties."

The P-47 "Jug," so called because of the rotund shape of its fuselage, had climbed to a couple of thousand feet above and in front of the bombers. Its pilot had never attacked an enemy four-engine bomber, scarce as German ones were, but recalling the concept of avoiding a bomber's defensive cones of fire learned in training, he envisioned those of the B-17. While he knew slugs wouldn't be coming his way, he was, after all, that day in a teaching mode.

The captain thought, a little frustration on my first pass will be good for them. Then a few more to build confidence and hone their skills to finish up will be perfect. There'll be plenty of time to make that lecture after all that.

Maneuvering into the bombers' twelve o'clock, he dove in a sinuous series of banks and turns to keep the top turret gunner wildly guessing. That was the only station that could get any bead at all on him coming in on them high and on the nose. He was above the arc of fire for the chin turret, and the cheek guns would get only a glimpse as he eased right and then left overhead. Only a few seconds, and he was gone, pulling out of his shallow high-speed dive, giving the same treatment to the gunners in the rear. Only the radioman with his single gun could at all track him as he flashed by overhead, at a combined speed of about six hundred miles an hour. The waist gunners couldn't see him, and neither could the tail gunner who, by the time he saw the diving fighter, was unable to depress his twin fifties enough. Of course, the other planes in the flight were able to track his speeding P-47, although only for a few seconds.

The fighter ended up making identical passes on the others of the flight, and then finished with head-on approaches from directly in front, then doing a "Split-S" and diving away, a *Luftwaffe* favorite.

When all had landed, and were stowing their flight gear, Bobby exclaimed, "That was really an education! If the Jerries are anything like that, we could be in for a rough time. Although it's easy to track a fighter coming straight on, it's tough to follow those quick side to side gyrations."

"Yeah," said Zito, the Engineer/top turret man. "And we can't use more than three or four guns on each pass, it's over so fast."

"That's right," Danny cut in, "But remember, just as we're a team on board our own plane, all the planes of each element also have to work as a team. While a fighter is a more than a match for a lone Fort, remember, a tight formation is designed to cover its neighbors, and as in our case, the belly of the lead plane."

"That last is essential, for sure," Bobby remarked, "Without a ball turret, there's nothing to protect us from below. Just another reason to be nice to our squadron-mates."

"OK, let's get to the lecture." Danny interjected. "I understand it'll be another one about fighter defense. Very appropriate in view of what we've just been through."

* * * *

The fighter ace giving the lecture was a typical hot-rock type. Wearing his flight suit, he looked as if he had just returned from combat.

The Colonel introduced him as from the 56th Fighter Group. "These boys have often escorted the 390th, and in the process he's shot down twenty enemy fighters. Every flier here has, one way or another, already met him. Today, as a matter of fact, over The Wash."

Amazed at the revelation, all applauded the equally amazed captain, who began by complementing them on their tight formation flying, adding, to some laughter, "I hope you'll give me more leeway during this lecture than the room you gave me to fly through your formation."

"I'm told this talk is for those in lead training and given just before its completion. You've now seen something of fighter tactics, and I think that if you remember the lesson learned today, with the speed of the attack, you'll realize that to bag a fighter is a rare prize for a gunner. Remember also that with the USAAF escorts mixing it with the German fighters, they look, for all the world, alike. Be sure that when you fire your machine guns the target is one of theirs.

"More often than not, on an escorted mission, the toll taken by your little friends can be as much as five times that of those actually shot down by the bombers. So don't count mere smoke trails as kills."

All were appalled by the captain's assertion, with its implication that the gunners were claiming victories that either were rightly due the fighters, or were actually padding their accounts, as it were. Danny, in his loyalty to his own gunners, and all the crews of the Group, rose to object.

"Sir, do you mean to say that claims by gunners in general are fabrications, or is it your position that because all may be shooting at a given Jerry that starts smoking, each is likely to claim him as his kill, thus mistakenly multiplying the actual toll by the number of gunners shooting?

"Yes and no. They're not lying, but in the melee of a high-speed fighter attack, so little time is available to observe the effects of their tracers, that they get confused. Fighters are equipped with gun cameras, and our claims have to be verified either by film footage, or someone observing the craft actually crashing."

Danny persisted, "Was such 'Kill Inflation' the case in the famous 1943 mission to Münster, when the 390th claimed the record for a single combat, sixty-two Jerry interceptors destroyed?"

"Probably so, in my opinion. It seems to have been based on making such mistaken claims. The 390th has to be honored in slogging through all that flak and over two hundred enemy fighters, but I understand the actual German losses in the air were precisely twenty-six. If that's true, subtracting the twenty documented victories of the boys from the 4th, 56th and 78th Fighter Groups, whose Thunderbolts came to your aid, it leaves only six downed by the bombers."

A chorus of disapproval followed, as the audience voiced its objection. After a few moments, the Colonel stood up, silencing the dissent. "At ease, gentlemen! What we just heard is certainly controversial, but remember, the captain is a veteran of over sixty sorties against the *Luftwaffe*, and at least half of those have been in escort duty with our Thirteenth Wing, and that includes the Münster mission, where he accounted for two Jerries.

"To date, he's downed twenty Nazi fighters, mostly in our defense. Never forget that he flies as an indispensable 'Little Friend,' so please, give him the respect due him and his fel-

low fighter pilots. Somewhere in between the truth may ultimately be known, but it may not come out until the enemy's
defeat. Remember what we learned the other day, they didn't
pile all that armor on their *Sturmbocken* just for the fun of
it. They sacrificed agility and speed, so crucial in a dogfight,
for protection from our gunners, in their primary mission
against our bombers.

"And don't forget, our B-17s did one helluva job at
Münster, damaging the key railroad yards, fulfilling the objective of disrupting transport from the vital Ruhr Valley by
destroying the core of the city. Our losses were a record that
still stands for our Group, eight Forts in all. But again I must
emphasize, many more would have fallen victim to the enemy but for pilots of our escort like the captain here. Look
at the Schweinfurt missions and Regensburg. We had no escorts at all over the target then, and everything that could fly
was sent up against us. Because of that, the overall losses for
the Eighth were sixty bombers each time. Now let's give our
guest a round of applause, and hope we can encourage our
gunners to improve that ratio he talks about."

Turning to the guest lecturer, he then said, "Thanks,
Captain, for coming to Framlingham to further our education. Good luck. We've all learned a great deal. I think your
words will go a long way to improve our reporting of enemy
kills, and your flying lesson earlier today will increase our
accuracy."

Bobby and Danny lingered in their chairs after the rest
of the class had gone. "You've had plenty of experience in the
RCAF, Danny, probably including fighter encounters, what
about all that he said?"

"My experience was with night raids, so visual sight-
ings were few and fleeting. You know too, that the Lancaster

Bomber is almost blind below, and since we flew alone, we had no support from the rest of our squadron. The Jerries knew that as well, and they devised a method of flying along under us, out of sight of our radar and tail gunner, while we were silhouetted against the sky. They would shoot upwards with a pair of twenty or thirty mm guns mounted at an angle to their direction of flight. If they were on target, and it was hard to miss, that was it usually for the targeted plane and crew.

"One time they caught us, but we were lucky. God, that was frightening. A complete surprise, just when you think you're home free, and then to have all hell break loose. Tracers blasting past you like white Fourth of July fireworks. We were all scared shitless, and the gunners were wildly firing at everything. Illuminated smoke, searchlight beam reflections, you name it. I could never believe they saw a night fighter for more than a second, yet the shouts of elation, over their fancied bagging of yet another one created a continual din over the intercom. At debriefing after our return to the field, it would invariably be reported that our Squadron had downed at least a dozen of the *Luftwaffe*.

"Now, in the daylight, if we're ever attacked by the *Sturmbocks*, we'll certainly be able to track them, and be able to get in a few rounds on each pass. But if they bear in head on, they'll be gone in a flash, and almost as fast if they dive from off the wing.

"Hits by a Browning fired from our nose might not cause smoke to mark the damage until the Jerry had flown through most of the formation. By that time how many gunners will have been shooting at that plane? The gunner in the front of the plane might not see the results, but the others would. How many would think he was the lucky one?"

Bobby nodded. "I get your point. What beats me is how the big brass could be taken in by the inflated Münster kills reported by the gunners."

Danny smiled, "Ever consider the value of a bomb group being awarded a Presidential Unit Citation? The 95th got one because of its bombing on that mission. As for the 390th's reported kills, it's a record that still stands. Morale was ebbing in those days, because at the time, there was less than a fifty-fifty chance of surviving the required twenty-five missions.

The big boys had to pump up the crews so they could keep on fighting. And that's what they did. Four days later, the Schweinfurt mission earned a unit citation for us, and the crews ate it up. Now, over a year later, we're still itching to get at those fighters and down them in the same numbers."

* * * *

By the time the crew had finished lead training, the toll at Schweinfurt, Regensburg and Münster they had heard about was ancient history. The 390th hadn't seen a Jerry fighter for two months, and the morale of the fliers had consequently reached an all-time high. Many even envisioned final victory before the winter really set in. Bobby, along with Danny and the others, was hopeful, but as they reminded each other, "It ain't over 'til it's over." And then they'd have another beer.

Their last mission of 1944 was on December 28, and was his crew's first as Squadron leader. Their co-pilot would move to the tail gunner's position to observe the rest of the squadron, while the Squadron Commander, Lt. Col. Armstrong, checked on their efficiency. The prospect was therefore more exciting than usual.

When they arrived at their hardstand, all were taken aback that the plane sitting on the concrete was not the new Fortress in which they had trained to hone their pathfinder skills, despite having been promised that beauty by the Colonel himself.

"Jeez," Bobby exclaimed in disappointment, "It looks like one of the original Forts with the old experimental *H2X* radar unit. I thought we were past having to depend on the Pathfinder Unit at Alconbury for our lead planes."

Danny wasn't happy either. "As usual, we have to take what they give us. At least it has the radar we need."

It was named *Satan's Second Sister*. With a name like that, which required a biblical scholar to figure out, it was no surprise that most of the crew were a little more wary of the mission than previously.

The operation started in the usual way, but with the shorter distance more welcome, their objective revealed during briefing to be near Koblenz, in the Rhineland, at the confluence of the Rhine River, the Mosel and the Main. They had been surprised to hear that over twenty percent of the *Reich's* transportation was by water, and that one fallen bridge, blocking a waterway, could cause great delays in the war materials and fuel reaching the front by that means.

The primary target was nearby Stadkyll, a small crossroads town, but an important communications center. There, in addition to causing bomb damage to essential transmission stations and lines, rubble from the collapsed buildings would help block movement along the busy traversing highways.

The strategy was a new concept to Bobby and his fellow officers, but as it turned out, of no importance, as all that could be seen through the *H2X*-linked bombsight was open farmland. He was dumbfounded, until Lynch, the navigator, apologized for an error he had made in plotting the course. Off only a mile, their course did put them over cloud-shrouded Koblenz itself, the secondary target, where the Squadron dropped its bombs at Bobby's signal. The bombs were aimed at what were thought to be marshaling yards, but as usual, bordering built-up areas of the city. This did not distress him as much as it had previously, mollified as he was by the knowledge that not only did that city contain vital rail and water links, it was also important as a manufacturing center.

Flak, as usual, jolted the air around their plane throughout the bomb run as Bobby intently bent over his bombsight, calling out, "Bombs away!"

As the ship shook with the continued bursts, he exclaimed, "Christ, look at all that flak ahead!"

"Easy men," Danny called out, "Hang on, we're getting out of here!" He put the B-17 into a shallow dive to the left, gaining speed, taking them out of the burst-pocked air over Koblenz.

They were lucky, happily for them, although the groups ahead caught it, losing four of the nearly four hundred planes sent out that day. One gunner from the 390th was killed as his plane received several fragments from a nearby burst.

No fighter resistance was encountered, as it appears that the Nazi controllers had misdirected their defensive *Sturmgruppen* elsewhere.

On the flight home, after they had left hostile territory, and at a time when all were allowed to use the intercom to help relieve the tension, the tail gunner, Firof, who knew his Old Testament, filled everyone in on the plane's name, regarding Satan's sister.

Her name was Lilith, supposedly Cain's twin. According to him, those relationships were so confused, with Cain's character also interchangeable with that of Satan, and with his taking his own sister, Lilith, as his wife, that it might be best that they didn't know the whole story.

Danny burst in, laughing over the intercom, "Satan would have married the second sister too, adding bigamy to the incest charges."

Bobby then added, "Very funny, but you guys are missing the obvious point. Satan had no second sister until they named this Fort."

He was disappointed regarding that mission, and at the next chance, he spoke to Danny about it. "God, even with the Mickey, I'm still sick about not seeing well enough to pinpoint our targets, dumping on built-up areas of nearby cities, which we can see on the radar, because of their size, as our secondary targets. Dropping bombs from high altitude does have a certain impersonal aspect to it, but those explosives have to be killing people, some not involved in the Nazi war industries. Toddlers and other little kids. You just don't see the immediate results or the gore. Even when you bomb visually, a veteran bombardier told me, seeing the explosions blowing things all to hell isn't like shooting someone. I wonder, will I ever get used to this? One thing I do know, I just gotta talk this out."

Danny was not without understanding. Because he had heard that before, somewhat impatiently he said, "Bobby, you know I have two kids, one a toddler still, and the thought of my family being subjected to bombings curdles my blood. But this is the only way to finish the war in the shortest possible time, and you know it as well as I." Referring to the failed plot to assassinate Hitler, he added, "Now if the people, not just a handful of disgruntled officers, had made some effort to overthrow him, I'd have more sympathy for them."

"But how can any population," Bobby asked rhetorically, "As regimented and as repressed as the Germans, ever force their government to surrender?"

* * * *

With the end of December, practice flights and classes, plus the critiques held after missions with the group's returning combat crews took up all his time during the day. This made things too busy to get into London, forcing Diana to visit Framlingham to see him in his off hours.

She took leave from her work over New Year's, staying at the little Inn on the triangle-shaped plaza that passed for the central square. During that time, when there was no mission scheduled, and after his practice and study obligations had been discharged, he could usually wangle a pass into that little town, only three miles away. If he worked it right, he could even stay overnight. There were fewer thoughts about Denise, but the reasons for her choice to go back to Wheelie still bothered him. At the same time, any pain was always banished by Diana's presence.

Much of their spare time was at the Crown Hotel, either in bed together or at the pub downstairs, where the food was plain but hearty. They would go for walks up the gentle slope past the old church, Saint Michael's, to Framlingham Castle, sprawled at the top. It was interesting to see the ruins from the ground for a change. The weather was not ideal for such excursions, but being alone together went a long way to make up for the cold and the wet.

They would sit in the pub and sip beer or cheap *Triumpha* Port or Sherry. Appropriately, the label depicted the ancient Briton Warrior Queen, Boudica, pointing the way to victory. Otherwise undistinguished, it did impart that wonderful feeling of warmth as it went down, so welcome in the early English winter.

The rooms were very cool because of the year's record lows and the wartime shortage of coal. Again, it was a repeat of Diana's flat, where one could get only "Half warm," sitting next to the flames. As usual, the cheery English fireplace promised more than it delivered, most of the heat going up the chimney.

They read some of the history of the area, especially the lore surrounding the long-ruined castle. Diana had found it ironic that instead of siege, its partial destruction was by its last owner, who had specified in his will that it be demolished upon his death.

One cold afternoon, in the pub after they again had taken a stroll to the castle, the owner overheard their conversation about the ruins, and asked if they would be interested in hearing the story. It turned out that he was chairman of the local castle committee and quite a historian.

"With the invasion of East Anglia by the Danes," he began, "The building of strong points for defense became necessary. The original castle, built by the Saxons, resisted the invaders for hundreds of years until finally being overwhelmed. Its defenders were executed, including Edmund, the Saxon king, and its walls reduced to piles of stone."

Diana asked, "Isn't that how the town of Bury St. Edmunds, west of here, got its name?"

"Right you are, Miss Howard. King Edmund is actually buried there, and it was a Saxon shrine until the Norman Conquest in 1066. After the Saxons were driven out, the Norman nobleman, Hugh le Bigod, started the new castle. It was a more formidable structure, using much of the original stone, plus a great deal more of the hard local flint, and even stone from as far away as Normandy.

"Unlike most castles, with a central citadel, or Keep, surrounded by walls with corner towers, this one was designed with extra-thick walls and many strong towers without a central redoubt."

Turning to Bobby, he said, "The number of towers wouldn't do for you Yanks. You probably wouldn't have approved of there being thirteen of 'em in all."

"With most Americans, you'd be right," he agreed. "At home, buildings of over twelve floors skip that number and go on to fourteen. That's just ridiculous. For me, it's a lucky number, but not so much due to any mere superstition. When I was that age, I survived quite a number of scrapes, any of which could have done me in." Turning to Diana, he said affectionately, "More recently, I've had nothing but good luck."

Taking a gulp of his ale, the Englishman continued. "It was Sir Hugh's grandson, Roger, reputedly quite the ladies' man, who put the finishing touches on the castle, strengthening its walls and developing the moat you now see. Also, he erected a building within the enclosure, used as a lodging for wealthy travelers.

"It is rumored that with time," the pub owner added with a sly smile, "The family name evolved from the French Bigod to 'By God,' thus giving rise to that limerick, 'Roger the Lodger.'"

"Oh, come now," Diana objected, eying Bobby expectantly, "Stick to the facts. You know how such liberties are apt to set off uncontrolled ribaldry in any Yank within earshot."

"Sorry miss, couldn't help that one. But to go on, the castle came to form a center of power for the Dukes of Norfolk, including your namesake, Sir Thomas Howard. But the power of the castle didn't save two of the Howard family, Ann Boleyn and Katherine Howard, beheaded on the order of their husband, Henry the Eighth."

Bobby looked at his companion then. "Sir Thomas Howard! Any relation, Diana?"

She smiled demurely, and then turned to hear more, as their host continued.

"Later, a more royal, but equally threatened Mary Tudor, Catherine of Aragon's daughter by Henry, was given the castle by her half-brother, the sickly Edward the Sixth. She sought refuge in it, while her Catholic supporters in London set the stage for her ascension to the throne after Edward's death.

"We know her as 'Bloody Mary' more than the official Mary the First. Despite her ownership of the castle, and her executions of the hundreds that stood in the way of bringing Catholicism back to Britain, no blood was ever spilled in her name at Framlingham."

Diana interrupted. "Those were executions for religious reasons, which called for burning at the stake. The bloody beheadings were for such civil crimes as treason. Seems to me she should have been called 'Burning Mary' instead, wouldn't you agree, Bobby?"

"Burning or bloody," he replied, "As with Shakespeare's rose in *Romeo and Juliet,* an execution by any other name. And what's that about the castle never falling to attack?"

"It's true," the storyteller went on, "At one time it was one of the largest castles in England, but its fall wasn't by force of arms. You see, ironically, this castle, unlike its smaller Saxon predecessor, never underwent siege. This was due to its owners' lack of resolve, giving in short of that.

"It was a prison for a time, during the Elizabethan years, and later a poorhouse. Now, it's the town meeting hall, but the cost of maintaining the ruins has become so dear, that the Town Council is trying to induce one of the national preservation trusts to take over."

"Whatta story," Bobby exclaimed, "I have to hand it to you English. In ruins for three hundred years, and most of its stones still there."

The Englishmen replied, "During the last century, and before that, the governmental uses to which it was put kept scavengers away, otherwise local builders would have accounted for all except the odd stone. More recently, they would have started in on the walls themselves, except for the Town Council. But, you've noticed the local church. It wasn't built close to the castle and with that same stone by chance."

Enthralled by the story, Bobby exclaimed, "Thirteen towers! We turn over the castle on our approach to the airfield, and I've been over it many times, but never bothered to count." Jokingly he added, "It must be my lucky castle."

"My dear," Diana declared, "What it must be is your superstitious Irish blood. It's a wonder indeed that you're able to function at all unless the auguries are right."

Bobby looked at her in amazement, "Oh, come off it," he said, "English history and literature are full of superstition. And speaking of Bloody Mary, that superstition of calling her name thirteen times into a mirror at midnight to make her appear, originated right here in England. And for a fact, I've seen you, sweetheart, avoiding cracks and lines on sidewalks."

Thanking the pub-keeper, she said, "That was a fascinating account indeed." Then, finishing her Sherry, she looked expectantly at her companion.

"Fascinating, I agree," Bobby said, "Especially that part about Sir Thomas Howard. Is the connection just a co-incidence? You told me your family had been poor, and I gathered that your affluence now was due to your dad's achievements alone. Could the Howards have fallen so far?"

Slowly shaking her head to his first question, she rolled her big green eyes at the second. "One question at a time, please. What would you expect, as a result of two of their young women beheaded? The Howard name itself became suspect. Still, the family was able to remain in possession of Framlingham Castle until they fell on hard times, and it had to be sold. In time, our branch of the family was left with very little indeed. Some fell into debt and were imprisoned, and, as perhaps with your Taylors, others were forced to work out their debts in the Colonies. The Howards originally came by their power in the Norman Conquest. Our position of affluence now is by dint of long hard struggle, finally rewarded by the recognition of the brilliant work on the part of father."

Reflecting on that, Bobby finally observed, "I'm happy that some of your ancestors stayed home, so that we could meet as we have. I don't know how I could have gotten along without you."

At that, she leaned over to him, and snuggled with her head on his shoulder, whispering, "I'll wager that some other female would have come along before long. You could never lack for attention in Britain."

"Oh, sure," he replied, "Overpaid, oversexed and over here." Playfully kissing her on the nose, he added, "But let's forget all that, and get something to eat. I'm feeling underfed at the moment."

* * * *

The New Year was a cause for celebration, the news especially good. With the weather clearing over the Western Front, Allied forces were able to slow, and then stop, the great German offensive that had been launched before Christmas.

Known as the "Battle of the Bulge," because of the penetration the Nazis made through the thinly defended Ardennes Forest in Belgium, it became a salient nearly half the way to Brussels and Antwerp.

It was the greatest land battle of the entire war for the Western Allies. The German objective was Antwerp, a vital port of supply. They almost succeeded. Under cover of the clouds and fog, their offensive surprised our forces, enabling them to take thousands of Americans prisoner.

One reason their thrusts were finally repulsed was because of support by planes of the Allied Air Forces. Starting on December 24, air attacks on the Nazi columns were resumed. That day a thousand plane flyover of the front was staged by the Eighth Air Force, including elements of the 390th, as a morale booster, on their way to bomb German supply lines.

The Nazi Generals, expecting American resistance to quickly crumble, had counted on capturing fuel supplies along the way, short as they were of fuel and oil because of the Allied bombings of Germany. They had even resorted to horse-drawn vehicles to move their supplies. It was a huge miscalculation. With clearing skies, stiffening resistance by the now air-supported ground troops excluded the Germans from the fuel dumps. As a consequence, the *Wermacht's* motorized units were halted far short of their objectives, and many tanks and artillery had to be abandoned in the subsequent retreat.

Bobby was, in addition, much encouraged, as perhaps better visibility over the German homeland would be good enough to engage in the pinpoint bombing in which he had excelled in training.

* * * *

Their trysting was cut short by Bobby's next mission on January 7. Although eager to return to combat, he still found it hard to get up in the darkness and the January cold, and found it difficult to tolerate being awakened by that intrusive flashlight. He had understood that lead crews were to be given special privileges, and had hoped that one of them would be a civilized awakening. After breakfast, which was welcomed as it soothed the hollow aching in his stomach, he finished putting on his flight clothes, and then went to briefing.

When the curtain covering the map of Europe was pulled back, their target was shown to be Rodenkirchen, southeast of Cologne on the Rhine River. He reflected on the losses to flak that they had suffered on their first two missions to the big cathedral city nearby, but decided that the relatively short distance from their base tended to make up for that. It was just across the Belgian border.

Their target, it was emphasized, was the site of an important triple span bridge, which if knocked down, would paralyze traffic supplying the Nazi armies. After being stopped during the Battle of the Bulge, they were now in retreat, much of it on foot and without their armor.

As the briefing officers pointed out, visibility might still be poor, making the lead plane all-important, because of the expected dependence on radar. Bobby's crew looked at him expectantly, as in his role of lead bombardier, his pinpointing the bridge was the whole purpose of their work that day. It occurred to him that if their bombs were accurate, the effects could shorten the war, sparing many lives, even their own.

When they were dropped off at their hardstand, they found the B-17 used in recent training was again theirs for their first mission of 1945. A near-new plane, familiar now, another year, and the possibility of clear weather, at last.

When taking off for Germany, the B-17s were always heavily loaded, but there had never been a close call for their Squadron. There *had* been a wipeout at the end of the runway at the end of December, when a B-17 of one of the other Squadrons of the Group had engine failure on takeoff. That ended in an immense explosion, scattering parts of the plane and its crew for a quarter mile.

Take-off was always the most critical part of flying, and with all that gasoline and high explosives, the event was, needless to say, tense. Bobby's position in the nose of the Fortress had always heightened the excitement, and this day was no exception for him. He was unable to relax even partially, until they were securely airborne and the wheels were tucked up with their characteristic thump into their housings behind the inboard engines.

It was only then that his grip on the chin turret control yoke and the bombsight was relaxed. They were based only ten miles from the North Sea, and it was just a few minutes before they passed over the mist-shrouded white cliffs south of Norwich. On Danny's orders then, all the guns were tested with short bursts. Bobby fired his guns also, after which he could lift the yoke up out of the way. He then attended to his bombsight, checking its connections to the plane's controls and to the Mickey radar.

After they reached ten thousand feet, and throughout the flight at altitude, he had the added duty of periodically checking on the crew. It was not infrequent that an oxygen line would become disconnected, resulting in a flier slipping into a coma. Such could occur without the slightest inkling on the part of the victim.

When they reached the prescribed altitude, they formed up at the Rally Point with the other planes of their squadron, taking their place in the Group without incident, despite the usual clouds. All the way to the Rhine he noted the high layer above, muting the sun, and those below that they had climbed through earlier, billows and wisps of soft white. As with everyone else, he constantly searched the skies for signs of *Luftwaffe* fighters. Because of the bombings, the enemy had become chronically short of fuel, and that day they were conserving it.

Despite the cloud cover, they knew they were nearing their destination when, picked up by the enemy anti-aircraft radar, the formations of the leading group ahead entered a "Box" of flak, a barrage of bursting 88 mm shells, thrown up into the path of the attacking bombers, with the knowledge they couldn't deviate from their course during the bomb run.

Soon they reached the IP, where they turned toward the objective. Danny put the plane on the Automatic Flight Control Equipment, or AFCE. This turned their flight path over to the automatic pilot, linked to the bombsight, until the bombs were released.

Bobby couldn't see the target through the clouds, but the accurate flak found three of the bombers in the Group ahead of them, along with one of the almost two hundred escorting Mustangs. He watched in horror as the nearest of the stricken Fortresses slowly went into a flat spin and began its long plunge down towards the clouds. Horrified, he envisioned them helplessly immobilized by centrifugal force of the spin, as none of the crew was seen to escape.

As the 568th entered the wall of flak his eyes riveted on the bombsight's radar image, his adrenaline, always a factor in combat, began to pump. There, outlined by the distinctive curve of the Rhine, where the target bridge was known to be, was the blurry image of the city. But nowhere to be seen was the sought-after bridge, not even the railroad tracks that were known to cross the river on it.

"Dammit," he complained, an almost sick feeling of frustration in the pit of his stomach, "How can they expect us to hit a target not more than thirty feet wide through the clouds, even with this *H2X*, when we can barely make out the outlines of the city?"

Calculating from his aerial maps where the bridge should be, he dropped their bombs, the signal for the following Forts of the Squadron to release theirs. It was only a minute or so, but seemed forever, as the dirty black bursts of flak continued in their path. Bobby thought, we've gotta be over the target, or the anti-aircraft wouldn't be there either.

As soon as bomb-drop lightened the plane, Danny took back the controls, and put the ship into a shallow dive to gain speed, making a steep ninety-degree turn to the north. Bobby closed the bomb bay doors, and resumed his vigil with the gun yoke once more in front of him. The only fighters they could see were again the Mustangs of the 357th, staying close, depending on the Fortress navigators, until they had the cliffs of the English shore in sight once again.

* * * *

There was another opportunity for Bobby and Diana to get together after that mission, but because of a possibility of his flying the next day, if a break in the weather came, he had to remain on the Base.

She was not about to let that keep them apart. The Air Ministry provided Base maintenance for the Americans through the British Base Works Directorate, conducted by the Royal Engineers. In that way, she was able to secure accommodations for a few days at Parham Hall. Normally used for the occasional base function, such as providing accommodation for the women helping celebrate the 100th and 200th mission parties, it usually stood almost empty.

It did house the caretakers, Mildred Carpenter and her two teenage daughters. They looked after the interior and the needs of any guests, while the detachment of Engineers did the maintenance and cared for the grounds. Conveniently, it was only a half-mile from the 568th Squadron area.

During the autumn of 1944, more than usual atrocious weather conditions had prevailed. Parham Hall therefore served as a makeshift sleeping facility for other crews forced to land at Framlingham when their own fields were socked in. At such times the largely unfurnished rooms were hastily outfitted with spare beds borrowed from the squadron areas, along with the necessary bedding. Not often used were suites upstairs, kept furnished in a luxurious manner, for the occasional VIP.

Diana knew about Parham Hall and those accommodations. Using her Royal Engineers connection with the Air Ministry, she secured quarters there during a tour of inspection that she was to make. Her romance with Bobby appealed to the female staff, furthered by her gift of a bottle of Scotch.

Winter was the off-season for VIPs, and aside from Mrs. Carpenter and her daughters, she had the run of the whole floor, as well as her suite of two fine rooms and a bath. The windows faced away from the airfield, minimizing the noise, although never blotting it out entirely. Bobby could easily walk to meet her there, classes and other duties permitting, and when her own work allowed. Their privacy was such that he spent the nights there one weekend. The Carpenter women, taken by the romance of the two lovers under their care, did their best to make their stay a memorable one.

On the Base, Diana wore her uniform, showing the rank of Leftenant, equal to Bobby's own. Teasing, she reminded him that she was his senior in grade, having held the rank for more than a year, beginning a good six months before Bobby's own commission. They saw each other several times that week, and were growing even closer. She would snuggle with him when he first got to her room despite how cold his skin and clothes were. They talked of the war, with the momentum building in favor of the Allies, about their families, and their respective childhoods. The Great Depression had been a thing remote to her, but she was impressed with the way Bobby had come through it, receiving an excellent education despite a shortage of money. He laid the privation part on a bit thick, recounting his fare of oatmeal, and at times sliced cold oatmeal sandwiches.

Actually, he admitted, under her skeptical questioning, that he was never really hungry more than a couple of hours before the next meal at home. His problem was that he never had anything for his sweet tooth when he was first in school, and had no spending money for candy. He recounted to her how this was remedied temporarily by occasionally switching his peanut butter and lettuce sandwiches on whole wheat bread for a jelly on white when, at school lunchtime, a tray for surplus food, donations for the poor kids, came around. His mother would have almost disowned him had she known, health food nut that she was. It was a fair trade, he maintained, as he got something sweet, and some truly hungry kid got a really nutritious lunch.

These discussions would almost invariably end with some playful clowning around on Bobby's part, ending, sometimes suddenly, in making love as if they had just discovered each other. And with only a couple of hours together on some days, the time flew.

TWENTY

War Comes To Framlingham

Inevitably, Bobby had to fly, and with improvement in the weather, their trysting was interrupted by his twelfth mission, on January thirteenth. The usual awakening had become easier in the lead Squadron's quarters when quiet was no longer necessary, since all were scheduled to fly. At least by then, the CQ's flashlight pointed at the ceiling, rather than into their faces. It was still that ungodly hour, around four AM.

Breakfast was the usual, after which they attended briefing, learning the day's mission. The American Third and Seventh Armies had requested that the bridges crossing the Rhine be taken out, to hamper the supply lines of Marshall von Rundstedt's *Wermacht* forces, still retreating from the Ardennes. They were to bomb them at Mainz, with Bobby's "B" Squadron to find and drop the important Gustavburg Bridge into the river, if the "A" Squadron, ahead of them failed.

That day, they had greeted a new addition to the Thunder crew, Richard K. Brown, their permanent Mickey operator. He came well qualified in everything except combat experience. Still, when he hopped off the truck, he didn't show any of the signs of the first mission anxiety the young gunners often exhibited.

Unlike Brown, a 2nd lieutenant, the men were more than usually worried. This time, it was that number, the thirteenth

332

of the month. Bobby tried to calm them with assurances that he himself would be coming through okay. "After all," he told them, "Thirteen is my lucky number. Because you men are on the plane with me, you'll come out of it okay too. Besides, we're part of the Thirteenth Combat Wing, and have been all along, coming through safely every time."

No one liked the idea of overly jittery gunners. They had enough to worry about as it was, although the formations again were untroubled by fighter attack, escorted by a large number of P-51s. The flak was accurate, however, and a half dozen Fortresses of the Group were damaged, four of them badly, although no losses were suffered. As always, the cloud cover was frustrating, and the bridges proved elusive.

The "A" Squadron couldn't even find the target area, ending up in nearby Euskirchen, dropping bombs on suburbs and some tracks. Crew one's navigator, Lynch, told Danny the lead Squadron of the Group was off course, and instead of following them, they continued on to Mainz where, even with the radar, Bobby could not make out the bridge itself, but at the point in the river's bend where the bridge was known to be, toggled his deadly cargo as he signaled "Bombs away" for each plane's six one thousand pounders, the size best for bridges. Nothing was seen of their hits through the overcast at that time, but bombs later were found to have struck suburbs and the important rail yards next to the bridge, which linked the city to Darmstadt and Frankfurt.

* * * *

The blue flag was flying when they landed that day after mission number twelve, denoting another for the next day. Hurrying to the bulletin board after debriefing, they found their crew prominently listed, confirming that the flag flew for them.

Diana, waiting in the lane leading to his quarters, couldn't stand being away from him for even that one night, and followed him. She was wearing her Royal Engineers uniform, over which she had wrapped a heavy dun-colored issue woolen cape. The only indication of her rank was worn on her cap, where the color of the rough British Army woolens complemented her blond hair. He was tired, but overjoyed that she was there, and took her to officers' mess.

The spaghetti and meatballs were not bad, but it was too noisy to talk there, so after finishing the meal, the next stop was the Officers' Club. Because the bar was closed to him in deference to the mission in the morning, she was the only one of the couple to be served.

As they found a table, in answer to her offer to share her pint of beer, he replied, "That's nice of you, sweetheart, but I'm okay. I got more than the usual single shot of Scotch they pour for debriefing. That should hold me, thanks."

They had picked a secluded corner, still under the curious glances of the drinkers not tapped for the next morning's mission. As they sat down, she squeezed his hand.

"I heard at the Air Ministry about the increased security now being instituted at the airbases in East Anglia." Smiling wryly, she added, "Your Yank MPs have certainly taken it to heart here. Can you believe I've been stopped for identification twice already, just coming over from Parham Hall?"

"I can believe that," he laughed, "Every one of those jokers would jump at the chance to talk to you. But I *have* noticed they've beefed up their detachment here this last week. Framlingham, as you know, is only ten miles from the North Sea. They're concerned about last-ditch sabotage of our bombers by Nazi infiltrators, I think."

"There's that possibility, I grant you," she replied, "But wouldn't bombing the field be more workable? While they've lost their naval bases along the Channel as well as the whole of the Belgian shore, they still have *Luftwaffe* concentrations in Holland."

"Good point," he observed, "And it wouldn't be a first time for Framlingham. Early last spring there was an intruder, a twin-engine Messerschmitt 410, which had been circling the base, looking for targets in the darkness of the wee hours.

"As it happened, a mission had been scheduled for the 390th to Augsburg that morning, the thirteenth of April. Before we got our own Mickey-equipped planes, most of the Pathfinder Forts, with the radar units, were obtained from the 96th Bomb Group at Alconbury, fifty miles from here.

"That B-17 was in its final approach, but as soon as they turned on their landing lights, the enemy pounced, knocking out their controls. They crash-landed off the runway into a brick wall. The plane caught fire, and they all would have died except for the heroics of nearby British soldiers. As it was, three of the crew were killed, and the Jerry escaped, because of the red tape getting clearance to fire." Watching her sip her beer, Bobby continued, "Luckily no one else died, but it was just pure luck. The field defenses then were equipped with potent 40 mm anti-aircraft cannon and a couple dozen .50 Caliber machine guns. But the word to open up on the Messerschmitt didn't come down in time from Air Division. It seems too many RAF planes, returning from their night missions over the Continent, were being shot at, and the diplomatic way was to get clearance from the British."

Diana shook her head. "I can just see it. It would make good comedy if it weren't so tragic. But the chain of command has always been festooned with red tape."

They laughed then, but were brought back to reality by the late hour. Neither wanted to part. He considered inviting her to his Nissen hut, but that was out, as his fellow officers were there, either trying to sleep or writing letters. But he did have to get back to the Squadron area.

On leaving the club, he meant to say goodnight, but she wouldn't let him go. As they passed Parham Hall, she broke the silence.

"I have something important to tell you, Bobby," she said excitedly. "I wanted to tell you sooner, but the security thing interfered. It's something I've always wanted. I think I'm carrying your baby. I've never, ever missed my monthly until now. In fact, it has been almost seven weeks."

Elated, Bobby gathered her into his arms tenderly. "That's wonderful news, darling! I love you so."

He still had as many as twenty-three missions to go, and while he and Diana had decided to tie the knot, he had always thought that marriage before finishing his tour would be out of the question. But now, because of the love he had for her and the responsibility of her pregnancy, that had to change.

He recalled his decision to put off marrying Denise until after finishing his education, and that mistake had to be avoided this time, or he could end up losing Diana too. Now it looked like he could be another one of the thousands bringing English war brides home. And what a bride!

In a soft voice, almost whispering, he asked, "Diana, how do you feel about coming home with me to California?"

With the moon shrouded by clouds in the blacked-out night, he could just see her face, lighted by an open smile.

She happily whispered her reply. "Of course. I'll go wherever you go, forever."

He already knew that, and was quick to embrace her even more closely, whispering, "Diana, will you marry me after tomorrow's mission?"

Her enthusiastic "Yes," was all she said, and all that was needed. She then clung to him wordlessly with an increasing passion that despite his fatigued state was exciting beyond belief. Overwhelmed with passion and joy, they frantically coupled, standing there against a wind-sheltered corrugated metal wall in the dark and frosty night. After the urgency subsided, he held her close as they repeatedly kissed.

"Come back to me tomorrow." She whispered.

He promised that with a final kiss. "Our marriage can't be soon enough for me," he replied.

When he returned to his bed. It was late, and in the dark, he just threw his clothes into his laundry bag, got into another pair of long johns, and hit the sack.

Despite his fatigue, sleep didn't come easily. He was worried, more so than before any other mission. All sorts of anxieties were whirling around in his mind. He pondered his failure to attend confession as Father Lenahan had suggested, and as he had halfway meant to do. Well, hell, he thought, what good would that have done, considering our making love just now? He hadn't attended church since Christmas, and then, it was Diana's Anglican one. He reflected on that wonderful emotional experience, uplifted as he had been by the Christmas holiday spirit, the stirring music, and his nearness to her.

He had chided the teenage gunners for their concerns regarding their mission that day, on the thirteenth of the month, pointing out to them the futility of such superstition, but wryly reminded himself of his own regarding his fancied lucky number. Well, they had survived that day, and mission number thirteen was next. That brought him again to reflect on how his superstition concerning that number had started

The events when he was thirteen returned to him, and he realized it had to do with his age when he survived so many accidents and misadventures. His parents, concerned with his safety, had labeled him accident-prone. But it was entirely due to carelessness and bravado, just a stage in his development, as nothing like that ever happened in later years.

Hit by a car when turning in front of it on his bike, suffering a concussion and a broken arm. Attempting to go hand over hand along the telephone cable between utility poles in front of the house, only to lose his grip and fall to the curbing. Again a concussion. Then there was that breakneck run in his would-be Soapbox Derby racer, the *Brown Bullet,* starting up on Mountain Avenue down super-steep Alameda. That ended in a slide of thirty yards along the rough pavement when the coaster overturned and he was thrown out. He survived all that, although his jeans and some skin did not. And he was thirteen. He shook his head considering the logic of that one.

It seemed longer, but sleep did come after only a few minutes, as his thoughts drifted back to Diana. Finally, the wonderful warmth she brought to his life seemed to cover him like a soft downy comforter.

＊ ＊ ＊ ＊

After they parted that evening at the 568th Squadron area, Diana headed back toward Parham Hall. Just as she reached the lane that led there, the moon, high in the sky and almost full, made a rare appearance from behind the ever-present clouds, lighting up the Group's planes on their hardstands in the other direction for a few minutes. On a whim, she walked back to get a closer look. One in particular caught her attention, and due its silvery reflection, the sight captivated her.

As she stood admiring the Fortress, and thinking of Bobby's mission in the morning, as an experienced plane watcher, she noted the domed radar antenna, housed where the ball turret usually was. Displayed on the vertical stabilizer she could see the letter "E," just below its serial number, and the big "Square J" of the 390th.

Thinking it must be Bobby's plane, she went around to the nose, kissed the fingers of her right hand, and then, reaching up, touched them to the cold metal of the little hatch.

As the scene was eclipsed by the moon's disappearance once more behind the clouds, she turned and started walking back toward Parham Hall, hurrying because of the cold. Worrying about Bobby's safety, she was stopped by a sudden barked order.

"Halt, or I'll shoot!"

It was an MP. She hadn't seen him because of the darkness and her pre-occupation, but now up close she could just make out the white helmet, which had led the British to call them "Snowdrops."

"Put your hands in the air," he said brusquely, "And don't move!" Advancing with his .45 automatic in one hand and a flashlight in the other, he saw her tousled hair and her rumpled officers' uniform.

"Ma'am, I'm sorry, but you have to show me your ID, please. You must know this is a restricted area for everyone except ground crew and tomorrow's flight personnel."

Embarrassed in being caught like that, and in her disheveled condition, Diana fumbled around in her shoulder bag, saying, "Please help me with your torch, soldier, I can't see a thing in the dark."

He holstered his pistol, and as they looked into her bag, the sound of an aircraft circling caught their attention.

He mumbled, "Must be one of your big RAF Lancasters returning from a mission. They fly over here often on their way back from night raids over Germany."

Diana saw the young open face of a boy illuminated in the light. She was momentarily speechless. So young, these Yanks, she thought. Then it hit her.

In an urgent tone, she remarked, "It's too early for their return, and it's not one of our heavies. That's not the sound of Rolls-Royce Merlins. Switch off your torch soldier. Don't you see, it's a Nazi intruder! Alert Base Defense, and be quick about it!"

Her crisp ring of authority jolted the MP into hastily grabbing his walkie-talkie from his nearby jeep. Getting the OD, the Officer of the Day, at Base Defense on the line, he hastily explained, "Sir, Corporal Denver, with the MPs. I have the word of an AMWD officer here that a twin-engine plane is circling the field, and must have seen a light. She thinks the aircraft is a Jerry intruder!" He didn't mention that the light was his.

The barked answer, "Keep her there, I'll be right along, corporal!" could be clearly heard through the receiver.

"No!" Diana shouted into the radio, "There isn't time for that. I'm Leftenant Howard, with the Air Ministry. Alert your base anti-aircraft batteries on the *Tannoy,* your PA system, and check with the control tower. They won't pick up a friend or foe signal, because it's a Bandit!"

Everything then seemed to happen all at once. Alerted by the loudspeaker's air-raid warning, all not asleep on the base heeded the signal, although most not on duty, including

Bobby, accustomed to the constant noise, almost always slept through any commotion.

Several searchlights suddenly pierced the blackness, projecting discs of white on the low overcast. They quickly caught a twin-engine plane, which Diana saw was a Junkers 88 fighter-bomber. It was just east of the field, not more than a few hundred feet up, plainly showing the German cross on its wings as it banked.

The officer on duty had been through the previous attack. As he gave the order to fire, his only thought was that last spring's *SNAFU* wasn't going to happen to him.

"Damned if we're gonna let this sonofabitch get away," he shouted, to no one in particular.

As the enemy plane banked toward the field, intent on a bombing and strafing run, the base .50 calibers opened up, their red tracers flashing toward the attacker from several directions. At that height and distance, they could hardly miss. Still, the Junkers came on, losing altitude directly over the main runway, its pilot intent on dropping his bombs.

Both engines were on fire. The ground crews, still preparing B-17s in that area, scattered. The Jerry pilot, blinded by the searchlights, missed the obvious targets and misjudged his height. Just before reaching the end of the runway, the plane slammed down onto the concrete, engulfed in flames.

Diana saw what was about to happen, and shouted a warning to the corporal, each diving into the ditch on either side of the narrow road. As she lay there, she watched in wide-eyed terror as the flaming wreckage, led by one of the engines, skidded in her direction, seemingly almost in slow motion.

At the last moment she ran, as one of the intruder's bombs exploded in the ditch where she had taken refuge, leaving a huge crater in the lane, filled with acrid smoke.

With the explosion and fire, the Squadron's quarters were emptied of their sleepy occupants, most in long johns or various combinations of flight clothes used in attempts to get a warm sleep. There wasn't much to see, except the scattered and burning remnants of the Ju-88 around the bomb crater and the shattered jeep some distance up the lane.

"God dammit," Danny exploded, "That bastard almost got us. Just a bit more to the left, and he would have hit squarely among our planes!"

Standing next to him, Bobby, sighed with relief. "You know what a bomb would have done to any Fortress it hit. By now they're all filled with Hundred Octane and loaded with two or three tons of high explosives. And us less than three hundred yards away!"

Danny nodded, remembering the havoc caused at the end of the runway when that B-17 crashed on takeoff the month before.

"At least it wasn't one of ours this time," Bobby mumbled wearily to Danny, as he began to shiver. It had become even colder than when he had turned in. Keenly feeling the need for the sleep that had barely started, he and his fellows returned to their sacks.

TWENTY-ONE

The Thirteenth Mission

Reveille was at four AM, only a couple of hours later. Carefully dressing, he went to the mess hall with his fellow officers to down some breakfast. Bacon and fresh eggs, still reserved for those scheduled for a mission that day. The saying, *the condemned man ate a hearty meal* was not lost on them. Nevertheless, countering their unease about the danger they were soon to face, they mostly attacked the fare with healthy appetites, unlike before their earlier missions.

All the talk was about the downing of the Nazi intruder. Rumor had it that Base Defense had been alerted by an officer who had been visiting. For a moment Bobby felt a dagger of fear in the pit of his stomach. Diana? Nah, it couldn't have been her. She would have been back at Parham Hall by then, he told himself.

They then proceeded to their briefing, their stomachs full, but again with their concerns accompanying them, playing on their imaginations. Where were they going today?

Someone said, "Hey, maybe it'll be easy—a milk run for a change." From their previous experiences with flak, the idea of an easy and risk-free mission had to be just wishful thinking. When had one of those ever been their luck? The fact that they had never had any fighter opposition did help, but when the map curtain was pulled at briefing, showing the route to be almost all the way to Berlin, among the usual groans were those of Bobby and his fellows.

They were somewhat reassured by the Intelligence Officer that because their assignment was "Low priority," there would likely be, as usual, no fighter opposition. Further, the escort of several hundred Mustangs for the eight hundred plus aircraft in the bomber stream was certain to keep the *Luftwaffe* away.

Three Squadrons from the 390th would take part, and unlike their previous missions, no flak was expected. Their assignment was an underground facility that the enemy chose not to betray by surrounding it with anti-aircraft batteries.

While concerned with the distance they would have to cover to reach their target, over six hundred miles, most began to envision the proverbial milk run from the impression given by the briefing officers.

Immediately recognizing that there was a problem, Bobby whispered to Danny, "Our IP is Belzig, a town about fifty miles southeast of the target at Derben, making our flight path appear to be aiming for Berlin. What are the enemy air controllers going to think? Is the Eighth Air Force trying to bring Nazi fighters up for our escorts to pounce on? It's as if they're using us as bait, the real objective being the *Luftwaffe*. He just said Derben is a low priority target. Otherwise, why fly deeper into Germany, and then turn homeward to drop? Sure, we've always feinted away from our target, but now we're flying fifty miles deeper into the most heavily defended region of the *Reich*, and then almost another fifty back. Over ninety extra miles!"

During the question and answer session for the pilots that followed the general briefing, Danny, with what Bobby had said in mind, stood upon being recognized by the Group Commander.

"Colonel, sir," he said, "Lieutenant Thunder, lead pilot for the 568th. I'm puzzled and troubled by the route planned, coming so near Berlin. We've just been told ours is a low priority target. Most of the personnel are talking about a milk run. If that's the case, why risk bringing down the entire Berlin Air Defense force on our Group? Why not a more direct approach from the north, leaving the main bomber stream earlier, with our Wing turning south to follow the Elbe River, rather than the Havel, so close to the German Capital? That way our target at Derben, on the Elbe, would also be nearly a hundred miles closer."

"Lieutenant," the Colonel replied, "I've asked the same question of General Partridge up at Air Division, and while for us the route looks ill-planned, we have to consider that almost a thousand bombers will be involved, with only our Thirteenth Wing going to Derben. There is safety in numbers, so we all fly together in the bomber stream as far as possible, escorted by our little friends, the Mustangs, until we reach the IP at Belzig. Then we turn back toward our target, while the other Wings of the Division and the rest of the Eighth head for theirs, Berlin, Leipzig, Mersberg, or wherever. Remember, this is a team effort, and the over-all good of all our forces takes precedence over that of any one Group. Your point is well taken, Thunder, and I would agree with you if the 390th were the only group involved."

As Danny sat down, the Colonel added, "Oh, and we've decided to have a Command Pilot serving as co-pilot with you today. Captain Bean here has more missions in command than you have as lead. I'm sure you'll find him most helpful."

It irked Danny that with all his experience in the RCAF, they were saddling him with someone who didn't fly more than once or twice a month. And why a Command Pilot anyway? They would be the "C" element in the Group, bringing up the rear, and with only eight Forts.

After the general briefing session, as with the pilots, the bombardiers in each crew met separately, for further specialized information. In Bobby's case, it was with the Group Bombardier, going over maps and photographs of the target area on the Elbe. As the lead bombardier of the Squadron, he received special instructions.

Since the production numbers for radar units had allowed a lead crew in every squadron, the Eighth Air Force had, with attrition, replaced many of its bombardiers with enlisted men. These had been trained mainly as gunners, with the added attention to the routines required for those in charge of the bombs. These men were called "Toggeliers." After all, every plane's bombs, whether toggled by a bombardier or his substitute, were now to be dropped on signal from the Squadron lead. Among the bombers put up that day by Bobby's 568th, theirs and only one other carried a bombardier.

By that time, they were becoming a rare breed, and they didn't like it one bit. The rationale, that with only one radar-equipped Fort per squadron, the expertise of a bombardier was wasted on any plane aside from the lead and the designated deputy. Concentrating on their gunnery, toggeliers could become expert on the chin turret, crucial during the head-on massed attacks the *Luftwaffe* had favored. Otherwise, all they had to do on the bomb run was to open the bomb bay doors and then trip the bomb release switch when the lead plane dropped its bombs.

Bobby sat next to Frank O'Neil, a fellow 2nd lieutenant, bombardier of the deputy lead crew. They were on their 29th mission, expected to be the next to last for them, despite arriving at Framlingham at the same time as crew one. While Bobby and his mates had been training those six weeks for Squadron lead, Frank's crew, in *Mississippi Mission*, had been on sixteen additional combats.

That morning, due to some screw up, no toggeliers showed up for the session. Bobby leaned over to O'Neil, whispering, "What happens if both our planes fall out of formation? The others would be next to useless."

O'Neill replied, "I guess they'd just have to catch up with the next squadron and its lead plane. But that's not likely to be necessary. Remember, Taylor, they're telling us this mission will be a milk run."

Because of the intruder's attack, coupled with the damage suffered on the previous mission, the Squadron inventory of serviceable Forts was depleted. Usually, any given Squadron in the 390th would have at least eighteen Fortresses on their hardstands, or in the hangers undergoing work. This gave flexibility in selecting the most airworthy aircraft, from the total number available, for the next mission. Usually the crews of one of the four Squadrons would stand down, while three would fly. Normal for a Squadron to put up was twelve, but the number would vary. This usually depended on whether the maintenance crews could repair and service them in time, working around the clock quite frequently to get the job done. Occasionally a maximum effort on the part of the Group would be called for, necessitating the use of every available combat-ready plane, making up a fourth and even a fifth squadron instead of the usual three.

Before the cold morning of the Fourteenth dawned, it became evident to Engineering that they were coming up short. The 568th didn't have the numbers. Some of the planes were so full of holes from the damage from the intruder explosion that trouble-shooting and repairs would have to wait for daylight. They counted only seven serviceable craft, hardly Squadron strength.

The 571st, located away from the crash site, was in good shape, and lent an eighth B-17, an un-named orphan, identified only by its serial number, to the 568th. In that way they could participate with the minimum number of eight bombers, judged barely adequate for their mutual protection from fighter attack, lacking the usual low flight of four.

As their truck was driven past the still smoking wreckage of the intruder, in the early morning darkness they could only make out some investigative activity there. When they were dropped off at their usual hardstand, they found yet another Mickey-equipped craft. Not much different than the others, aside from the ID letter on the fuselage and below the "Square J" on the tail, serial number 46480. That this was yet a different aircraft was greeted with mixed feelings, but tempered by the idea that the third of the new planes they would fly had to be the proverbial charm.

It certainly looked perfect, with its still shiny aluminum skin, a lack of patches and only light oil stains. The Engineering Officer at briefing had certified all the planes to be in perfect condition, and their crew chief told them that it had served well on its first and only previous combat the week before. Everything had checked out flawlessly that morning.

Unfortunately, careful inspection missed a single impact of an explosion-propelled fragment that had dented the aluminum impeller housing of the number three engine's turbo-supercharger, where tolerances were only a couple of thousandths of an inch.

Bobby, as the armament officer for their crew, had to see to it that the gunners picked up their machine guns and had properly fitted them into the mounts at their stations. He and Lynch supervised the handling of theirs as well. He then inspected the bomb bay doors enclosing the deadly cargo and checked the solidity of the Plexiglas of the nose.

Encumbered by his bulky flight clothing, he expertly, if not effortlessly, hoisted himself through the front hatch, after finally emptying his bladder. This was again into the Brussels sprouts that grew right up to the concrete of those particular hardstands, and which resulted in a suspiciously more exuberant growth there than elsewhere. By that time, it had become almost a tradition for the crews.

From his position over the bombsight in the nose of the Fortress, in the decreasing dimness of the misty dawn, enhancing the green side of the spectrum, similar patches alongside several of the parked planes stood out. He mused about how the farmer felt about that, until that trivial thought was erased by the enormity of the impending incursion deep into the *Reich*, the realization hitting with the usual hollow feeling in the pit of the stomach.

He proceeded to check the bomb-load, seeing that all ten of the five hundred pounders were fused and on safety, taking time to go over the radar equipment with Brown, the new Mickey operator. He then returned to his station to make a final check on his gun controls and other connections.

In the din of whining starter motors, ending as the engines caught in coughing clouds of blue-white exhaust, the lead planes of the three squadrons began to taxi. One by one they began to move out to the perimeter taxiway. Bobby had finished checking out his equipment, wiping the lenses of the Norden bombsight carefully with tissue. He then checked his oxygen, electrical heating outlet, finally bringing down the yoke that controlled the twin fifties in the chin turret beneath him. As always, that was comforting, as along with the bombsight in front of him, it gave him continued support, mostly moral, on his little stool, in case sudden deceleration occurred. He still wasn't completely convinced that their new plane would perform flawlessly.

On the way to the runway, they taxied past the others of the 568th, each Fortress waiting its turn to fall in behind. Only one was an "Old friend," as they affectionately regarded planes in which they had previously flown. There were O'Neill's *Mississippi Mission, Cloud Hopper, Starduster,* and *Girl of My Dreams,* none of which Bobby had crewed.

They passed *Little Butch III,* the one in which he and fellow crewmembers had been welded into a fighting unit. On those missions they had found there was nothing they wouldn't do for each other. They had become literally a flying brotherhood in that Fort.

Bringing up the rear, most often the case with newcomers, was the loaner from the 571st, carrying the letter "Z" and only its serial number. In a gesture of welcome, Bobby saluted them appreciatively as his Fort taxied by.

As they turned onto the runway, after the tower's green light indicated their turn for takeoff, the rest of the Squadron followed at thirty-second intervals. Just at sunrise, Danny lifted the heavily loaded craft through the light mist to the prescribed altitude, at the airspeed and manifold settings calculated to space the bombers safely as they gained altitude. Visibility was good for a change, but it was reassuring to see that the abbreviated 568th and the rest of the Group had learned well, lessons essential for collision-free assembly when they had to pass through dense clouds, as almost always had obscured their climbing out.

The Squadrons formed up behind the Group lead, with Bobby's element the low Squadron again. At the Rally Point, as with most of the previous missions, they joined the bombers of the other Groups making up their Air Division, the Third, and headed out over the North Sea in a long train.

In the nose of the ship, he couldn't see the elements following them, but the leading formations of bombers, their aluminum skins glinting golden in the rising sun, were so numerous that they resembled strings of Christmas tree lights. Moving ever forward, they were mere specks in the distance, fifty miles ahead.

The bomber stream would be over a hundred miles long, they had been told. Along with the fighters, the great numbers of Eighth Air Force planes involved lent a certain feeling of security. Something like herd immunity was a thought that occurred to him. In numbers there is safety, he kept thinking, helping to allay that ever-present anxiety.

Still, the fact that their Squadron, with only eight planes, was short its low flight of four was disquieting, making it more vulnerable to fighter attack, despite the reassurances by the big brass. Four of the 568th's Fortresses had been damaged by flak on the raid only the day before to Mainz-Euskirchen. The others, initially ready to go, being nearest the crash and explosion of the intruder, might have sustained only minor damage, but couldn't be thoroughly inspected until daylight, and thus couldn't be cleared for action in time. They did give his lead plane extra attention, as in this game one couldn't be too careful.

Oh well, Bobby thought, enemy fighter resistance had always been absent for them. Thus far, almost the only danger had been German anti-aircraft fire, the weather and the possibility of mechanical failure. The thought occurred to him, a rationalization really, that whether they had twelve planes or eight made no difference to the gunners who might be waiting for them as they crossed the enemy coast. Still, he couldn't shake the worry about fighters, and the lack of a full compliment of twelve planes. Their incomplete umbrella of defensive fire would certainly make them a more attractive and vulnerable target for the *Luftwaffe*.

Although Belgium had by then been mostly liberated, the Netherlands was not free of enemy flak and fighters. To avoid them, their course continued well out over the sea as they proceeded on a northerly bearing. For a change, the weather was perfect for visual bombing, with hardly a cloud, except for a thin layer a thousand feet below, at that time to the northeast of their course. Bobby envisioned actually seeing the results of his efforts, and found comfort in the greater assurance that his bombs would not be landing on homes and schools, but squarely on target. It again occurred to him that all those clouds on their previous missions, which had been so frustrating for him because of the lack of target visibility, could be part of the reason that they had not had much in the way of fighter resistance, or more damage from flak.

When their escort of Mustangs from the 567th joined them high above, over the German coast north of Cuxhaven, near the Danish border, they were much heartened. At that point, they were almost two thirds of the way to the target, save for the extra miles demanded by their questionable IP at Belzig.

Just after leaving the coast, with the Group maintaining an altitude of 26,000 feet, the 568th's lead Fort suddenly had a drop in power. Danny, over the intercom, called to the top turret Gunner/Engineer just behind him.

"Zito, check this out! The instruments tell us that everything's still running smoothly, except we've lost manifold pressure in number three."

Leaving his gun platform behind the pilots, Zito peered over Danny's shoulder.

"Sir, it has to be the turbo. The engine isn't smoking, and oil and fuel pressures are normal. No way can that be fixed in flight."

Danny exchanged glances with Captain Bean, who had displaced their co-pilot for the mission. Shoving the throttles forward, he tried to compensate with the other engines, pushing them to peak output, nearly restoring their speed.

That lasted only five minutes. "Dammit to hell," Danny shouted, looking at his instruments, "They're overheating. The other three R-1820s can't take much more of this, flailing away in this rarified atmosphere."

Little by little they began to lose altitude, loaded down as they were, dropping farther behind the "A" and "B" Squadrons.

Zito said, "It's probably not the bearings, because the oil pressure is up. The temperature is off the scale, though, meaning the impeller has seized up. Twenty thousand RPM's can build white heat if the housing has been dented. Don't ask me how the preflight inspection missed that."

Turning back foremost in his mind, Danny instructed Cardone to radio Gerald Johnston, the deputy lead pilot in *Mississippi Mission,* who replied that they were ready to take over. The 568th would number only seven, but by increasing speed, leaving the faltering Fort, they could still close up with the rest of the Group ahead.

Bean yelled, "Hold it! What in hell do you think you're doing? I'm the Command Pilot, and my orders are to complete the mission as planned."

Danny looked at him incredulously. "There's no way we can make up for the loss of that supercharger at anything over twenty-one thousand feet, carrying this bomb load. We have to turn back. We can't risk the rest of the Squadron by insisting they throttle back to our speed."

"We're going to stay as close as we can to the rest of the Group, regardless, Bean shot back. "Give the engines emergency power."

Danny almost exploded. "Dammit, you can see I've done that, and they're already overheating. Much more of this and we won't have any engines at all. If you insist on continuing, we'll have to jettison our bombs. That way we could regain our position in the Group, and at least be able to signal the drop for our Squadron."

The Command Pilot exclaimed, "Lieutenant! This is a bombing mission, and bombing our objective is what each plane will do. Returning prematurely is cowardly. The Eighth Air Force has never been turned back by the *Luftwaffe!*"

His eyes widening with disbelief, Danny retorted, "The *Luftwaffe!* What's turning us back is a major mechanical defect. Aborting is our choice, not forced by any action of theirs!"

As if he hadn't heard that, Bean loudly continued, "A lone Fort would be a prime target for enemy fighters. It's over three hundred miles back across the water, and we're half way to Derben already."

Danny countered, saying firmly, "We're turning back. All eight of us will be sitting ducks if their fighters find the Squadron. You know what they can do to isolated elements. Can't you see? You're jeopardizing not only us, but also those seven other Forts and sixty-three crew. As a single plane, we can hide in those scattered clouds below on our way home if Jerry fighters make it necessary."

Bean objected, "Look at those contrails up there. Hundreds of Mustangs. And remember our briefing. This mission will be the milk run they described. We're the lead Fort, and we'll continue to lead. Radio our deputy to get back into position and the others to continue following us."

Danny started the one-eighty that would begin their flight home.

"Lieutenant Thunder!" The angry Bean shouted, as he tried to counter Danny's superior strength on the wheel and rudder pedals, "Did you hear me? Turn this Fort back to its original heading, or else!"

Danny looked at him in disgust. "You're forgetting that this is *my* plane. For some unknown reason, probably so you could log an easy combat mission, they've put you in that right seat. Technically, you're only here to command the Squadron, and since we can't keep up with them, you won't have a squadron to command."

Enraged, the Captain screamed, "Turn this bird back on course! The Squadron will stay with us if I say so. I'll have you court-marshaled. You could be shot as a mutineer! Now, as superior to you in rank, I'm giving you one last chance. Do you understand? You will continue on course. That's a Direct Order."

Seething, Danny complied. Not even he dared defy a Direct Order from a superior officer, but still he retorted,

"You're wrong Bean. Direct Order or not, Army Regulations state that in case of mechanical failure, the decision to abort is the sole prerogative of the craft's pilot. They also say that in the case of the pilot being unable to make that decision, the officer next in line of command, the co-pilot, shall make the decision. You're the co-pilot on this mission, Bean, not the pilot. I'm here to make that decision, which you've already heard."

Before the angry Bean could respond, a chorus of voices came over the intercom, with a single message of support for Danny.

"Shut up, you guys," Danny replied firmly. "This is not a mutiny. It's a disagreement between the Captain of the ship, and the Admiral of the fleet. This Fort is in trouble, and we should turn back. That's why we have a deputy lead. But for some unknown reason, Bean here has been sent with us to run the squadron, such as it is. When we get back, I'm bringing charges. You can back me up then. This guy is risking not only all our lives, but everyone behind us."

"I'm writing you up as soon we get back to Framlingham, Thunder. You'll be lucky to keep your commission after this!"

"We'll see, *if* we get back," Danny replied through clenched teeth.

The lead Fort flew on, and the rest of the Squadron stayed with them, all dropping lower and farther behind. The fighter escort, at a much higher altitude, after joining them at the coast, lost visual contact when that high thin cirrus cloud layer, which had been slowly moving southeast came between them. During that interval, as the lagging 568th lost more ground, the escorting Mustangs flew ahead, keeping pace with the main force.

As the flight continued, with the heading still over the Elbe River, taking the bomber stream on a course north of Berlin, their little element remained unmolested. It was only when they turned south, and began following the smaller Havel, that it looked certain that they were headed for the Capital, rather than the target, Derben.

From over twenty-eight thousand feet, the Nazis were waiting for the main body. In they came, wave after wave of single engine fighters, in line abreast. Those bombers received the protection of their Mustang escorts, engaging the enemy and driving them away in a swarm of deadly dogfights. Occasionally, German planes broke through, attacking the tight formations bearing down on their objectives.

Without anti-aircraft fire, they could fire on the Fortresses before, during, and after their bomb runs, although not without hits by the gunners of the hundreds of B-17s. That defensive fire, coupled with the huge toll taken by the Mustangs, limited the losses along the bomber stream.

Bobby could see the fighting ahead, but not the very large mass of enemy planes that happened upon the straggling 568th. Firof, at the tail guns, saw them first.

"We're sitting ducks! There must be a hundred of them, mostly single engine 190s."

Danny shouted through the intercom, "Cardone, radio our fighter escort for support!"

The Radioman/Gunner made the call, clearing his machine gun at the same time. "This is *Cavort*. We need fighter support. Repeat, *Cavort* calling, Jerries coming in! Urgently require support!" But in the melee, the Mustang pilots, above the thin obscuring cloud layer, didn't hear that desperate call.

Initially, and surprisingly, the Germans came in from the rear, six o'clock high, trying to hide their approach in the contrails of the huge bomber force ahead. Later they came from every point of the compass. While slow and low, the 568th was at first in perfect formation, and ready for them, their total of 102 .50 cal. machine guns forming an almost perfect umbrella of fire. Perfect at first anyway, as a couple of fighters in the first wave fell away smoking.

The first Fort to be downed was destroyed by a fluke, but for those witnessing it, it was almost demoralizing. They had just tightened up the formation when the attacking fighters were first seen.

"Wow! Firof cried, "I just got me a 190! It's smoking badly, but Jesus, he's misjudged his clearance and has rammed the waist of our friend from the 571st. And, holy shit, the spinning propeller just chewed its way totally through the fuselage!"

The radar officer, Brown, manning one of the waist guns, exclaimed, "Good God, I can't believe it! The tail section is flying, but the rest of the plane is falling like a rock. Look, the tail gunner is still firing. Come on, guy, hit the silk before it's too late!"

"He made it!" Kelly, at the other waist gun, called out, "Just in time. See, the tail section is starting to tumble!"

In the nose of the Fortress, leading the formation, Bobby could see little at first, his heart in his throat, pumping with adrenaline. They were under attack, marked by the excited chatter of the gunners on the intercom, and the vibration of the plane with the firing of their guns.

Crouching over the bombsight, and with the control yoke of the twin fifties of the chin turret in his hands, he was ready when one of the fighters that had attacked from behind passed through the formation into his field of fire. It was amazingly easy, a quick burst, just a short squeeze of the firing button. He could see the tracers tearing shreds of metal off the tail surfaces, then "Walking" up the fuselage, followed by the jettisoning of the canopy, as the pilot bailed out, his falling form quickly lost from sight below.

That they had been hit in the first pass was apparent, as he felt the multiple impacts, but the plane continued on, keeping its vectored course toward the IP. At twenty-two thousand feet, they were almost able to match the speed of the rest of the Group, still far ahead, two thousand feet higher, and partially obscured by the thin cloud layer between them.

Just behind Bobby, Lynch, the navigator, in between firing his cheek gun, was frantically studying his charts. Amid the shaking of the plane by defensive fire and bullet impacts, he continued calling out the checkpoints below over the intercom.

Now, as the leader of the formation, they were being given the treatment Nazi fighters gave all pathfinder planes. The Jerries had quickly learned that the radar antenna had eliminated the ball turret in the plane's belly, allowing the lead Fort to be more easily attacked from below. As long as there was protective fire from the accompanying Fortresses, and the formation remained tight, the enemy could attack that way only at great risk. Except for the most aggressive or foolhardy pilot, an attacker would think twice about that approach.

One tried, and fortunate to have avoided the supporting fire from the other planes in the Squadron on his steep climb, lost speed, just forward of Bobby's position.

He's stalling out, he thought, about to go into a spin! It was too high for the chin guns, so he grabbed the cheek gun on that side, and as he squeezed the trigger, saw the stream of fire, at point-blank range, almost cut all the way through the 190 behind the canopy. He could see the startled look on the pilot's face, just before the cockpit was engulfed in flames. The craft then dropped off in a spin, exploding three hundred feet below.

The seven aircraft remaining in formation were swarmed upon by at least ninety assault fighters, now attacking from every direction. The first victim to their cannon fire was *Cloud Hopper,* which fell into a steep dive.

The right waist gunner, Frank Kelly, called out, "I see three guys dropping away!"

Just then, Lynch said over the intercom in a strangely calm voice, while tapping on Bobby's shoulder to get his attention, "It'll be another three minutes to our Initial Point."

At that moment, the Fortress in number four position, directly behind and below the lead plane, hit during the first wave and trailing increasing smoke from a fire somewhere, suddenly blew up. There was a white flash followed by an orange ball of fire, scattering burning fragments in all directions, each trailing smoke like the burst of a huge, malevolent skyrocket.

"It's *Starduster!*" cried tail gunner Firof, adding, "But look, two, no, three, hey! Six made it out. The lucky bastards! How in hell did they do that?"

Bobby, using either his chin turret, or the left cheek gun, depending on the target, could only see the battle in front. The cloud layer above was thinning out ahead, giving a better view of the two other Squadrons of the 390th, and the rest of the Thirteenth Wing.

He was concentrating on the approaching IP, where his request to Danny would put the bombsight and autopilot in control of the plane. He was almost totally oblivious of the destruction of his own Squadron, which ordinarily would have frightened anyone. But in the heat of battle, every man was too busy for fright. They had felt that beforehand, as all sane men did, and it would return later—if they survived.

Lynch called out, "The IP is two minutes away."

Just then, the number six Fortress, to the left and behind them, under attack by two fighters, began trailing flames from one wing. Several men were seen to bail out from the waist. Then, the entire plane became enveloped in flames, a ball of fire. It was *Girl of My Dreams*. Almost miraculously, six or seven parachutes were seen to blossom far below, according to the excited chatter of the gunners in the rear.

"Lucky S.O.Bs," one shouted, "Just in time!"

Brown, the Mickey operator, still manning the left waist gun, called out, "Where's our number three? They were there when I was peppering those 190s coming in!"

"Yeah," yelled Zito from the top turret, "It just disappeared. It was that new, un-named job piloted by Lt. Morman."

In the nose of their similar bare metal Fort, sitting behind Bobby, Lynch called out, "One minute to the IP."

The Jerry fighters kept coming. Winking muzzle flashes of their cannon were answered by the vibrating roar of multiple fifties. There was less defensive fire now, with the loss of half the Forts. The air in the plane was filled with smoke, reeking of cordite, but not affecting the crew much, breathing as they were through their oxygen masks.

Little Butch III was next. Now with two engines on fire, the craft fell from its exposed position in the formation. It hit the snow-covered ground far below, in a ball of flames, but not before half the crew were seen to bail out. It was the second 390th plane that day to crash at the little village of Goerne, off to the right. One Fortress, from the 571st, the element just ahead, had led the way. *Good Ol' Yank,* carried five men down with her. They fought to the last, until starting that long fall earthward. Midway there it exploded, taking with it an enemy fighter that flew into the falling debris, the wreckage of both planes crashing nearly together far below.

The IP! Intent on his gunnery, Bobby was oblivious of the landmarks until that very moment. He didn't see O'Neil, their deputy lead bombardier, and his other three surviving crewmembers bail out of the burning *Mississippi Mission,* behind and to the right in number two position, over the little town of Garlitz, where it crashed.

Lynch called out the IP, giving the new bearing to Danny. As the plane turned towards their target, it became time to enter the flight data into the sight's computer for the beginning of the bomb run. Bobby left his guns and began. Airspeed, altitude, wind drift. He could see the target far ahead, under the Norden's cross hairs. Black smoke was already boiling up thousands of feet into the air.

Finishing his calculations, and getting on the intercom to Danny, he said, "We're on target, just make sure our airspeed remains steady so my calculations will hold. Those boys ahead have made some hits. Let's hope the target can still be seen when we get there!"

He wasn't able to contact Brown, the Mickey operator. Noting the continued gunnery vibrations and the extra clatter, he had decided he was needed more on his fifty at the plane's waist than in operating the radar unit. Hell, he thought, conditions have been visual all day anyway as far as the ground is concerned.

Bobby kept hoping for their little friends, who, like the cavalry, would come to their rescue in time. But most of them were above the obscuring cloud layer, protecting the main body, and failed to see the plight of the 568th. The Mustangs assigned to the 390th when the battle began were by then busy with the Messerschmitt high cover, mostly from *Jagdgeschwader* 300.

The plane was being badly pounded in the continued fighter attacks, as they approached the target. Bobby wondered what was holding it together. He was encouraged that the battle had not been entirely one-sided. He could see several smoke trails made by falling enemy fighters. More than just my two, he thought.

Now, on the bomb run, he had a job to do. He put everything else out of his mind, except the oil facilities, keeping the bombsight's crosshairs on the objective ahead.

Danny called out, "Watch for changes in speed. Number three's smoking badly now. You may need to change what you're feeding into the Norden. I'm hitting the remaining engines for emergency power, at least until after bombs away."

Bobby detected grimness in the voice of his old buddy, correctly surmising that up there, in the left seat at the controls, things were as rough as he had it in the nose. And that was plenty rough.

Lynch could only switch from one cheek gun to the other, depending on the direction of the attack, or as was often the case, when an enemy fighter shot ahead of them. It was a wonder there was still ammunition left, Bobby thought. No gun had more than six hundred rounds, only a minute steadily firing a Browning Fifty. Even with bursts of only two seconds, would there be any remaining for withdrawal?

At that moment, in a frontal attack, a 20 mm cannon shell from an FW-190 shattered the right cheek window, passed through the navigator's chest, killing him instantly. It then exploded on the number two engine, where its nacelle joined the wing. A second round would have hit Bobby too, but he was saved by being bent over the bombsight. It creased the back of his flak vest, almost pulling it off, sending him into Lynch sitting behind him, his lifeless arm still gripping the right cheek gun.

Danny tried to feather the propeller, but oil was spewing out, its loss foiling the attempt. He was able to shut the engine down, but the prop continued to windmill, shaking the entire plane. This was a real threat to the already badly damaged craft, but they were for the moment saved by another 20 mm, exploding as it hit the propeller hub. The impact, combined with the torque of the un-feathered prop, broke the shaft, sending the propeller spinning away, missing the fuselage by a hair.

Bobby then hit the switch for opening the bomb-bay doors. Nothing happened! The red indicator light remained off, and they were rapidly approaching the aiming point. He shouted over the intercom for the radioman Cardone. "Gus, Get on those cranks that open the doors manually!"

No answer. Much of the communication system was out, as a shell had hit the radio room, taking out some of its critical circuitry. Bobby hoped that someone would think to use the cranks. There was no time for him to get back up there to the manual controls to open the doors himself. Obviously, he wouldn't be able to drop their bombs unless they went around again. But he knew they would never be able to complete the 360 Degree turn needed.

Frantically he tried to contact Danny. The emergency release to drop the bomb bay doors was located just behind the pilot, near the top turret, so the bombs could be dropped automatically.

Neither Danny nor Bean responded. He had no idea if they were still alive, since the bombsight, through the AFCE was controlling the plane. That would continue, barring damage to the system, until it was shut off, releasing the autopilot.

It was time! There was only one thing he could do then, as lead bombardier. Right on target, he fired the flare that signaled the remaining planes to drop their two and a half ton burdens. Hell, he thought, the 568th will still score today, maybe big-time.

As the drop was signaled, he felt a keen disappointment in the plane's failure to lighten with the usual elevator-like surge when relieved of its bomb load. He did experience a sense of accomplishment that the deadly cargoes of the remaining planes, as much as ten tons perhaps, were on their way to the mark. As he switched off the Norden, their wounded Fortress began to turn. No longer glued to the bombsight, Bobby twisted on his stool to count the other ships in the formation. To the left, he saw nothing except an element of Jerries, gathering for another pass. He swung around, thinking, the following Fortresses must be taking a wider turn. Still nothing! Just then, Firof, in the tail, exclaimed, "All the other Forts are gone!"

"My God!" Bobby shouted into his oxygen mask. "We're the only ones left!"

And then the fighters bored in again.

It crossed his mind that his job then, in addition to defending the plane, would be navigating for the flight back. But they were heading east, toward Berlin. Forget Framlingham. Considering their desperate position, he would settle for any safe haven on the ground.

Protected only by the fragile transparent nose, and exposed on his stool, Bobby tensed himself for a pair of head-on attackers, firing the last of his ammunition as he saw the first winking of their muzzle flashes. In three seconds they were gone, but not before a couple of 20 mm shells perforated the Plexiglas nose, one exploding on contact, spewing fragments and shredding the aluminum skin on one side, the other detonating behind in the bomb bay.

God, he thought, it was suddenly even colder, with a howling icy blast filling the nose compartment. A shell fragment had cut his oxygen line, pulling off his oxygen mask and nearly taking off his ear.

He reached for the mask and a portable tank, but couldn't find them. An all-pervading chill came over him as the electrical current failed in his thermal suit. He could barely see since his goggles had frosted up. As he tore them off, the frigid jet of air from the plane's perforated nose hit him full in the face in a blinding flash, making matters even worse. And behind him were the flames.

In the pilot's seat, Danny struggled with the controls, putting the Fortress into a dive in a desperate move to extinguish the fire.

"What the hell are you doing?" Bean yelled. Before Danny was heard to answer, the intercom failed completely.

It was then that Bobby realized that they were finished. He was struck by the irony that after all his agonizing about blind bombing, this mission was the only one where he had been able to clearly see the objective, and place the crosshairs perfectly on the aiming point. And then to be unable to drop their bombs!

He began to pray for the first time in years, as he grabbed his parachute and attached it to his harness. Lynch's body was still slumped over against him. The aircraft continued its shallow dive to the east. He thought, why are we heading for Berlin? Is anybody at the controls? And then the ship began to spin, the centrifugal force pinning him to the overhead, unable to reach the escape hatch in the floor.

How slowly time seemed to pass. His first thoughts were of Diana and their unborn child, and the plans that they had made for a life together after the war. He thought of his mother, and even of Denise. He wasn't drowning, but might as well have been, as the lack of oxygen began to take effect, enhanced by his now uncontrolled shivering. There was a great sadness, but with a physical detachment somehow.

He felt neither the force of the Boeing exploding nor pain as the shock wave propelled him forward, through the shattered Plexiglas nose, out of the big bird. It was as if only the memories of his life, as they flashed through his brain were real. Then everything became bathed in a lovely white light, coupled with a feeling as if he were floating on puffy, paradoxically warm white clouds, as shock set in and his brain became starved for oxygen and blood flow.

TWENTY-TWO

Recovery

When Diana regained consciousness, she was in the infirmary, thinking she was dead. At first her vision was blurred, and everything surrounding her was white. Somewhere there was music playing, or was that just ringing in her ears? Then, moving in bed, she felt the pain in her ribs and shoulders, quickly bringing her back to reality. Her first thought was of Bobby, and then of her baby.

"Oh God," she breathed in sudden realization, "Let them both be alive." This led to a gentle hand being placed on her forehead. As her vision focused, she made out the smiling face of a young nurse in white.

"You're in the hospital. You've been through quite a lot, but the doctor says aside from some ribs, nothing was broken, and you don't seem to have any internal injuries either. Now that you've come out of it, you'll likely be able to return to your unit very soon."

Diana considered that a few moments, and then asked, "Did the doctors have anything to say about my being pregnant?"

The nurse, surprised, responded, "I expect that wasn't part of their evaluation, as you certainly don't show it. I'll inform them, but I doubt that it would change anything."

Leaving Diana's side, she soon came back with the doctor, who wore the uniform of an Air Force Captain under his white coat.

"Hello," he said in a friendly voice. "I'm Doctor Latshaw. You're one lucky lady. No serious injuries, despite what you've been through. And you believe you're pregnant? We could run a frog test, but that would take too long, and by that time you'll be home for a well-earned rest."

"Doctor, I don't remember anything after the Base guns were turned on the Nazi intruder. Will you fill me in on what took place?"

He smiled then, saying, "You were found where the JU-88's bomb blast had thrown you. Most of the explosion's force was absorbed in the roadside ditch. That's what saved your life. Your heavy woolens protected you, both from burns and the severe hypothermia to be expected after those hours in the open." Then, laughing, he added, "It didn't hurt that you landed, in of all things, a newly harvested pile of Brussels sprouts!"

That evening, as she was sitting up in bed for a meal designed for postoperative cases, melba toast, tea and some sort of fruit-flavored gelatin, she received a visitor.

It was the Group Commander of the 390th. After introducing himself, he said, "I have to congratulate you for your brilliance in alerting the Base about that Nazi intruder on the early morning of the fourteenth. If it hadn't been for you, there's no telling how many people might have been killed. I'm recommending you for promotion, but that's up to your British superiors. I do have the authority to confer a decoration, however."

Reaching into his overcoat, he produced a shiny black case and snapped it open, displaying a five-pointed star, on a red, white and blue ribbon.

"This is the 'Bronze Star,' which reflects your presence of mind and coolness under imminent threat of enemy fire. Your actions at that time saved Station 153 from severe loss of life and the certain destruction of a number of aircraft."

As he pinned the medal on her hospital robe, rather than pride, she felt a little ashamed. She couldn't help thinking that had it not been for her impropriety in being out there, the young Snowdrop corporal's torch would not have betrayed their location to the enemy bomber pilot. If she had known then of the fate of Bobby and his Squadron, indirectly caused by that same intruder, she would have refused the honor, her actions serving only to re-arrange the casualty figures for the day.

The next day, she was visited by her immediate superior, a captain of the Royal Engineers. He had taken over her inspection duties, plus the supervision of repairing the bomb damage, a routine job for Base Maintenance. An older professional officer, he reminded her of her father.

First congratulating her on her Bronze Star, he took her hand, asking, "How are you, lass?"

She detected a certain concern in his tone. "Oh I'm fine, sir. Sorry about my being unable to carry on. Are things coming along satisfactorily at the airfield?"

"Well yes," he replied, "We've been able to repair the damage to the runway quite nicely, but there's bad news, too, I'm sorry to say. It concerns the raid the Group flew that day. An entire Squadron was wiped out near Berlin. All eight Fortresses and seventy-two brave chaps are missing."

Her ears still ringing from the explosion, she cried, "Good Lord! What did you say? Eight what?" Nearly overcome with dread, she quickly added, "Oh, I'm sorry sir," unsuccessfully trying to fend off the tears. "It's my ruddy hearing, the bomb blast, you know. Please say it wasn't 568th Squadron."

The captain saw the tears confirming an emotional connection. "I'm sorry," he said apologetically, picking up his cap to leave. "Yes, I'm afraid it was."

At that moment Diana's world crashed down around her. "Oh God, please, not Bobby!"

Almost overcome, all she could do for the rest of the day was to cling to the hope that he was still alive. She couldn't eat, and had to have a sleeping pill during the night. When awakened by the nurse the next morning, her first thoughts were that it was all a horrible dream. Then a glimmer of hope found its way into her thoughts. She began to heed it, recalling the known fact that on average, somewhat more than half the men of downed Fortresses survived to be taken prisoner. Was Bobby a POW? Then she prayed for that.

Two days later, the word was that she was to have a month's leave for recuperation. The nurse, still contending with her patient's depression, inquired whether her family had been notified. When she answered that she didn't know, she was then asked about her husband. Oh God, Diana considered, did she mean the baby's father, or her long-lost RAF bomber pilot?

Choosing the latter, she replied, "No, he shan't be coming. You see, I'm one of those war widows." Then, attempting to relieve the poor nurse's embarrassment, she hastily added, "My parents are in London, however. They've always been there for me in time of need. You needn't worry, I'll ring them up."

* * * *

She continued to worry about Bobby's fate and the circumstances that had led to the demise of the 568th. Details were delayed, but she found from official records mention of the huge number of planes that had been dispatched on January 14th to the regions around Berlin, seeking oil and other targets. The bombers had flown through nearly clear skies the whole way, all bombing visually. 186 B-17s, including the three Squadrons from the 390th, were sent to Derben, where the underground oil storage complex lay, forty miles west of Berlin.

The 357th Fighter Group, for breaking up the attack of around 250 Jerry fighters, received a Unit Citation, bagging an almost unbelievable confirmed fifty-five of them.

Unfortunately for Bobby and the rest of the 568th, their escort didn't manage to reach the lagging Squadron to break up the attack of the swarm of Nazi FW-190s that wiped them out. The Mustangs lost five of their numbers in dogfights as they diverted most of the *Luftwaffe* fighters from the main bomber stream.

After Group Command in the control tower at Framlingham had waited in vain for the return of the Forts of the 568th, an inquiry was held as to the causes of the disaster. In the de-briefing of personnel of the two surviving Squadrons, they learned little. Those aircrews had had their hands more than full due to fighter attacks.

The investigators were aware of the supercharger problem from radio communication. They questioned the decision to continue on, while acknowledging that by the time they had lost power, the Group was more than two thirds of the way to the objective. The Brass ignored the fact that at briefing that morning they had led the crews to believe that the mission would be a milk run, the reason that the other planes of the 568th stayed with their Squadron leader. They knew nothing of the conflict between Danny and Bean, or why fighter protection had broken down.

The judgment didn't take long. It wasn't the first time for the Eighth Air Force that an entire Squadron had been wiped out, although it was the greatest single-mission loss suffered by the 390th. The conclusion came down that it was due entirely to pilot error, just as Bobby had predicted in one of his letters during flight training about where blame would be placed. Ironically, it was Danny, and not Bean, who was implicated as being responsible.

The official account of Mission 243 on that fateful day was soon released:

"The 14 January assignment was the underground oil storage facilities at Derben, in the Berlin area.

"It should have been a routine assignment, but, like Münster, it developed into one of the Group's great battles.

"After numerous missions in which no enemy fighters were even seen, on this date 100 fighters attacked.

"At the time of the attack, "A" and "B" Squadrons were in good formation; "C" Squadron was minus a low element, being composed of only eight aircraft. One of the superchargers of the lead ship of the "C" Squadron went out, and the Squadron fell behind, and about 2,000 feet below the rest of the Group.

"Using no apparent plan of attack, a hundred Focke-Wulfs and Messerschmitts concentrated on "C" Squadron. In the fighting, which lasted for thirty minutes, all eight of the B-17s were shot down. Thirty of the fighters attacked "A" Squadron, while twenty-five hit "B" Squadron and added a ninth Fortress to the victims. It was the Group's greatest casualty figure, but all the fighting was not one-sided.

"Twenty-four fighters were destroyed, two were probably destroyed, and four were damaged by our gunners. And like Münster, the known toll would probably have been much greater if the crews shot down could have accounted for their scores.

"Bombing results were difficult to assess, as most bursts landed in the smoke of preceding Groups' bombs. However, some were plotted in the southern portion of the target area.

"The Group's efforts against Derben are best shown in a comparison against the background of 841 heavies which the Air Divisions sent out. The bomber total was 20 planes lost, while claiming 31 enemy fighters."

After the war, more details were learned from a letter to Bobby's mother from the Mickey operator, Richard K. Brown, who, with the radioman, Cosimo (Gus) Cardone, survived to become prisoners of war.

Brown, graphically and in detail, described their last aerial battle in his description of the events, noting the final blow to be a 20 mm shell exploding in the bomb bay, perforating oxygen and fuel transfer lines, starting an uncontrollable fire. Seeing the conflagration, he and Cardone bailed out just in time. Brown wrote that as his chute opened, he looked up, hoping to see other parachutes, only to witness the final destruction of the plane as it blew up.

The wreckage of Bobby's Fort and its remaining crew crashed at Ketzin, a suburb of Berlin. The local Catholic priest, seeking post-war CARE packages, also wrote Bobby's mother. It seems he was on hand to officiate over an impromptu burial of the crew locally. This was far from the primary target, Derben, forty miles to the west.

The fates of the other ships of the 568th have been clarified since, by input from some of the survivors who were able to bail out. All of these survived the brutality often faced on the ground from angry civilians, the meager rations in the *Stalags,* or prison camps, and the unbelievable hardships to which they were subjected just before the end of hostilities. These were in the Nazi-ordered forced marches, with the aim of keeping them from liberation by the advancing Allies.

From Bobby's property, as with that of the other missing men, uniforms were quickly expropriated, usually the case when personnel failed to return. Only his underwear, stockings and dirty laundry, plus his diary and other personal effects, remained to be sent home to his family. Among these was that last letter from Denise, dated two weeks before Bobby's final mission, but which hadn't arrived until that very day. It remained unopened until it was returned to his parents in Burbank with what remained of his possessions.

December 31, 1944

Dearest Bobby:

Forgive me for not writing these last couple of months, my life is in such a mess. You should know that I'm carrying your baby, making it impossible for me. I can't put down on paper the names Wheelie calls me. Mom tries to help, but Dad vows that he never even had a daughter. Without you here, life is no longer worth living. I can't take another day of this, much less the time needed for our baby. Please, please, forgive me, for what I'm about to do. I pray that somehow all three of us will be together some day, in a better place than this one. Until then, good-bye.

All my love, forever,

Denise

EPILOGUE

There has been much debate as to the value of the American and British bombing of German targets, focusing mostly on the British "Carpet bombing" of the cities, resulting in the firestorms of Hamburg and Dresden, with such great loss of life. A few radicals even leveled accusations of war crimes at the RAF. Many have also questioned the effectiveness of American daylight "Precision Bombing," pointing to the fact that by the end of 1944, German aircraft production had actually increased despite repeated attacks at great cost to the Eighth and Fifteenth Air Forces. Of course, that doesn't take into account what the production figures might have been without those same bombing raids. Mostly ignored by the critics of the Allied air war were the pressures on the *Reich* to put up an effective defense against the USAAF and the RAF, draining other theatres of the conflict of sorely needed men, artillery, and aircraft in the process.

The critics also largely ignored the destruction of synthetic fuel and chemical production plants as well as transportation facilities in the daytime strategic bombing by the Army Air Force. German documents have since shown that bombing had cut production of those essential war making elements by the conflict's end to a mere eighteen percent of what it had been. As a consequence, the *Luftwaffe* could not spare fuel to train new pilots adequately, and the *Wermacht* had to retreat from the Battle of the Bulge and the Eastern Front without much of its armor, having run out of fuel. Panzer divisions without fuel had become mere scrap iron.

The final word came from Hitler's military economist, Albert Speer, director of the *Reich's* war production. During post-war interrogations, he testified that even with the colossal losses the Germans suffered at Stalingrad and Kursk, amounting to more than half a million troops, sealing Germany's fate in the East, the destruction inflicted by the Allied bombing campaign was by far the greatest lost battle of the war.

In addition to the thousands of *Luftwaffe* aircraft, and the personnel needed to fly and maintain them, he revealed that German air defenses employed more than a million men on the ground, and utilized almost twenty thousand artillery pieces that could have been decisive factors on the Russian Front. Despite all that, the rain of bombs, virtually all from the Western Allies, devastated his homeland. He added that the most telling and significant destruction was by the Americans, in their systematic daylight bombing attacks on factories, transportation, communications, and oil. Acknowledging the hugely damaging British night attacks that had created firestorms in population centers as well as in industry, he concluded that it was the American bombers that delivered the deathblow.

Victory was not achieved without great loss of life, especially for those involved in the air war. The saying that the greatest danger for an Allied fighting man in Western Europe during World War II was to be in a heavy bomber over Germany is undoubtedly true.

Bobby seems to have reflected on this, as his poem, printed in *The Daily Trojan* at USC when he was called up in 1943 suggests.

Little Boy Brew

The bottles and glasses are covered with dust, and sober as hell they stand

And the little tin shaker is covered with rust, untouched by his loving hand.

Time was when the bottles were new, and the vintage passing fair.

That was the time that Little Boy Brew drank from them, and put them there

Now don't you go, he said to all, and don't let anyone in.

And he left to heed his draft board's call as he drank one last shot of gin.

But as he fought, a bullet's song stopped cold our Little Boy Brew.

The years are many, and the years are long, but the bottles and shakers are true

Aye, faithful to Little Boy Brew they stand, each in the same old place

Awaiting the touch of his shaking hand, and the slap-happy grin on his face.

And they wonder while waiting the long days through in the dust of the little bar

Whatever became of Little Boy Brew, since he drank there and left for afar.

While his father replaced Bobby's blue service star with a gold one, to accompany the blue of his other four offspring in the front window of the family home, his mother never gave up the belief that he had survived somehow. Perhaps he was in an amnesic state somewhere in Europe, she hoped.

After his father died, she traveled extensively throughout the world, and while she did visit the countries bordering the Mediterranean, she never toured Northern Europe. Thus, she was able to avoid the truth of Bobby's death, ignoring his final resting place, the U.S. Military Cemetery at Neuville-en-Condroz in Belgium, nine miles from Liege.

In a renewal of life, Diana went on to deliver a healthy baby boy on August 11th, 1945, the same day that the 390th completed its return to the U.S. She named him Philip Barr Taylor the Third. Again, it was much too big a name for a little boy.

She was content to raise her son by herself, with a little help from his loving English grandparents. And they, and everyone else, called him Bobby.

Ω

ACKNOWLEGEMENTS

The author is grateful for the patience of his family in putting up with the demands placed on them during the completion of this work. Without the editing and encouragement given by a number of them, this story probably could never have been finished. Included is my dear wife Eivor, along with sons Patrick Jr. and Erik, and daughter Karin. Thanks also go to cousin David Sheeley, for finding key archival material.

A debt of gratitude is also owed to the Research Department of the 390th Bombardment Group Memorial Museum in Tucson, Arizona, for their fine online database. The volunteer personnel there were most helpful in gleaning information concerning the operation of that Group during the war over Germany.

Some of the details could never have been gathered, except in the imagination, but for the input from those now departed. Their letters to my mother and me, during and just after the war, and other personal communication since then have been an invaluable source of information.

Thanks also go to fellow members of the Bay Area Independent Publishers Association for their helpful advice regarding self-publishing at their monthly sessions.

BIBLIOGRAPHY

390th Memorial Museum Foundation, *The Story of The 390th Bombardment Group,* (H) Third Edition, Turner Publishing Co., Paducah, KY, 1947

390th Bomb Group Members, *The 390th Bomb Group Anthology, Vol. I & II, 390th* Memorial Museum Foundation, Tucson, AZ, 1983 & 1985

Albertson, Bill, *I Flew With Hell's Angels: Thirty-six Combat Missions in a B-17 "Flying Fortress" 1944-1945,* Heritage Books, Westminster, MD, 2005

Alling, Charles, *A Mighty Fortress: Lead Bomber Over Europe,* Casemate, Drexel Hill, PA, 2002

Astor, Gerald, *The Mighty Eighth: The Air War in Europe Told by the Men who fought it,* Dell Publishing, New York, NY, 1997

Ayres, Travis L., *The Bomber Boys: True Stories of B-17 Airmen,* AuthorHouse, Bloomington, IN, 2005

Bowman, Martin W., *Wild Blue Yonder: Glory Days of the US Eighth Air Force in England,* Wellington House, London, UK, 2003

Bowman, Martin W., *Echoes of England: The 8th Air Force in World War Two,* Tempus Publishing Ltd, Stroud, Gloucestershire, UK, 2006

Freeman, Roger, *The Mighty Eighth: A History of the U.S. Army 8th Air Force,* Doubleday, Garden City, NY, 1970

Freeman, Roger, "B-17 Flying Fortress," chapter in the *Great Book of World War II Airplanes,* Wing and Anchor Press, New York, NY, 1984

Grinnell, Robert, *Focke-Wulf Fw190,* chapter ibid

Hawkins, Ian, *Münster: The Way It Was,* Robinson Typographics, Anaheim, CA, 1984

Hess, William N., Johnson, Frederick A., and Marshall, Chester, *Big Bombers of WWII,* Lowe & B. Hould Publishers, Ann Arbor, MI, 1998

Kershaw, Alex, *The Few: The American "Knights Of The Air" Who Risked Everything To fight In The Battle of Britain,* Da Capo Press, Cambridge, MA, 2006

Lorant, Jean-Yves and Goyat, Richard, *Jagdgeschwader 300:"Wilde Sau" Vol. Two,* Library of Eagles, Hamilton, MT, 2007

Miller, Donald L., *Masters of the Air: America's Bomber Boys Who Fought The Air War Against Nazi Germany,* Simon & Schuster, New York, NY, 2006

Morgan, Robert, (with Ron Powers) *The Man Who Flew The Memphis Belle: Memoir of a WWII Bomber Pilot,* New American Library, New York, NY, 2001

Morris, Rob, *Untold Valor: Forgotten Stories of American Bomber Crews over Europe in World War II,* Potomac Books, Washington, DC, 2006

Myers, Jack R., *Shot At And Missed: Recollections of a World War II Bombardier,* University of Oklahoma Press, Norman, OK, 2004

Neillands, Robin, *The Bomber War: The Allied Air Offensive Against Nazi Germany,* The Overlook Press, New York, NY, 2001

Nichol, John, and Rennell, Tony, *Tail-End Charlies: The Last Battles of the Bomber War,* 1944-1945, St. Martin's Press, New York, NY, 2006

Novy, Jack, *The Cold Blue Sky: A Gunner in World War Two,* Howell Press, Charlottesville, VA, 1997

O'Neill, Brian D. *Half a Wing, Three Engines and a Prayer,* McGraw-Hill, New York, NY, 1998

O'Neill, Frank, "Second to Last Mission," chapter in *World War II Stories: 390th Bombardment Group, Eighth Air Force,* Arizona Lithographers, Tucson, AZ, 2008

Pons, Gregory, *8th Air Force: American Heavy Bomber Groups in England,* 1942-45, Histoire & Collections, Paris, France, 2006

Reschke, Willi, *Jagdgeschwader 301/302 "Wilde Sau" In defense of the Reich with the Bf 109, Fw 190 and TA 152*, Schiffer Military History, Atglen, PA, 2005

Smith, Starr, *Jimmy Stewart: Bomber Pilot*. Zenith Press, St. Paul, MN, 2005

Stevens, Charles N., *An Innocent At Polebrook: A Memoir of an 8th Air Force Bombardier*, Charles N. Stevens, Bloomington, IN, 2003

Sweetman, Bill, "Avro Lancaster," chapter in *The Great Book Of World War II Airplanes*, Wing and Anchor Press, New York, NY, 1984

Taylor, Frederick, *Dresden*, Harper Collins, New York, N.Y, 2004

Whiting, Charles, *Hitler's Secret War: The Nazi Espionage Campaign Against The Allies*, Pen & Sword Books, Barnsley, South Yorkshire, U.K., 2000